Praise for *The Palace of Angels*

Vital, brutal and tender, *The Palace of Angels* is written with the urgency of breaking news and the delicacy of poetry. This is Morsi at his passionate best.

—Geraldine Brooks, Pulitzer Prizewinner

'Twenty Two Years to Life' [the second story in this volume] is a moving and heartbreaking tale based on a true story. It brings new meaning both to steadfastness and the human suffering within the mega prison of the Gaza Strip. The level of the occupier's cruelty is matched by the fragile humanity of the occupied—in a way that can only be appreciated with the personal narrative so beautifully spun. The human complexity turns and twists and is then exposed in this powerful tale of the clash between love and hate, revenge and compassion, within an impossible and abnormal reality of occupation, colonisation and ethnic cleansing. *The Palace of Angels* is a trilogy of gripping tales that challenge our preconceived ideas and identities.

—Ilan Pappe, Israeli historian and author,
Professor of History, University of Exeter

With all the sympathy one might feel, it is impossible for an outsider to imagine what it is like to be a Palestinian living in the West Bank or Gaza today. Morsi affords one a revealing glimpse.

—Daniel Gavron, author, former editor,
Israel Radio and the Jerusalem Post

It does not matter which part of the world we belong to if we consider ourselves a supporter of peace and equality, but it matters that we do not close our eyes to the fatal truth of the regime of Israel, Syria, Iran, Myanmar, Iraq, North Korea, Afghanistan or some of the Africa
countries. It matters to listen to the independent vo
these countries. And this novel is one of those voices.
of those voices that provokes our conscience.

—Shokoofeh Azar, shortlisted author fo
Queensland L

The Palace of Angels was hurting, shaking, made me dizzy and uncomfortable, gave me hope and filled me with despair, all at once.

—Kobi Tuch, Israeli educator

Morsi, writing with tremendous empathy, has distilled a political conflict into a very human, visceral story. The dichotomy between love and oppression echoes through this powerful narrative, taking the reader on a shifting journey between the delicate and the devastating.

—*WritingWA*

'What is Past is Dead' is about desperate actions we sometimes take to counter desperate events. The best thing about this novella: it is an intimate portrait of one man's life. Had Morsi painted this work on a bigger canvas, it would not have worked nearly so well as what he has done instead, which is to present us with a very fine cameo.

—T.D. Whittle, Author

A captivating tale of the human power of loving and yearning for freedom. Morsi's depiction of Palestinian life is heart wrenching because it's the truth and nothing but the truth. A story that resonates with all humanity.

—Rana Shubair, author, Gaza strip, Palestine

These novellas bring to mind Picasso's nightmarish 'Guernica', but Morsi's palette bears more vivid colours and his canvas is stretched across the measure of years. Only a great artist could plumb the relentless horror of the Middle East conflict with the immediacy Morsi achieves here, and that he simultaneously captures and celebrates the eternal beauty of love is testament to his mastery.

—Ken Spillman, award-winning author

About the Author

Mohammed Massoud Morsi was born in Copenhagen in 1975 and promptly started a roving lifestyle, moving to Egypt with his Egyptian parents, then back to Denmark to further his schooling. He was drawn to writing from an early age and found his calling in places far beyond the news fronts, and into human wastelands—light years from the trodden tourist runs.

Morsi spent almost two decades as a freelance journalist and photographer immersed in communities with forgotten people and conflicts around the world. He primarily worked for NGOs and published feature articles in Danish newspapers. Along the way, he also held a wide variety of jobs (airline programmer, forklift driver, fisherman, etc.) and expressed an entrepreneurial flair establishing a photographic academy in Copenhagen, building a school in a Phnom Penh slum, growing herbs guerilla style and farming rabbits in Egypt.

Morsi's intimate images, whether from the edge of an AIDS hospital bed, from a rubbish dump with rubbish pickers in Cambodia, from the turmoil of the Gaza Strip or in South Lebanon, all reflect his deep sense of justice.

Morsi's life experiences have given him a rich matrix which looks to important questions, finding what is quintessentially human within much broader struggles. He is a natural storyteller with compelling authenticity and an exquisite feeling for romance, at once sensitive and earthy.

Morsi's fiction and non-fiction have appeared in Australian and international publications. He has authored three novels and five non-fiction books. He lived in Europe, Africa and Asia before taking up residence in Australia in 2011. Now a citizen, he continues his writing and lives in Perth with his son, Zaki.

0-7-2021
Dear Jimmy,
May this travel
with you &
through you!
Morsi

THE PALACE OF ANGELS

MOHAMMED
MASSOUD MORSI

Published by Wild Dingo Press 2019
Melbourne, Australia
books@wilddingopress.com.au
wilddingopress.com.au

First published by Wild Dingo Press 2019
Stories first published separately by *Living in the Strange* 2016-18

Cover Design: Debra Billson
Barbed wire: Claudio Divizia/Shutterstock
Branches: Irtsya/Shutterstock
City line drawing: Babayuka/Shutterstock
Foreground trees: Naeblys/Shutterstock
Background: David Methven Schrader/123rf.com

Editors: Jim Magnus and Catherine Lewis
Printed in Australia.

Morsi, Mohammed Massoud, 1975- author.
The Palace of Angels / Mohammed Massoud Morsi

A catalogue record for this book is available from the National Library of Australia

ISBN: 9781925893045 (Paperback)
ISBN: 9781925893106 (ePdf)
ISBN: 9781925893113 (ePub)

Acknowledgements

I'd like to thank my publisher, Catherine Lewis of Wild Dingo Press, who has indulged my long emails and untimely phone calls. I am forever grateful for her hard work, support, advice, understanding and most importantly—believing in my work.

I would like to thank my father for never failing to support me in following my calls for adventure. Every one of them, with their triumphs or failures, have led me to live a life filled with purpose. Thank you for teaching me how to stand up for myself and for justice.

I am grateful for my mother whose painted landscapes decorate my home with an aura of peace and innocence. Thank you for teaching me that art bound in love is the most liberating form of creation.

I thank my sister for teaching me how to eat slowly and discover the wonder of languages, the grace of classical music and the power of hugs.

I would like to thank the heavens and the earth, Mahmoud Shikuku, Tawfiq Al Hakim, Ismail Yassen, Salah Jahin, Doria Shafiq and so many more, my gigantic family—those still with us and those whom I miss dearly—for enriching my life with the laughter and vibrations which resonate with that part of my soul I call Egyptian.

I also cannot express how much it has meant to have Jim Magnus patiently working with me through long hours, philosophising, editing and supporting me in writing these important stories. I want to thank Tanami Magnus for honestly and critically reviewing my work and offering her valuable insights as an advanced reader.

Most importantly, I want to thank my son Zaki for reminding me, every single day, that wisdom comes from below and not from above.

I am forever grateful to Omar Majdalawi, whose humour, courage, and quest for justice—whose tears brought my ship to his world. His people, the Palestinians, also became my people. Their struggle also became mine and as all other struggles, it roots within us all—in our oneness—equally deserving of a life lived in freedom and in dignity.

I am forever grateful to Kobi Tuch for sharing with me the dreams of his people, for teaching me about Tikkun Olam and all the beautiful—and often forgotten traditions—which can bring about a reality rejecting hatred, basing it on kindness and a true understanding of what it means to be human.

Finally, I am forever grateful for the giant mystery of being alive, to have my senses and their rewards, experiences—to be engaged in the world from beginning to end. I am grateful for the minuscule part of the universe that looks out through my eyes—seeing a beautiful humanity only clouded by an illusion that we are separate from each other.

Dedicated to you, whose tears fell into the well of my soul,
whose voices planted stories in the depth of my heart.

Disclaimer

Although based on true stories, all three novellas in this work are works of fiction. Names, characters, places, and incidents are either the product of the author's imagination or are used fictitiously. Any resemblance to actual persons, living or dead, events, or locales is entirely coincidental.

Contents

WHAT IS PAST IS DEAD

(A PREQUEL)

إحيِينِي اِلنَّهَاردَة و موِّتْنِي بُكْرَه

Let me live today and kill me tomorrow.

1

It was so silent I could hear the air flowing through my nostrils. I took out a lighter from my trousers and turned the spark wheel. It sounded as if I had opened a shaken can of Coke. The flame was straight and sparks rose from the specks of dust coming off the stone. I lit my cigarette, then flicked the lighter again and watched the flame. It was dead straight.

Mido was scanning our surroundings, squinting as if he was trying to make out something on the ridges above us. In the light of the full moon, I looked up but couldn't see anything.

'Mido!' I whispered, urgently.

'Ye…es,' he replied, slowly, exhaling a plume of smoke.

'Where is Ahmed?'

I hadn't seen him leave. We had only just stopped the van. If he had gone anywhere, I wanted to know. This was his plan after all and the whole way I had sensed that he hadn't told me all the details. I had had the same sensation the last time we did this, and I didn't like it.

I put the lighter back in my trousers and felt a piece of thick paper on the back of my hand. I pulled out a tattered airline boarding pass and the two familiar lines read Vienna-Cairo. I had arrived two nights earlier and was still wearing the same pair of pants. I curiously searched the rest of my pockets and found another crumbling piece of paper, reading Copenhagen-Vienna. I held them like a pair of aces, then stuck them down the rear pockets. I didn't want anyone else to find them.

Mido flicked his cigarette and resumed his gaze.

'So, where is he?' I said somewhat edgy, almost dropping my cigarette.

'I don't know. He went that way,' said Mido, still looking up, waving his arm in the direction of where the road made a turn as it slithered through the narrow valley we were in.

⟡⟡⟡

I couldn't see past the bend, so I left Mido and walked a short distance along the road until I reached it. There I stopped. I had been here several times before but this time, in the night, the moon cast creepy shadows on the rock faces around us. It felt as if I had entered a gallery run by Satan himself. A tapestry of cruel theatrical masks glowered at me as far as I could see. I froze, even though every bone in my body was screaming at me to leave that place. To run all the way back to the airport, past the corrupt immigration officers and the dubious security, until I could move no more, firmly strapped in a seat on a plane out of here. Instead I stood there and all I moved were my lips.

I said his name in a careful tone, not loud, not whispering.

'Ahmed? Ahmed?' I called softly, and heard my voice echo back from the rock masks around me.

Then Ahmed's voice sounded from the blackest of shadows: 'Come here...'

I saw the glow and smelled the hashish he was smoking before I could see him. He had crouched down with his back to the cliff. The white of his emerald black eyes looked up at me like a beast of prey ready to spring, laden with thin red veins, looking even more ominous in the sheen of the moonlight. I felt a stab of anxiety, as if I was walking on the ledge above us, not knowing if my next step would send me plunging to my death.

I stood in front of Ahmed in the dark and though I wanted to ask him what was wrong, I didn't. I looked back at the van with Mido standing there, as if posed for a tourist brochure in the moonlight, dramatic backdrop and all. Except that the entire floor of this van was packed with the same stuff that Ahmed now passed on to me.

The best hashish you could find in Egypt.

'I don't know who will meet us today,' said Ahmed in a low voice while staring at the dusty ground.

I sensed in his voice the squirming fear that had made him leave us to squat down in the shadow of the rocky cliff, to calm himself. Smoking hashish nudges the doors of perception or pulls out a drawer in which one's fears may be shut away.

I wrapped the tip of my lips around the butt of the joint, took a calm deep breath, and held it in.

'Why don't you know?' I asked him with a muffled voice, exhaling the smoke into the moonlight.

'I mean, why am I here? Why did you want me here?'

'Are you joking?' Ahmed snapped. 'You know why. Because you speak like a foreigner and you even look like one.'

I felt a pique to my pride. After all, I was Egyptian. My nurture in being Egyptian was acquired through speaking, eating, talking and smoking with my Egyptian peers. I almost took the bait—to jump head first into bickering about something quite irrelevant. We were out in the desert, the border of Israel just hundreds of metres away.

Instead, I replied: 'The last time you did it yourselves. What's the difference now?'

'I don't know who is coming today. That's the difference.' Ahmed's face loosened in a sad way and he continued.

'Ever since we began trading, we have met the same soldiers. The last time everything went smooth. We met, did our exchange, got money on top as we had expected, and they even asked us when we could trade again. You would have liked it. You might have even liked the soldiers as well. The first time we met them we were all nervous, remember? It was different last time. Mido and I almost began to like them. What do you think of that? Then somehow, all of a sudden, both my contacts disappeared. They were the only ones I could trust to make arrangements with the Israeli soldiers. I spent weeks trying all channels to find them, but they were gone, Allah knows where...'

Ahmed smiled for a second, staring into space, picking up a pebble and taking a deep breath.

'Ayman, the hero in Rafah, remember him? He was found dead in a tunnel with his guts cut out. The Jews, the Palestinians—even we would not claim him.'

I didn't say anything. I heard what Ahmed had said. I had heard that Ayman, who we'd called 'the hero', had been brutally murdered. The Ayman we had dined and laughed with, with whom we had lain on our backs, stargazing on a Gaza rooftop, imagining a free Palestine. That Ayman was no more. I heard what Ahmed had said and also what he hadn't. Ahmed knew why he had been killed and I knew what that meant. Ayman had been one of the best movers of goods through the tunnels under the desert floor between Gaza and Egypt. But someone had been watching him … watching us.

Ahmed struggled, pushing himself up against the cliff as he got up. His breathing was weary.

'*Yalla*[1], we need to go and unbolt the floor. I need your help. They'll be here soon,' he said and began walking back to the van. Ahmed had deliberately not told me about Ayman before we left Suez. I strangled an urge to scream in anger.

'What about Mido? Does he know what is going on?'

'No, and he doesn't care either. Mido is a happy guy. Happy to get the hashish, happy to go on an adventure, happy to get his share, happy to spend it. Mido doesn't know what worry is.'

◈◈◈

I was tense.

I knew Ahmed as well as I knew Mido. On the outside Mido appeared as if he didn't have a worry in the world. Mido was the joker. Everybody loved Mido. He got into just as much trouble as the rest of us but nobody ever got mad with Mido. All he had to do was just smile his big, radiant smile, and you couldn't help but smile back.

---

1 Let's go. Or: Hurry up.

He had such a good nature. He was always telling jokes, making faces, impersonating people. But always with a good heart; he never cut anyone down, and the only person he ever made a fool of was himself. He could be tough too; as tough as Ahmed and I. But Mido would rather make friends than pull a knife.

He had this hair, this beautiful brown hair. Everybody else's hair where we came from was black or at most dark brown, but Mido had this beautiful head of thick, wavy, almost reddish brown hair. He wore it a bit long, combed it straight back, and always kept it very neat with a red comb that he carried in his back pocket. Even that gesture—fully extending his arm, then drawing his hand slowly back over his head with his comb—was a joke on himself. He did it all the time, with this serious look on his face, his lips slightly pursed. And then he'd burst out laughing. And if any girls were around, well, they'd all be getting weak at the knees.

Yet Mido was also one of the most perceptive guys I knew, and he saw the worried look on my face as we approached the van. He was just about to say something, when Ahmed spoke.

'Come on, let's get ready before they get here. We want to finish this thing quickly.'

Ahmed handed out three big Phillips-head screwdrivers and we began to undo the screws that held the false floor in the back of the van. Some of them were angled wrong and needed care not to wreck the thread. On some, the head was almost gone, and a couple we couldn't get out.

All the time we were working, Mido kept looking up behind his back as if someone was watching us.

I looked, as well, but I couldn't keep my eyes off the rock faces, with their sinister mien in the blueish hue of the moonlight. I tried to let my forebodings go. I felt stoned. I shouldn't have smoked.

The light in the van was weak and kept flickering above our heads. I was sweating so much the drops ran from my forehead into my eyes and burnt like acid. I looked at Ahmed whose eyes were still crimson red. The drops on his face escaped, chasing each other along his jaw, disappearing down his neck. He must have seen me from the corner of his eye.

'Are you ready?' he asked, and I said, 'no'. He wanted to know if we were ready to lift the floor out. Mido gave up on the last screw and huffed: 'Ready!'

'We'll pull out the remaining screws as quietly as we can,' said Ahmed. The floor was a thin metal sheet, so it would move a bit but couldn't be bent. We'd have to put it back on again as soon as the deal was done, just with the few screws that would go in. No soldiers or policemen were going to look too closely at the bottom of the back of a van. Most of them looked as if they had been bought from a scrapyard and resurrected to live another life. There were no seats, Ahmed and Mido had removed them. Passenger vans made regular cargo runs so no one would even suspect anything in an otherwise empty van with windows all way around. If all of that didn't work, Ahmed knew pretty much every guy at every checkpoint in Sinai, and quite a few dollar bills had already passed between shaken hands on our way to the border.

The last screw came out with a bang. We all froze and stared at each other, still holding the metal sheet. The silence seemed to be waiting for another abrupt sound but nothing came. I helped Ahmed with the front part. It came off easily and we slid it out the slide door quietly.

One of the screws had pricked the palm of my left hand and I watched as a pool of blood formed. I thought to tell Ahmed but he had already begun unloading the van with Mido.

From the front of the van, I took a rag T-shirt and wrapped it around my hand, holding it high.

As the blood coloured the fabric, I saw him.

2

About thirty metres above us a very tall man appeared. He stood still at the cliff's edge and looked down at me. He had long hair and for a second, I thought perhaps it was a woman; but he was massive like a bull on two legs and he towered up, revealing a body of strength. I was going to speak, make a sound or something, but Mido and Ahmed were still busy counting the stash. I looked up again and heard a slight sound of a bell, a little tinkle bell. It was faint, very faint. The man held a rope that slacked as a goat came up behind and stood next to him. They both stared down at me.

I froze to the spot as I felt the warmth of my blood flowing in a sticky trickle through the cloth and down my arm. After we had looked at each other for what seemed an eternity, the man, with the goat on its lead, began walking along the ridge and away from me. Not thinking, I left the others and followed.

Walking slowly at first, then faster and faster until I was almost running to keep up with the man above; I was drawn to him, to his steps and to the tinkle of the goat on the lead. The ridge suddenly disappeared into the distance and within a few steps, the tall man and the goat were also lost in the gully of darkness that lay between the opposite ridges.

I waited a few seconds, thinking they might reappear again on the other side.

Nothing happened, so I slowly crossed the road and walked into the dark.

◈◈◈

Ahmed and Mido's voices faded into the background as the crunch of my steps on the sand beneath me echoed from the cliff faces.

I saw the ridges above narrowing as I walked further on. Ahead, a spot on the desert floor was lit by the moonlight, like a theatre stage under spotlights awaiting entry of the villain. I went to the light and stopped.

I heard the sound of the bell and the tall man's footsteps approaching. A mysterious darkness cloaked the ray of light like a black curtain. I shivered as my skin was pulled, as if the moon was pulling out every strand of hair on my head, on my entire body.

The man and the goat stepped into the light, facing me. I almost stopped breathing as we stood feet apart. He towered high above me and I looked up at a face that was crossed with deep cuts, even across his eyes, like an unpolished rock of blood marble. He had a wide, defined chin. His skin stretched over his face and looked like leather. His breathing was heavy like a maddened bull's and every time he exhaled, I felt it on my face. He looked like a man who had been on fire and survived.

'Are you ready?' said the tall man. The goat looked at me as if it, too, was waiting for an answer.

'I just wanted to see where you were going,' I said with a shaky voice, adding tremulously in my most polite Arabic: 'I think I have to go back to the others now. Please allow me...'

'I expect that you are ready, then, but also scared!' he said. 'If you can tell me what your purpose of being here is, I will accept your excuse...'

What a predicament I was in and what a peculiar way of talking to me. Who was this person to make any demands? His eyes were bulging, his coat was dusty and dirty and his hair long and tattered like an old horsetail.

'I am here, travelling my country with my friends, just like what they call camping,' I replied.

The man's eyes bulged as if they were about to pop out, the scars on his face thickened as if each and every one of them was about to burst from the blood rushing into them.

'*Kefaya!*'[2] he roared. The goat jumped in fright and so did I. 'Neither of us has time to stand here and play games. Let's get on with it. Come here!' he commanded.

I hesitantly took the half step towards them. The man seemed even taller, bigger, and I am by no means small. He was huge. I stared at his chest and it was moving like a giant swell on the ocean.

'I am not sure what you would like me to do?' I asked as I stood deferentially in front of him. I was confused. I was thinking that at any moment, Ahmed would slap me across my face and I'd come out of what seemed like a bizarre flight of my mind.

The man moved his jacket to the side and pulled out a large knife from its sheath. He had tucked it in behind the wide belt that went around his waist. He took the knife out, flipped it and handed it to me, holding its blade with his bare hand.

I took the knife. I don't know why but I took it.

The double-edged blade shone in the moonlight, one side sharp, the other side, serrated. The handle was round, highest in the middle of my palm and felt like rubber. It felt good in my hand.

A real Rambo knife, I thought.

The tall man spoke: 'From death we return to life; and the purpose of life is death. One sacrifice must be made to please God. It is now your turn to take this life.' His tone was ceremonial. He handed me the lead to the goat, which skipped towards me, looking at me with pleading eyes.

I stood there with the knife in one hand and in the other, the lead to the goat that I assumed I was meant to sacrifice. I thought of just turning around and walking away, but somehow that didn't seem to be a choice. I thought of escaping into the dark, but then what? Ahmed and Mido must have noticed my disappearance by now. Ahmed might be thinking that I'm sabotaging the whole operation. Perhaps Mido had already seen this man? If so, I could calmly explain what had happened and they would surely believe me.

---

2 Enough!

'Would you like me to kill the goat!?' I asked.

'Or you can choose another life, perhaps your own. The choice is yours,' he answered calmly.

There was no way I was going to kill the goat. The idea of taking its life just to propitiate some god seemed antiquated, from a time when the Earth was flat and belief in the Universe got you burned at the stake.

'Hold on!' I said, agitated. 'You just said I am ready. Ready for what, then?'

'Ready to choose. So, choose!' the tall man growled.

I stared into his eyes. He was in the form of a man but there was something about him that seemed from another time. His carved face looked as if it moved around his eyes. The scars pulsated with his breath and his whole body moved, as if at some point his coat would be blown to shreds and a fiery dragon would emerge.

I looked at the goat again. No, I could not kill it. I looked at the man and thought of what a dragon could do to me. I waged a war within myself; whether I was weak or strong, regardless, I couldn't kill the goat. The goat moved closer to me and rubbed its cheeks against my thigh.

I looked up to give my answer to the tall man, only to find him gone. Vanished. Without trace. I shivered right through my bones and suddenly the only sound I could hear, was the goat chewing its cud and Ahmed and Mido in the distance cautiously calling my name.

Ahmed and Mido!

I had lost track of myself.

I hurried back, with the goat's lead in one hand and the big Rambo knife in the other.

I kept looking back, expecting a tall figure to loom out of the dark, morphed into a dire dragon, swooping down on me and the goat, engulfing us in a furnace of death.

3

Ahmed and Mido had indeed been looking for me. I will never forget their faces. Their mouths froze open and for a second they looked as if they had seen a ghost. A picture of them in that very instant remains frozen in my memory.

'What is this?' he asked in a baffled voice, looking at the goat.

'Where did you get the knife from?' said Mido as he reached out and I opened my hand to let him take it.

'I am not sure how to explain this but there was this very tall man and he—' I began to say before Ahmed, looking at me with a big question mark in his eyes, interrupted.

'Actually, we don't have time to hear about this now. Tell us later; they'll be here any minute.'

Mido kept examining the knife.

'It's carbon steel. Very strong,' he said, studying its details as we walked back to the van. I still had the goat by the lead.

'I can't believe this! What's your plan with that goat?' Ahmed asked, clearly stressed. 'Let it go, let it go!'

I let go of the lead as we all stopped. Ahmed grabbed a rock and threw it at the goat. It ran a few steps away then stood there, waiting. We turned around and started walking again. Almost back at the van, I felt a lick on my wounded hand. I pushed it away but the goat kept coming back, licking the blood, rubbing itself against me.

Ahmed saw it, looked at me, then at Mido and back again.

'Tie it up then, quickly. Tie it to the back fender,' Ahmed sighed.

A look of resignation came over him and he shook his head. Facing me he said, 'We'll take it to old Hassan's place. He'll be eternally grateful.'

Ahmed and I were cousins and also best friends in our early years. Then life took my family and me to Copenhagen so we were separated for many years until one day we reconnected, at the main microbus stop in Suez. I was in my early teens but I clearly remember watching my cousin from a distance. He was wearing a brown leather jacket and black trousers. It was a winter day—sunny, almost glary. He wore aviator sunglasses which made him look cool. He was sitting in his van, talking to some other drivers and waiting for his ride to fill up. The van was white with wide tyres and low-profile rims and the interior had cosy lights for the night shift. It was clean and the large dash mat was embroidered with Arabic letters making up two words: *Allahu Aḵhbar*[3].

I got in and sat up front in the passenger's seat, lightly jumping in and out to let another passenger grab the middle seat next to Ahmed. Ahmed turned from his window talk, counted heads in the rear-view mirror and looked over the man between us. I didn't let him see my face. A last passenger jumped in the back before Ahmed drove off.

My cousin was tough but very just-minded at the same time. He treated everyone in the same way. I never heard anyone, in all the years Ahmed and I were friends, say a single bad word about him.

A large family hailed the bus, and Ahmed slowed down. The cabin in the rear was almost full. He loudly announced more space was needed and asked some young guys in the back to make room. The mother of the large family quickly shuffled all the children around the available seats before sitting down in the row of seats facing the cabin. The father and what looked to be his eldest son were the only ones left outside.

I put a one-pound note in the hand of the man beside me and said: 'Let's take the next one'. He understood straight away and put the note in Ahmed's hand. We both jumped out and let the father and his son take the front seats. The father thanked us gratefully.

---

3 God (Allah) is most great. Used by Muslims in prayers and as a general declaration of faith or thanksgiving.

Ahmed slowly put the van in motion while looking at me intently, leaning his body forward to see past the son and the father next to him. As I finally looked at him with a big smile, he stopped the van with a jolt, shaking everything and everyone.

Flinging the driver's door open, Ahmed ran around the van and we embraced and kissed on the cheeks several times. The people in the van didn't mind—they smiled and laughed and were happy for us. Comments and jokes were made, and Ahmed turned his head around several times to explain who I was.

'This is my brother! This is my brother! He lives in Denmark!'

Ahmed was so happy. I was happy. I had lost my own brother in my early childhood so Ahmed was the closest thing to a brother I had.

4

The stash that didn't fit into the crates under the back floor, we packed into three of the same half-sized Russian 82 mm mortar crates. We had tied these crates between the front seats and the rear compartment of the van. There were seven crates in all, each holding four bars across and four down, or sixteen bars altogether, each weighing in at thirty-six ounces. A bar is a block of compacted cannabis resin, or hashish. The first time we went and picked up that same amount of hashish from Mido's family in the Delta, it was packed into regular nine-ounce bars. They looked like a mountain of plastic gold bars and were extremely hard to pack.

The first run turned out better than we'd expected. Our enemies—also our buyers—paid us almost street price although it was clear to them that we didn't really know what we were doing. But they didn't know what they were doing either. Their trade was two crates of M16 assault rifles, twelve rifles in each crate. Each rifle was worth about 10,000 US dollars on the black market at that time. Two boxes of twenty-five modified M26 hand grenades and an Israeli postal sack with five freshly dated sandwiches of explosives, labelled SEMTEX. A large number of complimentary bullet rounds for the assault rifles were also added.

On this occasion, what was to be our last run, the calculation was easy: 2,500 US dollars per thirty-six-ounce bar of hash times sixteen bars (minus one we kept for ourselves), times seven crates, equalled 280,000 dollars. Out of that amount, roughly 220,000 dollars would be delivered as arms and 60,000 as cash. How they got the weapons and the money, they didn't say, and we didn't ask. And how we got the hashish and how we paid for it, they didn't ask, and we didn't say.

Once the deal was done we would head to Rafah, where we

would give the weapons to our Palestinian brothers to use, ideally in their fight for liberation from the Israelis. Not once did any of us consider reselling the weapons to make money. We kept the cash in a box with Mido's rooftop pigeons—enough to buy the next load of hashish—and shared equally what was left.

Without Ayman, the hero, we would have to rely on one of the most powerful men in Rafah, Ahmed Al Haffar, to ensure the weapons went straight through one of the countless tunnels into Gaza. On the other side, Khaled Abu Mohammed would make sure they went to men he trusted: who would not use them against each other. It was said he did this, but we couldn't know for sure. Khaled was a man with a loud voice, a large firm belly and a long beard, who made a very good living from making sure the right things went to the right places.

The only time I met Khaled was at a wedding on the Palestinian side of Rafah. I remember thinking there was no way I could ever lie to this man. The way he shook my hand and looked into my eyes felt as if he was reading my inner secrets. He didn't do small talk, but asked me straight up about my origins, family name, relations. He was known to interrogate you straight away and I was no exception. His networks in both high and low places decided who I was and whether or not he would want to deal with me.

I presume that he learned everything he needed to know.

We stacked the crates neatly next to the van. Then we waited.

5

Where the road makes a long S-bend, the moonlight shadow from the ridge above draped us in darkness. We were out of sight from anyone travelling the Taba-Rafah road. We could have met them on one of the dirt tracks that led all the way to the border with Israel but we dared not venture there. Where we were was already risky enough. A van travelling at night next to the border would surely be watched closely.

The border between Israel and Egypt was surprisingly quiet and thanks to the Camp David agreement in 1979, the Egyptian military presence on the Peninsula and in certain areas was very limited. There were only occasional light troop movements. Israeli military, however, moved in and out of the Sinai as they pleased, especially in the area where we were to meet.

We were sure they knew we were there. The first time we traded, we had turned on the headlights of Ahmed's van for the soldiers to see us, but then realised they could see us in the dark anyway. Could someone have our position pinpointed already and could alarm buttons be going off in all sorts of control rooms across the border? After all, our enemy was armed with some of the most advanced surveillance equipment in the world. We realised, though, that power and money play the same roles for most of us. And no one would be trading with us unless they thought they could get away with it. Ismail, a good friend of mine who served his military duties on the fringe of the tiny village of Nekhel in the Sinai, advised us of all the Egyptian movements on the Peninsula, and sometimes even that of the UN peacekeepers, in exchange for some fine hashish. Killing time in the Sinai was difficult, especially stuck at a base in the middle of a scorching desert with only the occasional weekend leave to look forward to.

It served us well. His information never failed us.

6

They came in an off-road truck, sand-coloured and steel-plated. The windscreen was partly covered by thick steel mesh on the passenger side and the only openings on the front doors were small hatches. The back of the truck was a large steel box with a small airconditioning unit on the roof, steel bi-fold doors at the rear and small narrow windows high up along both sides. It was ugly.

We called it 'the box'. It reminded us of the type of vehicle the Egyptian intelligence service, the Mukhabarat, and also the police, would use to pick up dissidents, criminals, demonstrators or anyone they felt like tormenting. The Egyptian 'box' was usually a modified Toyota Hilux with a black canvas canopy covering the back.

As young men, the police could stop us at any time and take us with them to the local police station. Most of us returned after a tough talk with some high-ranking officer, who told us not to flirt with girls. Some of us got beaten up because we said or did something wrong. Others ended up spending a few nights in a cell; and then there were those who we never heard from again.

Ahmed had once told me the truck had a name. The Israelis called it the Abir. In Hebrew it meant the knight or the brave man or something like that. It was used in all sorts of ways; young Palestinians would be taken in the back of these trucks to share the same or a much worse fate than their Egyptian compatriots.

Coming from the south, the truck made a large slow U-turn, then drove straight up to us and stopped with its front facing the opposite way to our van and its back aligned with our open side door. Its brake lights lit us up in red.

Two men stayed in the front with the engine running. We could hear them talking. A short time after, when the door latches were released, the voices grew louder as the passenger door opened slightly.

The diesel engine was turned off and the truck shook to a final thump.

I could make out Hebrew mixed with English but I couldn't understand what they were talking about. One of them sounded convincing and very confident. I was so anxious I was sure my voice would tremble and shake the moment I opened my mouth.

However, they almost seemed relaxed. Like they had just parked at their local store and were finishing a discussion about whether to stuff or grill the chicken for supper. Perhaps with some dip on the side.

After a while, the two men stopped talking and stepped out.

They were carrying short-barrel M16 rifles with their fingers on the triggers and both looked very fit. One man was dressed semi-civilian, with army pants and boots and a T-shirt with a large Star of David encircling a guy doing some sort of karate trick with the motif 'IDF Martial Arts'. The other man was in a combat kind of outfit. It looked expensive; not the usual cheap issue recruits were given. He wore sunglasses.

'*Shalom*,' the one with the sunglasses murmured in a deep voice as he stepped up to me.

The other guy didn't talk.

'*Aleikum Al Salaam*,' I replied. I should have stopped there, just moved on with things.

Not thinking, I said: 'Yet, how can we greet when we can't see each other?'

Without a flicker of change in his voice the man offered: 'What? Do you want to die, too?' He meant it. This was not just someone with a machine gun. Before me I saw a myrmidon, who could kill me, just like that, and sleep well afterwards.

My heart was pounding.

Too? What did he mean? Had he just come from a day's hard work, shooting Palestinian children in the head from a comfortable distance?

I heard my own breathing, I heard Ahmed's breathing, I heard Mido hardly breathing and I heard the air flowing through the large nostrils of the man in front of me and felt the air brushing the sweat on my face as he released every breath.

The goat murmured a quiet 'maaaah, maaah'.

I watched his finger shift on the trigger. His reflexes moved. He looked at the goat tied to the back of the van, glanced at the other guy and cast an idiotic smile straight in my face.

'Let's trade instead,' I said with a straight voice, breaking the standoff.

Lifting up the lid of a crate, I took a bar in my hand and handed it to the man in front of me. He shook his head.

'Give it to him,' he said and nodded in the direction of the other man.

Both had removed their name tags. I wondered what had happened to Baizer and Aberman, the soldiers we had traded with earlier.

The other man pushed his weapon to the side, took a small spring knife from his belt and cut open a bit of the plastic. He smelled the hashish, looked up and nodded.

These men weren't smokers; the best way to tell the quality of hashish is by smoking it. Smelling only tells you that it's hashish. There are other indicators, too, but the only sure one is to light up and try.

As soon as I saw his nod, a nod saying 'it smells good I guess', followed by a look for acceptance, I knew. Something bad had happened to the other soldiers. These guys weren't here to make money. They wanted to know who we were.

❖❖❖

We were being watched.

The one with the sunglasses said something in Hebrew and opened the back doors of the truck.

The first thing we saw was her red-brown hair. I looked at Ahmed and Mido and they were already looking at me with their eyes wide open like question marks.

She had honey-coloured eyes and a pretty face. A leather strap across her chest emphasised her breasts, tight pants displayed curvaceous legs and a slim top drew the line of her athletic body. She pulled the rifle on her back to her chest and exited the low roof of the truck.

She never smiled. I looked at the man with the glasses, obviously the one in charge. Then he glanced at the other man who swung his eyes to the girl, who turned to the man with the glasses. Then they all looked at us.

And there we were, Ahmed, Mido, me and a goat, a Rambo knife and a stack of hashish in a desolate part of the Sinai, less than a mile from the Israeli border.

'All good?' I asked to break the silence. I wasn't going to ask about the young woman.

'Do you have it all there?' the man in the glasses asked.

I pointed to the crates, gave him a quick run-down of the contents and asked if he brought what was agreed as well. I had no idea, of course. Ahmed was the broker. I didn't know who he had talked to, or what had been agreed upon precisely, but deals like this weren't subject to chance.

'Give him the money,' the man with the glasses said. The other man stepped over, opened a cargo pocket in his pants and took out two hard rolls of US dollars in a zip-lock bag. He handed them to me. I gave them to Ahmed who immediately climbed into the passenger side of the van and began counting.

'*Yalla*, move fast.' The man with the glasses commanded, motioning with his rifle for us to shift the weapons to our van. I looked at Mido before stepping over to the back of their truck.

The young woman opened the driver's door and flicked a switch, illuminating the back in a blue light.

Hand and finger marks in dried blood were daubed all over the walls. Towards the back doors, blood had run from a large splattered blotch on the wall, down to the floor. A small pool had formed and dried up. Straight in front of me, on the back wall, someone had written something in Arabic. It had clearly been written in blood and was all smeared except for a small part.

I made out: 'Tomorrow the sun will shine and I…' and then the line of the last letter was dragged all the way to the side, ending in a blotch of blood splashed in every direction, like the remnant of a blast. The floor was full of dried-up blood pools, drops and smears, scratched and marked with bare feet and boots.

Whoever had been in there had either been bludgeoned or taken their last breaths. The comparison with the Mukhabarat my mind had previously conjured, suddenly vanished. I watched Mido swallow deeply and he looked over at me with the most terrified eyes I had ever seen.

I wanted to say something, but at the edge of my vision were three soldiers with smug grins on their lips.

I grabbed the rope handle on one end of the large crate in front of us and gave Mido a reassuring look, as if to say, 'come on, let's get this over with'. He grabbed the other end.

We loaded the first dozen rifles into our van.

◈◈◈

Ahmed had counted the money and jumped out of the van as we finished loading the weapons. We spread the crates evenly from the front to the back and tied rope to the chair mounts in the floor to hold them down. Before we pulled the ropes across, I jumped up and opened each crate to check for any surprises, any hidden trackers or explosive devices. I threw a reassuring glance at Ahmed and then looked up at the three, armed soldiers watching our every move. We tied the crates down.

I looked back at the man with the glasses. The crates of hashish were still on the ground.

'One of you has got to let go of your gun…' I said, in a deliberately calm tone.

A wave of confused looks passed between the three of them before the girl released her rifle and rested it against the back wheel of the truck, just within reach.

They clearly had the upper hand. We were unarmed. They could have just flicked the safety and shot us on the spot. When the previous soldiers came to trade, they had left with a smile. These soldiers, however, were grim. They were on a mission and they were not going to fail.

The young female soldier blew a strand of hair from her left eye as she lifted the last of the crates into their truck. They were heavy. She was sweating and cursing in Hebrew. The two men grinned stupidly at each other. Hebrew tongue is close to Arabic and the three of us looked at the three of them who knew we could make out what was going on. Their grins turned into grinds again. She picked up her rifle and we were all done. I untied the goat, loudly protesting, and heaved it into the van where I tethered it short, then slammed the side door shut. I wanted to leave. It felt as if I had held my breath ever since we got there.

I turned around and stood beside Mido. Ahmed started to move. He looked at the three of them, but they remained silent. He walked around, got in and started the van. The old diesel engine puffed out a plume of suffocating smoke before it settled into its monotonous chuckle. I was waiting for the soldiers to turn around and get into their truck, but they didn't. They just closed the back of it and stood there, clearly wanting us to leave first. And we certainly wanted to leave.

I grabbed the handle by the windshield and pulled myself into the middle seat in one go. Ahmed let his foot off the clutch as Mido followed, grabbing the same handle, ready to jump in as the van slowly moved away. We did this all the time. Once in, we'd close the door and we'd be off.

I leaned towards the door, extended my hand just in case and watched Mido lift himself up, one foot on the step and in the usual way, we looked at each other, I made sure he had his legs firmly placed, he made sure I was making sure.

7

There was a short loud 'crack!'

I was looking straight into Mido's eyes when his head burst open. His forehead detached from his face in a violent blast, pieces hitting my face and flying all over the cabin.

It all happened in a flash, but it felt as if time had stood still. I felt the heat of the bullet, still burning hot, passing within an inch of my eyelids, and continuing with tremendous force out the windshield, leaving a large hole. I shut my eyes in reflex and a split second later I opened them to see Mido's eyes still staring at me. His body crumpled to the ground, sliding out of the van like a rag doll.

I was still leaning over, still had my arm extended. For a moment I was barely able to breathe.

'*YALLA, YALLA, YALLA!!!*' I heard Ahmed yell as he floored it. The van jumped as we hit Mido with the right back wheel. I leaned all the way over, not considering another bullet flying through my own head. I grabbed the door when it slammed shut as the van accelerated. We hit the edge of the road so hard the van jumped into the air and my head with it, crashing into the armrest. I lifted my head up slightly and through the corner of my eye, through the shaking rear view mirror, I saw the men and the woman still standing there, as if nothing had happened.

Not another bullet was fired. No one chased us.

8

We headed north as fast as the van would go.

The time, from when we abandoned Mido's body, to the time we saw an opportunity to stop, felt like an eternity. We took a dangerous dirt road shortcut that led us south again to reconnect with the main road leading through the Nekhel pass back to the Suez Canal. If the Israeli sniper hadn't had the time to put a bullet through all our heads, perhaps the Bedouins might. We felt like sitting ducks, exposed on all sides to hungry drug dealers, armed to the teeth and nesting in the caves that dotted the hillsides.

As the first rays of sunlight began to show the world around us, the blood and bits of Mido's brain and skull that had been spattered in the cabin became horrifyingly evident. The hole in the windscreen had been made by a very large calibre, high-speed projectile. Its force had left a near perfect hole and symmetrical cracks extending out.

Mido was dead.

I touched my eyelids.

I had been in such haste to leave, I hadn't cared about leg space, nor waiting for Mido. On all the other occasions I had been sitting in the passenger seat, nearest the door. I was always the last one to get in, Mido comfortably positioned between Ahmed and me, the one with the long legs.

Ahmed and I didn't say a word to each other. We cried in silence and at the first chance we got, at a wide, open part of the desert where no one would be watching us, where no one would expect anyone to stop, we stopped. We didn't have to talk about it. We knew exactly what we had to do. We opened the side door and pulled out all the weapons from the back and left them there. On the side of the dirt road.

It was already getting hot and Mido's blood, mixed with my own sweat, ran into my mouth and onto my tongue, down my throat and into my stomach.

We kicked out the windscreen and used what drinking water we had to remove the largest pools of blood. With a wet rag in my hand, I looked into the side mirror of the van. The whole right side of my face was caked in dried, cracked blood. It had fully covered my ear, and bits of brain had slid, in the blood, down to my earlobe to hang there like dried grapes on the vine. A larger piece was cemented in the bottom of the intertragic notch and was still mushy. Fragments of Mido's skull had dug themselves into my cheek, and I pulled them out like splinters with my fingertips. My right eyelashes were covered in a red-brown mascara made of his blood.

With the wet rag I tried cleaning them, putting them between my fingertips and pulling gently. Many of them came out. It hurt. I looked into the mirror a final time. I looked down and didn't look again.

We made it back to the main road having seen nothing but camels against the endless backdrop of the desert. We counted our blessings to Allah quietly and bribed our way through the last checkpoint before entering the open road leading to the Suez Canal and the Ahmed Hamdi tunnel. We pulled over at a roadhouse, ordered food, cold mineral water and a couple of shishas and sat there silently throughout the relentless heat of the day, speaking very little.

The keeper was more than pleased to have our business. I saw him looking with curiosity at the van several times, so I went and shook his hand with a couple of large notes stuck to the palm of my hand. He approved with a glance. He kept the coal hot on our shishas, tied the goat to a shady post under a tin roof, and put a pile of clover and a bucket of water in front of it. He looked at me and my torn eyelashes. He looked at both of us and the blood on our clothes, then wished us Allah's protection for all of our lives and for our further travel. The words were profuse and beautiful; and every one of them struck a knife through my heart. As soon as the sun fell behind the horizon, we got in the van and headed straight for Suez.

As the hot air blasted our faces, I watched the last moments of twilight and darkness descending upon us once more. Hearing a sound amidst the noise, I caught the eye of the fed and satisfied goat in the back of the van.

I saw a tiny house by the side of the road and asked Ahmed to stop. A boy and his father lived there. They were poor. I took the goat by the lead and handed it to the father.

He kept reiterating Allah's blessings to our names and our lives.

❖❖❖

Once we had gone through the tunnel, we were no longer in Sinai. Not keen to be stopped by the police, we had to get the window fixed before driving into Suez. We were both exhausted.

Ahmed knew of a guy who fixed cars for microbus drivers that had gotten themselves into trouble. He didn't ask questions, couldn't hear very well, did an excellent job and charged accordingly.

It was night by the time we reached Abu Hamama. When his wife opened the door there were an uncountable number of children around her. We waited whilst she woke her husband, and as in every Egyptian home, she brought us water and food and turned on the stove to make tea. We tried to refuse, to say we were in a hurry, but she just smiled at us and acted as if we were family.

It looked like any other house in the farm areas north of Suez; dirty and full of flies with the smell of rotting rubbish suffocating the air. Abu Hamama greeted us with half-open eyes and a stale breath, then went outside and opened a gate which was so heavily draped by plants, I hadn't noticed it.

I drove the van to the back and parked it where he pointed. He closed the gate behind us.

It only took him ten minutes to put another windshield in. Spare parts abounded for this model Toyota. The smell of the polyurethane didn't seem to bother him; he inhaled it, together with his cigarette, while stopping from time to time to sip sweet tea from a small glass.

'May Allah forgive us for not doing what we must do,' he said, still engaged in his work.

His wife brought us a pair of shirts, some matching trousers and some more tea. The clothes were clean. We changed into them, in turns behind the van, and drank the last bit of tea. She took our dirty clothes and threw them in an oil barrel full of twigs and plastics and other things to be burned. She didn't say a word about them. She just did it. Abu Hamama looked up at us, threw a glance at me, then at Ahmed.

'*Yalla*, may Allah bring you safely home,' and clapped the side of the van.

I paid him five times the usual price. He looked at the notes, kissed them, gestured to his forehead with them and then gave them to his wife. We left.

Ahmed drove the last bit back to Suez.

9

She screamed a long agonising scream. Then a short scream, broken by sobbing. She went on like this for some time. As soon as the man tried to approach her, the barber's razor blade in his hand, she would kick her legs about so violently that the two large women trying to restrain her lost their hold, and the man would back off once again.

'No! No! No! No! No!' and then piercing screams.

In the end the two women gave up. The kitchen door was opened, and they called in two men and her mother.

'No, Mother. No! No! No!' and this time she kicked over the small table the man had prepared for the procedure. On it he had placed a couple of cotton buds, a little metal tray, a few torn sheets of cloth and a glass of water. Clearly, he had done this before.

The stuff went everywhere, and in the commotion, the girl jumped away from the table and pulled her dress down. She ran towards the kitchen but couldn't get through the doorway with all the people watching. She looked like a trapped animal, her eyes wide and bewildered. Then she tried to run towards the balcony. The ladies yelled and screamed, fearing she might jump. The two men rushed, grabbed her by her arms and legs and carried her back to the table, still screaming.

One of them sat on the table and one took the girl and lifted her by her arms onto the other man's lap. She kicked all she could. The man sitting down had his arms in a bear hug around her. Then the man standing lifted her legs right up and gripped them as hard as he could. Her mother tried to comfort her, but the girl looked at her with the most hating eyes and screamed once more. The man with the blade moved in quickly.

I closed my eyes when he cut her, and in that instant, she somehow managed to move her legs so violently that the man holding her lost his balance and he released one of her legs. It went straight into the head of the man cutting her and while still being held down, she kept kicking his head with one leg and screaming without pause.

The razor blade missed its mark and went in. Her blood began to flow, fast.

Voices ordered everyone out. The mother started praying loudly to Allah for forgiveness and the lady who had been called to sound a traditional ululation, began asking for her money. The man sitting under the girl lifted her up and the other man took her legs.

The girl's screaming had turned into a painful cry. Her blood dripped heavily on the floor. The man sitting under her had his crotch covered in her blood. As they carried her out, she saw us.

She looked straight into my eyes.

Her eyes became Mido's eyes. There was silence, then her head suddenly exploded. Blood came flying at me. I curled up as if I was still in my mother's womb. We ran out through the living room. We had been watching through the slit of a slightly opened bedroom door. We ran past everyone. Someone yelled at us. 'You children of dogs!' Hands tried to catch us.

My cousin ran down the staircase. I stopped in the hallway. The phone on the dresser was ringing. It was an old phone with a turn dial but its tone was modern like a cell phone. It kept ringing. The voices around me faded and there was only the sound of the telephone.

I lifted the handle.

10

I opened my eyes to the bedside table. The phone was ringing and spinning. I grabbed it; vibrating in my hand I looked at it. It was Ahmed. I pushed the button and put it to my ear. The clock radio in front of me read 06:13.

'What's wrong?' I said.

Ahmed was crying. I had cried just before I fell asleep. I was in no mood to hear him cry. I felt anger creeping up.

'What are we going to do?' he said, almost sulking. 'What are we going to say to Mido's parents?' and he continued with a run of questions that I had already asked myself. I didn't have an answer and neither did he. 'We all knew the risk.' I said in a cold tone.

An uncomfortable silence followed.

I wanted to throw the phone out the window or just pass it to the ladies I could hear chattering on the balcony next door. I wished for the phone line to suddenly cut out as it so often did, but nothing happened. I could hear Ahmed's breathing with an occasional contemplative murmur, as though just about to speak. On the neighbours' balcony, Mrs Badri was reminiscing with her friend about her late husband's early morning habits. I'd heard this story many times myself. How it had been a hot morning, how he had made himself a cup of tea and how the cigarette was still between his fingers as he quietly slipped away with a smile on his face. Usually her friend would then console her but that morning it was different.

'*Khalas ba'a! El Faat, Maat!*' she said to Mrs Badri in an annoyed tone.

What is past, is dead.

What is past, is dead.

What is past, is dead.

Suddenly there was a puff of cool air amidst the brewing morning heat. The ladies praised the coolness and the discussion turned towards the changing of the seasons and the welcoming of cooler weather.

Ahmed finally broke the silence.

'Stay at home today,' he said. 'I know what is going to happen and it will begin today.' What Ahmed meant was that people would begin asking questions about Mido's whereabouts.

Had the bullet gone through my head instead, it would have been easier. Nobody would immediately ask about me and a story could be made up about why I was not there. I was, after all, *living in the strange*, as it's said of an Egyptian living abroad. Mido was a familiar face, with many friends around the city and a large family. The first phone calls would be made that day.

'What is past, is dead.'

I got up, had a shower, packed my small bag, ate some *ful medammes*[4] my cousin had left for me before going to work, knocked back four strong teas with heaps of sugar and chased them down with a pea of opium that I placed under my tongue, before jumping in a taxi and heading straight for the bus station.

◈◈◈

The man sitting beside me on the bus made strange hand movements. His breathing was silent, interrupted by loud snorts and throat clearings that jerked me out of the sleep I wished to fall into.

'I'm going to go crazy!'

He was talking to me but I really didn't feel like talking with him or anyone. Except for his dilated black eyes, his face was expressionless. His rotten teeth foretold his rancid breath that hit my face, making me hold my own breath in defence.

---

4 *Ful medames*, or simply *fūl*, is a dish of cooked fava beans served with vegetable oil, cumin, and optionally with chopped parsley, garlic, onion, lemon juice, chili pepper and other vegetable, herb and spice ingredients. It is a staple food in Egypt.

'By Allah, I love her. I have spent years in pain and never once have I asked Him to take me!'

The man slapped his thighs, then rocked back and forth with his upper body.

'*Insha'Allah*,[5] everything will be good. Allah is kind,' I said. I was exhausted. Eventually the man turned his face away from me and looked out at the desert whizzing by.

'Life has become so costly! Everything is so expensive, and the cost of living is unbelievable…' He turned his troubled face towards me again. 'Living is expensive, so may God take it! It's a crime it can be so! Don't you think it's a crime?' The man was beginning to unnerve me.

I nodded. He kept talking. 'Why do we have to have so much grief? Isn't it enough we're eating rocks in this life of ours? What kind of life is it anyway? Two births and both times twins—four children with a bottomless pit for the money spent on them. Six people on one wage living in a chicken coop. Should I have cut myself into pieces?'

I kept silent, doubting he would even hear me anyway if I spoke. He continued.

'My children were naked and we needed one thousand and one things. Yet, we went on with what we had. What else could we do? What!? Hamada, a man working with me, is a hard worker. He really is. But Hamada sells drugs after work. That is how he survives. I couldn't sell a chicken, with Allah as my witness! I couldn't even steal and yet they have cleaned me out. They have left me out to dry!'

I took out my pack of cigarettes and offered him one. 'Here, have a smoke. *Insha'Allah* things will get better.'

'By Allah!' he said. 'First, I gave up drinking, then I gave up smoking. What else can I give up? My life?' The man buried his head in his palms. And then raised it slowly. 'I don't blame her;

5 If God (Allah) wills it.

she is a much better person than I am. If it wasn't for her, the dogs would have eaten us. Yet my children…'

'Yes, the children…' I said in a soft voice.

'What do we do when the children are sick and we cannot pay for medicine? This is just one thing and this is how our life is. Tell me what to do. Tell me! Imagine it, my good man! She said it was our only solution. Either she's crazy or I am!' He was slapping his thighs and his eyes were flickering in every direction. I began to think the man was out of his mind. I was going to ask a question but then he began to smile.

'Believe me, the worst thing to do in life is to bottle it all up. I've been in Hell for the last couple of years, ever since she told me that she wanted to work. I thought she wanted to use her training as a nurse but she suggested something else.' The man's face was beginning to turn yellow. At the same time, I was curious as to what he wanted to tell me, though I was in no state of mind to feel any empathy. I kept quiet. He leaned towards me and lowered his voice.

'Had I known what she wanted to do I would have lost my mind there and then. She came one day and said, "*Habibi*,[6] our children are hungry and our life is hard. I wanted to tell you so you wouldn't say I was betraying you. It would be easier for me to lose my children than to do what I have done." We both cried that night. After that I thought of killing her but even that I couldn't afford.' The man leaned back in his seat and exhaled. 'She said I was the only one in the world and that every time she had closed her eyes and imagined it was me…' A tear was brimming in the corner of his left eye. Another outburst followed.

'May God curse a life in poverty. No man is worthy of such a life, no matter what!'

His voice was shaking. And whatever I wanted to say remained inside me as the first buildings passed by the window, signalling the

6 Can either mean 'friend' or 'beloved', depending on the context and intonation.

outskirts of Cairo. A short time later, the conductor walked down the aisle, rapidly announcing the first stop, Dar Al Eshara.

The man rose to his feet and I got up and made room for him to exit. He looked at me and said something that I didn't hear amid the commotion of exiting passengers. As I didn't react and just greeted him farewell, he turned around and made his way towards another passenger who had been seated a few rows ahead of us.

A woman had stood up and joined the exiting queue. She turned around and looked at him with an extraordinarily beautiful face. She put her hand up to her waist and moved her palm, rotating from side to side. An expression of curiosity was followed by disappointment as she looked straight back at me with large black eyes.

I didn't get up.

※※※

As the bus began moving again, I slipped the conductor a *bariza*, a ten-pound note, and told him I wanted to get off as soon as possible. I would have got off at that first stop and caught a cab to the airport but I knew I had to stay put. A crying husband with a beautiful wife in love, in despair, trying to survive, was a familiar fate I didn't want to get involved in. I just needed to get out before we passed Almaza and began entering the inner-city parts of Cairo. A journey to the airport from there would be lengthy, if not worse.

I stepped out of the bus and jumped straight into a cab. As we set off, a brief squabble about the airport and entry fees was quickly resolved with a generous addition to the fare. I didn't have the time nor the patience for the Cairo taxi driver game.

'You're not from here,' the driver said.

'No,' I said. 'I am in exile, my friend. Have been so all my life and it's time for me to leave again.'

'In safety, by the will of Allah, by the will of Allah,' he iterated.

The drive was short, and I felt relief being at the airport. I wanted to catch any flight to Europe so tried a dozen airlines before I found an empty seat. I could fly to Vienna with EgyptAir and connect onwards to Copenhagen with the stand-by return ticket I'd had since leaving Copenhagen. I paid in cash and the young lady at the ticket office put on an extra fat smile as she handed over the business class ticket and boarding pass as well.

'*Insha'Allah*, you will go swiftly through immigration. Just show them your ticket and they will work quickly.'

She had obviously not tried to leave her own country yet.

My heart beat like a drum as I approached the immigration officer. A European couple were ahead of me at the counter. The officer entered their information into the computer, glanced at them briefly, stamped their passports and handed them back with a smile. They were young, sunburnt and going back to a world the officer could only imagine.

The next person in line, an Egyptian roughly my age, was spoken to with curt disrespect, even though he used the 'sir' every few words to try and avoid any offence or delay. I prepared myself for like treatment.

As the officer stamped the man's passport and handed it back, not even looking at him, I straightened my back and was about to move forward when he looked at me and raised his hand, telling me to wait.

He got up, looked annoyed, and yelled out a man's name in a crude way: 'Methat, Methat!'

Another officer appeared and relieved him. This officer had a big belly, his uniform looking ready to burst around his waist and neck. He sat down, fiddled with some papers on the desk, checked the computer and took out a handkerchief to wipe the sweat off his entire face and neck. Then he looked up at me and used his index finger to signal 'come here'.

I was unctuously polite, taking the lead from the young man before me. I put down my Danish passport with the business class ticket inside it. He glanced at the ticket, then at me. Then he began entering my name onto the computer slowly, using only one fat index finger.

'What were you doing here, Mohammed?' he asked me.

'Visiting family, sir,' I replied, trying to convince myself that that had actually been the purpose.

He put my passport through the hole in the wall and asked me to go to a line of chairs and wait. I politely made him aware that I needed to hurry to catch my flight. He acknowledged.

A tall officer in an army uniform approached me shortly thereafter and led me to a small room with a desk and a computer and a portrait of Hosni Mubarak seemingly watching my every step with an imposed authority.

'Do you have your military discharge papers on you?'

For a second my heart stopped, then I quickly got my bearings. I knew that if I stayed more than six months, I would need the military's permission to leave the country. It transpired that my passport had been stamped incorrectly by immigration as arriving two years earlier than my actual arrival, less than a week earlier.

'Sir, someone has stamped my passport incorrectly. I just arrived a few days ago. My aunt is sick and asked me to come and see her. Surely the airline can sort this out within minutes.'

The officer picked up the phone and called a number.

'Yes, okay, fine.' He noted something on a piece of paper and called another number.

'Hassan, I have this young man here and there was a wrong stamp in his passport. What can we do?' A few more nods, a few more acknowledgements before he put down the phone again.

'Mohammed, unfortunately you have to go to the discharge office in Al Zagazig and they will write you the papers you need *for me* to allow you to leave the country.'

His tone was sincere but what he was asking me was crazy, as he well knew. Telling me that I needed to cancel my flight, leave the airport for Al Zagazig—a good five hours away by bus—just to get a piece of paper that most likely wouldn't be handed over straight away, but would demand a whole day's interrogation. And I would probably be sent back to Cairo to request the airline for a copy of my initial itinerary on arrival. What he was suggesting was impossible, and he knew it.

'Sir, is there any way I can expedite this? My flight leaves in thirty minutes, the gate is closing in ten. I will lose my job if I don't return today. My family needs me to provide for them and it's a disaster if I don't make this flight.' I kept as calm as I could and I let my voice choke up a bit.

The officer looked at me and rolled the ball point pen between his fingers, as if pondering how to help me. 'I can send a man to Al Zagazig with a copy of your passport and I will let you return to your family now.'

'Thank you! Thank you, sir!' I exclaimed.

'He will do so, only because I tell him. Do you understand?'

I nodded. 'Of course! May Allah keep you, sir! May Allah keep away hidden evil from you, sir!'

I laid it on thick. He picked up the phone again.

'Hassan, come down here, please.'

Moments later, Hassan came into the office and greeted me and the officer in a friendly way. The officer explained to Hassan, a skinny guy with leathery skin and a burgundy shirt tucked into a pair of oversized pants drawn all the way up to his waist, that he must go to Al Zagazig and finish my paperwork for me.

'Yes, sir!' he said without hesitation.

The officer handed me back my passport and ticket. I rose to my feet and shook his hand. Discreetly, I slipped a couple of hundred-dollar notes into the passport. 'Greet our friend a "good morning" appropriately and he will lead you all the way to the gate'.

'Please?' Hassan said, extending his hand.

I handed over the passport and the ticket to Hassan. He opened it, looked at the notes and closed it again. Then he nodded to the officer.

I quickly followed Hassan as he squeezed his way in between the crowds of people waiting in line for immigration. He walked me straight through security and straight to the gate where two staff members waited for me. Hassan handed them my passport and the ticket without any words exchanged and the sound of the paper tearing was as if I had found a key to the jail cell I'd been thrown into.

I shook Hassan's hand and thanked him.

'*Be'salaama insha'Allah!*'[7] he said, wishing me a safe journey.

I ran down an empty jet way and was met by two female flight attendants wearing too much make up. They quickly ushered me aboard and as I entered the aircraft, they pulled the door shut.

'Boarding completed,' a voice said as I was shown to my window seat and served an ice-cold orange juice. The plane was quickly pushed back and within minutes we were waiting in idle for take-off. It felt like an eternity until the captain fed the engines and the plane roared down the runway before finally letting go of the ground in a smooth rotation.

As the plane climbed through the smog, I looked down at the ganglion of life moving around below. I could almost smell the food cooking for dinner, sense the children playing in the courtyards, see the streetsellers carting their produce through a narrow alleyway, and taste the sweet shisha in my life. The plane banked sharply as it continued its ascent. I looked to the east and watched cars fade into the desert.

In the reflection of the window, I looked into my own eyes and cried in silence.

---

7 With safety, God willing!

11

It was a bitterly cold and dark winter's day in Copenhagen. I will never forget it. I hadn't talked to Ahmed for some months and as I was turning the key, about to walk into my second-storey apartment, the phone rang. With the key still in the keyhole, I waited. The only people who knew the number of this phone were my family. I waited a bit longer. In the end I turned the key, convincing myself it was my parents who always let the phone ring out. I picked up the handset.

It was my aunt, Ahmed's mother.

She told me that shortly after I flew out, Ahmed had had a serious car accident. Road workers had left an excavation unmarked and Ahmed had driven into the deep pit at high speed. He had been rushing a group of German tourists back to their cruise ship, anchored south of the Suez Canal. She told me how the government had quickly covered the hole and tried to blame Ahmed for the accident, saying he had been drinking. She also told me that Mido's parents had been frantically trying to come up with an explanation for their son's disappearance and that his mother would often come and sit with her for hours, crying.

Unable to receive treatment in time, Ahmed's body was paralysed from the waist down and sentenced to an existence horizontal in his bed at his mother's home. His sister would change him and his mother would wash him like a child. His wife had left him and left his family to look after their daughter as well.

'Every time he knows Mido's mother is coming, he asks me to not sit in his room. I don't understand,' my aunt said. I could only imagine.

'We all know what happened to Mido...' she said, and I held my breath. 'Like thousands of other young men, where else could he be? Of course, they must have taken him on the street, flirting with a girl or something and ... well, you know...' and then she went quiet.

I almost fainted as I waited for those words. Of course, the obvious explanation would be that Mido had disappeared in the back of a Box, like so many others. A young man in the wrong place at the wrong time who fell into the hands of bloodthirsty policemen.

It was such a plausible explanation that believing it almost made it easy ... not to feel bad any more.

EPILOGUE

I stayed away for almost two years, eventually returning to Suez, occasionally, to spend all my time in Ahmed's small room. The same room where years earlier, we had formed the idealistic plan to help the Palestinians in the second *Intifada* by getting them guns. So they wouldn't die in the street like dogs, but could fight back, like men. How the three of us in a room with a TV and a blanket of hashish in the air had made it happen, was a blur.

Ahmed stayed in his bed for nine years. He was no heavier than a small child when I carried him down the steps from his mother's apartment in Suez. He looked at me with dilated wet black eyes. I didn't mock him. I didn't tell him he'd be fine. I told him the truth. I told him I loved him, in Danish—'*jeg elsker dig*'—and laid him on the back seat in the red Hyundai. We took him to the hospital in Cairo, where he passed away a few weeks later.

Not long ago, I returned to visit his grave. It looks like a small brick house—four walls and partly covered by a concrete roof. The family name is written next to a set of steel gates. Inside, the ground is tiled and the steps leading to the underground chamber's entrance are exposed to the sun and filled with sand, covered with palm leaves. I burned the old dead leaves and paid a young man to lay fresh leaves on the graves. He was laying them sparsely, so I told him off. I put a five-pound note in his hand. 'Make it well. It's important.' The young man smiled and recited a rehearsed line of praises from the Koran. I looked around. The cemetery resembled more a market than a place for dead people. Cars were driving in and out through the dusty narrow lanes. Boys and young men were trying to sell everything from Koran readings to cold drinks.

The young man finished. I bought a prayer recitation for another pound and had to stop him, as it seemed to never end.

I walked back to the main road leading into Suez. The traffic from Cairo was coming in fast, yet a car slowed down. It was an old man.

'Where are you going to, my son?' he asked. He looked at me with kind eyes, as if I indeed was his son. 'To the beginning of the road.' I said. 'Or the end of the road for me,' he said, and smiled.

I can't remember his name but the old man was from that other time, one I had watched on TV, when Egypt was a country of the arts, where there were cinemas and theatres and no enemy to hate, and where the mosque called for prayers through human voices, not megaphones from China. From the time when Ahmed and I were kids.

I returned to my cousin's apartment and there I lay, sleepless, through the night. I reached under the bed and pulled out the Rambo knife. I clenched my hand around its rubber grip and tried to close my eyes, but all I saw were pictures gyrating as in a kaleidoscope. The harder I tried to close my eyes, the more pictures of what *was and is*, kept exposing themselves on top of each other. My eyelids tired, and the images faded away … until they appeared again.

I went back to 'living in the strange', as a stranger, and now I am as far away from home as I can possibly get. But it doesn't matter where I go. Mido is dead, Ahmed is dead, and the past is dead. Yet three o'clock in the morning is very much alive and it has found me sleepless, seeing Mido's head exploding in a billow of blood, over and over again.

Hearing the crack. Feeling the heat of the bullet. Its closeness to my eyes.

TWENTY TWO YEARS TO LIFE

إتْلَم اَلمتْعُوسْ عَلَى خَايِبْ اَلْرَجَا

The unlucky and the hopeless
have come together.

1

I am looking at the light of the brightest star in the sky. I am feeling dazed, as if I am floating on air. The star is moving towards me, approaching me from an immense distance. Its light is getting brighter and brighter. I hear my son whispering into my ear, *I love you, baba*, and I whisper back, *I love you, too*, just as there is a bright flash and the light of the star devours me.

❖❖❖

I drove so slowly down that pot-holed street. The water poured down from a grey sky. Rivers crisscrossed the asphalt and drains were gurgling with muddy water. The limping pace of the one wiper working, brought cover instead of taking away the rain. It dripped from every corner and crevice inside my father's old Mercedes Benz and I could hardly see past the hood of the car.

A bell rang. A shadow ran past the front of the car. Then another and another. I hit the brakes as a stampede of children came charging out of a school, hidden somewhere in the heavy rain. I sat there for a minute, listening to their excitement through the sound of the raindrops beating on the roof of the car. I caught a glimpse of some of them, running, smiling and screaming in a high pitch, all at once. I laughed quietly to myself.

Within moments, as if someone had turned the lights back on, the clouds cleared, the downpour eased to a light sprinkle, the noise of the children faded into a serene silence and bright sunbeams reflected in pools of water. I had to cover my eyes. The change was so strong, so sudden. A perfect rainbow appeared, following the fast-moving clouds like a soothing companion.

I watched in awe. Rainbows were rare. The smell of the sewer overflowing, however, was not, and the pungent odour quickly rose as the sun began to heat the ground. I was about to set the car in motion when I saw the road ahead had been washed away. A river of mud charged across it from the higher grounds in the west. I lifted myself up, hanging on to the door and balancing on the doorstep, just to take a closer look. I turned towards the school. A small group of people were standing there. I thought to ask them for a different way to the border, and it was then I laid my eyes upon her.

She held a pile of papers and binders against a white long-sleeved shirt—tucked neatly in—and wore a dark green skirt with a belt that had a golden buckle. Her legs were covered in black nylon stockings and she stood in small, slightly raised, stylish black shoes. She had long eyelashes, stunning brown eyes and long, straight black hair that was bound in a ponytail and almost reached her waist. Her face was covered with tiny drops of rain that made her dark skin shine, and I was sure she had been showered with gold dust. I saw her, she saw me. I looked cautiously around, making sure no one was watching us. She did the same. We smiled.

❖❖❖

We took our engagement vows six months later, at a small mosque in Al-Bayuk which at some time had been hit by a shell. We said the words, repeating after the imam[8], under the stars; and held our wedding a year after we met, on the beach in Al Mawasi. We had both just turned twenty and for a while our families thought it was going to remain at the engagement. We left the wedding party to consummate our marriage according to tradition, even though we had succumbed to our desire for each other months earlier. Her brother, Mahmoud, began seeking permits for every conceivable person that might come to our wedding. He would call me every second day, asking me for ID card details of my side of the family

8 A worship leader of a mosque and Muslim community among Sunni Muslims.

and my friends. He was also making sure I wasn't getting cold feet. The Israelis had their Gush Katif settlements surrounding the whole town, which meant they restricted the movement of the small native population as they pleased and didn't allow any visitors without prior permission.

I laughed every time Mahmoud asked me and he laughed as well. I kept telling him not to worry and he kept telling me he was honoured to have me in their family. Both families were accepting of us which was unusual considering our age and that our families didn't know each other. I would like to think it was because of our love for each other—and, of course, that was part of it. But we were both well-mannered and our families appreciated each other from the first day; and these were probably the main reasons no one objected.

From the day I met her I kept returning to the school every chance I got, even when I didn't have papers to take to the Egyptian immigration office at the border. She would meet me outside the school and later on, at a nearby mosque. It was safe there; we would talk for hours, and eventually, we decided it was time for our families to meet. Once they'd met, we could be closer to each other and it didn't take long before they left us by ourselves. And when that happened, we knew we didn't want to leave each other again. Her name was Farida and her family were originally Bedouins, having settled in Al Mawasi at the turn of the nineteenth century.

◈◈◈

The first year, we counted our blessings. It was our time and we didn't want to have children, just then. Our family and friends kept asking, but we managed our times of intimacy so it wouldn't happen. Farida was still working at the school and I would drive past once a month to file more papers, applying for permission to live across the border with my family on the Egyptian side of Rafah.

After two years I went to the doctor without telling Farida. I just wanted to know myself, just wanted to make sure. She did the same, of course. It didn't matter which doctor we saw or how many tests we did. The result remained the same. We were both fine.

Ten years later we were still praying for it to happen. Then came the first *Intifada* and it changed everything. A taste of freedom was replaced with a sense of fear. We had to be careful of our ways, even our thoughts. I bought us a very small apartment in Gaza City and accepted that I wouldn't be able to move to Egypt. I joked about buying the apartment and said it was just like lighting up a cigarette when waiting for the bus. The bus will arrive, but the child didn't.

2

The first *Intifada* ended in 1993 and when the second began at the turn of the millennium, we had saved enough money to go to Canada to see a specialist. It had taken months to secure the permits to travel to Cairo to be able to fly to Montreal via Paris. Bahir, my uncle, would help us with our asylum; at least that's what he said. He didn't come to meet us at the airport, and we were stranded in a frozen January Montreal with only halting English to our names.

After waiting for hours, we decided to walk to a nearby hotel. Not to get a room but to sit and wait in the lobby. We left a note with a young woman at the airport information counter. She was very kind, and with hand gestures and slow speech, told us she would keep an eye out for the man we described in case he turned up. The airport was empty at two in the morning. She surveyed us with pensive eyes, obviously not dressed for the cold, and asked if we had more clothes, but we didn't.

As the sliding doors to the outside opened, the warm air was sucked out. I remember the first breath almost hurt. That's how cold it was. We didn't make it to the hotel. Halfway there, in stumbling amazement of the falling snow, Farida slipped on the icy ground and broke a bone in her hand. A car stopped and a man got out, asking if we needed help. He looked at Farida holding her hand and asked us to let him take us to the hospital. I said, 'No, no hospital. Waiting family,' but the man wouldn't accept my answer.

'I'm sorry, I have to insist. You will freeze to death out here.'

We followed the man to his car; James Hoey was his name. He was large, looked strong like an ox, and spoke with an English accent I'd never heard before. He took us to a large red brick building with windows in rows and told us it was called Richardson Hospital. He spoke calmly to the Emergency reception in French. We didn't understand and we couldn't do anything but sit and wait. Then he turned to us a final time and said, 'everything is taken care of and they will see you shortly. Good luck, and welcome to Canada!'

We were exhausted, and the only thing we managed to express was a 'thank you'. And then he left, and we never saw him again. Shortly after, we were led to an examination room. It was the cleanest, most well-equipped hospital room I'd ever seen.

They must have known we spoke Arabic. The nurse's name was Aziza. She had chocolate round cheeks and radiated goodness. She spoke to us in Egyptian Arabic, asked us every possible question, and we answered as if we were being interrogated by Israeli soldiers. She kept cracking jokes about it, asking us to relax, but somehow, we didn't know how to. Perhaps it was bewilderment over being in a place where we hadn't yet been harassed. We were at the mercy of the people around us, as we had been from the day we were born. That day was the first time we had seen what life could look like outside Palestine.

After having done everything possible for Farida, the nurse asked us to wait in the waiting room. We took our two large suitcases and followed her to her car. She took us to her home and kept us like family—in our eyes, better.

◈◈◈

Dr John Mousley looked puzzled the last time he spoke to us as a doctor.

'I have been examining couples for almost thirty years and I don't know what to say…'

He shuffled the papers on his desk, silently gazing at test results. He took a deep breath and sat back in his chair.

'You're both fine. We tried other eggs, we tried different semen on your wife's eggs. The egg is fertilised. Yet when we try with the two of you, nothing happens. It's like you meet and stay together and eventually perish together. We've tried many times over with the exact same result. I have never seen anything like this.'

Tears ran down from Farida's eyes. I wanted to put them back.

'Is this the final answer for us?' I asked, pleading.

'I can only recommend you go and see another specialist. Perhaps it's some sort of hormone deficiency. Or it could be something entirely different.' He paused for a second. 'There are some very good people in the US. I can give you their names if you'd like?'

We had used up all our money, been refused entry to the US and had a return ticket to Cairo a fortnight later. We knew our time was up. I looked at Farida. She was staring out the window, the reflections of the passing clouds mirrored in her eyes. She was praying silently.

I looked back at the doctor. He had been genuinely interested since the day we came to him. He knew how far we had travelled, and without saying, he hadn't billed us for many of the examinations, but kept asking us about our lives, how we'd met, and what it was like living in Gaza.

'Thank you, doctor. We need to go home soon. You have been very helpful and kind to us.'

Dr John shook our hands and kept standing as we closed the door behind us.

He invited us to dinner before we left Canada and we accepted. We went to a large two-storey home in the hills overlooking Montreal, the light of the city sparkling from below in a breathtaking view. Dr John had two beautiful children. Tim, the oldest, was studying nanoscience and Anika ran a successful eye clinic in the centre of the city. They were both in their twenties. His wife, Jody, was caring and genuine, and had put a lot of effort into the dinner preparations. She had made us *Maqluba* and *Zibdieh*[9], traditional dishes from Gaza; as I tasted the food, tears ran uncontrollably down my cheeks. Farida looked at me and we held each other in a close hug—our next stop was our home and at the same time, our prison.

---

9 *Maqluba*: An 'upside-down' dish, made with fried vegetables, meat (chicken/lamb) and rice. *Zibdieh*: Shrimp cooked with red peppers, garlic and peeled tomatoes.

Dr John and his family stopped eating and quietly waited for us to compose ourselves.

'It's so good, it made us think of home!' Farida exclaimed with tears in her eyes. Everyone smiled and sighed with relief.

Dr John took my hand and looked me in the eyes as we were leaving their home.

'I will pray for you and Farida. Sometimes we can't understand everything, and I believe, sometimes we're not meant to. I know there is a God and you both know this, too—in fact, we share the same God… May Allah be with you.'

3

The Israelis were leaving their settlement. We watched it on the news: settlers not wanting to let go of what they had stolen from our families in the first place, chaining themselves to anything possible. The scenes bore no dignity. Adult women, screaming at the top of their lungs and beating the soldiers that came to unchain them, were dragged down the street kicking as if they were being moved from one insane asylum to another. We sat with our friends in Gaza City and watched in silence; and some of us cried in silence. The anchor woman was reading the news as if we had triumphed in war, but the Israelis did everything they could to make sure we heard what dignified thieves they were, telling the world how we would turn their paradise into a dump. I didn't care. I didn't understand the occupation and I didn't understand the *Intifada*. I was driven by a strong wish to feel happy, to go through the four seasons of the year with a smile and to be able to breathe deeply.

Farida broke the silence in a serious tone: 'I wonder if they will leave the swimming pools?'

We all knew what the answer was, and we all laughed loudly. Even Farida.

The Israelis demolished everything.

4

On the 14th of November 2005, we moved to Farida's birthplace without having to apply for permits. Up until that day, Al Mawasi had been known as the 'Prison within the Prison' because not only had we been treated like animals—going back to Gaza through roadblocks and checkpoints but also within the community itself—the Israeli army would impose the same kind of indignity. There had been a ring of ten-foot-high fencing with razor wire and every conceivable type of surveillance surrounding the Israeli settlements. We had previously only stayed for short periods of time; it had been too difficult to live there. Visiting my family in Rafah just a couple of kilometres away meant going through four checkpoints, two roadblocks and a border crossing, and spoken to through a megaphone by Israeli soldiers on elevated ground, like the chosen overlords they truly believe they are. Spending time with Farida's relatives, less than a kilometre away, had meant going through either a roadblock or a checkpoint, and sometimes that hadn't been possible. Life in Gaza City, had by comparison, been peaceful.

We didn't know what to expect but we had prepared our personal numbers, just in case. Without those numbers we hadn't been able to enter or exit Al Mawasi. Mine was 877, Farida's 107. I felt like a cow: branded with a number and having to queue up to enter the stable my imposed master controlled. We arrived in the late morning hours. There was no pillbox covered in black netting, no rifles sticking out of its dark hole, no high concrete wall slabs and no megaphones shouting commands at us. Until that day, the Israelis had completely enclosed the large settlement from us but still forced us to go through a checkpoint every time we wished to enter or leave our own homes. The wire fence that had separated us and served as our viewing platform to the chosen people, had now been removed. The road that used to run along their side of the fence had been shredded; no army jeeps or latest model SUVs were dotting it anymore. The road on our side of the fence still looked the same, still single-laned, still with beaten-up rusty vans dodging the large holes in the bitumen at a tedious pace.

We opened our eyes to a scene of destruction instead of the lush gardens and homes we had driven past when the fences were up. The settlements had been demolished down to the last brick. We didn't care, instead we began clearing where we were to build our first home, where Farida's grandparents had once lived before being forcefully expelled by the Israelis in 1968.

Lifting a brick repeatedly up and down over my head in joy, I turned to Farida and smiled: 'We will have a home! A home!'

Farida laughed, lifted up her skirt and danced around me: 'And we will fill it with the laughter of children! *Ya Allah, ya Allah, ya Allah!*'[10]

10 My dear God, my dear God, my dear God!

5

The electricity had been out for two days and the hot winds of that early summer, mixed with the moisture of the ocean, made the heat suffocating. I hadn't been able to sleep well. I stayed in bed for a while and looked at Farida next to me, little pearls of sweat covering her face. She had her arms under her head and had tied her thick long hair up. Twenty-two years had passed since I first laid eyes on her and still I soaked her up, every day.

Farida had for a while been filling out nicely. Soft rings had formed on her neck and her breasts had grown voluminous. Her appetite was dressing our life with contented evenings. She'd cook our favourite dishes and we'd make love, quivering with pleasure and satisfaction. My work as an agricultural engineer endowed me with an abundance of kind and humble farmers who provided me with free produce of all kinds in exchange for irrigation parts, pumps and other equipment that ill-managed donation programs had left deteriorating in warehouses. Cigarettes were exchanged for a pump, then exchanged for a couple of plump chickens. It worked out well for everyone.

I got dressed and took the four flights down the stairs, my footfalls clattering at a quick pace. We lived in the neighbourhood of Shuja'iyya, just to the east of Gaza City. I made my way to the main road, Salah El-Din, to try to hunt down a streetseller with bread. If I didn't make it in time, I could spend close to an hour in a queue, trading UN food assistance coupons for reconstituted bread that contained more sand than flour. I had money, though. I was lucky—it was rare that I had to stand in the queue. Dignity meant allowing the men with children to purchase the bread before myself, often returning to Farida empty-handed.

It was still five in the morning, and men greeted each other with an unsettling haste while on their daily mission to secure bread. Azeem was at his usual spot. I liked him; he was always informal with me and if he didn't have bread, he'd shoot off some kid to go and find me a loaf somewhere. He had just arrived, was laying out *barseem* (greens) for his donkey and I was the first to greet his morning.

'*Sabah el-kheir*,[11] ya Azeem.'

'*Sabah el-kheir*, ya Fathi.'

Yet there was no morning of blessings, I thought to myself. Azeem only had two loaves of bread on his cart, most likely awaiting pickup. Strangely, there were a couple of eggs there as well.

'Are you selling eggs this morning for me to make my own bread?' I asked, pulling a smile.

'You are always the joker! No, that would mean we have to ask the UN for more yeast and if we do that, they'll put it on the banned list. Allah forbid that!' he said, loudly laughing, almost dropping his two last rotten teeth.

'Fathi…' He then said in a quiet voice, leaning over towards me. 'Khokha suddenly began laying eggs. I was about to butcher her when I saw an egg, so I left her. And look…' He pointed to the eggs. 'An egg every day… And you know how much fresh eggs are…' and then he leaned back to a standing posture, looking content and self-important.

'May Allah give you fortune and happiness,' I said, still smiling.

Azeem had already sold the two loaves of bread but decided the customer picking them up would still be grateful for a single one. He would find a good excuse, he told me. We haggled back and forth over the price of the two eggs, and they ended up dearer than the loaf of bread. I took my shoe off, removed the sock from my left foot and put the eggs in it, like priceless crystals.

---

11 Good morning.

Farida was still sleeping when I came back. I prepared a large breakfast for us, and when I went to wake her up, I realised I had lost track of time and it was getting late for work. I got organised hastily, made myself a couple of sandwiches, put the rest of the food back in the fridge, left her a loving note and closed the front door gently.

I drove through Al Bayuk. The mosque with the missing roof where Farida and I had held our hands on the Koran twenty-one years earlier had been reduced to a pile of rubble. Heavy bombardment from the Israelis had laid waste to a large part of the small community, and though it should have been busy at this time of the day, it was quiet. The hot air had already made its way from the Sinai and small whirlwinds formed, twirling rubbish and dust around. I stopped. The engine idled irregularly, and the barking of a stray dog broke the steady tune of the wind.

I stepped out and walked over to what had once been the entrance of the mosque. There were all sorts of papers scattered on the ground. Letters, certificates, applications and dozens of different types of books. Religious learning books, fictional books and even comic books. Most of them were badly damaged but you could still make out what they were. I crouched down and picked up what looked to be a children's book, but it turned out to be a cover with a drawing of a man and large woman with a big belly, smiling.

The title read, 'How a baby is made', in Arabic.

I laughed to myself. Judging by the print, the book was a local copy, one of many that printers in Gaza used to translate from English to Arabic and sell through street vendors and private bookshops. I wondered what had happened, when even books like these were now considered *haram*[12] by the regressive line of religious dogma that had been imposed on us.

---

12 Forbidden or proscribed by Islamic law.

For a few moments, I went nowhere. Images from the past turned through my mind like a kaleidoscope. I got lost in the memories of my life, drifting through an iridescent ocean shining the hues of times long gone in kindred thoughts, emotions, places and people. I slowly settled back into the port of my senses and the words before my eyes. I put the book down again and walked back to my car.

I was late.

◊◊◊

I parked next to a large black Mercedes that looked as if it had just come out of the factory. The windows were all black-tinted, even the front. I heard voices from afar and saw three men in the distance, standing in the shade of an olive tree. I tried to make out what was happening. I sat there watching them, looking back at the expensive car next to mine, finishing my cigarette. Perhaps the men were using the tree to hide and watch some sort of trouble that I couldn't see. Perhaps an official was visiting and, if so, I had to look my best. The farm lay very close to the Rafah border crossing to Egypt, less than a kilometre away, separated by a rusty fence with barbed wire on the top. I felt lethargic. I wanted to go home and have a nap next to Farida but I needed to finish what I came to do. I had to write out a licence for a piece of farmland that the owner wished to build a house on. I got out of the car, flicked away the ash on my shirt and approached the men, walking calmly, greeting from a fair distance.

'*Asalaamu aleikum.*'[13]

Abdul Ghani, the farmer, was the first to turn to me, then another man I didn't know and finally the third man, whom I knew. Khaled Abu Mohammed.

All three men replied in unison: '*We aleikum a'salaam*'.[14]

---

13 Peace be upon you. A standard salutation among Muslims, whether socially or within worship and other contexts.

14 Response to above greeting: And upon you be peace.

Abdul Ghani was a skinny man of about forty-five, although he looked more like seventy-five. He had wrinkles all over his face and his teeth were almost gone so it was sometimes hard to understand him. Every time I saw this man, he was wearing a beanie. I'm not sure how he could manage it in the heat, but it looked a part of him. He had lost all his hair in sorrow of his mother's death, or so the story went. I couldn't imagine this man sad, though—light seemed to shine from his face. He ran over to me half hunchbacked and we exchanged cheek kisses. At the same time, he shook my hand fiercely. The palm of his hand felt like a leather shoe.

The man I didn't know was a friend of Abdul Ghani. He introduced himself as Hisham and he seemed as kind and humble as his friend. He kept his hands behind his back, only extending the right one to greet me and then keeping silent, just smiling at times for no apparent reason. I finally shook Khaled's extended hand. He didn't let go but stopped shaking after a moment, staring directly into my eyes. I felt uncomfortable. Abdul Ghani stepped in.

'This is my good friend, Fathi,' he said as he tripped on a dead branch and ended up hanging on to my shoulder instead of clapping me on the back as he usually would. 'Fathi works for the ministry of agriculture and we are always honoured when he visits.'

Khaled looked at me and lifted his eyebrows. 'I have heard of you. Someone told me they call you by…by…by…' and he kept flicking his fingers, showing he was trying to remember a name—which he knew did not exist. When boys enter the rows of men, they are also called by the name of their first-born child. He was Khaled, father of Mohammed. I was Fathi. He continued making a mockery of me. 'When Allah chooses the day, you will receive your good name,' he said as he looked up to the sky with the palms of his hands facing up, as a symbol of praying.

I wasn't taking the bait. I kept silent.

'Look up, look up!' Abdul Ghani said excitedly, still hanging on to my shoulder. I looked up and in the tree, two chickens were perched. They looked old, patches of feathers were missing on their bellies. Other than that, I couldn't see anything. I was puzzled.

'When I came into their nest with the axe in my hand, they went running. I didn't lock the door and you know how slowly I move, so I let them go and they went up the tree and have been there ever since.'

'Why don't you get a stick and drive them down. We can catch them for you now.'

Khaled and Hisham laughed and Abdul Ghani followed suit. I was about to head back and leave; Khaled's remarks had triggered an increasing feeling of frustration. I didn't even need to be there. I knew what the farm looked like, I knew where Abdul Ghani wanted to build. I was just peddling bureaucracy. He wanted to place a barn over the desert, but even if it was fertile river land, the department wouldn't care less, as long as they received the fee for the permit. The fact that it was a desert and the fact that Abdul Ghani was poor, just meant I needed to sign it off with the smallest fee possible.

'*Habibi*, I was going to slaughter them, but Allah has sent me a blessing. They started laying eggs!' Abdul Ghani was radiating with joy.

'Eggs!?' I exclaimed and looked up at the two old chickens flicking their heads from side to side, eyeballing another spectator.

'Exactly. Eggs! Who would believe Allah is capable of such miracles? *Allahu Akbar!*[15]'

'*Allahu Akbar, Allahu Akbar…*' Both Hani and Khaled followed suit. Then I did the same, in a slightly muffled and dragged out voice.

'*Allah-hu Ak-bar…*'

That day it appeared Allah had decided to give every old chicken a second chance.

---

15 God is most great. Used by Muslims in prayers and as a general declaration of faith or thanksgiving.

God, what do you have in store for me next?

I came to my senses before I let the thought reverberate through my mouth. Khaled looked at me, then signalled his leaving by beginning to walk towards his car.

'*Insha'Allah*, you will be blessed too. I can understand you must be afraid of saying *Insha'Allah* now, but have faith. *Insha'Allah*, Allah will give you your good name!'

I kept calm and stared deep into Khaled's eyes. And while he slowly walked past me for what seemed an eternity, I said: '*Insha'Allah*, may Allah hear your kind words. Do you want something?'

He stopped briefly, not once removing his eyes from mine.

'May Allah keep you Fathi. But keep your white penny for your black day.' Khaled said as he placed his right hand on his heart.

'Do *you* want something?' he asked.

'May Allah keep you,' I replied in a polite voice.

'*Yalla, Allah maekom*,'[16] Khaled farewelled, as he walked back to his car. I only turned my head when I saw the plume of dust chasing the black dot like a wave until it finally engulfed it as he stopped on the main road and headed towards the border.

I looked back at Abdul Ghani. His eyes flickered and his voice shook slightly. I could have asked him the reason for Khaled's visit, but I already knew. Abdul Ghani was a poor man. Building a barn on desert land, especially with very little produce in need of storage, only meant one thing. Abdul Ghani had agreed to let Khaled Abu Mohammed cross the border to Egypt underneath his land. And what better place to hide an entrance than under the roof of a poor farmer's barn.

Abdul Ghani refused to let me leave without me accepting the first two eggs his chickens had laid. I didn't want to take them but eventually I decided not to hurt his pride. I had only a signature in return to offer him. A signature, however, that would prevent him from starving. To me, the paper was worth less than the eggs.

16 Let's go, God be with you (plural).

To Abdul Ghani, it represented sitting next to the chickens—a second chance. To Khaled Abu Mohammed, it meant more business, more power. If I didn't sign the papers, he would make sure I didn't get to sign any other ones. He only turned up so I would know I was dealing with him and not a poor farmer. I finalised the documents on the spot and had Abdul Ghani sign to pay only a symbolic fee.

6

Spanning two countries, Rafah was split in 1982 when Israel withdrew from the Sinai. The town lies at the bottommost tip of the Gaza Strip. On both sides of the border with Egypt, a wide strip has been bulldozed and the rubble left to form hill-sized mounds with jagged peaks. Without the children playing on them, they would resemble a landmark of concrete dunes. Squalid buildings in grey Portland cement colour are separated by narrow rubbish-ridden alleys that are crowded with frustrated, unemployed, bloodshot-eyed men in their prime. On the 12th of November 1956, one hundred and eleven Palestinians were shot dead in a cold-blooded massacre by Israeli soldiers, which left the town in the grip of revenge. Rafah was the home of martyrs.

I drove along the border. A dirt road, parallel to what the Egyptians so aptly called the metal road, gave away its location next to the steel fence separating us. I avoided going through Rafah city, not wanting to be seen in case someone else from the department was there. Usually I would have faith in people, but in Rafah I knew I was also better off avoiding the alleyways leading to Tal Al Sultan, a large refugee camp north of the city. They were full of people whose lesser fortune created a whole set of different rules that were based on self-justice. This is where Mohammed lived, not because he had to, but because he chose to. It was his home and the people of the camp spoke his language. I had grown up on what was now the Egyptian side of Rafah and as I approached one of the roads leading back into the camp I could see across to where my uncle Zaki and Aunt Fatma lived. It was probably less than a kilometre from where I turned, separated by the rusty steel fence and the ideas of fearful men.

I glanced at the fuel gauge. The needle had been resting on empty for a while now. I was almost out but didn't want to get fuel before I left my car. Not in Rafah. Thirty kilometres is a long way in Gaza and fuel was something that was scarce—at times so that I couldn't do my work. I knew the fuel station at the border was empty so the one in Rafah city would be as well. And in case I managed to get fuel somehow, I couldn't leave my car out on the street. Thieves would be walking past, shaking it to hear if it had enough for a quick grab. I'd have to wait and hope I would get lucky later. The department would allow us to buy 'illegal' fuel if needed. It would be smuggled in from Egypt or Israel and then sold in either ten-litre jerkins or one-litre bottles.

I weaselled my way through horse carts, donkey carts, young men in tight jeans with arms clinched, girls wearing high heels and giggling behind their veils, seeking eyes biting their nails and street-corner watchmen who followed me with walkie-talkies in their hands whilst boys played football as if the streets were empty.

◈◈◈

I heard voices behind the door as I leaned my head on it. I knocked and waited. Four large bolts were shifted with a heavy metallic sound. Mohammed's wife, Sarah, eventually opened it and sent me a big smile before swallowing the last bit of food in her mouth.

'Mohammed, come and have a look,' she said, as she turned her head away from me.

'What! Who is it? Do you really want me to get up? Can't they hear we are eating?' Mohammed spoke back loudly, clearly with his mouth full of food, clearly agitated.

'Just come and look!' She said, walking away from the door. I remained standing there.

Mohammed held the food back behind a strongly muffled voice as he tried to exclaim his joy at seeing me. He put his hand up like an upside-down flower still not open, signalling me to wait a second while he swallowed. He extended his right arm to me with the hand bent downwards, as it was greasy. I took it and he dragged me in.

The smell of roasted chicken filled the air and I smiled.

'It's the day of the chickens!' I loudly pronounced as I took his arm and we kissed each other twice on both cheeks and looked each other in the eyes.

I asked him how he was.

'*El hamdullah*,[17] ya Fathi,' he said smiling, and returned the question.

'*El hamdullah*, ya Mohammed. *El hamdullah,*' I replied with a smile.

'It is the only thing we can do, to be grateful to Allah. *Yalla*, come, join us! Sarah, prepare for *Ustaz*[18] Fathi!' Mohammed's voice shook the air like a drum.

'May Allah bless you, Mohammed, but I must get back to Farida soon and she is making me … Chicken, I think!' I said laughingly.

Mohammed was a tall and handsome man. His eyes were like honeycomb on fire, his hair pitch black in contrast. His skin was coloured like rye and his beard—as black as the rest of his hair—followed the lines of his square cheeks. Sarah was Mohammed's second wife. Zeinab, his first wife, was killed when the taxi she and their children were in, stopped at a jam-packed intersection. It was rush hour. Kids were crossing the streets in all directions, young men hastily trying to sell handkerchiefs or washing windscreens as the cars came to a standstill. An Israeli F-16 fighter jet with a pilot that followed orders without question had already locked in on the car right next to them and pushed the button. In the time it would have taken the missile to ignite, fly through the air, reach the car and explode, Zeinab and their two sons, Abdul-Halim and Haydar, would only just have managed to look out the window and chase the roar of the fighter jet. Then it was all over.

---

17 Praise be to God (Allah).

18 Honorific title for a man in the Middle East.

The explosion created a large hole in the street and in it, the car that had carried a family of four, not some prominent military figure, had been turned into a mash of shrapnel and body parts. The other cars had been crushed against each other and the carnage suggested that of a human slaughterhouse. Flying glass had cut into scores of people, and although most survived, those surrounding the bullseye were immolated.

I had to get four other men to help throw Mohammed to the ground and we tied him up against a lamppost, screaming and kicking, until I had removed his children. Words fail to describe the silent conversation I had with death when I removed the two six-year-old twin boys who were left frozen in an incinerated pose of shielding themselves.

Both Haydar and Abdul-Halim were in their first week of school and had been carrying their little plastic backpacks. The explosion had melted the bags onto their skin and turned their clothes into ash. Haydar was still warm, charred beyond recognition. I knew it was him because he was the one with the large appetite. He was stiff and his skin felt hard and brittle under my fingertips. A man from the Red Crescent helped as we wrapped both of them in towels to be taken to Zeinab's parents.

I went back to Mohammed who, tied to the lamppost, looked like a crazy animal: foaming mouth, kicking legs and twisting body, screaming at me with his mighty voice to let him loose, threatening to kill me if I didn't. I got on my knees, unable to stop shaking, and looked him in the eyes. I tried to utter something, just one word, but nothing came out. Mohammed fell to sobbing as he stared back at me, tears running from his eyes. I went around to his back and untied him. He got up and straggled his way towards the taxi. Several men surrounded him, some wanting to stop him, some telling the others to wait and let him be. I didn't move. I watched my childhood friend try to lift the body of his beloved Zeinab out of the car, only to have her tear apart like a papier-mâché Catrina with warm pulp bursting out from inside.

The following day Mohammed tried to touch Haydar and Abdul-Halim, but every time he came close, he stopped an inch away from their black bodies as if trying to find a place to lay his strong hands without hurting them. Instead, he prayed a single prayer, kissed the bodies of both his sons gently on the forehead, whispered something in Zeinab's ear and stroked what was once her face with the back of his hand, like running a feather on soft skin. He didn't shed a single tear. He rose like a lion standing upright, and then fainted to the ground.

We buried his family in a silence of low muffled prayers.

7

Mohammed had, once upon a time, been my hero. He would throw himself in front of anyone who tried to force themselves on me. He would swing the fists I did not know how to swing, and he would fire the words I had never heard at home. As we grew up and discovered the reality of our lives, we developed a bond like brothers. Circumstance had chosen us, as if it was meant to be; I was the brain and Mohammed the brawn. We would always look after each other. Mohammed would find promising business deals that involved some sort of risk and with his physique, his commanding posture and voice, he was the man on the scene while I was the brain with the numbers and connections. In the late nineties when I took up my position in the department, I knew it would secure me a fair salary and a certain amount of immunity in our dealings across Gaza. We traded everything from sugar to fertilisers, anything from shovels to spare parts. However, as the second *Intifada* came, most of our dealings were rendered unviable or impossible. In the volatility that followed, it was Mohammed's brain that freed us from the daily food coupon frays as he found a new source of income, which although highly risky, also afforded financial security for our families.

'I saw Khaled today...' I said slowly, after we had finished catching up on past and current news. Mohammed stayed silent for a moment. I glanced over at him. He was gazing down at the piece of chicken in his hand. It was only him and me sitting there. Sarah had begun to clear the floor setting, and his son, Abdallah, was watching a cartoon on TV.

'So... did he say anything?' Mohammed uttered, tearing off small strips of meat from the piece of chicken, putting them slowly into his mouth, chewing even more slowly.

'What was he supposed to say, Mohammed, tell me?' I said, now waiting for him to look at me.

'They must have caught them. Maybe even killed them. The last shipment never arrived. Khaled didn't have anything for me last time, so I began asking around and one of the men at the border told me the Egyptian army had found Israeli weapons in the desert not far from here.' He finally raised his head with a worried look on his face.

'Will our names cross the border?'

'I am not sure, Fathi. They need Khaled as much as we do, but…' He stared straight ahead.

'But what?' I asked, feeling like I could taste war regurgitated.

'You know how they work. You know that if they want to know, they will know. If you are asking me what will happen now—I think nothing. The shipments were all clean, we never found any tracking devices, and nobody knows about us.'

Mohammed took a deep breath after saying it all without a pause.

'There's still Khaled…' I watched Mohammed's reaction.

'Abu Mohammed will do what he needs to do to survive. We knew that and it hasn't changed.' He sighed.

I drank the last bit of the tea Sarah had made for me and let Mohammed get up and wash his hands. She brought another tea out as Mohammed came back from the bathroom, drying his hands and face with a towel.

'Thank you, but I have to go…' I said, politely, to Sarah.

'I have fresh water, you fool!' Mohammed said with a laugh.

We went to the balcony. Our sweet tea was made with clean spring water from Egypt. Most of the tap water in Gaza was salty. We'd bathe in it and wash our clothes in it but had to buy desalinated water which we used for cooking and even drinking at times, although it tasted awful. I took another sip and looked over the railing. The street was busy, and from the fifth floor, it looked like any other street in Gaza. The movement, the sounds and the smells were comforting from that level. It brought about a sense of freedom, of detachment, only watching it like a bird, not having to land.

'In Canada, the streets were empty,' I said as I was looking down.

'What do you mean: empty?' Mohammed asked in a puzzled tone.

'They were empty. It was so cold that people were either in their cars or walking inside in the underground city I told you about … And even there it was empty. It felt as if every man, every woman, every child was in their own world. So quiet. So clean. So empty.'

'Did you want to stay?' Mohammed asked after humming, as if trying to understand what I was really saying. However, I had no other meaning intended. I was merely preoccupied—for the second time that day, wondering if happiness was simply accepting that circumstances had chosen one.

'I didn't and I did.' I looked at Mohammed. He had sat down cross-legged and was looking at me, listening.

'We went to Canada for help but we also saw an opportunity—a place where you can live without worrying that you are closing your eyes for the last time every night you go to bed. And we also saw unhappiness like we'd never seen it before. As if they invented something to worry about, because they had nothing to worry about.'

I looked at Mohammed staring past his glass into nowhere and decided to stop talking about Canada. I only had an idea of where his mind might have drifted off to.

'*Ya akhi!*[19] Let's talk about something else,' I said and sighed.

'How is Farida?' he asked me.

'She's as beautiful as the day I first saw her. Mind you, a lot more like a ripe plum these days!' I said, chuckling pleasurably.

'May Allah keep her for you. Even like a ripe plum!' Mohammed's smile stretched across his face and radiated as he leaned towards me and whispered.

'I'm not supposed to tell anyone yet, but Sarah—'

---

19 My brother!

I interrupted Mohammed before he finished what he was about to say.

'*Mabruk, mabruk!*[20] May Allah give you another beautiful child and keep them for you!'

I was so happy for Mohammed that I forgot the loudness of my voice. Suddenly I saw Sarah's hand hit him on the shoulder with a clenched fist. Half his tea spilled out and he cringed to avoid more blows. They were both laughing.

'Well, *ustaz* Fathi, you are the first to know. Not even my parents know yet,' Sarah said, smiling with her entirety, staring at Mohammed with a flirting demeanour.

Less than a year after Zeinab was killed, Mohammed had married Sarah, her younger sister.

I congratulated them both until Abdallah interrupted me. It was just the right time for him to come and sit on his father's lap. There it was, right in front of me, like the photograph concealed in the glove compartment of Mohammed's car.

In the same place, with Haydar and Abdul-Halim on his lap, Zeinab standing next to him.

20 Congratulations!

8

With the jerrycan of fuel Mohammed poured into the tank of my car, I headed back to Gaza City. It was becoming dark and I was sure Farida was getting worried but there was no signal on my cell phone. I drove slowly past an old man making a living selling calls from a desk with an old rotary telephone on it. I gestured, querying if he was in business, to which he answered 'no' with a wave of the hand. I left Rafah.

Darkness engulfed me like a black cocoon. The headlights made a curved line which faded into the unknown ahead. I kept my eyes peeled as I pulled the black cloth closer and closer to me, rolling over the bitumen at a firm pace. Only dim flickers of light were visible in the far background. There were no fighter jets, no explosions, and besides the rattle and shake of the car, I was breathing in an eerie silence through the open window.

I almost hit him as I veered around a large pothole. It was a flash. Was that a boy sitting curled up in the sand? Although it lasted only a split second, I took in what I had seen: dirty, small. I had already let my foot off the accelerator but hadn't put my foot on the brake yet. I hesitated for a second. Did I just imagine it? I stopped. No other car was in sight. The heat from the engine rose up the side and made me squint as I tried to make out any movement in the side mirror. Nothing. I began reversing and kept looking to the far side of the beam that filled with the dust the tyres picked up. As I hit the pothole I had avoided earlier, the car turned sharply and I hit the brakes. The dust settled in the beams of the headlights and there he was, sitting right in front of the car, holding his hand up in front of his eyes.

For a minute we both sat there. I turned on the interior light and he got up.

He walked straight over and put his small hands on the windowsill. Dried lines of tears ran from his eyes and were rubbed out with dirty hands, halfway down his thin face. His cheeks were flat, his eyes were yellow, almost golden-coloured and his eyebrows, nearly grown together, framed them in a fuzzy way. His ears stuck out a bit and his hair was curly and light brown. He wore a nylon sports singlet, FC Barca, like every other kid in Gaza; but his was torn and rank. His grey jeans showed no sign of having been washed and his worn slippers hung onto his cracked feet. He was restless, moving his whole body as if waiting for a handout or an order.

'What are you doing here? Are you waiting for someone?' I asked him. He didn't answer. Just smiled with large teeth that were in need of care.

'What's your name, my son?' We were face to face.

'Aboud, sir.' His eyes flickered randomly, looking around the inside of the car. I wasn't sure if he was telling the truth.

'Where is your home? Do you want me to take you somewhere?' I asked, inquisitively.

'I will go with you if you want sir. Do whatever you like, sir,' he said slowly.

For a second I was confused and then it struck me that he was offering himself to me. He needed money. I felt blood rushing to my face, disgusted by images my mind created of the pervert sitting in the previous car. I collected myself, then looked at him sternly.

'I can take you wherever you want to go, but don't ask me what I want, again.' I meant my voice to be firm and kind and gentle at the same time. Aboud stood there for a while, looking back at me, looking sideways and back. I wasn't a customer and he had a choice, perhaps for the first time that day—perhaps for the first time since somebody had been the first someone. He kept scratching his groin, putting his hand back up to the car, then down again. Pulling, scratching. His face had turned from a pretentious smile to a large question mark.

'Can you take me to Gaza?' he finally asked.

'Yalla, quick, I am late already!'

He ran across to the passenger side, opened the door and got in.

Aboud didn't take much space. His legs didn't reach the floor and he was pulling himself up to look out as we drove on. He looked skinny, and judging by his breath, probably hadn't eaten all day.

'Are you hungry?' I said

'Yes!' he replied eagerly.

I reached for the lunchbag on the back seat and pulled out a sandwich with hummus and olives and Za'atar. When I passed it to him, he sat there looking at it, looking at me. I reached back once more and got him the large coke bottle I had filled with clean drinking water.

'*Yalla*, eat! And here is water.' I put the bottle on the seat next to him.

Aboud took a small bite first, chewed on it for a while, then swallowed as if it hurt. I paid attention to the road, only glancing at him with the corner of my eye. He opened the bottle and drank a sip. He stopped and caught his breath, then put the bottle back to his mouth and kept drinking as if he had just crossed the desert. Then he finished off the sandwich, almost without breathing, and followed it with the rest of the water. I glanced at him and smiled.

'*Bel Hana We'shefa!*'[21] There is another sandwich if you can eat it.' I said with a smile.

Aboud stared at me, breathing heavily, still holding the empty bottle. He didn't move.

'Take it!' I said, grabbing it and handing it to him. He held it for a bit, then he began eating, slower this time. And judging by his smile, enjoying the sweetness of the fig jam. I took out my last cigarette and lit it.

With the sandwich in his hand, Aboud got on his knees and put his face to the wind. He was just a kid, maybe ten, twelve years old.

21 Enjoy your meal!

I don't know why, but my thoughts began drifting off. What if I took him home? Did he have parents, or had they been killed? Life might be stronger than death but in Gaza death haunts you at every step. Warding it off and skipping over its snares is with deep gratitude to Allah. Yet I knew this kid would have escaped death in ways I could only imagine. And maybe it was all just shame that had forced him to where he was. Shame and all its open wounds. I turned my head slightly and looked again at him. I wondered what it was like, being a father, having my son next to me looking out the open window at the black horizon and the stars in the sky coming together.

I switched off the interior light as we approached Gaza City.

Aboud sat down again and looked at me.

'Can I have a cigarette?' he asked.

I drove on in silence. The city encircled us with its dim lights and bullet-scarred walls. I was just minutes from home. The long, dusty, narrow road leading up to it was full of kids playing soccer in the light of the few bulbs burning. They stopped the ball as we approached them, looking into the car as I drove slowly past. Older men stood in the background, arms crossed, following us with their eyes, like hawks. Judgement and the subsequent repercussions of the lynch mob could be administered swiftly and without questioning. These people, my neighbours, my fellow countrymen, loved their prison. For lack of any other, it had become their identity and their sense of security; and it was ruled by a dogma that had become our collective conceptual prison. Even mine. I knew what it took to survive. I turned out and away, driving back to the main street and crossing towards the west of the city. I parked halfway down a side street near an open corner shop. Cars on both sides had stickers on them, pointing out their allegiance to either international NGOs or the UN mission.

'I'm going to get cigarettes. You stay in the car,' I said to Aboud and got out.

'Do you want anything?' I asked, stooping down to see him, as I still held the door before closing it.

With his eyes, he spoke the truth.

I know that you want to help me, but you can't. Tell me if I matter. Just tell me.

I stood there, and he sat there. And time stood still for a moment as if we were both wise old men, knowing our free will was squeezed under a colossal black boot.

'May Allah keep you, *Ammu*[22],' he said.

I took my time in the small shop: walking around the narrow aisles, picking small bags of nuts off the shelves, reading the product descriptions and occasionally asking the shopkeeper about the prices of items I had no interest in. It was a well-stocked place with prices considerably higher than in the rest of the city. There was imported food with prices that only foreign workers or business owners could afford. I stood in front of the fan at the cash register and closed my eyes. The sweat on my forehead evaporated quickly and I imagined I was in a place with cool spring breezes, green hills and easy living.

'I praise Allah every day the organisation next door lets me use their electricity,' the shopkeeper said as he handed me a plastic bag with the nuts and cigarettes.

'May Allah be with you; you deserve the praise,' I replied and left the shop.

I walked back slowly, half my usual pace. I looked down, only glancing up when I could see the windscreen of my car coming into sight. The driver's side against the footpath first, then the passenger's side. I peered up to see if it was Aboud's head I could make out, but it was too dark. As I got closer, I resumed my normal pace and reached the car, looking down at the empty passenger seat.

I took a deep breath and exhaled, as if granted pardon for a hideous crime.

---

22 Uncle. Also a respectful way of addressing an elder.

9

Golden light streamed in from the west, softened by faint clouds as it changed to a light magenta. The rays began to sift through the alleyways, almost resembling a sun which had grown tentacles, trying to hold on to the apartment blocks as if pulled by darkness in their eternal battle. Eventually it would slip, grab on to another building and slip even further until conquered by its arch enemy.

I sat on my own on the balcony, smoking a cigarette, drinking a tea and reading the newspaper. Farida had left early in the morning, as the sun made its first return. When I finally got home the day before, I had found her in a rather strange mood. She was happy to see me, angry I was so late and questioning so interrogatively about my day, I wondered if she thought I was having an affair. Then, before I knew it, she apologised and went to bed. I got a bit of hashish from a jar in the kitchen, heated up some coals on the stove and enjoyed a shisha on the balcony, listening to the fading sounds of a darkened city, exercising a dream of life in Canada being in Gaza. In the end I had so many hiccups to this vision I ended up coughing and laughing loudly to myself. When a man's cry from the dark a few levels down told me to say my prayers and go to bed, I did.

Farida spent every Thursday with her sister. She would take the bus to Al Mawasi and stand in line to cross at the Tufah checkpoint. It only opened twice a day but in that time the Israelis would often close it on a whim. If that happened on her way home, she would return to her sister and stay there until the next day when she would try to exit in the morning.

I heard the key turning, then the front door opening and a rustling of plastic bags and other heavy things being set down on the floor. I was just putting down my cup of tea to see if she needed a hand when she stepped out onto the balcony.

'*Habibi*, make me a tea. And get me some water. Please.' Farida said, catching her breath.

'Thank God for your safe arrival.' I replied. 'Did something happen?'

I got up to go to the kitchen and she was just about to turn around to lead the way, when she looked me in the eyes and said, 'yes, I will tell you, but let me first throw water on my body'.

She tugged me into the apartment by my hand, fixed her eyes on me again and gave me a soft kiss on the lips, then went into the bathroom and closed the door.

I went to the kitchen and watched the aluminium kettle being caressed by the blue gas flame, drifting off into a land of nothingness.

❖❖❖

Farida had long hair with thick, soft black tresses. She would make a tight ponytail which she skilfully rolled into one of those cake-looking things on the back of her head. Sometimes I'd sit and pretend to watch television in the living room. Adjacent to the bedroom, I'd sneak up to lift a hanging rug on the wall and, like a voyeur, glance at her naked reflection in the vanity mirror through a large crack that had opened when a bomb hit the building next door. When we made love, I could feast my eyes on her for as long as I wanted and relish her long hair as it brushed my face.

I was hungry for her now, staring at the kettle, listening to the water boiling and watching the flames twitch to yellow as the water squirted onto them. I made a pot of tea, arranged a platter for two and went back to the balcony.

Farida came out and sat on the adjacent chair, combing her wet hair in front of me. I watched in silence as I poured her the tea. Neither of us said a word. She took a sip and looked around the balcony. The shisha was still there. She looked out at the fire-red sky and then at me once more, then at the shisha. I had only seen Farida act like this once before, when her mother had passed away.

She was smiling and then her smile turned into a grin that duly turned to laughter. She put her hand to her mouth and tears began flowing down her cheeks. I didn't know what to do, to laugh or cry. I put my arms around her and she buried her head into my chest. Her crying turned into sobbing. I didn't speak. Finally, she stopped, then she looked deeply into my eyes.

'Do you love me?' she asked. 'Just answer me honestly now, don't think.'

I didn't need to think about the reply, I was curious about the reason.

'Farida … I don't know why you are asking me this right now … But yes … I love you.'

Farida fell into a sob again.

'I am not in doubt. I just wanted to hear it.' Her face was still buried in my chest.

Silence followed. Farida left her head on my chest. Her eyes were open and just looking out into thin air. She dried her tears with the back of her hand and lifted herself up to look me in the eyes again. Tears brimmed once more.

'I am pregnant.'

She dropped her head onto my chest once again.

I heard words I had resigned myself never to hear. They didn't make sense, so I found myself locked in an unbreakable silence. I didn't know whether to laugh or cry. Farida lifted herself up once more and I looked her in the eyes. Tears coursed her cheeks like tiny rivers. Her eyes glistened, her tears like liquid diamonds. I drowned in the truth of the moment as tears streamed down my cheeks. I took Farida's soft hands and walked her back inside. She followed in silence. We looked at the adjacent buildings and, in the absence of onlookers, we closed the balcony doors behind us.

There we stood in the last touch of twilight and spoke without words. We removed our clothes and embraced for a long time, stroking each other, kissing, and listening to the silent conversation of our hearts.

10

Farida held her large stomach as the bus shook. From Gaza City, it took an hour to reach what had been the Tufah checkpoint. As we left Khan Younis, we were all leaning sideways, peeling our eyes at the horizon through the windscreen of the bus. A few men got up and walked down the aisle to stand behind the driver, then the rest followed. I stood up, holding the seatback in front of me to balance myself as I tried to peek over all the heads in front of me. I left the seat and joined the men, holding the shoulders of those in front of me, feeling the hands of those behind me. Suddenly there was a cry.

'*Al bahr! Al bahr! Al bahr!*'[23] And there was a great cheer. I felt the goose pimples crawling on my skin as the bus turned and the Mediterranean Ocean presented itself to us. In contrast to the yellow sand, it sent blessings for our arrival, wrapping us in its tranquil deep blue blanket. As long as I could remember, we had been denied this view by the towering wall of concrete the Israelis had built on the high vantage point entering Al Mawasi.

I was filled with ecstasy as I looked over at Farida who was blushing with a big open mouth and sparkling eyes, as she looked out the window. She still had her hands on her belly. Six months had passed since our lives began moving backwards in time, and Farida had been over three months into her pregnancy when she went to the doctor. She told me that her body was telling her all the time but she could not believe it, and when the medicos confirmed it, she spent more than an hour laughing and crying.

---

23 The sea!

Farida saw me looking at her and smiled, tears welling in her eyes. Large drops let go and began rolling down her cheeks, sliding to the corners of her mouth, her lips pursed as she tried to control herself. We kept looking into each other's eyes as my own tears fell and as everyone on the bus was engulfed in a joyous sea of embraces and kisses.

The same night, when we walked into a blackened ocean holding hands and giving thanks to Allah, Farida got her first contractions.

Hamada was born early in the morning on the 15th of November 2005.

11

The Mediterranean had swollen up, the colour of the sea had turned brown. The froth of the waves broke off in chunks of foam that hurled through the air as cold winds from the north bore their way across the water. In the distance Israeli warships patrolled, rolling like floating corks on the shifting horizon.

Hamada ran ahead of me, yelling at the top of his voice. The waves thundered as they broke onto the sand.

'Baba! Baba! *Yalla! Yalla!* I will be first!'

Hamada threw himself into the belly of a brown wave and disappeared for a few seconds, only to emerge with a scream on the back side of it.

'Woooooo! Cold! So cooold!!' he yelled, waving at me to follow him.

I laughed as I took a deep breath and charged the first open wave. I opened my eyes and peered through the inferno of bubbles in the muddy water before I shot up like a rocket.

'Allah have mercy! The water is freezing, my son!' My voice was quivering from the shock.

'Wait and then it is not so bad!' Hamada laughed back.

As a giant wave came crashing down, we both dived under it and emerged victorious on its back. Hamada kicked himself to a backflip, laughing in sheer elation. My lips were getting numb.

'Baba, your lips are blue!' Hamada yelled as he threw a lump of foam that landed on my head. He broke into laughter as we both went up and down with the waves, clear of the break.

'Two minutes and then you come in!' I said, before I rode a wave back to shore. Wrapping a towel around me, I kept watching my son as he frolicked like a dolphin. He would wait for a big wave and then surf it with his body. He'd do it again with a lump of foam on his head, get ditched on the shore and then jump straight back in. I let him play for a while longer, but I knew how cold the water was. When I waved him in, he came running, shaking all over his tall skinny body as I wrapped two towels around him.

'I love the sea, Baba! One day I will be a professional surfer! Just like the man with the green eyes!'

'*Insha'Allah*. Remember to say, *Insha'Allah! Insha'Allah*, all your dreams will come true.'

'*Insha'Allah*.' Hamada looked at me adoringly as we walked back home.

I looked back at the raging sea and my eyes couldn't help but fall on the ships in the horizon. I looked at Hamada again, then pushed away the fears that entered my head.

I could smell it; war was brewing again.

12

March usually signalled the onset of spring but that year it was unusually cold. I had returned from my early morning beachcomb where I would collect anything that could burn: pieces of wood, paper, rubber, plastics. I would also get wood from old crates at work through my usual trades. To Hamada, collecting materials and making the fire was exciting. His zest for life was indescribable. A large bright smile, two radiant light brown eyes and rich bushy hair that would cover his ears most of the time. His nose and eyebrows were his mother's—his eyes, ears, head shape—mine. He was tall and at his age, he was the strongest in his class—or so I believed as his father. Hamada was everything we had ever dreamed of in a son and much more. He was meant to be. No other children followed, and when we celebrated his eighth birthday, Farida and I looked at each other and gave our thanks that we had been blessed with him. He was our first and only son and his soul was entirely his own, as if he had chosen us to be his parents. We would joke that the only way we really knew he was our son was because he had our features.

Hamada loved the sea. He loved it so much that Farida had me build him a little box for towels outside the front door. He also had a small surfboard I'd got him from a group of surfers calling themselves the Gaza Surf Club. He would come running back from school, throw his bag down and run straight for the water. Any chores waiting for him would be done in such haste you would think he was being paid. All he ever thought about was the ocean. One day, a man from Australia who was working for the UN, came to visit the department. When he opened his briefcase, I saw the front page of a surfing magazine. I knew it was a surfing magazine, not because it had a surfboard on it but a picture of the man with the green eyes that Hamada had shown me. He had had a school assignment to write about sports and the whole class was taken into Khan Younis to another school that had Internet. Hamada's assignment which he called 'Winning the world championship surfing', was awarded the best story in the class. Kelly Slater was the man's name and Hamada was going to beat him. I was a proud baba.

Life in Al Mawasi was like paradise when I compared it to Gaza City. Some days I would ask myself how I could feel such gratitude. My only answer was in my faith, that this strange thing called life was no more than a door. One that would suddenly open, by a divine force in absolute symbiosis with what we call the universe, to give those who receive it a glimpse of that universe. To understand that it is the universe itself that looks out through our eyes and endows us with love through the cycle of death and birth. And to accept the outlook, no matter how good or bad, and then depart back to the nothingness of the universe, who we really are. Regardless of what awaits when the door opens, happiness is felt when one forgives those who have caused pain.

'*Menkum lelallah!*'[24] I said the day I carried Mohammed's charred children. And through the corner of my eyes, in the eyes of the men around me, I sensed the lack of understanding for those words of simple forgiveness.

I never said it out loud again.

---

24 From you to Allah! A phrase asking Allah to judge someone, implicitly forgiving that person.

13

In Gaza, the years following Hamada's birth were in contrast to his life-loving nature. They were ridden with violence and death. Fighting an oppressor brings out oppressors among your own kind whom you didn't know existed. The oppression against ourselves was evident yet we could not confront it nor was there room for discourse. Anyone who argued would instantly be labelled a traitor, perhaps even an informer. The Israelis were bombing us regularly and we would hear of pathetic retaliation bids that each and every time were hailed as great victories; we all knew, though, that we were fighting the Moloch of war with a machete. The Israelis' retaliations came without warning—brutal and indiscriminate. One day I slowly drove past a sign on a wall that proclaimed:

Who cares about an innocent prisoner? Not his inmates nor his capturer.

Two days later I drove past it again and someone had machine-gun sprayed the entire concrete wall full of bullets, effectively removing the writing. I didn't slow down this time.

That cold spring in 2014, Hamada, alongside every other child in Gaza, talked about *el zanana*, or the drone. Instead of planes, the Israelis were using drones more than ever. In the middle of the night you could hear their loud humming. The operators, men and women, were sitting safely far away, probably like someone playing a video game, looking at a screen whilst flying their advanced remotely controlled toy over houses, setting coordinates on heat signals or firing their missiles. They were hard to see at night, flying fast over the rooftops and suddenly, seemingly ignited from nowhere, the white light from a missile's fuel burning, would set the sky ablaze and blind you as it charged towards its target.

A group of men leaving a shop with furniture for the newlywed groom. A group of people surrounding a man selling smuggled goods. The faraway operators followed orders and took these people out. To them their targets weren't living breathing human beings. If so, they wouldn't be able to push the button. *Or would they?*

I used to tell Hamada that they were big insects but one day when he was six, a drone fired a missile in broad daylight above our heads. As the missile flew into a building at the end of the road, I had already taken Hamada in my arms and turned my back to the imminent blast. It hit me like a brick. I was lifted off the ground and luckily, tossed in the air, to land on my back with broken ribs, my son still in my arms. He got up and shook me, thinking I was dead, amidst a scene of shattered heads, severed bodies and a savagery he had—until that day—only heard of.

When I woke up at the hospital, Hamada was standing next to me crying. I couldn't hug him.

'They are very bad, those big insects, but see, I am fine!'

Hamada spat out a laugh and wiped his eyes. And then he laughed more. And then I slipped a laugh as well, but the pain was so excruciating, I had to stop.

The drones became more drones and what little I had preserved of innocence in Hamada's childhood vanished in the reality of that day.

14

Distinct beeps from the small shortwave transistor radio signalled the news bulletin on Radio Cairo. When the local radio channels, electricity and phones were cut at the same time, we would know something was happening. The only way to find out would either be through Radio Cairo or Radio Damascus or sometimes, the Vatican. If the men in robes across the sea began to air certain prayers in Arabic, we could almost count the hours to when the sound of fighter jets would turn our heads to the sky.

Farida laughed mockingly as the speaker said the words, *the United Nations.*

'United for who?!' She asked angrily as she got Hamada ready for school.

The phones had indeed been cut and the power was out. If the Israelis were going to bomb, the safest place for him would be school. It wouldn't be the last place but surely not the first they would hit. That much we knew. It was one of two small schools in Al Mawasi and acted as a shelter as well.

The looks Farida and I sent each other that morning were like a judgement of our faith. Life in Gaza wasn't about making decisions because regardless of which decision you ended up making, you would be faced with circumstances that you could not predict. The only thing we could do was to live our lives and do our best to avoid becoming the victims of a game where we were already held hostage.

I tried to imagine how our lives would look in Gaza, had we had the routine of life in Canada. Eventually, I concluded that I didn't have any recollection of life in peace. I simply didn't know what peace was about.

Fear brewed in my gut as I realised that my own son would grow up in the same, or even worse, situation. Never living in a time of peace.

That year we had seriously begun to question our future in Gaza. The Israeli blockade had made life almost unbearable. The tunnels had been targeted by both the Egyptians and the Israelis and although many still held they were out of our reach. The dealings we had across the border had almost foundered and there were rumours of an order for Khaled Abu Mohammed's head. We were prisoners and at the mercy of a hand that could see us starving at any time. The collusion in apathy of the world outside, the lack of will from those we called our brothers and sisters, was no longer speculation, it was a fact. We were alone, and even the 'we' were divided. The Israelis ran a classic policy of divide and conquer, and our resistance resembled more and more that of desperation.

And it was bold desperation. We were desperate.

15

I heard the first F-16s around noon, two of them. They came in low over the department office in Gaza City and flew out over the ocean where we watched them turn around. It was like a déjà vu; we knew what was coming and it wouldn't be good. There was no time to hide. Everyone in the office ran down the steps and out onto the street, continuing to run as far away as we could possibly get from what we guessed was their path. The jets accelerated and blasted their sonic boom straight over us. Glass shattered and dust lifted as if the whole world was an old dusty rug being beaten with a giant bat. No bombs or missiles were dropped, their path didn't deviate as they disappeared straight back to Israel. It was just a display of what was to come.

Three Israeli teenagers had been killed, perpetrators unknown, and we knew it meant terrible collective punishment, wholesale indiscriminate vengeance. We knew our lives counted for nothing next to theirs. Nobody in Israel, nobody outside Gaza ever took much notice when three Palestinian teenagers died, when three Palestinian children died or when three Palestinian babies, still in their mother's wombs, died. They were numbers, rarely were they given names. Mostly they were without stories, without a life anyone could relate to, and of course, they were without faces.

Ismail, one of my colleagues at the department, leaned over and showed me his phone, waist high with Netanyahu's tweets. I looked at the profile picture. It was tainted with a smug smile. It was a man who had been waiting for his chance and here it was being handed to him on a silver platter. He didn't hesitate and the disproportionate force in which he retaliated was poetically described on a wall in front of me. As the words passed before me, I saw the eyes of the only two people I shared my soul with.

With the injustice of tomorrow we shall live but with the justice we will be served now, we will die like animals.

I looked back at the phone Ismail was reading loudly from. I wasn't listening, my ears were still ringing from the sonic boom and I could hear my own breathing, as if I was trapped inside a cardboard box, hidden somewhere in a dark space. I looked at Ismail talking, I looked back up at the words on the wall. I looked back down at the screen of the mobile phone and watched Ismail's thumb scroll through the tweets slowly as he read them.

They were abducted & murdered in cold blood by human animals.

Vengeance for the blood of a small child, Satan has not yet created. Neither has vengeance for the blood of three pure youths who were on their way home to their parents who will not see them anymore.

As I read the words on the wall once more, my cell phone rang. It was Mohammed.

'Put me at ease, my brother…'

'Two F-16s, how many at your end?' I answered as my heart raced.

'Two.'

Since the kidnapping at the beginning of the month, every day had been a trial. The sound of the drones in the night gave warning of what would come. Sleep came in periods of silence, sometimes minutes, and on good days, hours, until a hum or a roar or a deafening explosion would wake us up like animals on guard. At the end of the month of June, our lives didn't feel human any more.

Exactly one week after the jets threw their warning, the massacre began.

16

My hands rested on Hamada's shoulders. I looked at his face in the reflection of a wood-framed glass door that separated the shopfront from the back as Abu Ahmed, the butcher, was about to slaughter a lamb. A boy had become a man or perhaps a girl had become a woman; perhaps someone was celebrating the return of their son from an Israeli prison. Hamada's eyes didn't move as Abu Ahmed said his prayer to Allah and cut the arteries and windpipe in a single swift thrust. The blood flowed in a heavy stream onto the tiled floor and formed a creek that grasped the straight grout lines on its path to the floor drain. Nidal, his assistant, slowly released his grip on the animal as its eyes closed and all life ebbed out.

'Baba, has he gone to heaven now?'

'His soul has. I am sure of it,' I answered, stroking his shoulder.

Abu Ahmed left Nidal with the lamb and stepped out through the glass door. His face met Hamada's and he sent him a big smile. His hands were all bloody and his apron was that of a butcher, laden with bits of meat and intestines. Where his large belly would rest against the workbench a clear line marked a thread of drops trailing all the way down to the edge of the apron. His boots were covered with a thick layer of hardened blood, recoated by a fresh layer from the *Zabiha*[25] we had just witnessed.

Abu Ahmed ran a small butcher shop on the outskirts of the Khan Younis camp. It was the best and closest butcher to us and, like every other butcher in Gaza, he was rarely busy. He was a very

25 Arabic term for the Islamic way of slaughter.

religious man and in every sentence there would be at least one praise to Allah.

'*Asalaamu Aleikum!* Allah has gifted me with your visit, Abu Hamada, and may Allah keep him for you.'

The beginnings of my reply, '*We aleikum*—' were the only words that left my mouth as a deafening blast brought our greeting to an end. The ground shook violently, and the large shop windows shattered as if they had been dropped from a great height. It all happened in a split second yet instinct made me take Hamada, already in my grasp and throw myself to the ground. Abu Ahmed did the same. I sheltered my son in front of me, my back to the street and we covered our heads, awaiting another blast.

For a moment the world stood still. The fear inside me screamed and I was praying in frantic iteration, 'Allah, Allah, mercy, mercy, mercy!' Hamada was curled tight, pushing himself towards my chest, still with his hands over his ears, whining: 'Baba! Baba!'

The silence was indescribable. Every man, woman and child was doing exactly the same thing. Either the explosion had claimed their life or they were thrown to the ground, curled up, awaiting another blow. After a short time, a scream broke the silence. I removed my hands from my ears. It had happened before, a scream and then another blow. Awaiting in tension I dared not get up. My eyes met Abu Ahmed's lying on the ground face down close to us. He looked at me then looked up and watched bits of concrete sprinkle down from the ceiling. The long fluorescent lights above our heads had burst and tiny bits of glass and dust covered us and everything around us.

'Nidal! Nidal!' Abu Ahmed cried out. Nidal came out, rushing to help him get off the ground. I cradled Hamada in my arms, got up and ran out. I knew what was coming.

'*Yalla, yalla!* Quick!' And both Nidal and Abu Ahmed followed us.

I squeezed Hamada close to my chest as I ran out onto the street. And as I was taking in the sight of the bloodbath in front of me, the shockwave from the building collapsing behind us forced me to my knees. A cloud of concrete dust charged its way from the falling debris, turning the street and the air around us into a suffocating fog. I stayed put, still on my knees and sat Hamada up to face me, lifted his T-shirt over his nose and did the same for myself. I squeezed him tight.

'Breathe through your nose! Don't open your mouth! Close your eyes!' I cried out through my own shirt. The dust penetrated and I coughed violently, trying to keep myself from breathing through my mouth. Hamada hadn't stopped crying. My eyes were streaming tears from coughing and he squeezed himself to me, clasping his arms around my body.

We stayed put, right there in the middle of the street, unable to look each other in the eyes.

I prayed for what felt like an eternity, enveloped in a world turned grey.

❖❖❖

The rays of the sun danced as if we were under the surface of the sea. Through the cloud, the fingers of light moved in random patterns as a light wind slowly lifted the dust up and away. I opened my eyes, squinting. They felt as if they had needles in them. I took Hamada and removed his hands from around my body, pulled his shirt down from his face and blew hard.

'Open your eyes slowly.' Hamada's tears had run down his cheeks and had taken with them the concrete dust. I got up from our kneeling pose and lifted him up as well. He kept hugging me, didn't want to open his eyes, didn't want to let go of me.

'My son, the soul of my heart … *Khalas, khalas*[26]…' Dust rose from his T-shirt as I ran my hands on his back, consoling him. He was still crying as screams, cries of help and long repetitive, agonising moans surrounded us.

---

26 Can be used in different ways: It's enough. Or, It's okay.

A water pipe had erupted on the side of the collapsed building that minutes earlier had held Abu Ahmed's butcher shop. Twisted through boulders of concrete, it was still releasing a steady stream of water. I lifted Hamada up, carried him in my arms and staggered with shaking legs towards it. With my right hand, I threw water in my eyes. Hamada still grasped onto me and held my left arm tightly. The water was salty, and I replaced one stinging sensation with another, as my eyes cleared. I pushed Hamada's head back from my chest and threw water on his face. He didn't protest but kept his eyes closed as both the water, the sun and the cacophony of mayhem would have taken him on an express elevator, straight to hell. I knew how it felt, I had been a child in Gaza as well, and as I looked up, I only wished for him to keep his eyes closed.

Abu Ahmed was sitting on the ground, wailing, looking at his shop. His back was covered in blood and Nidal was limp on the ground next to him. A big gash ran across the top of Nidal's skull which was facing me. He was dead. I turned my head the other way and looked across the street. The carnage was spread out as if a tree had been shaken upside down to shed its bodies on the ground, splitting them like overripe fruit. A man lay on his side facing me. The skin on the front of his body had been peeled from his feet all the way to his head, like the cadaver mannequin at a doctor's office. A woman was lying on her back, her ribs sticking up through her clothes like spikes, her intestines lying on top of her as if placed deliberately. There were at least a dozen bodies, some still twitching, others deadly still.

Memories of violence are not like other memories. They burn themselves into the soul. My mother, may Allah have mercy on her soul, was my first memory. I watched her scream to death, trying to brush off flames that had covered her as well as my older sister and brother. I was five when an Israeli shell hit the adjacent building with an incendiary head. My father carried me in his arms and raced down the steps. I was looking back over his shoulder, and as we made it to the ground and out the front door, another shell hit, the fire splashing through the large openings of the staircase like blazing water. I watched my father lose his mind, like Mohammed had lost his when he saw the remains of his family charred, wanting to pull them out, being held back by other men and eventually sagging to the ground on his knees. I watched my father as I grew up, always in another world, with that single moment etched into his soul. Even though I would stand in front of him, he didn't look at me, not once, not until the day he died. On the morning of my twentieth birthday, he woke me up, as if nothing had ever happened, looked me in the eyes with tears welling in his own, congratulated me on my birthday and apologised for having been so withdrawn. Then he gave me a hug and the keys to his car.

Later the same day he smuggled himself across to the Israeli side of the Sufa crossing where, wearing a vest of soldered tin cans and armed with an AK-47 rifle, he took the lives of three soldiers. After he had spent all his bullets, he charged at a soldier firing at him, taking the man's life by tearing his throat out with his teeth, like a wild animal, before being killed himself.

Abu Ahmed got up and humped over to where I was standing. He put his hand on my shoulder.

'Allah be praised!' He spoke without looking at me, staring at the bloodbath around us. 'Take your son and go now, *yalla*!'

He was right. I looked down at Hamada, still clenching his eyes tight. I held him to my chest, walked away, down an alley, onto the main street leading back towards Al Mawasi and got on the bus. As soon as Hamada smelt the ocean, he carefully opened his sticky eyes, looked at me and smiled. Then he closed them again. As I approached our home, having walked the long way back from the bus stop, Farida came out running towards us, crying.

I took her in one arm and held her tightly to me. Hamada had fallen asleep, with his head on my shoulder. Farida kept kissing me, kissing Hamada, kept crying.

17

I couldn't think. The days had all formed into one long stream as if blood were raining from the sky and chasing down endless gutters. Sleep had turned into an enemy and we all fought it. Fought it so we wouldn't die in a nightmare. We would keep our ears pinned, waiting for the roar of a fighter jet approaching. Holding our breath, waiting to hear if the drone that had flown over our house would render a blast. And when I heard one, it was so far off I could exhale in relief. Seconds later, I would turn to Farida and see her do the exact same thing. Hamada would follow suit and then climb into our bed.

'If you stay awake, I can sleep and when I wake up, you can sleep. Okay?'

He would speak those words half asleep, almost every night, and then curl up between Farida and me, like a baby in the womb.

Schools had closed, work had stopped and most forms of human interaction, except with near neighbours, had stopped. We were sitting ducks in the true meaning of the word. We couldn't move, couldn't visit anyone. The streets were deserted. Only when it looked as if the bombing would stop, would people venture out, just like ants. Suddenly the streets would fill up, as if we were prisoners on a lunch break, congregating in groups until a sudden blast would force us running back inside. The bricks around us offered little protection but somehow, we believed they could save us.

Our elected party and its nepotic branches were rousing us to fight. But there was no real fight—we were being slaughtered. The Israelis had firepower vastly greater than ours. Most of us were unarmed and if fighters had used puny New Year's rockets, the Israeli persecutors would still have painted themselves as 'the victims', the restorers of peace. To them, it was the perfect drama triangle. I would have liked to believe that it was our brave resistance that finally exposed the Israelis as the cowards they are. But it was *their* own ferocious brutality that cracked through the apathy of the outside world. Suddenly, speakers on the shortwave radio were expressing shock and disgust that we had only dreamt of hearing. Even the Pope. We knew they were just words but then, when every day felt like being held in a human abattoir, those words offered hope. We hoped the rightness of our resistance would be credited, that someone would come and stand by us against the tyrants. We had faith that things would change, but for a long time they didn't, at least not as we had hoped. Meanwhile, the world watched on as the Israelis, in diabolic hatred, pulverised and slaughtered us like the animals they considered us to be.

Three weeks had passed since the first planes threw their sonic boom. Two weeks had passed, watching bombs being dropped to the east and missiles fired over our heads from the west. The same day we survived the attack near the butcher shop, Ibrahim Sawalli, with eight other young men, watched what we, as Palestinians, dreamt of participating in. They had arranged for the broadcast of the World Cup semi-finals game between Argentina and the Netherlands and it was to be a moment of cautious celebration. Mohammed and I used to meet where they were gathering, just north of Al Mawasi, at the Waqt al-Marah[27] café. It was a makeshift place, full of laughter and salt drenched bodies, cheap umbrella shades and plastic chairs. Ibrahim had only advertised airing the game, by word of mouth. I had told Salim, Ibrahim's brother, to ask Ali, my car mechanic, to lend him a charged car battery so he could run the small transportable TV for the evening. I was going to go. I was going to call Mohammed after returning from the butcher.

27 Time of fun (literally).

I didn't, of course.

The Israeli missile left a crater so big the ocean filled it from below. Salim was never fully recovered. Parts of his body were exposed by bulldozers the next day. He was young. They all were. All nine young men, watching a game in the World Cup, like millions of other people around the globe that same night.

The only reason they died was because they were Palestinians in Gaza.

18

'*Illy beheb maa beyekrah*,'[28] I said to myself as I lay on my back, following the sound of the *zanana*. With my hand stroking Farida's, moving up and down with the tip of my fingers, I was wide awake. Farida had her eyes closed yet I sensed she was awake.

Hamada was sound asleep in his room. I'd promised him an early morning swim. I didn't want to think about it. As long as the Israelis were bombing, even the beach was now a dangerous place. We were almost into a month of shelling and life had become one long prayer to stay alive. Exactly a week after the café bombing, four boys playing soccer were killed on the beach. They were cousins. The first shell didn't kill them but as they fled, running on the beach, the angle of the second shell was adjusted to strike right in their midst.

'Baba, why did they kill the boys on the beach?'

'Because they are cowards, my son.'

'Why?'

'Because for men who believe God *only loves them*, it's easy to kill.'

The drone flew quickly over once. North to south. I counted the seconds, as if awaiting the thunder. It returned south to north. Slower this time. Then I heard it turning and I wasn't sure whether it was the sound of it or just a resonating sound of a drone, in my ear. It came back from the east, swept over us again and turned south to climb higher. I couldn't hear it any longer. Or could I? I was sure there was a faint buzzing somewhere. Perhaps not. What were they looking for? What was the drone operator thinking? Were they just taking pictures of our area? And if they were, why?

---

28 The one who loves, does not hate.

I looked at my watch. It was a quarter past three in the morning. Every inch of my body wanted to sleep but I couldn't. A silence of primed ears, of murmurs in the distant background. That is how it was, every single night. There was a gentle knock on the front door. It was Hani, our neighbour three houses down, asking for some sugar for his tea. He offered me a tea, so we went and sat outside his front door in silence, watching the stars far above.

'I haven't found an answer for why our stars look different from theirs,' Hani suddenly whispered.

I heard every word he said, yet I was unable to answer him. Hani, the farmer, asked a question so profound that I was left mute. I contemplated a religious answer but stopped myself. I wanted to move my lips, console us both, but wasn't able to. The words he spoke were the ones we all thought but couldn't find the words for.

I looked up and noticed a star darken, then brighten again. Then the next star in line did the same and the one after it. And then I made it out. It was tiny.

The drone was still there, high above our heads.

◈◈◈

When the unmistakable sound of the F-16 fighter jet reached us, I jumped up and looked to the dark sky. The roar was approaching and descending. I tried to pinpoint it, to determine its direction.

Finally, I saw it as it crossed the light of the half moon. It was coming in fast, angled to throw a bomb yet before I had finished the thought, a spray of bullets lit up, fired at it from the ground, two houses behind ours. The jet roared back up towards the stars and another one came in behind it.

I felt the tea glass break and cut my skin. I had been clenching it, making a fist, forgetting it was there. My hand opened in a reflex and the thick pieces of glass fell to the ground. I left Hani and ran to our front door as fast as I could. He had already turned around and charged through his own. There was no time to think. It was instinct. The only thing on my mind was to get my family out. My blood-soaked hand didn't even register.

I shoved the door in with the weight of my body and fell over. As I got straight up again, my eyes fell on Farida, sitting in the bed, staring at me, at my bloody hand. Her eyes were wide open, and she looked at me with a frightening stare, motionless.

'Out, out, out!' I yelled! 'Hamada, Hamada, Hamada!!!' I ran towards his bedroom but before I made it to the kitchen, the blast hit the house like a giant fist.

I was thrown to the ground and almost fell unconscious. I couldn't hear anything, one ear felt hot and the other was ringing madly. I opened my eyes but could hardly see. The air was thick with smoke and concrete dust. I coughed and spat out dust, wiped my mouth with my bloody hand. I lifted up my shirt and covered my nose and mouth. I could make out Farida's feet moving. She had been thrown to the ground as well. I turned on to my stomach and pushed my body off the ground, supporting myself against the wall. My feet felt like lead, dragging me along as I staggered towards Hamada's room.

'Hamada!!!!' I yelled through the shirt. 'Answer me!! Hamada!'

There was no answer.

I felt my way through the doorway to Hamada's bedroom struggling through the rubble. A large hole had been smashed in the roof and in the strip of pale moonlight streaming in, I saw my son. He was on his back. The bed had been hit in the impact and was bent like an inverted A-frame. Hamada was still on it, bent in the same shape, settled halfway down an impact crater in the floor. I stopped.

'Hamada...' I whispered ... 'Hamada...'

Hamada was covered in rubble. His eyes were wide open and so was his mouth. His blood was dripping rapidly from the lowest point of the bed. I walked down into the small crater, knelt and gazed at him before I pushed my arms and hands under him, into a hot pool of blood. It was dark, my legs were shaking fiercely.

Cradling his body the best I could, I lifted him up, then turned around, and fled the room, moving as fast as my legs would carry me. Through the smoke I ran down the hallway, straight into Farida and, through the inferno of a screeching sound in my ears, I could hear her screams. She put her hands on Hamada, moving them frenziedly, tracing his body.

'My son, my son … Hamada! … Wake up, Hamada! … No. No. Allah … No!'

Farida fell to the ground, loudly wailing, her whole body shaking violently. She clung on to me as I kept walking, dragging us forcefully out through the front door. We had barely got out, when a second jet approached for the kill. Hani came running towards us with a torch and stopped abruptly a few feet away.

In the light of his torch, I looked down and saw Hamada's head resting on my arm. Only a small strip of flesh and skin kept it from coming off. His windpipe and arteries had been severed, the spine in his neck had been torn apart, leaving a blank space and most of his intestines were hanging out of his abdomen, resting on my stomach.

I looked down at my son for the last time and that was what I saw. There was no spark of my Hamada. What was left made me retch uncontrollably as I clasped his body tight against mine. Hysterically screaming, Farida collapsed in front of me and in that same moment I found myself looking down at us from above—as my soul departed from my body.

Hani was yelling at me, signalling me to run but I couldn't speak nor move. The only thing I heard was my heartbeat searching for its soul. Hani turned around and ran. I knelt with Hamada in my arms, put him down next to Farida, lying on her side, and embraced them tightly.

A knock-on-the-roof bomb is a bomb without an explosive head. It's designed to warn people that a real bomb or missile is imminent. The warning time can be anything from seconds to minutes to hours. It penetrates with the same brute force as a real bomb, tearing through concrete, furniture and flesh.

Hani, his wife and two children ran the opposite way and doors were opening all around us. Our neighbours were coming out onto the street. Some were still in their nightgowns, children in their arms, running away from their homes. Why our home had been targeted, only the Israelis knew. There was no warning except for that knock on the roof.

The roar of the second jet was deafened by the blast of the bomb it threw.

The shockwave hit my back like a giant boot on fire.

19

The sea surrounding us was black and frothing. The waves breaking around the island of large boulders, resembled a necklace of barbed wire. The sky above was clouded with an unnatural red hue to it. The clouds themselves were black and moved with furious speed. A tall shape in the figure of a man carrying a satchel on his side and dressed in a black *thawb*[29] stood before me. His legs were covered, and his arms were crossed low, tucked inside the dress. There was no shade or sun and his face was shaped like an egg with no hair, painted with two black eyes, the balls of which were stark white without a single vein. His face parted and what I hadn't seen were lips, moved. The teeth behind them shone at me like polished diamonds.

'Come closer … I'd like to show you something' he said in a deep voice.

'Why?'

The man's lips moved, then paused half open.

'I see. Perhaps you don't know what I can offer,' he said. 'Do you know where you are?'

'No,' I said firmly, feeling strangely present.

'Come closer and I will show you. Please.'

I stepped closer as he opened his hands and faced the palms up. A light streamed out of them and in the light I saw Hamada swimming, with a smile on his face. After a short while, he closed his hands again.

---

29 An ankle-length Arab garment, usually with long sleeves, similar to a robe.

'Where is he?!' I asked in a demanding tone, feeling my anger rising within.

'Be calm … I am the Messenger, the carrier, most of the time. I have taken him to the place where I was told to take him. I can take *you* to the same place. From there you have to ask *them* to go to where he is. That is, if they'll let you…'

'Who told you?! Who are *they*?!' I wanted to force him to tell me but somehow my arms wouldn't move. I didn't have control over my own body.

'You still don't know where you are, do you?' he asked calmly.

'No!'

'You are where you can choose to come with me and all I ask, is your soul. I can take you to where I took your son, but I can't promise you they will take you to the same place.'

I had the choice of dying, right there and then. A sense of clarity came about, and I felt peace streaming through my body.

'You will take my soul, anyway, won't you?' I asked as I looked at the dark head in front of me.

'Yes, I will. I just can't choose the time. That's up to you.'

'I understand,' I said and then saw my life flashing before me in a rapid retrospective.

Was this it? Heaven or Hell? And even there, faced with giving my soul away to death himself, I couldn't be sure. What a hierarchy, what a preposterous way of dealing with life, I thought. There I had been, born into a life of no comfort, with few or no opportunities, in a community imprisoned by circumstances. Certainly, I had stolen and traded the same weapons I despised, but I did it because I wanted to live. I wanted to give my family a life worth living.

Or was that a crime as well? We were blessed with a son when we no longer expected it; or was that merely a mockery? My love for my son, my unconditional love for him, how could that not matter? In any case, I would still end up here. And this dark person, man, woman or whatever being lay behind the shape, would take my soul, good or bad, and my destination would still be unknown to me.

I had had enough: the death of Hamada, death I had witnessed in life. Death could wait.

'I'm not ready to come with you.'

'Have you made up your mind? There is no saying that you won't be with you son if you come with me now,' he replied.

'The only thing I wanted for my son was to be happy. You just showed me that he's happy. I am content with that. I need to make sure Farida is well now and—'

He stopped me and continued.

'And have your revenge. Well, that is something you have to barter with the devil about. I can't help you with that. I can only promise you that I will wait for you at the end. Do you understand?'

'Yes,' I said.

'Go and do what you must do then and we will meet again when the time comes.' He added: 'Soon, I sense'.

The clouds moved faster and faster, and a storm turned the sea to a fury. Black foam raced across the surface of the water and I covered my eyes. The red hue of the sky turned darker and darker. The wind pressed at me from all directions, forcing me to my knees.

I put my face to the ground and covered my ears from the howling wind which circled me as I saw the darkness turn bright.

◈◈◈

When I opened my eyes, there they were. Her eyes.

She didn't say a word. We looked in each other's eyes. And there we were, in the same place we had met, when our lives were full of hope. She put her hand in mine and squeezed gently. We both cried silently, both with heavy tears streaming down our cheeks.

I wanted to speak but felt a piercing pain throughout my back and chest. Farida put her finger to my mouth, signalling for me to try not to speak.

'Hamada will be buried tomorrow…' She said and began sobbing immediately. 'He was going to be buried today, but no digger would go there.'

Farida took a tissue out of her purse and wiped my tears, then wiped her own face. She was struggling to control herself.

'The doctor said you can leave today. They have removed the shrapnel from your back and you only have three broken ribs. Be grateful to Allah…'

'Grateful to Allah…?' I muttered back. The pain in my back was excruciating.

A doctor and a male nurse came to my bed. They spoke together in French—I recognised it from our time in Canada. Without introduction, the doctor began examining me. I didn't speak. The nurse asked Farida a few questions which she quietly answered. Pieces of reinforcement steel, concrete and other shrapnel had lodged itself in my back and taken over four hours to remove. I had been unconscious for almost a day.

The nurse finished changing my bandage and told Farida we could leave as soon as I wanted.

'What about his pain?' She asked him pleadingly.

'We only have Ibuprofen left. I can give you a strip but that's all we have. I am very sorry…' The nurse answered sincerely and patiently waited for Farida to speak but her silence ended the conversation.

The painkillers were barely working as Farida helped me to sit up. I was sure I wouldn't be able to move, every breath felt as if a gang of thugs had stabbed me in the back. Yet what I saw when I turned my head dulled my pain more than the pain killers. What had felt like a blow of cruelty—the nurse telling me to go home—faded away as I took in the ward full of critically wounded men and boys.

The sounds of crying, wailing, screaming, suddenly appeared to me.

I was in the waiting room of death.

20

Farida was on the phone. Room had become available, especially for small bodies, not taking up much space. They asked if they could put other children there as well, with Hamada, perhaps underneath or above. Still in excruciating pain, I slowly put on a white shirt and told Farida I was going to wait for her outside. Each breath was felt as if I were lifting a heavy suit of armour.

The cemetery was bombed in the early morning. A large crater had formed and the simple cement blocks that carried the names of men, women and children had slid down and piled on top of each other. Body parts, still decaying, were thrown against nearby houses, and bones were scattered like driftwood after a storm. The cemetery was on the outskirts of Khan Younis. It lay on a slight slope, surrounded by olive trees. Like most other graveyards in Gaza it carried the word martyr somewhere in its name.

There was an eerie silence between the fall of two bombs in the distance. I walked around the large crater, passing people who were picking up bones and frantically putting half rotten body parts back into the ground.

The young man digging, sweating heavily through a dirty shirt, complained loudly from the pit.

'With Allah as my witness, I must dig six feet for one boy, and you are asking me to dig for three? How will I feed my own son, or shall I lay him here as well?!'

'Good man, with the blessings of Allah, make it deeper,' a man said. 'Here!' And he handed him a bunch of curled up notes. The digger put the long-armed spade to his chest, counted them swiftly and resumed digging.

I stood in the back and didn't say a word. I wasn't burying my son yet, I waited for him to arrive with Omar, Farida's uncle. I felt a shiver of excitement—to see Hamada.

The procession arrived, in all its hurry. Israeli drones were eyeing us from afar and people were muttering in prayer. Suspicion of a wrapped body being a missile, would promptly bring another bomb down from the sky.

First a young boy named Youssef was buried. He was six years old but you couldn't really tell, he had been burned alive so the shroud was tainted black around the ties. He was rested on his side, facing Mecca, and a foot of dirt was thrown on top. Once more, people argued that it wasn't enough. I watched as they squabbled like leashed hyenas over the amount of dirt that could or couldn't be placed over a dead child according to the religious code. Eventually another boy was buried at the same depth, resting on his right side as well, and both were covered enough to satisfy everyone. '*In the name of Allah and in the faith of the messenger of Allah...*' and the imam ran off a long line of religious quotes. He finished it off with: '*Allah Yerhamak we yenawarlak el kabr we yegalak rawda men el ganah*'. May God forgive you and shed light in your grave and make a room for you in heaven.

'*Allahu Akbar.*'

Then came Hamada's turn.

Farida took my hand and squeezed it hard. I looked at her. She was devastated. I knew though, that Hamada was in a good place and that he wasn't being buried. It was just a body. I let go of her hand and went to take my place in the line of men. Farida looked at me quizzically with large wet eyes. She was clearly puzzled over something I was saying. I explained to her that I had already seen Hamada swimming. She began crying.

People parted to the side as Omar came towards us carrying the small body shrouded in layers of white cotton. The body had been washed, wrapped from head to toe. Clearly the head had detached as it was lolling in every direction underneath the fabric. The prayers to Allah became louder as I approached Omar.

'Allah! Grant peace to Mohammad and his family as you did to Ibrahim and his family. O Allah! Bless Mohammad and his family as you blessed Ibrahim and his family. Truly you are most glorious and most praiseworthy.'

'Are you sure this is my son?! Are you sure my son is dead?!' I put my fingers on the cloth and shook the body. The head remained in its separate place.

'Why are you telling me you are burying my son?' I asked Omar. 'Are you sure he is dead?! Are you sure?!' 'Why are you burying my son?!'

'Fathi...?' Omar pleaded.

People began crying. Omar began crying. I looked up and around me and looked back at Farida as she cried. I didn't cry. This was just some body, some thing, some one. I knew I wouldn't find my son under the piece of cloth. Omar passed the body to a friend, took both my hands and looked at me with tears down his face. He didn't say anything. The digger, other people I didn't know and some of my friends from the department surrounded us and slowly moved me away from the grave.

'Allah have mercy on us all. Allah, give this young soul a place in heaven ... Allah...'

'Why are you so sure he is dead?! Are you really sure?!' I kept yelling as the men pushed me backwards. I looked into Omar's eyes, full of tears. His own son, Mohammed, was the same age as Hamada, born a week apart. He had looked after Hamada as his own, never forgotten a birthday and always asked if he needed anything. He made sure that I knew how much he loved Hamada. He made sure that I knew how much I was respected for my love for Farida.

'Fathi, pray upon the prophet. Pray for his place in heaven, Fathi,' Omar pleaded.

I felt a surge of grief. The tears welled in my heart until they burst out through my eyes, like a river in flood. I waited for my heart to stop, for death to push the men aside and take my soul from my body, but it didn't happen. Instead there was a moment of clarity and the earth, the sky and sea came hurtling towards me. I looked into the eyes of the young man who had dug the hole for my own son; he stood amongst the men. It was Aboud.

'Pray for his place in heaven, Ammu,' he said.

I held Farida's hand and we floated on our backs under the surface of the sea, the rays of the sun diffracting at our eyes as Hamada appeared and dived to meet us with open arms in a warm embrace.

Together we drifted off into a fearless world. I felt at peace.

❖❖❖

The first time Hamada saw a weapon was in my hands. It was an AK-47 assault rifle, brought in through Egypt, most likely all the way from Libya. I had promised Mohammed to deliver it to one of Khaled's distributors but when I arrived at his house, I found that he had been assassinated and the building was full of confused police officers with no one to arrest. I kept the rifle in the boot of the car and as I was opening it one day, Hamada saw it. He curiously asked me what it was for. I told him it was meant to shoot a bullet. And like every other child, he asked why, and like every other parent in Gaza, my reply was: 'Because sometimes we have to speak the language of our enemies, even if we don't wish to do so.'

This opened a can of worms. Question upon question that eventually led to a termination of the discussion. The reality of life in Gaza, living besieged and treated like a lower order of humanity, was too cruel to lay upon a five-year-old child. I had watched television in Canada where parents discussed one of the hardest things in life: telling one's child that we weren't always that nice to each other as human beings. I remembered Farida looking surprised and asking me: 'Is there a war here in Canada?!'

The rifle didn't leave the boot of my car for a long time. I had wrapped it up and laid it in plain sight, except for a cover of folded black cloth. The day after the funeral was quiet, only distant blasts of artillery on the far side of Khan Younis had penetrated the stillness of the night, and the rockets fired in retaliation sounded like strong bursts of wind through the olive trees. I walked out to the car while Farida was still asleep, unfolded the cloth and looked at the weapon. It was fairly new, kind of small, as well. I looked around me and picked it up, releasing the clip. It was fully loaded, thirty rounds. I put the clip back in. I felt its weight, rested it against my arm, put my finger on the trigger and aimed at a star in the sky before putting it back again.

I needed more ammunition.

21

Farida opened her eyes slowly. She had been crying in her sleep. Dried tears ran sideways across her cheeks and her eyelashes stuck together on one side as she opened them. She was on her side with one hand under her cheek. She moved her tongue around her mouth and looked at me with lost eyes:

'Water me, please...' A gentle asking to bring her some water.

I had a glass already. I handed it to her. She drank slowly, stopping a few times to wet her dry lips with her tongue. She looked back up at me, didn't say anything. Eyed me up and down, rubbed her eyes clear of dry tears and sleep, then looked at me again.

'What is it, Fathi?' she asked and kept looking at me. 'Do you need me to bring you something? You look as if you are going somewhere. Where are you going...?'

I just sat there, on the small wooden chair next to the vanity in the remains of our bedroom. I had moved it so I was facing her. The truth was I had nothing to say.

How could I have described to her the feeling of being between two worlds? How could I describe how much I missed the part of my soul that we had brought into life? How could I tell her that I felt our home had turned into a living hell? How could I explain the pain in my soul in that devastating moment I saw my son dead? How time had stood still since then. How my entire memory had been crushed and I was left with only that one moment to occupy me, day and night. How could I describe the desolation of my heart, never to find its companion? The moment when I was on my knees and looked onto my own son and couldn't hear him, couldn't find him. How could I describe the rage I felt, carrying him, held together by the threads of his skin, his body severed as a chicken is butchered? He didn't choose his circumstances and neither did I and neither did any of us. How could I tell her that I couldn't sleep at night as I wondered how those who killed him could sleep? How any of us could sleep knowing our children were being killed? How could I explain that I no longer had any hope? The hope which had carried me through, which had given me my life resilience. All had stemmed from this hope, not religion and never anger.

'Fathi?'

'I am sorry. I was just … I just woke up early and I didn't want to go back to bed and …'

Farida kept looking at me. I was afraid of asking her how she felt.

'I love you …'

Farida didn't reply. From resting on her elbow on one side, she sat up, stretched her arm and put the glass of water on the vanity.

'Where are you going?' Farida asked.

'I am not going anywhere right now … Tomorrow, *Insha'Allah* … I will go and see Mohammed. He couldn't come to the funeral. I want to talk to him …'

Farida didn't say more. It had been three days since we had buried Hamada's body and we had only spoken a few words to each other. The whole first day we were outside of ourselves. People kept coming through to what was left of our house, the bedroom. The day the hospital told me to go home, I asked Farida where we were going, and she just said 'home'. We arrived at a ruin; the only thing standing was the bedroom with half of its rear wall collapsed. Hani had marshalled a group of men to throw up the remains as a shelter for our return. A large black cloth had been stretched across the missing part of the roof; and the rear wall, adjacent to the kitchen, had been rebuilt by stacking pieces of rubble. They had swept the entry and mounted a piece of plywood as a door to our bedroom, which had also become a front door. All that remained was a broken vanity, our bed, a wooden chair, the radio, a few pieces of clothing and some kitchen utensils that had been piled together in the back. A dripping tap had been mounted to a pipe twisted out of the rubble. We lived in our own nightmare. Without Hani and the other neighbours bringing us what they could spare of food and water, I am sure we would have chosen to drown ourselves in the sea.

The second day the shelling around Khan Younis was heavy. Halfway through the day Farida and I looked at each other and walked hand in hand to the beach where I used to swim with Hamada. Every time a bomb fell, Farida would pull her shoulders, embrace me and close her eyes with her head to my chest. The smoke from the east was black and moved over us and out across the ocean. We lay on the sand with the waves caressing our legs until sunset and I hoped, at that moment, we would be seen and ordered dead. Farida spoke my hope.

'Allah, please take us now. Please. Please let us see our son again.'

As the sun cast its farewell over our empty beach, we kissed each other with open eyes. A drone flew over us and returned but didn't fire. Perhaps the man watching through its camera had a real beating heart in his chest and let us live.

He should have killed us.

22

The Israelis had moved their frontline into Gaza ten days before they killed Hamada on the 27th of July 2014. The radio said they were destroying tunnels, but the truth was monstrously different. They destroyed a hospital, a water plant, they hit a UN refuge, killing women and children, and even destroyed a biscuit factory. The more people the Israelis killed, the more support they appeared to get in the news. The words of hope we had initially clung to were as ephemeral as the voices that had spoken them. The radio kept saying the Israeli Defence Force, the IDF, the IDF, the IDF and the Iron Dome, and the flabbergasting oxymoron of supporting Israel's right to self-defence as an occupier of Palestinian land. Never the Palestinians' right to defend themselves against their occupier. Propaganda is repetition, so the BBC got the nickname, Brother Bibi's Channel, since no one was ever in doubt of their devotion to the Zionist agenda of Benjamin Netanyahu.

We were surrounded by enemies. Hamas fighters raided Al Mawasi in the middle of the night, looking for Fatah followers and others whom they believed or suspected were traitors. They were executed on sight. Farida and I lay in our bed as the boots trampled past our ruin. We held our breath as the voices came to a halt close by. A male voice commanded a door knocked in. Hani was dragged out on the street in front of his family. His wife, Afaf, screamed, pleading with the men to leave him. We heard her being forcefully thrown to the ground. We looked at each other in the trickle of light shining through the black cloth above us. We heard the shots and Hani's body dropping to the ground in the silence of a life being taken.

Then followed the screams, the wailing, and the boots moving on.

23

The first day of the month of August, Farida took me to Khan Younis for lunch. It's a bizarre affair trying to feel alive when you are being bombed, when drones armed with missiles fly over your head and children smile, playing on top of what once was their home. Our scars were, if not visible on the outside, deep and constant inside. Our hope was a touch stronger than the pain, so Farida decided that morning to nourish the hope, even in the midst of our agony. After Hamada's death, I replaced my feelings of hope with feelings of hatred. The love I felt for Farida was my only torment, as it kept asking me to love her, to hope and to believe.

Farida took my arm in hers and we walked into Malak's restaurant. It was a small place that served some of the best local dishes in Gaza. Farida and I had met there through the years and when we had brought Hamada with us, we told him stories of how we would flirt with each other. He would laugh until his eyes watered.

We ordered a selection of small dishes and began eating. Farida's appetite made me smile. She looked up at me.

'*El hamdullah!* Where have you been hiding that?!' she cried loudly.

'It's your beauty, while eating, I can't resist!'

Farida covered her mouth as she laughed. I laughed as well. We looked at each other. Suddenly her expression changed, tears began brimming, overflowing, dropping. I felt the tub overflowing as well.

'It must be the onions!'

Farida's smile returned and the tears that fell were once more of love.

A rocking explosion nearby brought the war back. Everyone in the restaurant stepped outside and we, who were sitting outside in the shade, looked up. Take shelter or run? People began paying and leaving hastily. We lingered on, kept sitting on our plastic chairs sipping our coffee with a piece of *kunafa*[30], watching the commotion. I felt as if we both had decided to live for just one day. Even forget there was a war going on.

The fighter jets roared across low in the sky and we felt a tremor as if an earthquake was building. We kept sitting. I smoked a cigarette and followed the jets eastwards with my eyes.

Just wait, you sons of dogs…

Farida took the cigarette out of my hand and had a few drags. I smiled.

'When did you start smoking?'

'Right now. Why not? What else have you got on you?'

Farida was flirting and the staff at the restaurant were amused and happy about it. Happy we stayed, happy other people saw us and followed suit. Those who could afford a small treat like ourselves. Those who wished to live for just a bit. While life was still there.

We returned to our bedroom. Barricaded the door with the wooden chair, whispered as we undressed and entangled ourselves on a heavenly bed dressed with see-through netting and pillows of feather. Holding hands, we fell asleep in exhaustion and walked on through to another world.

Hamada ran towards us, smiling, rising from the waves. We closed our eyes and the war had never been.

❖❖❖

My love,

I woke from my sleep one day to find myself in the dream of loving you. Days turned into nights, as it came true. I have been blessed with love from the minute I saw you in front of the school on that rainy day. No other woman ever caught my eye and my heart has been yours, still is and will forever be. I hope for your forgiveness as life now asks me to

---

30 Arabic cheese pastry.

leave you. I have asked Mohammed to bring you safely to Egypt and he has arranged for your papers. Our family in Rafah are expecting you. If I could have come with you, I would, but I can't, so I am setting you free from the hell we're living in. The door is open so take the chance and run! The walls will come down one day, I know they will and if you see this moment, please tell me everything about it. I have never known it, we have never known it. It's the only thing I always dreamt about, how it would be, to live as a free man. I have walked in the light of our hearts since I met you and now I will walk down the road of darkness that ends in a shallow grave.

I have to see Hamada again, I promised him that if we ever got lost from each other, we would meet again in heaven. I was promised that I would at least be taken to its gates. I hope they open for me. I have no other choice but to hope. Hope you will be safe in Egypt, hope heaven has given Hamada bliss and hope I will be granted a moment at least to keep my promise to him, if my Maker doesn't judge me first.

I did everything I could. I did everything to keep us happy and safe. I was grateful for what was and what became. We did indeed know what life our son would be born into. Perhaps Allah will judge us for that? Perhaps that's why he took Hamada from us again? Were we bad people? Did we ask too much? What did we do to deserve our life? And may Allah forgive me for asking that. I am grateful. To have seen my own son, to have loved him.

I am grateful for the love he gave me. I am grateful for you.

I love you.

Fathi

24

I parked outside Mohammed's apartment and looked up to find him waiting on the balcony. I walked up the steps. There was dust and pieces of concrete littered about. A shell had hit the adjacent building. The noise of my feet dragging across the grit bounced off the walls and sounded as if someone was following me. I stopped several times and looked behind me. The rifle was tucked under my left arm, pointing to the ground. Mohammed opened the door and stepped out. I reached him and we stood before each other. Then he pulled me towards him and embraced me. My tears erupted uncontrollably.

Mohammed consoled me, looked at me and said, 'Khaled is here.'

I wiped my tears quickly and composed myself, took a deep breath and followed him in. We were on our own; Sarah and Abdullah weren't there. I didn't ask where they were but stepped into the living room where Khaled sat, hands folded, on a living-room chair. He was abstracted, in another place, looking into thin air. As I walked in, he remained seated for a second, then got up and extended his hand. We shook hands and kissed formally on the cheeks.

'*Salaam Aleikum*, ya Abu Hamada.' He looked at me with changed eyes, almost defeated.

'*We aleikum al salaam…*' I replied.

I could tell he wanted to say something but stopped himself. He kept looking at me with his usual stare, although his eyes flickered a hint of redemption. He let go of my hand. Mohammed ushered us back to our seats. We sat down. There was a moment of silence, then Khaled spoke.

'Mohammed asked me to come here. I was told you need a favour.'

'It's not a favour. I won't be able to repay any debt to you.'

'That's an interesting proposition. So, tell me what I can help you with and I will tell you the price.'

'I need more bullets and I need a man who can bring me close to the enemy.'

I unshrouded the rifle on my lap and looked at Khaled. Khaled looked at me and at the rifle. He didn't speak. Mohammed offered tea. We both accepted and then he disappeared into the kitchen. Khaled kept looking at me, at the rifle.

'Why are you asking me?'

'Because it's time for you to repay me, Khaled … My black day has arrived and you need my white penny.'

Khaled paused. My counterstrike had come to this man whose past arrogance in power was notorious. I knew his position in Gaza had fallen. He had lost several of his men, and most of the tunnels he had funded had been destroyed. He had very few ways, if any, of paying back his debts—and those people Khaled owed money to, had even less patience when there was a war going on. I had heard he had also lost one of his sons, but I decided to leave it. After all, he had called me Abu Hamada.

Khaled looked at me in the examining way I knew too well. I looked back at him, stern, facing him off.

'I want one thing from you.'

'I am under your command.'[31]

'Fathi … I don't want to see you again.'

There was silence, only broken by Mohammed's stirring of the glasses in the kitchen. He stopped for a second and then continued, placing them on a tray. I looked back in silence.

'From my eyes, Fathi… From my eyes…'[32]

---

31 A saying in Arabic meaning: You are valued.
32 A saying in Arabic meaning: I promise.

I am sure Mohammed heard every word spoken. He came back and served us the tea. His eyes were shiny and he gave me a pleading look as he extended the small tea glass, rattling on a carved glass saucer. We discussed the war and the losses we all had suffered. Khaled told us of his eldest son's death, then left shortly thereafter.

I will never forget the calm movement of his lips, his eyes pierced, as if he had decided once and for all, to walk in the light of day.

❖❖❖

Like a blazing furnace, the afternoon crept slowly by. After Khaled had left, I sat with Mohammed behind a shade cloth on the balcony. The hashish we smoked was a pleasant relief to the pain in my body and its cerebral effect was calming. The street below was empty. An old man stuck his head out from the entry of the apartment block across the narrow space, scanned the skies, and ran to another building. I remembered doing the same thing.

I looked towards the east. Two Israeli tanks were moving north at high speed, dust rising behind them as if they were a herd of wild animals in a stampede. A helicopter flew ahead of them in the same direction and another passed above, heading south. The Israelis avoided any low flying towards the west in the afternoon, even the drones were deployed a bit higher. Once the sun was in their eyes, the battleships would take over and begin shelling from the ocean. They didn't care where their bombs fell, as long as they killed a Palestinian. This was obvious to us, obvious to the photographers and journalists who dared to venture away from *the Palace* as we called their hotel in Gaza City. Those who did saw what we saw and many of them were killed, just like us. The Israelis didn't care; they would say that our fighters used them as human shields—and that apparently meant they could use bigger bombs.

The phone rang. I thought it was Farida, but the number was hidden. I picked up.

'Allo…' I said, pressing the phone hard against my ear. A couple of seconds passed, enough to hear the caller breathing heavily, a few kids' voices passed him, his shoes rubbed against dust, walking up a dirty staircase.

'Allo,' I said once more.

'*Asalaamu aleikum*,' a deep male voice penetrated.

'*Asalaamu aleikum*,' I answered.

'I will meet you in three hours. Bring only what you need. I will take you to where you want to go.'

'Where will we meet?'

'I will send someone to bring you to me. He will come soon and give you the directions. Follow them and leave your phone. If you bring it, I will know, and I will not be there. *Yalla, Allah maak*.' He hung up.

Mohammed looked at me, lit up a cigarette and took a deep breath.

'I can't ask you not to go,' Mohammed said slowly.

'I know. I don't want you to ask me, either,' I replied, looking down at my phone.

I had already left my last words to Farida and in those, part of my soul. I had left my voice and my love. I had left her my heart. If I called her, she would ask me to stay and I would be compelled to do the right thing by her, and return.

I kept staring at the phone, the smoke from Mohammed's cigarette passing over it, feeling the heat of the sun on my back and the sweat in my hands around it, holding it tightly, rubbing it like a wishing stone.

I switched off the phone.

After a sharp knock, Mohammed opened the front door of the apartment to a boy who handed him a folded piece of paper. The boy left and didn't ask for payment. We looked down from the balcony and saw him get into a beaten-up old Peugeot further down the street. The car took off hastily. Mohammed glanced at the note in his hand and handed it to me. He took a large breath of his cigarette and sat down with a sigh, exhaling all the smoke with his head bent down.

In the name of Allah, the merciful. The enemy is close. Your vengeance will be a victory to us all. I will take you to them. Al Jalaa square. Walk around the rocket at eight o'clock exactly. No other cars will stop.

Allah is great.

Kader

I straightened my back and looked up at Mohammed watching me silently. The cigarette had burned down to a strip of ash between his fingers and the wind broke off bits of it, one tiny fleck at a time, swirling them around the balcony.

'Do you want to know what it says?' I asked. Mohammed stayed put, the cigarette still between his fingers.

'I know what it says …' Mohammed answered. 'I wish it didn't have to be so. I wish we could leave right now and go to the beach. Have a swim and laugh. I wish all of this never was and that we opened our eyes to a different world every day.'

I couldn't answer Mohammed, for I shared the sentiment of his words.

'Where is Sarah, Abdallah?' I asked instead.

'They are with her parents. Tomorrow they will go to Egypt with Farida. *Insha'Allah* they will all be safe. The men on the border won't get their money if it doesn't happen, so it will happen.'

'Promise me.'

'By Allah, I promise you, my brother: Farida will be in Egypt by this time tomorrow.'

'*Insha'Allah*,' I said

'*Insha'Allah*,' Mohammed said.

Mohammed went with me. He drove me all the way to Gaza City past broken power lines, craters in the street and toppled buildings. Al Jalaa Square was surprisingly busy with streetsellers and people out shopping while it was possible. I only had a short time left. We drove around the M-75 rocket monument, headed a few hundred metres north and stopped.

We both got out. Mohammed walked around the car. Our friendship from childhood to that moment as grown men: it all passed by my eyes. I leaned the shrouded rifle against the car before we hugged with clenched fists that we tapped on each other's back.

'I love you, my brother. May Allah be with you.' Mohammed held his tears back to the point where every vein on his face bulged as if about to burst. Then he got back in the car without hesitation, took a last look at me in the side mirror, and drove off.

I held the rifle close to my side and watched him drive back towards the monument. The brakes lit up as he made his way around it, entangled with everything else on the street, moving in the same direction.

I glanced at my watch, then looked up.

The light of the day made way for the golden blanket of the summer twilight.

To be followed by the eternal darkness of the night sky.

25

The second hand on my watch inched swiftly towards the minute hand and as they aligned, they skipped in unison to point straight up. Eight o'clock. I took a deep breath and crossed to the monument. Barely had I got there when a car I recognised pulled up. It was Khaled's black Mercedes, beaten up. Clearly, debris had showered it and bullet holes pitted a coarse line across the bonnet and windscreen on the passenger side. The door was opened.

A man hooded in a balaclava sat behind the wheel. He was wearing dark camouflage clothes from head to toe, and the only thing I could see in the light of the interior, were his piercing green eyes. His vest was packed with pockets and a hand grenade shook on the right side of his chest.

'*Yalla*, get in!'

I got in, put my rifle with its muzzle to the floor and leaned it against the centre console.

Al Jalaa Square is in the north of Gaza City. The home of the Izz Ad-Din Al Qassam Brigades, a secretive militant group, named after the man who homemade the rocket of the same name. Although the rockets did less damage than a high calibre bullet, they were beacons of the resilience and resistance of the Gazan people. Until that day I hadn't met anyone from this group but here I was, sitting next to one. He drove as if we were being chased by an invisible enemy, speeding through the dark streets and alleyways, keeping his eye on the sky as much as the road, heading southeast.

'*Salaam ya*, Fathi. I am Kader.'

'*Salaam ya*, Kader,' I replied.

'I will take you to the front. You won't have much time. The Israelis will send in their commandos tonight. Allah be praised, their arrogance cost them lives and everyone knows they will withdraw very soon now. So, they will come for their revenge today, the cowards. Allah is just and you will avenge your son as well, may Allah have found him a place in heaven.'

I was a dog on a leash. Not a rescue dog but a suicide dog.

Kader spoke quickly, without hesitation. His voice was crisp, determined. He was a fighter, cheekbones protruding and a trimmed beard, short but fit body and his clothes, although dirty, looked as if they were part of him. His green eyes, scanning the air and the ground, shone bravely. He cast no shadow over his will to fight.

In the dark of the night, Shuja'iyya was a rubble moon landscape. I couldn't even recognise where Farida and I had lived. A sadness ran through my veins. It looked like an earthquake zone. Very few buildings were standing, most were flattened in uneven piles or spread out around craters as if someone had whumped a fist in the middle of a cream cake. The floodlights from industrial diggers and bulldozers appeared like dusty umbrellas, revealing crowds of men, women and children under their giant claws and scoops, searching for bodies--dead or alive—belongings and mementos of the inhabitants under the debris. The Israelis had pounded the area for three days, killing hundreds of innocent people as they searched for a dozen lost soldiers. GPS chips, implanted in the shoulders of the Israeli soldiers, were removed by the Palestinian fighters who captured or killed them. They then used the chips to lead the Israelis on a wild goose chase that cost them dearly. The fighters kept coming out of the ground in places the Israelis hadn't mapped, and they fought heroically. The battle of Shuja'iyya had finished ten days earlier on the 23rd of July. The Israelis had withdrawn with losses they hadn't expected. In retaliation they levelled the entire neighbourhood and killed civilians without mercy, in cold blood—all in the name of protecting their soldiers and destroying tunnels.

Tunnels we were on our way to.

❖❖❖

Kader tore through a narrow alley at high speed. At the end he pulled the hand brake and drifted the car sideways towards a concrete wall. The words, *Allahu Akbar*, spray-painted on the wall approached my eyes on the passenger side before being pulled away as Kader put his foot on the gas, opened both side-door windows and drove into a large opening in the wall of a destroyed building. Two fighters pointed their rifles to our heads as we went down a steep ramp, straight into an underground compound. Kader looked up at the man closest to him and they both pointed their rifles downwards.

'*Yalla*, we don't have much time. We have to get you ready. Don't step out with the rifle.'

We both got out. Kader went to a man in the back of the low-ceilinged concrete basement, large enough for a car to easily turn around in. Two groups of men had their vests flat on the ground, filling rounds into empty clips, strapping them onto their vests. They were taking rifles apart, cleaning them, assembling them. A few glimpses were cast my way but besides that, everyone continued doing their work. Kader got me a vest.

'Take this. It belonged to the martyr, Badran. It's Kevlar, so will give you more time!' Kader clapped his chest with his right hand to signal the protection of the vest. 'He was a brave fighter, may Allah have mercy on his soul.'

I took the vest. It was heavy. Kader went in fast steps to the end of the room where several large crates were stacked. I looked at the vest again. I didn't want to know how Badran had died. I wore black jeans, a green T-shirt and black running shoes. Everyone around me wore dark to black clothes and I was going to wear a black military vest. I would meet with death in the colour of death.

Kader brought back spare sets of empty clips for my rifle, opposites facing, taped together, boxes full of bullets, a pistol and two hand grenades which he clipped onto my vest.

'You can get your rifle from the car now. Begin filling the clips, make sure you know where each one is on your vest so you can change them quickly.'

Kader showed me how to press a bullet into the magazine, then ran off again. I got my rifle out of the car, sat down on the ground and opened a box of rounds. I took one out and looked at it. It was shiny.

In the name of Allah, the merciful, take as much blood as was taken and may this be a just vengeance.

I finished loading the first two clips, taped them together, flicked the safety on, hooked one in and clicked it into place, then loaded the first bullet with a quick pull to the chamber and lay the rifle on the ground. I finished loading the rest of the clips, all eight of them, two hundred and forty bullets.

Kader returned, handed me a large assault knife and checked all the gear.

'You are ready.'

'I am ready.'

'We are all ready.' The men formed a line, I stood next to Kader, folding my hand to begin the last prayer of the day. I remained and kept praying to myself as one by one, the others finished. For the blood our children had spilled, for the strength to kill another human being, for trading with death and making the devil drunk with vengeance.

I asked for forgiveness.

26

I wanted to look the enemy in the eyes. I wanted him to fear my anger and his own imminent death. I wanted him to know that he was no closer to God than myself. I felt the sweat running down my neck; and the adrenalin pounded in my head as in my heart. I handed back the balaclava to Kader. He looked at me and took it without a word. Then I slid down the rope, head first. I just fitted into the dirt hole. The torch I had in my mouth revealed the bottom of the pit. I put my hands on the ground and pulled with my fingertips the rest of my body still upright down into the narrow tunnel. I could only just crawl, pulling myself by pushing my elbows and lower arms to the ground, raising my chest slightly and pulling. Each time I raised my head too much I scraped the ceiling and dirt crumbled from the walls around me. I avoided breathing through my mouth, I avoided thinking about anything else other than why I was heading for the light at the end.

Crawl at a steady pace. Don't stop. Keep moving, keep your chest up, remember your grenades, keep your rifle ahead of you. It will take you 10 minutes. Set your clock. The last crawl before going up is very narrow. Remember, turn off your torch as soon as you see the tunnel stops. Turn onto your back, pull yourself through with your hands and you will see the opening. Push against the wall with your legs and back and move yourself up. It's 3 metres. There are some pockets in the dirt where you can put your feet, but don't rest your weight on them. Once you're at the top, wait until the shots are fired, this way they will move into position and you can run straight towards them with cover from the buildings on both sides. Watch the rats. They bite, so just let them pass. May Allah be with you.

I crawled for what seemed an eternity, the sweat from my eyebrows running into my eyes. It burned badly. I wiped my face against my arms and felt the dirt stick to my face instead. The rifle began to feel heavy towards the end. Although I had become used to its weight, the safety, how to quickly change the clip, I still had to see a bullet come out of it and penetrate the enemy. For all the death and destruction I had witnessed in my life, I had never pulled the trigger myself. I felt no fear. I stopped for a second and felt it—no fear. My determination was fuelling my adrenalin. I moved even quicker, like a soldier, 1-2-1-2, until the beam of light reflected onto a brown dirt wall in front of me. I had come to the end.

I doused the torch.

The ground shook as I peered through the makeshift plastic periscope. It was stuck through a hole in the steel lid that covered the exit. I turned it to several directions, wiping the burning sweat from my eyes, brushing the dirt off my face with brisk movements. The air was suffocating, and the steel lid was like a furnace from having lain in the burning sun all day. I had to hold myself up, my back and legs shaking against the dirt walls of the narrow hole.

It was an Israeli tank that caused the earth to tremble. It turned its turret and pointed its barrel straight towards me. For a second I thought I had been seen but it rumbled past, so close, that the steel lid shook and moved to the side, exposing the night sky above. I ducked and pushed my legs hard against the wall. I shook furiously and held on tightly to the rifle. I had to get out of the hole.

As soon as the tank had passed, I looked through the periscope again. There were soldiers scrambling, being ordered in groups to spread. Two moved towards me and my heart began racing. I was waiting for the signal. The shot from Kader which would be my cue to attack.

I barely had to wait. As I scanned the buildings around me from my low vantage point, the shot came. There was a flash as the single shot was planted in the gut of a soldier running alongside the tank. He fell to the ground and held his hand to the wound. Commotion broke out, men shouted orders in Hebrew as soldiers ran for cover, including the two still coming towards me.

They hid behind the remains of a wall. I was coming out in the middle of the rubble of the same destroyed building and they were only metres away. As far as the enemy knew, there was no possibility of anyone coming from underneath. However, four tunnels remained, and I was given one of them. Kader and the others would exit from tunnels whose locations I didn't know. I didn't even know where they entered. If I were captured, the enemy would only discover one tunnel.

I closed my eyes. I clenched the rifle in my hands and slowly moved the selector from safety to semi-automatic, single shot. My heart raced, my blood was boiling, my head felt light. My legs shook uncontrollably, and I realised I couldn't move if I needed to, not until I could get the rifle and my arms above ground and pull myself up and out of the hole. I put my finger on the trigger, a bullet was already in the chamber. I put my head to the barrel, sweat ran heavily from my head down the steel. I moved the selector to automatic. I was ready.

In the name of Allah the merciful.

I shook so much, my knee tapped hard on the dirt walls of the hole. It hurt and made a tapping sound. One of the two men with their backs to me turned around and looked straight at me. He was young; his eyes were terrified. He opened his mouth—gaping mute. With my body and legs, still in the hole shaking, I rested my arms on the ground and pointed the rifle at him.

I didn't see the scared young man as I took aim. I saw the man who dropped the bomb which opened up the guts of my son, who unclipped his helmet off and flew home to dinner with his family, kissing his wife and kids goodnight, feeling he had done a good day's work. The soldier lifted his rifle, surprised, about to take aim. He still had his mouth open when I put my finger on the trigger. The other soldier didn't move, he was still looking ahead and up. Shots were being fired and hitting the wall they were behind. Kader was doing what he had promised. I tightened my body and looked the young man straight in his eyes as I pulled the trigger.

It was a spit of lead. A stream of bullets spat out of the barrel and through the young man's body, hitting him from his thigh to his chest. He dropped his rifle, fell to ground and twisted in agony to the side. His buddy looked down at him and turned his head towards me. Another set of terrified young eyes stared at me and before he could point his rifle, I pulled the trigger once more and hit him across his body, taking a finger off his right hand. Blood squirted out and he fell to the ground, grasping his bleeding hand.

I put the rifle on the ground and pulled myself out of the hole. My legs were a pair of shaking sticks that I dragged after my body. As I crawled flat on the ground towards the two young men, I felt a bullet graze my back and warm blood began running down my side. I didn't feel any pain and pulled myself as fast as I could until I reached the two soldiers. More shots were fired but all three of us on the ground were out of the line of fire. Their own couldn't take me out. Not yet.

The young man I had shot last, let go of his hand and took a small hand pistol from his belt. I held his arm, slammed it to the ground and grabbed the pistol. I pointed it to his heart from the side of his bullet proof vest, looked him in the eyes and pulled the trigger. The bullet passed through his body and his eyes lit up for a split second as I stared into them. I turned to the other young man and put one knee on his chest and one on his arm as I twisted his other arm above his head and pointed the pistol to his chin.

'Don't kill me! Don't kill me!' he pleaded in Arabic.

'Why? You are chosen by God, so you have nothing to fear.'

Hatred had consumed me. I didn't feel myself or my soul. I was a servant of death as I pulled the trigger. The head of the soldier opened up like a fountain and his eyes turned white in a fraction of a second. As I looked into them, I felt a surge of relief in my body.

It was a full shoot-out between Kader and his men and the Israeli unit. The tank rumbled back towards the end of the street and fired a shell that passed us by a hair's breadth. The shock wave threw me over the body of the young man I had just killed. My face against his open head.

Dust filled the air and the dim light of the night sky was covered, creating a hazed canvas with fireballs going off from here and there. Bullets with phosphorus rings threw deadly strips of light, resembling bright fireflies snaking their way through the air. I rose from the ground, feeling dizzy. Blood ran down on to my legs. I was bleeding heavily. I unclipped the two hand grenades, pulled the pins and threw them, one at a time, ahead of me towards the tank. As soon as they blew, I began running. Voices yelled and more shots were fired.

As I ran, I was hit in my left shoulder. I kept running. The cloud thinned out and I began firing in front of me. The clip ran out and I swapped it around, kept firing, kept running. I ran out of the cloud and there, right in front of me, taking cover at the side of a building, were another two soldiers. They fired and I felt a flash in my body. I jumped at the closest one and in a hellish rage, I took my assault knife and stabbed him in the throat. One, two, three times. I kept stabbing, watched his blood gush out in powerful bursts, as the other soldier kept firing his rifle, sending bullet after bullet tearing through my body. A warm sensation filled me as I shrivelled and was flung back by the fire penetrating me, hitting the ground on my back.

It was my revenge and the triumphant death of sorrow. My heart stopped as the heavens descended with their welcoming embrace.

And I ended.

***

I am looking at the light of the brightest star in the sky. I feel dazed, as if I am floating on air. I see Farida standing on the doorsteps of the school, and the rainbows chasing the clouds. I see Hamada running towards the ocean, looking back at me with hopeful eyes.

I feel his skinny body as I hold him in my arms. I listen to his voice and I watch Farida's eyes glow with happiness as we send him to his first day at school. I look into her eyes as I kiss her gently on the lips. 'I love you,' I say.

The star is moving towards me, flying through the vast distance down from the sky that is the same to all of us, every man, woman and child. Its light growing brighter and brighter.

Out of the darkness that surrounds us.

THE PALACE OF ANGELS

الطُيور اَلتى تُولَد فى القَفَصْ تَعتقِد أنَّ اَلطيران جَريمَة

Birds born in a cage think that flying is a crime.

1

It was damp and cold that night; and I could have been you. I could have been somewhere else. Anywhere else. Instead, I was stuck in a long queue, shouldered by deep-voiced grunts. Steamy breaths filled the air in the lit-up yellow of the night. This was the same queue I found myself in almost every morning and every evening of the week. Men heading to work, women and children on their way to see relatives, people seeking medical treatment or whatever. Every morning we were faced with traders offering us various goods, like a drive-through bazaar but on foot. Boys sold chewing gum or sim cards and calling credit, girls had better luck with snacks and napkins. There were contraband cigarettes, coffee and food from mobile kitchens. Chickens and vegetables from farmers, counterfeit jeans, underwear and socks. The circus unfolded as I, alongside everyone else, disappeared in the mass of the crowd and became another head, another faceless body edging towards a towering concrete wall dotted with watchtowers at strategic intervals. It looked like a maximum-security prison in an American movie; soldiers armed with automatic rifles, surveillance cameras and megaphones. We were the herd of inmates, pushing and shoving like cattle.

Each time we inched forward, the corridor enclosing us narrowed. There could be no turning back unless one was prepared to scale the barred fence and walk it against the flow, back towards the entry—without falling, without colliding onto the mass of people. We entered a steel cage topped with razor wire, winding zigzag like a snake. This was the waiting area but not as you might imagine at the doctor's. There were no chairs or call-outs and we shuffled our frozen feet slowly forward. When signalled, when told, we passed through revolving turnstiles that only allowed one person at a time. Medical cases had their own passage but that night, a pregnant woman had mistakenly put herself in the wrong queue. She stumbled to her knees, holding her swollen belly. The soldiers quickly surrounded her and distrustfully aimed their guns at her. Her water broke, spreading quickly from under her.

And darkened the concrete floor to black.

2

I was someone else that day. Someone other than who I am today. What endures are dreams and nightmares from a past life. A clutch of memories that keep calling me, nagging me. I took the risk of a new life, albeit one which was more promising than the one I was living. I took a leap of faith into the unknown and the unknown set me free.

My life began on a hot, late summer evening in the village of Budrus in the now occupied West Bank of Palestine. My mother wasn't expecting my arrival just yet. She went into labour while visiting a childhood friend. I opened my eyes the moment my face revealed itself to the world and scared the midwife so much she let out a scream that startled my mother, and I shot out like a rocket. Or so she told me.

I was born on the 29th of August 1987. This same day, the Palestinian cartoonist Naji al-Ali[33] died.

Amidst the blur of the early years, the circles in my mother's eyes were magical as was the ever-blue sky behind them. They were my first memory. Their expanding and contracting. Their shining in happiness. As my eyes began to focus, they became my haven and a place where I looked for answers. The movement of the circles spoke to me as they dilated or shrank, as they searched her inner universe for answers to my questions. The world appeared in circles to me, from those on my mother's breasts to that of the single lightbulb above my bed, shining so brightly it left a halo in the far corners

33 Naji Salim Hussain al-Ali (ناجي سليم العلي) Nājī Salīm al-'Alī (1938-1987), was a Palestinian cartoonist, noted for his political criticism of the Arab regimes and Israel in his works. He has been described as the greatest Palestinian cartoonist and probably the best-known cartoonist in the Arab world.

of my eyes. It remained as the lights went out, travelling in waves further and further towards the centre. I'd try everything to see where the halo would go to but I never made it and fell asleep with the pulsating blue of it in the black of my eyes.

Both my mother and father held me close, their heartbeats beacons of the world. When the tempo rose, I studied their faces and how they reacted. I'd turn to see what or who was causing the galloping in their chests. I'd watch them, the way they spoke, acted, the way their eyes flickered and how they watched me. I'd listen to the change in my parents' voices and I'd touch or press myself closer to them. As soon as the danger had passed, as soon as the angry voices had given up, as soon as they had let us pass, I'd listen and feel the change.

My father's heart beat would relax back into a safe thumping. My mother's would linger on, rising and falling as she'd kiss and caress me. And I'd keep staring at her, keep waiting for the moment she'd face me, the moment I would feel safe, myself.

In her circles of magic.

◈◈◈

I turned six to a world full of anger and hatred. Running home from school on my birthday, I found our street on fire. Car tyres were burning and rocks were ready, piled in mounds as ammunition. A barricade had been set against the occupation forces. One of their armoured vans came in and out of sight through the black smoke. I recognised Bilal, one of my cousins. His body looked like that of a fighter, lean and strong. He wore the black and white chequered *Kufiyah*[34] wrapped around his head, that left only his fiery eyes visible. He was passionate about the *Intifada*—the Palestinian uprising—and with his head held high, he spoke of how we would one day be free to walk the earth of our own homeland. To be equal to the Jews, whom

34 Traditional Palestinian scarf, most commonly known in the black-and-white-chequered pattern. It's also the general word for scarf in Arabic.

we once upon a time peacefully lived with. I looked up to him as if he were the gladiator of justice, although at the time that word was confined to a deeply embedded gut feeling of creating something much better for myself than what life had given me. I had become used to this sight, burning tyres, stones in the street and Palestinian flags being waved against Israeli soldiers who were armed to the teeth.

There were times when that world would disappear. I once caught a frog. A frog so small it fitted into my already small child-sized hands. I remembered it made soft croaks and looked at me pleadingly, turning the world into a magical tale. I carried it around all day, showed it to my friends and had conversations with it. Finally, my mother ordered me to return it to where I had found it. At the end of the day, together with my best friend Ali, I let it go. It disappeared into a moist patch of grass near an old olive tree and with it, the beauty of the wonder of life. The sounds and images that filled my days and my dreams returned quickly but I never forgot how that frog stopped. How it looked at me for the last time before it vanished back into its own world. Or perhaps it was me who looked at the frog and it merely wondered why I had chosen to set it free.

I wasn't far behind the men when the Israeli van turned and faced them sideways. A small steel flap was opened and a rifle appeared. The men threw themselves to the ground as several rounds were fired. The bullets penetrated smoke, tyres and eventually flesh. Two shots went through Bilal. One through his chest, close to his heart, the other one straight through his heart. The bullets kept going, reached me and continued through my thigh. I fell to the ground with blood soaking my brand-new school uniform, thinking I was on fire. The inferno that spread throughout my body turned into a warm blanket under which I drifted off to sleep. As I closed my eyes, I saw the van take off at great speed, shaking off the young men who had climbed on top of it as others pounded it with rocks in their hands. People rushed towards me as everything faded into grey. I was taken to the local clinic and I survived.

They told me Bilal became a martyr that day. He would gain a place in heaven, they said. He died resisting and rejecting injustice as I still resist and reject the occupation—but not with a rock in my hand. I had stood right behind him and could have died. If there is a place in heaven, I hope it's like they say it is, without hatred, without violence. Where peace is the currency and our differences the assets. A place where the angels truly exist and a place where Bilal can't leave me as a martyr.

Surviving that day didn't make any difference to my life. I did. At the end, I let myself be swept along by the wind of change. From its breeze to its raging storm I was given opportunities to choose. It was difficult to realise that I actually had choices. Choices, which in the beginning drowned in deafening confusion. I fought blindly until I finally let go and listened.

To the only part of me that remained free—my soul.

3

With heads intertwined, people in the queue wanted to catch a glimpse of the commotion on the other side of the steel-barred barrier. Standing on the outer edge of the waiting area in the winding snake-pit corridor, I watched the pregnant woman moan in agony. I put my fingers through the mesh that formed the cage around us and pushed the side of my face towards it.

There were five young soldiers, two of them were women. They stood around her, their rifles pointed at her. She pleaded with them loudly to get her a doctor and extended her hand, trying all directions. They kept their fingers on the trigger and took a step back except for one of the two young women. She was clearly hesitant as she shifted her attention between the other soldiers and the woman. But she didn't say or do anything. Two of the men laughed and said something to each other in Hebrew. One of them, the one who appeared to be the one in charge, suddenly spat in a deliberate manner on the ground and said in broken Arabic.

'Why should I help you? What is coming out is another *sharmuta*[35], just like yourself!'

He said it with his eyes trained on us. A pack of caged women, children and men. I felt blood surge to my head. I saw my fingers turning red as I tightened my grip on the steel mesh, clenching my jaws until my teeth hurt. Then, the realisation of where we were, what we could do and the consequence if we did, made me strangle my anger and dissolve my tension. I swallowed it. The agitation, the revolt the soldier was aching for, didn't happen.

---

35 An insulting slang term meaning prostitute or hooker.

Only an outraged murmur went through the cage, eventually fading into an eerie silence.

The woman on the ground whimpered through the stillness. In the cold air, drops formed at the tip of my runny nose. I let them fall onto my jacket, spreading like the water breaking from the wretched woman. Her sound filled the air in a broken tune of injustice that not even the enemy looking with fuming hatred into our eyes could ignore.

The lead soldier tripped back and forth between our cage and the woman. The opportunity at his feet obviously stirred him. His pace increased. He was frustrated. The other soldiers looked at him, looked at each other, not knowing what to do. We waited to see what would happen, that was all we could do. In the end he walked up to the cage and yelled at us savagely. His face went red, he took off his helmet and slammed it to the ground. He spat his saliva uncontrollably, yelling incomprehensible words in Hebrew.

The man had totally lost it.

A laughter spread around me and I, too, could have laughed but I didn't. I kept looking at the woman on the ground, palms to her face, sobbing. The other soldiers grinned at their colleague who was losing the plot. Except for that young female soldier—she wasn't laughing. While the others amused themselves at the predicament, she knelt down on one knee.

The pregnant woman, still looking down, turned quickly as the young female soldier gently tapped her shoulder. I couldn't hear what she was saying but the pregnant woman responded with surprise. They both looked up several times, clearly trying to act before the distraction of the laughter passed. The young female soldier stood up, her image cast under the yellow from the light above her. It appeared like a warm blanket had it not been for her breath, exhaled as thick steam in the chill of the damp night.

She glanced in our direction and that is when our eyes met. The meeting was short but defined. I saw her colours in the blinding ambience of the artificial light. I looked away and didn't look back until the laughter stopped. I heard her voice uttering something about an ambulance in a CB radio, the squelch, the silence, then the three-tone response. The other female soldier took a defensive stand as she faced us, raising her rifle slightly—as if we were going to take advantage of the situation and break through the steel bars, with rifles trained on us from all sides.

The voices on the CB radios kept issuing commands. The two male soldiers walked slowly up to their superior, talking to him without putting a hand on him. He didn't move, still boiling with anger, veins extruded, eyes hardly blinking. Saliva had run down his chin and onto his shirt. I made out his nametag, the Hebrew letters read SHARON A. I watched as he removed his earpiece and released the safety of his rifle. He lifted it from where it was hanging below his chest and pointed it at the cage. He was only a few steps away, packed like a mule with a vest full of bulging pockets, the heavy rifle with its strap around his neck, like the chain wrapped around the neck of a mediaeval slave. The soldiers behind him looked bewildered. Their laughter had only added to his anger. He looked humiliated. I could see that—we all could. One of the soldiers signalled to the two female soldiers with his hands, tacitly telling them to get help. They were all young, perhaps in their mid-twenties. They could easily have overpowered their superior, but they stood back. One of them let go of the trigger, swung the rifle in front of him and rested his arms on it.

Sharon A took a step forward.

We all took a step back where, really, there was no place to step back. Nowhere to run, nowhere to hide. We stood still. I had let go of the steel mesh but I grabbed it again. I straightened my body and stood firm. Sharon A took yet another step forward and all I could do was look him in the eye. His eyes switched among every man, woman and child staring at him. I felt defenceless, defiant and curiously fearless all at once. He let the muzzle of the rifle run across the steel mesh. Each time it skipped a wire he let it rest for a second before continuing. Every time, he quickly looked over the crowd.

I felt something brush my leg and, lowering my eyes, I caught sight of a few small fingers. A little girl was standing next to me, grabbing the mesh like myself. She was probably five or six years old. She had shiny black ponytails with magic wands for pins and was dressed in a red velvet winter coat. Her shoes were tiny white slip-ons with a buckle of golden stars underlined by a rainbow.

I was surprised she wasn't sleeping. It was four in the morning. I let out a smile and I caught myself doing so. I stalled. Held the smile back as if afraid someone might see me. For a moment, I feared Sharon A had seen me.

I made out the girl's face as she looked at her mother, who was staring at Sharon A as he moved past us. The girl turned, two large black hopeful eyes staring at me. The roundest cheeks. The benign radiance of childhood flooded me with memories and shone at me like a beacon, overpowering the dimness of the yellowed night.

She smiled carefully. At that, I let it go—I let the smile out. I couldn't stop myself. And something good happened right there and then. I don't know why but it did. Regardless of what would come next, I felt a sensation of peace in my heart. As if everything would eventually turn good. If not for my people, for my family, at least for myself. I didn't want to look up again. I wanted to stay folded in the warmth of my emotion.

Her mother stood, with striking resemblance, behind her. She held her hands across her daughter's chest. She didn't see me. She saw Sharon A. But he wasn't looking at the little girl nor her mother. He didn't even see them although we all saw him.

Sharon A walked back towards us again. I looked up. He stopped right in front of me, the rifle resting on the mesh. Pointed right at my heart. His wild eyes stopped flickering as he stared into mine. Here it was. I wanted him to pull the trigger. I stared back.

Pull the trigger.

⟐⟐⟐

Two Israeli nurses arrived and lifted the pregnant woman onto a wheelchair. Pushing at a rushed pace, they took her back to the medical entry on the Palestinian side of the crossing. Although she quickly disappeared from sight, it was known what would happen. Palestinian medics, if there were any, would place her on another chair. They'd be looking for options. An ambulance might be around, might take her to a hospital but most likely it would be busy with more serious cases. Women in the queues would attempt to help her give birth. An office or an empty storage container at the checkpoint could provide some sort of privacy. She might also find herself left on the ground, unable to enter the Palestinian side again. The nurses, whose call of duty is that of a doctor, might also lift her off the wheelchair and leave her at the gates. No matter whether the sun was blazing the inferno of summer or black in the cold of winter.

I had seen mothers like her several times. Once, I saw a woman give birth right there on the ground in front of the Israeli soldiers. She had just gone through the revolving gates, like the woman that day. It happened so quickly. The soldiers laughed as she cried loudly, tormented, pain ridden, pleading. Her pain and their chasing laughter bounced around the steel cage like the demons playing hide and seek in my nightmares. I felt a crushing sadness in my soul and broke into tears. The woman delivered herself, bleeding heavily. She held her newborn in a tender embrace and then she passed out. Palestinian nurses eventually arrived and put mother and child on a stretcher. The woman lay with her newborn in her hands, the baby stretched blindly on top of her. The nurses lifted the stretcher when the soldier pointed his rifle and nodded. He stopped them again straight after. The nurse in the back cried silently as he stared into the still eyes of the mother. The soldier lifted her *Kufiyah*, still on the ground, with the tip of his rifle and flicked it on top of the baby. He then smiled and ushered them along, with his rifle.

As I stood there, the mesh fading into white and disappearing before my eyes, a female voice echoed distantly as Sharon A faced me. Hatred shone out of his eyes. My heart, ever gripped in a life lived like that of a prisoner, was pounding. I had taken my yearning for freedom down the path of considering ending my own life, resolutely terminating the confinement. In that moment, I had found myself at the gates to freedom. The key to open them stood armed in front of me.

I couldn't understand the female voice. She was talking to Sharon A calmly, maybe trying to coax him out of his frenzy. With his rifle still levelled, he didn't take his eyes away from me, and at that point, everything but Sharon A—had disappeared out of my sight. It wasn't until I heard a roar from behind, like a warrior charging at his enemy. The people standing around me came into peripheral view again, the mesh reappeared and so did the young female soldier who had caught my eye earlier. Once more, we locked in on each other. Neither of us blinked. A fissure appeared in what was otherwise an impenetrable surface in hell.

Sharon A had already moved his eyes towards the roar. He shifted one leg backwards. He took aim. He didn't have to look any more, the target had come to him. The approaching cry crashed into a jangle of screams and I felt a sudden hard push to the side. A shoe planted itself in my arm and the body of a young man flew through the air between myself and the mother of the little girl. He threw himself like a lion against the mesh. But he had hardly touched it when Sharon A pulled the trigger.

It was a metallic thump.

My eyes followed the young man's body as it slumped backwards in a heavy recoil. The bullet went through his head, two jets of blood gushing in its wake. His body struck me and hit the mother too, as he flew through the air and landed on people behind us. The body couldn't go any further. I stumbled to the ground in the packed cage, part of it weighing down on me. His blood spilled onto my throat and spread under my clothes.

I felt warm.

The soldiers yelled at each other and pacified their superior. Their faces creased with fear. Sharon A lay wriggling on the ground, laughing hysterically. Guns were pointed at us from every direction, people's faces looked like those of animals frantically trying to escape their cage. There were pleading cries from parts of the crowd to remain calm, to avoid a bloodbath.

My mind drifted away and I found myself in a tunnel with the muffled sounds of the chaos surrounding me. I sat there in my sudden deafness, my hands on a young man I had seen many times before. Beneath the glistening layer of deep red was a peaceful face. He was finally free from the torment, from the haunting of his emotions.

This young man had made it out. Out of the enclosure, out of our daily pilgrimage to the feeding grounds we were forced to graze for survival. He chose the most desperate form of freedom and he had just beaten me to it.

I envied that dead man.

❖❖❖

The little girl stared. Her mother held her tight to her side, trying to force her to look away, but she kept turning her head to look. Her black eyes were flat, as if painted on. The glistening hope had been replaced with a piercing matte. Blood dotted her face, speckled her clothes from top to bottom. In parts it ran like trails of raindrops.

We were all being shuffled around at gunpoint. Sounds amplified and as I came out of the tunnel, I felt the sharp prod of a rifle in my side and the shove of a boot. I tumbled over and my hands let go of the young man. I heard his name spoken, the prayers to Allah, the kissing of crosses. I looked up to see a soldier wearing a kippah[36] commanding me to move away. For a second I just sat there, my hands bathed in blood.

36 A brimless cap, worn by Jewish males during prayer and by some Jews at all times.

Shoot me.

Two other soldiers grabbed me by my armpits, dragged me on the ground and dropped me at the feet of those standing. People had been pushed even tighter than seemed possible and others had been gun-forced through the turnstiles and grouped sitting on the ground. As I pushed myself off the concrete and stood up, the blood prints left by my hands resembled a backlit cave painting. Relics from an era of damnation. But for the soothing voice of an older woman, a voice reminding me of hope, I would have roared like the young man. She took out a cloth napkin which was passed across to me.

'Here, someone help him. Give him this to wipe his hands. Why are you all standing like this?'

I expressed a faint thank-you. We stood silent, watching the body of the young man. Everyone knew he got what he wanted. He didn't win though. Nor did the soldier who also got rid of the pain that burned inside him.

We all knew there were no winners.

I stood at the edge of a crescent of people. Between us and the young man on the ground, rifles still pointed at us. Soldiers from the Palestinian Authority would come and pick him up. No one else was allowed to approach him. Not even his relatives would have been allowed to touch him.

There was more prodding and more pointing of rifles. We turned in line and began moving. I looked straight into the neck of the man in front of me. The creases, the hairless spot. I had crossed this hell every day for so long I could even recognise the back of a man's head. The checkpoint had indeed been closed. As we moved in one direction, nurses, doctors, soldiers and other people rushed back towards Sharon A. Palestinian nurses turned up. Everyone before the waiting area had to return to the Palestinian side. Those of us still inside the waiting area were shuffled towards the exit. There was no time for questions. We were either allowed to pass or sent back with, as always, no reason given.

I looked down at my hands. Blood had dried at the edges of my fingernails. The cracks in the callouses of my hands were tainted in red. I kept looking down. As each person was checked and another allowed to pass a turnstile and then a long *sleeve*, the sounds closed in on me. I put my hands hard up against my ears and muffled the noise as much as possible. I looked at my feet, then I looked at the feet next to me, and in front of me. When they moved forward, I moved forward. I didn't look up. I inched the tip of my toes all the way, like a child trying to make a point.

It felt as if there was no body on the ground. As if this young life that had just closed was merely a dog that had been put down. That was it.

This is madness.

Through the corner of my eye, I saw Palestinian paramilitary officers arriving. There was little discussion, just a few lip movements from one of the Israeli soldiers. The four officers were then allowed into the waiting area. They grabbed the young man's body by the arms and legs and carried him back. No stretcher. As they passed us, his head flopped back, his jaw opened and his tongue fell and hung like that of a dead dog. Blood trailed in thick lines that didn't want to let go.

I felt nauseated and turned my head. There I saw the little girl. She looked at me, smiled widely and exclaimed:

'I am not touching the line, see!'

I looked down at her small shoes with blood stains on them. An almost invisible yellow line crossed the path beneath our feet, a relic from before the checkpoint was expanded. A buzzer sounded. The voice of the little girl's mother waved gently down and her small feet crossed the line. I heard another buzzer. I moved forward and put my hand on the steel bars, pushing myself through the narrow turnstile. It revolved around in random loud clangs—they all did. I felt a pounding headache. I closed my mind, tried to force the pain away but there was no escape. The sound of the steel tappers dropping felt like a sledge hammer inside my head.

I was driven into the ground like a human stake.

4

I'd often see my father shaking his head, talking to himself. Sometimes in the early morning, sometimes in gatherings of friends and family, sometimes at sunset. It was a conscious talk, as if in hope that an answer would suddenly appear.

'What did we do to them? Why do they hate us so much now? We used to live together like brothers and sisters ... *Ya Allah*, what happened? What happened?'

I remember my father talking about the end of racial segregation in South Africa. It coincided with the end of the first *Intifada* and the mourning of my cousin Bilal. The year was 1993. I was a child so what they talked about only made sense later in my life. Or rather it didn't make sense. Because neither the end of Apartheid nor the signing of the first Oslo Accords made any difference to our lives.

As a boy, all I knew was to avoid *Al-Yahud*, the Jews. Every time they caught us, we stopped singing or sometimes they stopped us *because* we were singing. When they did, they pushed us around but not like the older boys at school. They could speak Arabic but deliberately addressed us in Hebrew and when we said we didn't understand, they would say they knew who our parents were, where we lived, that we were being watched and that they would come and *take us away* if they wanted to. Of course, the threats were always in Arabic. Every time they lashed me with them, my heart pounded and fear muffled their words. I tried to forget the words they wanted me to tell my parents but I had no choice of escape. I was just a child and fear and terror were a daily part of my life. However, after Bilal's death, we stopped being children in the full sense of the word. We began to fight back.

One day, some soldiers grabbed us as we were running down the street to the daily alley-way soccer match. They dragged us on the ground as we struggled and screamed, pulled our shirts tight around our necks and then stood us up against their truck with rifles pointed at us. The usual blast of filthy words poured down. I turned my face to avoid the soldier's spit in my eyes. I looked at Ali next to me. He was my childhood friend, Ali. He stood up to them.

'Say that to your own mother!' He was defiantly yelling back. I watched as my friend faced his fears. He believed he was stronger than an adult, but he was only six years old.

Both the soldiers turned to him and struck him in the stomach with their knees. Ali fell to the ground with a squeal. He began to cry. I followed suit. I felt a surge of adrenalin and my heart raced as my fist hit the soldier who had hurt Ali. But the fist of a six-year-old is a puny thing despite my then fancy that I was as strong as a superhero. My fist hit a hard vest and a pocket with something even harder inside and then one of my small fingers made a breaking sound. I screamed as I saw it in an awkward position and felt the pain creeping on. The soldiers laughed, the one in front of me grabbed me by my neck and threw me down next to Ali. I felt no hatred in that moment. Only pain in my body and fear in my mind. There is not much reasoning in a six-year-old but there is most certainly fear. And I was afraid in that moment. That fear went deep into my soul and set roots there. Roots that grew into wretched wreaths of anger.

The soldiers laughed and as I turned my head and stared into Ali's scared eyes, the boots of the soldiers pressed down on our backs. Holding us down, dirt in our mouths. Then we felt their warm piss. The stream moved up my spine, and as it reached past my neck, I closed my eyes.

The smell was foul.

5

It was a slow, automatic motion as I undid the button of my jacket and reached for my ID card. Instead of facing it towards a camera or a dark-tinted window, I saw the boots on the ground, the rifle, the khaki. I looked up and there she was. The steel bars from the turnstiles, the monotonous scraping of shuffling feet, the voices of people, the radios, every sound gave way to a silent vacuum. Our eyes met. She inspected me from top to toe without a word. I took in her face. I sensed something familiar and my heart skipped a beat. A sharp spontaneous breath from within took me away. I saw a place, another time. A memory surfaced.

I was holding my father's hand, waiting for a bus. We stood in a line of people, separated from fast-moving cars by a slab of concrete wide enough to stand two people side by side. Traffic rushed past on both sides of the platform and the only way to get to it was to chase the breaks in the stream of cars. It was hot and I hid from the burning sun by pushing myself between the towering bodies around me. I was thirsty. I looked across the road and there was another bus stop—a stop for Israelis. A shaded overpass led to the platform with a staircase and an elevator at both ends. There was a water fountain next to the ticket machine. A woman let a clear stream of water fill her mouth, demonstratively, while looking at us. She used the back of her hand to wipe the water from around her mouth then casually walked to wait for her bus under the shade. As she looked, I stared. She took out a newspaper and in it, buried herself.

A row of children filled two adjacent benches. They were being watched by two adults. There were both boys and girls. They looked my own age. They were happy, jumping up and down on the chairs, tickling each other, talking and eating. I looked across the babble of rowdiness and stopped at a particular girl. She was preoccupied, had a small notebook in one hand and a pencil in the other. She kept putting the pencil in her mouth and twisting it around. I smiled. I was sure she was also biting it. I knew that feeling. It was good. She put it back to the paper and drew something, then repeated the motion.

Cars drove past, cutting my view into small frames, but suddenly there was a break in the traffic. The drone of car tyres chewing on asphalt was replaced for a moment, with the sounds from the opposite bus stop. I heard the children at the same time our wave of voices would have crossed the road. The girl took the pencil out of her mouth, looked up and straight at me. I smiled. She smiled. I carefully lifted my forearm and waved to her.

The other children weren't looking. Her legs swung back and forth over the edge of the bench as she removed the pencil from her mouth and waved back with small hand movements close to her body. I took in her face as best as I could from the distance. Her eyes shone with colour against her black hair. I couldn't make it out, she was too far away but they were blue or perhaps green or perhaps both.

The traffic returned. The voices faded. A bus came to a halt and blocked the view. The windows were darkened but I imagined she was looking at me again. I kept waving at the bus as it took off and left the stop vacated. The last thing I remember was my father smiling and asking me, 'Who are you waving at, my son?'

As I gave her the ID card with my right hand, I had unconsciously raised my left hand in a shy wave. She looked at me inquisitively. I quickly put my arm down and an involuntary blush pulsed through my body.

She glanced at my card quickly, then looked at me again, then back at the card. She had green eyes. She held the card between her index and long finger and handed it back to me. I took it in the same way, with two shaking fingers and saw her fingers doing the exact same thing. Her nails were painted deep red. I couldn't help but notice; there had been so much red already. We looked at each other again curiously. We held the card between us for a rather long time. She let it go first.

I left the checkpoint.

⬥⬥⬥

I was tired. I was cold. I felt used. And I was late.

I could have been taken to *the sealed room*: a room clad like a bank vault that scanned its occupants' bodies. The selection criteria for this honour was unknown. The room was only supposed to hold twelve people but often there'd be thirty or forty in there. I was never chosen but my friend Ali was. Several times. He was never told why. Often, they made him get undressed and pass through the scanner more than once. He told me he had nightmares about being left there, unable to see out, not knowing when he would be let out, fearing he was being radiated. The psychological terror—that I am sure was calculated—had its effect. I always breathed a sigh of relief as soon as I had passed it, although I had never set foot inside. We heard the Israeli soldiers as they selected people. Their name for it was *the death room*.

I had just seen a young man end his life at the hands of a crazed soldier. And there I was, waiting in the dark for the bus to come through the checkpoint as I did every morning. My hands trembled. I reeled under the sensations of the feel of the man's drying blood, his face, the faces of the little girl and her mother, the pregnant woman, the female soldier. I thought of the woman. Did she make it? Did she give birth safely? I prayed for her, then. Prayers for her protection. Then I prayed to Allah to have mercy on the soul of the young man. I knew I shouldn't, as God doesn't approve of suicide, but perhaps God knew better. Perhaps the young man believed he could actually take on the soldier, had forgotten there was a steel fence in the way. Perhaps. I was struggling to stay sane. God didn't make guns nor did he create borders or closed minds. Besides, who was God anyway if he did?

I got back on the bus. We had to get off to walk through the checkpoint. Everyone has to walk through the checkpoint unless they're over fifty-five or simply can't walk. I went down the aisle and found my seat—there were still empty ones. People were still passing the checkpoint. The engine of the bus was running, the heater on full. The warm air made my skin throb; I unzipped my jacket to let the warmth embrace me. I flopped into my seat and looked down, opening my blood-smeared hands. A large soft clot of blood was still curved around the nail of my right thumb. I looked down the aisle and saw the tired faces of people sitting down, dropping as if falling into invisible pockets. I felt part of a canvas of quiet exhaustion.

My thoughts turned to the female soldier, wondering what her name was. I hadn't looked at her name tag. She had been too far away most of the time and when I faced her, our eyes were locked on each other. Sharon A's nametag kept reappearing though, his pacing in front of me, moving back and forth like a tiger behind bars. I remembered the bus stop from my childhood once more. I wasn't far away from it. Nothing was far from anything where I lived. Travelling was a matter of *how hard* anything was to reach from anywhere else. I literally lived less than ten kilometres from my work, but in order to get there, it could take me at least two hours and in the worst case, longer than the entire working day. Like thousands of other Palestinians working in East Jerusalem, I made my way to the checkpoint in the middle of the night to avoid the chaotic early morning scenes. And I was still late. I slowly moved my finger and put it into my mouth. As my spit wet the blood, its taste spread as if piercing my tongue. The taste of blood was less satisfying than the thought of it.

My eyes grew heavier with the rumble of the idling engine and the blowing of the warm air ejected from vents under the windows. I put one hand in the other and rested them on my thighs. My whole body ached as it untied itself. The commanding people outside the bus sounded like a muffled whirlwind and I had found the calm centre of the storm.

I closed my eyes and fell asleep, forever over a hillside, soaring as always over endless plains.

6

I couldn't be sure but the walk and the form told me it was a woman who was coming towards me. She was veiled. Not religiously but more of a wedding-type of see-through veil. Her whole body was draped in the same fabric. It had iridescent lines that sparkled in various colours as if it was somehow 'alive'.

A mist of orange mantled the scene. Like an afternoon sandstorm but without the grainy needles in the air. Large majestic olive trees, much bigger than I had ever seen, covered a shallow valley. They were laden with ripe olives. Black orange-hue shiny olives. There was a slight breeze, gentle, warm, not hot. In the far background, a few goats roamed as the valley slithered into the distance.

I had no idea where I was or how I came to be here. I didn't know this woman. I turned and saw exactly the same thing. The woman kept approaching from behind as well or was this another one? I felt my pulse rise, sweat break through my forehead. I turned around again. And again, the shallow hillsides appeared mirrored alongside the moving soundless figure.

I turned around a few times. With every turn the woman came closer. Eventually I decided to stop turning and walk towards her. However, every time I felt I had gained some ground, she appeared still in the same place or even more distant. I quickened my pace and most definitely, she seemed to be further away. I stopped. She came closer once again.

I had to be going absolutely mad. What was the point of all this?

I sensed a great anger brewing. I hated her. I hated her because I didn't know her. I hated her because everything about her was strange. I hated her because she made me feel scared. I hated her because that made me hate myself more than I hated her. I hated myself because I was scared. And then I hated her. I hated myself and I hated her and I hated whatever I had got myself into; this mirrored inescapable world that I remembered having seen before.

I sat down and dropped my head between my knees. My panting blew the grains of sand at my feet. I watched as a perfect circle formed. The circle became shaded. There had been no sound. I almost fell backwards when I looked up to see an almost ghost-like figure. I pushed against the ground, thrashing sand into the air as I tried to distance myself.

After a few kicks I stopped. The air stopped. Everything stopped except the figure in front of me, shaped with the curves of a woman but without a face, the colours changing illusively on her dress. It was immaterial, almost ethereal. I thought the garment covered her entire body but in fact I couldn't tell whether indeed she had a body or whether the dress was merely a drape to convey a human shape. There were no footsteps and it seemed as if I had lost my hearing.

'Adnan…'

A distinct female voice sounded inside my head. My reaction was fear. I tried to back away in hasty kicks but couldn't. This figure, this she, remained right in front of me. I swung around quickly, and again the story repeated itself. I quickly realised that I couldn't go anywhere. I looked up at her again. She wasn't surprised by my reaction. She gestured for me to stand up.

I got up and I spoke, but the words sent out of my mouth made no sound, as if I were in a vacuum. I touched my head, as if I'd found a wire sticking out, as if I was surprised to hear her talking to me.

'Why have you come, Adnan? What's different this time?'

I understood her but I didn't understand myself. I didn't understand the question I had inside myself.

Who am I?

'You already know this. This is not your question. You just don't know how to believe it. You are yourself—and you are also fighting yourself. And you've been fighting for a long time. You could keep fighting and never win. Is that what you want?'

I thought, 'Of course, that's not what I want. Who would want that?'

I looked up at this glowing wraith. There was something essentially warm yet something inherently dangerous about her.

'You are part of me, aren't you?' I asked in my mind.

'I am in particular part of you.'

Her voice paradoxically, was both hopeful and hopeless.

'So … You want to know how to see yourself in the mirror? That's why you are here, isn't it?'

I understood. I felt what she meant, and it made perfect sense. As if someone had injected me with a potion of self-knowledge. I replied, stammering.

'I don't know. It's strange. I am…I feel…I…'

The words came slowly, as if draining through a whirlpool.

'I had had this moment. It was an accident. I saw my own reflection and when that happened, I felt sick. I realised it wasn't me.'

I looked up and wished there was a face. Reading my mind, her voice returned.

'It is only you who knows what you wish to look at. See the creation in your own eyes, see me as you wish to see me…' She paused briefly, because of course she knew where my eyes had fallen.

'And Adnan … There are no flaws when a heart loves another heart. Don't let your own heart kill you.'

Like a penetrating wind, the words passed through me. I felt a great surge of faith as I was swept and caressed by the invisible forces of the messenger.

Who, by their own nature do not judge.

⬥⬥⬥

Awakening but still dreaming, I wavered back to the bus. Toxic diesel fumes curled around like a grey ghost dragging a dirty blanket over the seats. A noxious alarm of haze and the cough that came with it. I opened my eyes to the mouth and rumbling voice of a huge man. He was walking down the narrow doorsteps in the back of the bus.

'Wake up, sweet prince. It's time to go to work or be told you have none!'

His leather jacket squeaked every time he moved. He laughed at himself and his voice thundered. Halfway through the door, he got stuck. Seriously stuck. He turned and twisted his great belly, trying to turn around but getting even more stuck. His leather jacket kept squeaking and men gathered from outside the bus, issuing commands to those behind on how to free him.

I closed my eyes again and slid as far down the seat as I could to avoid the diesel fumes. The scene unfolding was claustrophobic. The sound of the man's jacket crept through my mind like a snake with rough skin. A part of me wanted to get up, wanted to kick him hard. So hard, he would pop out.

The commotion increased. Through the windows, I saw a pair of Israeli soldiers waiting for the bus to empty. They were standing in the background watching and laughing loudly. One of them had a big mouth. I saw it as he looked up and laughed so hard his eyes went teary. His teeth were large and clean. His side locks were long and curly. Adornment to his ugly face. As ugly as a donkey braying, except this donkey was heavily armed and whipping us.

Two men were pushing the fat man from inside the vehicle. I couldn't see how many were outside trying to pull him out but it began to look like a crowd. I closed my eyes. I opened them again. The soldiers were still laughing, more people were approaching. More soldiers were approaching. I moved up from my slouched position, cleared the sleep from my eyes, crossed my arms on the seatback in front of me, and placed my cheek on it. I was snoozing, awake but half asleep. Not in a rush because there was no rush. That particular week it felt as if I had done nothing but work and sleep, and I couldn't tell whether I'd actually slept more on the bus than in my own bed. I opened and closed my eyes and for each movement I was hoping that the next time my eyelids would move upwards, I would see something else.

A few more soldiers came running as the fat man was freed. Their disappointed grins were followed by one of them yelling 'Go back in!' The pointing of his rifle made everyone freeze, but as they saw the soldiers' grins, they clenched their fists. A higher-ranking soldier stepped in. He must have wanted to finish his coffee in peace. The men were ushered along. Swear words were slung both ways.

I got up and alighted with dancingly light feet. It was always too late. There was never on time.

Not once.

7

I had been working there for a year as a carpenter, renovating the timber works of an almost thousand-year-old building. It had once been a monastery for nuns on their pilgrimage. As times changed and pilgrimage gave way to tourism, it was turned into a hotel covertly named 'The Palace'. Tiny rooms with colourful lead-encased windows welcomed its guests. Narrow crooked staircases, that often forced luggage to be left in the basement locker, took them through this three-storey maze. Picture upon picture, painting upon painting decorated every wall. There were portraits of revered popes and vintage photographs of world leaders smiling as they embraced The Palace owner. The genial and benevolent nature of this man was legendary. What the place lacked in space, it boasted in the rich history that endowed its very heart. People from all walks of life had stayed there. From poor pilgrims who were given free sanctuary to statesmen and wealthy priests who blessed the place and bestowed the means to keep it going.

My employer was indeed a gentle old man—a Palestinian whose strength in his Christian faith paralleled his non-conformity with the occupying forces. He had standing with the powers that be, even though the hardest of them, the hardest of Zionists, knew he saw right through them. For the criminals they were. Thieves in beards and black hats.

His spirit was free; he feared nothing but God. Not once did he treat me unjustly. Not once did I hear him question our late arriving or complain that we'd collapse in a corner in the middle of the day, fatigued by the hours lost crossing the checkpoint. I'd often wake up, stumbling in my dreams, still with a hammer or a pencil in my hand.

I'd find a plate of food and a glass of milk waiting for me. It felt like sleeping in. I'd feel a surge of gratitude for his kindness. He spread kindness equally to Ali and the other men and women working for him. Never did anyone take advantage of this kindness. Instead it was met with redoubled application. It worked well for all.

The Old City in Jerusalem is a winding maze of streets, hidden alleyways and tiny squares, extending into a web wherever you look. A tourist map held high, turned like a steering wheel in hope and at whim, was an icon. Visitors would get lost and often pause, spending long periods looking and being looked at before finally turning to someone for help. Man, woman or child. They would nervously enquire. They would turn and look to the soldiers with the black sunglasses. To no avail usually. These men often knew little more than how to enter and exit their positions. Dismissively they'd wave the tourists back to one of the languid characters dotting the crowded backdrop. The tourists would experience the standoff they had got themselves into.

I had long memorised the way to The Palace from the bus stop. I had also memorised detours, buildings with through-exits and alleyways. If I saw a group of soldiers, I'd deviate to an optional route and, if on one of those I'd see another group, I'd deviate yet again. Within a couple of months, the entire maze surrounding The Palace was in my head. I even knew where walls had cavities I could hide in if needed. I knew the popular food shops and when they were busy. No Israeli soldier would enter them, even with a rifle. They knew that a group of angry women were a greater peril than young men throwing stones. I avoided soldiers at all cost, not because I was afraid of them but because I could never win. If I argued with them, they would threaten me. If I were compliant, they would strip search me in public and humiliate me. If they were looking for trouble, whatever I did or said, whatever my posture, my reward would be physical—a kick from a knee or a blow from a baton. Then the procedure would be routine. I'd be dragged away, flung into the back of an armoured vehicle and left to fry in the sun; or taken for a ride that might end in being dumped on a ring road somewhere, having to get back on foot while being pelted with rubbish from passing cars.

As I turned the corner to The Palace I stopped abruptly. I stepped back to stay out of sight. In the distance outside the entrance, a large half circle of policemen formed a barrier. In full combat gear with helmets, batons and visors. People had gathered on both sides, their arms crossed, waiting. I looked up. The muzzle of a rifle poked out from the ledge of a rooftop. Snipers were in position.

I was safest to blend in.

'They're afraid we'll cut his throat!' a man said loudly to his friend across the barrier of men in black. A shiny black BMW with black-tinted windows was parked behind them. I made my way through the crowd. Someone *important* was visiting The Palace.

The armoured policemen were nervous. The police always were, even if the crowd was calm. Eyes were shifting in every direction. Backs were being covered. In black from the balaclavas beneath their helmets to the colour of their boots. Faceless men in the uniform of oppression. We saw the police as public protectors of the powerful. They were on hand for moneyed connections, pushing the boundaries of legality. To us they were but pawns who had different rules to move by from those of the men in khaki. They answered to Israeli settlers who pressured Palestinians to sell their homes with threats of legal action, claiming the property was Jewish during the First or Second Temple period, or invoking tales that dead people had told. Owners inevitably capitulated to the Israeli judicial system. The verdict was almost guaranteed to bring the loss of their home. Other settlers had simply occupied houses while the police protected them until they won their case of *ancient ownership* in a farcical Israeli court.

In East Jerusalem, there had been numerous *Intifadas* and we were in a period of rising tension and increasing provocation. Ever since I could remember, there was always tension. I cannot remember ever walking down these streets and feeling relaxed. There was constantly a nagging feeling. There were too many near misses. Too many confrontations, insults yelled at me as I walked by, and bored soldiers at checkpoints looking for trouble. Often, I'd be fatigued by the time I reached The Palace.

My workplace became somewhat of a sanctuary, except that I couldn't sleep the night there. I had to return to Mukhamas every day. This is how my life was. This is how most people's lives still are. I knew there had been another life, though. My parents' generation talked about going to the beach with their Jewish friends when they were young. I often imagined what my own life would be like if we were all friends. I imagined hanging out with this funny guy Eli, who worked at the building supplies store. When the shop wasn't busy, he would joke with me about his love life; the young Israeli women he met, 'with guns and narrow minds' as he put it. Beautiful as some of them were, he quickly moved on if their parents were orthodox, if they didn't want to have sex, if they wanted to get married. We would laugh about marriage. Even if I wanted to get married, I couldn't. I'd have to save up for the dowry. Eli's life was easy though. One day, he told me something I hadn't thought of before, searching my face as if he wanted to help me, but couldn't.

'It's hard enough to be Jewish in Israel but I'm grateful I'm not Palestinian…'

He knew what it was like for a Palestinian man with a West Bank ID. He was about my age. He had a short, left leg so limped a bit, but he was handsome. The military had rejected him, of course, so he hadn't been brainwashed.

The atmosphere in front of The Palace was tense, so I didn't want to tell the police I was late for work. Whatever was happening inside would mean work had stopped anyway and Raphael, or just Rafi as we called the owner, would know. He would understand. He always did.

A big man in a black suit with black sunglasses walked out of The Palace. He looked discontented. With giant strides, he walked directly to the black car. The driver stepped out, walked around to the passenger side and opened the back door. As the big man got in, the car sank with his weight. The driver got behind the wheel, the policemen changed formation and cleared a path as the car exited from the crowd and sped off, down the narrow, cobbled road. The policemen walked slowly back and suddenly disappeared as if swallowed by the ancient walls. As the crowd quickly thinned out, Ali appeared.

'Good morning, Nana. Where were you? I thought you were still in the nectar of your dream…'

'Good morning Ali. And what morning? And what dream? The one I'm living or the one I'm dreaming? Whichever one. *Yalla*, let's go to work before it's time to go home!'

With our arms on each other's shoulders, we swung the big wooden doors open.

And entered The Palace, laughing.

8

Ali and I circled between three villages as children. We lived with relatives and the landowners our fathers worked for. We moved from Budrus in the West, Deir Qaddis nearby and Aboud further to the east. Next to Deir Qaddis lies the Israeli settlement of Nili and near Aboud lies the settlement of Ofarim. They were both built before I was born, illegally, of course.

Ali's father and my father had been born at the clinic in the village of Aboud on the same day in 1956. Ali's father was named Fayez as he triumphantly arrived first, and my father was aptly named Khamis after the day of the week. They grew up together, closer to each other than to their brothers and sisters. And when they met our mothers or the other way around if you ask them, things went the way Allah had intended. My mother, Ghalia, and Ali's mother, Marah, met our fathers, picking olives. They all met on the same day and both couples were married on the same day.

They were skilled field workers, our parents. Both mothers and fathers did everything from turning the soil to sowing the seeds and harvesting. They called the villages *the circle of our life*. Our parents said *ours*. I said *ours* and my life remained intrinsically chained to Ali's.

I remember climbing some of the largest trees with Ali. One day we came across an enormous olive tree. It was three to four times taller than the average adult olive tree. Legends had been written about such trees. From a distance it looked like an out-of-shape walnut tree. The branches were thin on one side and thick on the other. There was a heart in the middle where no light shone through. It was dotted with a cover of ripening fruit. From there two giant arms reached for the sky like a triumphant athlete at the Olympics. It stood on its own in the middle of a field, surrounded by shrubs of lavender. The stems folded as the wind swept around the thick trunk but the tree itself stood fast. Only the thinnest branches waved, and the leaves appeared as if the whole tree was covered in fur. We told ourselves it must be a thousand years old.

The tree didn't yield its secret easily. We had to climb to reach the lower branches, that's how big it was. Ali stood on my shoulders and jumped up to the first one. And that was in a mess of smaller branches, poking and scraping him as he lifted me by my arms. As soon as I could, I pulled myself up to sit next to him. We almost gave up climbing any further, the foliage was so dense.

When I looked up behind me to break off a twig that jabbed my neck, I noticed an opening near the centre of the tree. It looked as if light was bouncing around behind the opening—a gentle flickering of light green. I stood up and moved sideways towards it, balancing between the branch under my feet and the one I had my hands on above my head.

'Ali, look here!'

He stopped swinging his dangling feet and jumped up beside me, squinting, peeking through the branches.

'You go first. See if there is room for both of us.'

Above the branch I was standing on, the tree looked like a bush. Almost impenetrable except for a small opening that seemed to conceal a cavity. I pushed my skinny arm through and felt around for a branch or a twig to hold onto. Ali turned his back to me for me to push my feet off. I put my other hand through the hole as well as my face. White stripes were scraped on my skin against the pointy dead twigs. I put my hands down on the bed of branches and pulled myself up the rest of the way. The soft branches closed up the hole behind me and I rose to my feet with the open mouth and wide smile of amazement.

'Ali, come! Come!'

I held his hand as he drew himself up through the narrow opening. He opened his scratched eyelids and his mouth as I had.

A space had formed in the centre of the tree. Almost like a giant ball-shaped cage. Tiny birds emerged and frantically circled before finding an exit. Once they had gone, there was only the sound of the wind, muted to let me hear my own breathing. Through the middle of the hollow, the trunk formed a central column. We could walk around it, stepping securely on the thick branches that formed its skeleton.

A secret cave! We were ecstatic, loudly celebrating how we would keep this tree house to ourselves. To the heart of our child souls, we had struck great riches. This cave in the sky became our other home.

When the wind blew, we would lie on our backs and listen. There were plenty of dried leaves and twigs to form a number of cosy arrangements. The flow of the air through the tree bore different notes according to its direction. Depending on where we placed our small bodies we could rule out one sound and bring in another. The light was perfect. On hot days, we'd have shade. We'd bring water and food and spend the whole day in and around the tree. It seemed invisible to the world.

Perhaps that's why it had grown to be so old and beautiful...

We got a rope and Ali's father gave us a pulley to hoist things up. We had to tell the adults about the giant tree. They all knew about it, of course, but we told ourselves none of them knew about the cavity. Perhaps they did, but they were just too big to enter it. And perhaps they didn't. A few other children would come and play around the tree. Even try to reach the first branch. We'd be hiding, silently breathing, waiting for them to leave. Not once did we reveal ourselves or the secret of the tree. One day, when Ali's dad came looking for us, we sat in our sacred space, watched through the cracks as he walked around it, looking up and about. He yelled out our names until, somewhat worried, turned around and walked away. We quickly climbed down and ran to him. He smiled with relief and asked where we had been hiding. We said we were just on the top, and pretended we had called back. He looked at us with a doubtful eye and kissed us both on our heads.

I'm glad that my memories of Ali are still so clear. I remember his face, the protruding nose and long chin, his piercing eyes that were almost blue on top of black. My mother used to say that Ali was gifted with his kind heart because Allah had been victorious. Satan had struck him the cruelty of his scarred face but failed to win him over. Ali was handsome but at the same time he wasn't. His physique, even as a child was impressive. He was the fastest runner, the best climber, the strongest wrestler. His face was that of the warlord from the Beqaa Valley who was drawn in one of my father's history books. His features were crude and even when he smiled, his large teeth looked as if a Neanderthal had meddled with his family tree. He was built like a rock, compact, and his grin, honestly, was quite scary. But underneath his rugged exterior was a gentle, creative soul. Ali never ceased to inspire me. In those childhood years up in that giant olive tree, Ali taught me everything about shapes, angles and knives. We were eight years old when we found our green-leafed haven and already then, Ali was the Michelangelo of Palestine.

Ali's father was very loving with him. He'd take him to his chest and gently clasp his large hands around his head when children had been teasing him. They called him 'the human donkey'—and remember, 'donkey' in Arabic is someone who is very stupid. And usually ugly.

Ali's mother didn't give him much attention. She adored his brother, Ismail, and left him in no doubt of that. Ali was the unwanted one. But Fayez treated them equally. He never allowed Ismail to think he was any better, but in the often heartbreaking reality of life, Ali grew up knowing his own mother looked down on him and that his brother was a stranger to him.

'Press your finger against the tip of the blade and move it. Don't push, just move it gently…'

Ali watched as I did as I was told. A thin slice of wood curled as the sharp blade of the knife carved a crescent in the trunk of the giant olive tree.

'I want to write *Ali* and I want to carve a heart…'

'You can write *Ali* and I will show you how to carve half of the heart.'

Those first summers up in the tree were a magical part of my life. The world was peaceful. There were no soldiers. No burning tyres or piercing bullets. No adults talking of wars. No broken dreams. Life had meaning and its purpose for me was to decorate our wooden retreat with my best friend, Ali. Most of the things we drew had hearts and angels around them. By the time we had carved the last piece, we were teenagers. That was on the day of Ali's sixteenth birthday, just two weeks before mine.

To the untrained eye, I am sure the entire cave would have been an awe-inspiring gallery of carving art. On the trunk, we had left space for our better pieces. Ali quietly carved two hearts on it. Each of the hearts was held by an angel. The angels faced each other. Under them, his knife edged the leathery olive bark in connected Arabic letters that spelled his intricate poetry.

Ali scraped and cleaned the carving, then blew hard at it with pursed lips and closed eyes as he brushed it with the palm of his hand. It looked as if it were drawn on paper. The lines were perfect. I read the words out loud.

'*Angels bring us our hearts. And when a heart meets a heart, the eye sees no flaw…*'

Ali stared at his work, the angels with hearts half their own size in the palms of their hands. He was silently crying. I looked around me. The wind was blowing gently through the cave. Leaves reflected shades of green onto the carvings. There were houses and planes, stick people and stick guns. There were faces with detail and there were hearts. Lots of hearts. There were words from the Koran and there were angels. More than anything, the cavity was full of angels.

On my birthday we returned to our cave. It would be our last time there together. In the years after, we were away from it as our fathers were forced to seek work elsewhere. It was a hot August day but our green-lit grotto felt cool. We laughed at the strangeness of that. We suggested names for the haven. It was magnificent. It was wonderful. To us it was a palace. Ali gazed at his carvings. The tree had stretched most of the earliest pieces. Arabic letters were forming in organic shapes. The palace was alive—a living thing as we searched to give it a name. The palace of wishes. The palace of prayers. The palace of peace.

The Palace of Angels.

9

Rafi had decided that the ancient attic of The Palace could serve as a grand suite. He set Ali and me in charge of the whole makeover. He had seen how we had renovated the timber works. He'd witnessed Ali carving the cornice of the great dining room with intricate detail. We weren't the fastest, but we worked with a passion that resonated with Rafi. Often, we'd wonder if he was paying us to do practical work or to decorate his beloved Palace with art. Regardless, it was an arrangement that suited all of us.

'I want this attic to welcome the angels…'

We had barely set foot in the attic when he said the words. He looked around beaming as if welcoming them, and then he didn't say more. He just looked at our faces and our dropped jaws. I was amazed at the space. The top of the building had a large dome in the centre and stout wooden columns that rose to the ceiling where they were held and encased in elaborately decorate cast-iron mountings. Plaster had crumbled onto the slate floor, exposing old walls of mortar, boulders and bricks. Beams of light shone through large skylights and a panoramic window assembly overlooked parts of the Old City.

Rafi clapped and my heart skipped a beat. He smiled, bowed and in a joking gesture, he rolled his arm grandly as he backed out through the door.

Rafi always smiled. Even when confronted with angry soldiers at the front door or if the municipality had threatened him with court action or even if powerful men in black luxury cars tried to buy The Palace from him. When they'd try to pressure him, he'd show them the door, laughing. I never saw him lose his temper. He was tall and skinny but he had an enormous appetite and there was a saying that he never cooked for his guests but for himself. What meant the most to me, to us, was that he was kind.

There was a rumour though. It said Rafi at a young age had found an ancient chest full of gold in The Palace basement. His father had made him spend the whole summer down there digging to create more pantry space. He was disciplining him, as he so often did, for his poor performance at school. They say Rafi took the riches and hired an assassin to kill his father and that he buried him where the chest had been.

Once, a guest had ventured down there and had come screaming back up again. She had tried to tell the other guests what she had seen but fainted as the words came out. Rafi had taken her to the hospital and arranged for all her things to be picked up. They say she left the country in haste shortly after and was never seen again. After that incident, Rafi had the doors to the basement bolted shut.

We were at the top of The Palace. Ali took out the carving knife he'd had since we were children. It had a short blade of carbon steel. A bulbous handle. He swept his eyes around the attic before setting them down in mine. Without a word we walked towards an old wooden support column.

'Let's welcome the angels.'

'*Yalla*, let's bring them in,' I said. We couldn't help but laugh.

Once again, we had found ourselves in a palace of angels.

10

I so welcomed the spring. It came on a special day when I smelt its sweet victory over its foe, the winter. It was like an aphrodisiac. Sitting outside the cafés, women bared their ankles. They threw smiles and eye-kisses as I walked by. Trees splashed out an explosion of colour and the air filled with mating sounds. A familiar feeling of hope crept up once more.

On that first day of spring in 2014, Ali met his soulmate. She literally stumbled into his back as we were crossing the checkpoint. They began talking straight away. I saw it. There was hardly room in the queue for Ali to turn around as she apologised. When he did, time stopped for them. I'm sure of that. He smiled. She smiled back. Her name was Farrah and in the sleepy-eyed hours of the early morning, those two found in each other their connection to life. By the time we had left the checkpoint they had arranged a meeting the next day. Ali didn't get pulled in to the sealed room after that day. I don't know what happened but for a short time, he walked this earth of ours with a straight back and a face that glowed with the amorous devotion that only the love of a woman can bring.

It wasn't long after Ali met Farrah that I met Linah again.

I'd left work for lunch. Ali was meeting Farrah and I felt like a stroll so I went to a small café outside the old city. It was called *Mount Carmel*. The lunchtime rush had already been and only a few people dotted the eye-boggling white and black setting of plastic tables and chairs. Adam served meals in printed wrappings that told you all about the dishes. It was a deliberate statement. By the 1970s, Israel had begun to appropriate many parts of Palestinian life, including cuisine, and had begun removing their origins from textbooks. I had a falafel meal whose wrapping said it came from

Egypt. The word *falafel* was Palestinian, but the chickpea version was now the national dish of Israel. I had time to smile about the fact sheet and I wondered who owned the café. I had a coffee and even time to look through a newspaper left on a table. I flicked through the pages looking for something interesting, an opportunity, perhaps. And, of course, hope. Instead, I found a mass of conflict, issues and problems. There was no positive message whatsoever. I stopped reading and closed the newspaper. As the back page stared at me with a picture of the Israeli Prime Minister, Benjamin Netanyahu surrounded by children, I felt sick. I paid and left.

It was a random stop on the main road leading back to the gates of the old city. *Pop-up Checkpoints* they are called. My ID card was in my hand. I'd rehearsed the motion. I'd pass the card and only look up when I felt it taken from me. The soldier would look at me quickly. Inspect the card. Pass it back. I'd already be looking down again. I'd walk along. No words exchanged. Not unless … Well, not unless *something*.

Apparently, there was something. Perhaps it was her shampoo or perhaps it was her sweat. I recognised the scent. Or perhaps it was because it was simply *nice*. There was definitely something. I couldn't see their faces. I had the sun straight in my eyes. They saw to that deliberately, if they could. I extended my arm with the ID card in my hand. One of them took it. I didn't get it back. They were two soldiers standing side by side. The one with the big boots turned around first. He spoke to someone a few steps away, apparently about an issue with another person's ID card. That's all I could make out from the Hebrew. The other pair of boots kept facing me.

The parts of her hair that weren't tied up or tucked under her helmet threw a shade of swirling tendrils. Stretched in the afternoon shadow they touched the shade of my own head. It was a beautiful sight as the mild spring breeze gently caressed my face. As I stood there looking down, I captured patterns for my carvings at The Palace. As I stood there, facing the ground, thoughts raced through my mind.

This is not how it should be.

I looked up. The sunlight was a glary backdrop turning her face dark. I closed my eyes. Blood rushed through thin veins and merged with her outline. My eyelids formed a backlit red canvas. On it was painted the face of a woman. The blood shone in yellow like gold and formed her face with soft curved eyes, full lips and sparkling flowy hair.

I heard the sound of her boots move past my left ear. I felt her hands on my shoulders. I jolted a tiny bit. She stopped for a second before turning me sideways. The sun was no longer to her advantage. The backlit red painting disappeared. I opened up my eyes.

And there she was.

We studied each other in silence. The steady breeze of spring softly wrapped around us without disruption, without resistance. With just enough white noise to erase commanding voices. It gave us time to face each other for some moments without words.

'Adnan Al-Rahal…' she said as she looked at my ID card. She turned her head around slightly. The other soldier was still engaged with the other man they'd stopped.

I glanced at her name tag. It read ABERMAN L. I could have guessed a million other names but the name 'Lina' popped into mind, followed by the Japanese cartoon we all watched as children.

'Lina. Is your name Lina?' I asked in Arabic. She opened her eyes wide.

'Linah. With an 'h' at the end,' she replied in Arabic—musical Arabic.

'Of course.'

'How did you know?'

'You said, Adnan, so I thought Lina—Lina-h,' and I stressed the 'h' at the end of the word.

'I don't understand?'

'It's a cartoon. The main characters were a boy named Adnan and a girl named Lina and… Well… It's not important. You don't know it. Just the reason I guessed your name Lina-h.'

Her lips stretched and she smiled. She moved closer. We were already standing at arm's reach from one another. 'What is your job?'

Soldiers were trained in interrogation techniques. They would ask the same question over and over again to see if you would slip up and answer differently. It was a standard question but the way she asked it wasn't. She bit the edge of her lips slightly. I felt my heartbeat rise.

'I'm a carpenter,' I replied calmly. She waited for a few seconds.

'And what are you doing?'

'Do you mean as in what am I doing in my job right now?'

'Yes'

'I am doing what I love doing.'

'And what is that?'

'I carve symbols into wood.'

'What kind of symbols?'

'Symbols that form stories.'

'Who can read them?'

'Anyone can read them.'

'It doesn't matter which language I speak?'

'It doesn't matter which language you speak.'

'You don't say?'

'It's true.'

'What do you do?' I asked her. She smiled widely.

'What do you mean?'

'You just asked me the same question. I told you I carve stories.'

'I mean, what-do-you-do, as in what do you do?'

'I'm here?'

'Besides that?'

'I don't understand.'

'Okay. What do you do right here, then?'

'I protect my people,' she said hesitantly.

It was the end of the conversation. Silence. I didn't know what she was thinking, but I saw confusion in her eyes. Part of me was very angry. Part of me felt sorry for her. I saw it every day in the eyes of the soldiers. Brainwashed with the gravity of their duty, but nonetheless human beings who would question their daily routine. Their checking of ID cards, their harassment of people and the whole system of segregation that employed them.

I forgave this soldier, at the same time I wondered if she had misunderstood me.

ABERMAN L became Linah to me. She took my card between her fingers and gave it back to me. Her fingernails were tinted in a pearly shade of white. Déjà vu. I held the card from the other end in the same way. We kept it like that.

'What happened to the red colour?' I asked her.

She drew her lips to the sides as a brief half-smile spread across her face.

'I'll tell you another time,' she said.

She let go of the card. I put it back in my pocket, taking in the last of her eyes. There was a small freckle inside a yellow line, encircling a sea of green. Another black line encapsulated that line. I stepped sideways and left her and the other guards behind.

Red nail polish, I thought, and smiled.

11

It was half past three in the morning when my phone rang. I was lying in bed weighing up whether to go to work or not. The second hand on the plastic wall clock was rattling. It was one of those types that didn't tick but I could hear it though it was across the room. As it passed the minute, the rattling increased—the cheap cogs in a tug of war with gravity. As soon as it reached the bottom it went quiet until it reached a quarter to. It began to rattle as my phone began to vibrate.

'Good morning, Ali...'

'Good morning...' Ali paused with a murmur ... The words to follow were on his tongue.

'So... Are you going?' he asked.

'Going where?'

Ali didn't sound tired at all. 'Work, my friend. Work...'

'I thought you meant...'

'No...' Ali dragged it out as if I had suggested something hideous.

'Will they let us cross?'

'Of course, not.'

'What about Farrah?'

'I'm with her family today.'

'What's the occasion?'

'Her brother, Abdullah.'

'Is he being released?'

'No, Nana... He... May you live—'[37]

'There is no God but Allah!' I swung my feet to the side and sat up on the edge of the bed. It made me dizzy while at the same time

---

37 Often said when sharing the news of someone's death (informal condolence).

questions flew around my mind.

'What happened? May Allah have mercy on his soul and give him a place in heaven…'

I grabbed my head, my words sinking between my knees to stop the room spinning.

'They haven't been told anything, as usual.'

'When will he be buried?'

'Not until tomorrow, earliest. They will not release the body until then.'

'Why?'

'There will be a demonstration there today—just like every year.'

'Stones against bullets…' I said, dragging my hand down my face, trying to rise from the fog of sleep. Then a thought came to me and I spoke it straight away.

'Ali, why are you awake?'

There was a short pause. I could hear Ali's breathing. There were no other voices.

'I can't sleep…' he said, uneasily.

I didn't question what Ali said though I put the phone closer to my ear, listening. There was only his breathing. It was calm and heavy at the same time. I wondered for an instant if the young man at the checkpoint had been breathing in the same way before he threw himself at the bullet.

'What am I thinking?' my thought slipped out.

'What?' said Ali.

'Nothing. Ali, I'm going to go back to bed.'

'What are you going to do?'

'I will spend the day with my parents. I will call Farrah later. *The rest to her life*[38].'

'May Allah bless you, Nana…' Ali's voice was flat and monotonous.

'There is only one God but Allah,' I said quietly, sadly.

'Mohammed, the messenger of Allah,' Ali replied.

---

38 One way of giving one's condolences.

I hung up. The death of Abdullah marked the end of the glorious spring. The deep blue of the sky faded as the days warmed. Sometimes a pair of pristine white clouds would drift in. Occasional patches of shade remained. Green turned yellow and the world appeared less dense.

It was the 15th of May. The day of *the Nakba*, the day of the catastrophe. The Israelis were celebrating the creation of their state. Their Independence Day. The Palestinians also commemorate that day. Hundreds of thousands of Palestinians were driven from their homes by Israeli troops, or fled. It was ethnic cleansing. Thousands were killed in massacres during 1948. This was how Israel was born. The arrogance of colonialism had stretched itself out again, this time in the name of Zionism. The first Nakba was in 1920 when the British, French and Italians divided the former Ottoman Empire into separate states along lines of their own fancy.

Accompanied by pink gin and military music.

12

I slept in: it was almost ten before I opened my eyes. I felt I had finally caught up with my shadow. I lay in bed as I heard my mother downstairs. We were in Mukhamas near East Jerusalem. We had moved there when I was nineteen. My father had found some work at a small bookbinding firm. Work in the fields was being replaced by machines and the wages were so low, they forced the workers to seasonally rotate or go looking for some other work elsewhere. The only time we'd return to the villages was during the olive harvest.

It was an old, small two-storey townhouse. A narrow staircase led up to a tiny first floor. Three rooms, a living room with a classical Arabic floor furniture setting and two bedrooms with king-sized cotton mattress beds. I walked out of my bedroom and found my father stretched out with a glass of golden tea in one hand and a book in the other. My father so loved reading. Even while working the fields he'd have a book with him. As soon as he could, he'd open it and lose himself in the worlds that filled the pages. He looked up at me and smiled.

'Morning of Blessings,'[39] he said.

'Morning of Light.'[40] I went and sat next to him, clearing the sleep from my eyes. Yawning loudly several times.

'I'm sorry. I feel like I could sleep until tomorrow morning.'

My father yawned in unison.

'Aren't you not going to work either?' I asked knowing the answer.

'No, the boss decided best to bolt up for the day.' I could tell he was disappointed, maybe disheartened.

---

39 How 'Good morning' is said in Arabic. Can be said in more ways.
40 Alternative 'Good morning'. 'Light' or 'blessings' can be used as both wish to reply.

My father closed his book and turned to me with a serious face.

'Nana, Ali called me today.'

'I know. He also called me. At three in the morning. I'm worried about Ali…'

'May Allah find Abdullah a place in heaven.'

'Well, he forgot to look while he was still with us…'

'Nana. That's not right… Seek forgiveness from Allah…'

The discussion stopped. Father knew how I felt about religion. I had seen death too many times to believe we would be resurrected at *Yaum al-Qiyamah*[41]. I remember questioning my mother one morning. I will never forget her face as I asked her what about all the people who lived before anyone even knew about the religions we knew? Which angels were going to sit on their shoulders and write out their good and bad deeds? If we are all waiting for the day of resurrection, of judgement, are we living to die? Are we living for the day where all living things will be raised and called in front of God? To go to either heaven or hellfire. What are we going to do there if it's the end of times, anyway?

My mother would put her hands up and utter a loud prayer for me. I would look up to where she was facing and see nothing. I often wish I could have. It would have made my life so much easier.

A part of me felt the sting. I had been taught that my thoughts were wrong. Never why they were wrong.

'*Yalla ya ebni*.[42] You need to get dressed. I've arranged with Fayez that we will meet at the prison and join the protest march.'

'Yes, father…'

I went downstairs. My mother was already dressed and at the same time preparing for the main meal of the day. She saw me and stopped what she was doing. She smiled. My mother had a kind face. She was thin, even though she had a large appetite. When she didn't smile her cheekbones protruded. When she did, her whole

41 In Islam, *Qiyamah* is the belief in the resurrection of the people on the Day of Judgment, whether Muslim or not. In the Koran, *Al-Qiyamah* refers to the resurrection. The day of resurrection.

42 *Ya ebni*: my son.

face stretched out in a wide welcoming embrace. Her eyes glistened, her teeth shone and her voice would call for attention with its intermittent giggle. My mother was a humble soul. She had light brown eyes and dark brown skin. She adored the colour brown in light tones and loved the end of summer for its browned pastel look. She wore a light brown hijab atop her light brown hair. My mum was a woman of the earth.

'Morning of light and jasmine… I will make you some breakfast my son.'

'Are you coming with us, mama?'

'Yes.'

I smiled. My mother was a fearless woman. She would stand up against the soldiers at the checkpoints without saying a single word. She'd disarm them by simply staring at them. She'd tell me that she'd be telling them what cowards they were, just by looking at them. 'No man should ever hurt a woman. And a man who carries a rifle and points it against a woman, who points it against a girl, a child—is twice a coward! His soul is weak and his mind even more.' As a child I'd watch the soldiers crumble inside when she'd walk all the way up to them, pushing them aside with her body. I'd hold her hand so tightly it would hurt her but she wouldn't say anything until we were safe. She'd always tell me I had to keep my soul healthy. It would always be my strongest weapon.

I was the only child. My younger brother died shortly after he was born. An infection almost took my mother's life but settled for her uterus. Ali became my brother. My parents knew that. And to Ali, my mother Ghalia, was his mother. Everyone knew that. Even Marah, his paternal mother.

'Mama, I am worried about Ali…'

'Why?'

'There's something about him that reminds me of a time when we were children. When his mother threw the weight of the world on his shoulders. It's like he holds two keys. One for love and one for a dark and sinister hatred. And I'm afraid he's got this key in his hands right now…'

'May God take us farther from the hidden evil…'

I rolled my eyes. My mother saw it. She let it go.

'I am sorry, mama.'

'It's okay. Forgotten. But thank you…'

'I don't know, mama. Ali's feeling peace with Farrah but it's like that peace is amplifying his silent rage… against the occupation… All I am saying is, I heard his breathing, today… The death of Abdullah has…' I stopped.

My mother chose not to worry. 'What's the point of worrying about what has not happened?' She'd often say to me. This is how she lived her life. It was infectious and full of hope. And in our daily life, as long as I can remember, we needed hope.

'What Allah has written, he has written, my son…' That was her reply.

There was a leftover boiled egg for breakfast. A bit of bread with hummus, but I had no appetite. I drank a glass of water. It had an awful taste of rust.

My father came down to the kitchen. He still had his book in his hand.

'What is written?'

There was no reply. I got dressed. We were ready to leave. My mother grabbed her bag; my father, his book.

13

As we approached Beitunia, the Ofer prison came into sight. That was as far as we got. We stopped. Traffic jammed. Something had happened. Every Palestinian road going into Beitunia and Ramallah was blocked by the border police and the military. I looked across at the Israeli highway. Cars were speeding across between Jerusalem and the illegal settlements. There was an off-ramp from that road onto the road we were on, leading into Beitunia. The prison was right next to the highway. We were in a minivan with other travellers, trapped like a single link on a stretched chain, unable to break free. Tanks blocked the road. Ambulances screamed past us. A large flock of people were moving away from the prison in the distance and back towards the city. Tiny clouds of tear gas dotted the hillsides. A helicopter hovered in the distance.

People tried to make phone calls. The cell network was blocked. My father took out his phone and looked at it. He held it in his hands, flipped it back and forth. We were being isolated. The demonstration had turned into a clash. And when people without weapons stand up against those with weapons, injustice becomes the 'justice' served.

We were forced to remain seated. Israeli soldiers patrolled the kilometre-long line of vehicles, making sure no one got out. Another helicopter kept patrolling the whole area. An aerial surveillance camera was permanently strung across high pillars over the highway. With the blue backdrop of the sky, its turning lens reflected the sunlight like the mirror of a castaway seeking rescue.

It was a theatre with no exit. No restroom. No intermission. No telephone. We were trapped in the minivan for the whole day.

My father opened his book. Four hours later he had finished it. He looked at me and asked without a word if I wanted to read it. I looked at the title. It was a fat book. *Once upon a country*, the title read. I knew the author. He was a peace activist, a philosopher and a Palestinian. Patient and forgiving. I had no space for those emotions. I looked at my father with admiration.

A woman opened a large plastic bag. It was full of sandwiches and food for her family. She spoke out loud.

'Oh Allah, give me strength and forgive me. This was for my daughter but it is *haram*[43] to let it go to waste.'

The woman handed out the kofta sandwiches. Not a single person declined. All of us were starving. No one had expected to spend eight hours in a crammed minivan. Water was passed around and for a short time we felt free, as a curbed audience imprisoned in a van, forced to sit through the spectacle outside—performed against a prison backdrop.

When you confine the human body, the human *being* finds other ways of feeling free. We talked about our relatives, where we were from, if our families knew each other. The theatre outside had become the only part of our lives that didn't change. We didn't talk about it, not at all.

Time passed and our bodies ached from sitting still. An older man cried in agony as a spasm went down his back. I felt my right leg turning numb and tried to shift my weight from side to side. My mother desperately needed to go to the bathroom. She whispered to two women in front of us. They were in the same bind. The whole business was organised respectfully. The bottom of a plastic water bottle was cut with a key and men took off their shirts or jackets. Pieces of clothing were tied together to form a space of privacy. The women took their turns, then two children and lastly the men.

As I peed into the bottle, a gush of seething hatred surged through me. I was the last and the piss was almost up to the rim. There was an awkward silence and a pervasive smell. I looked at

43 *Haram*: Food or actions that are proscribed in Muslim law.

my dad. His eyes begged forgiveness. I told him in the same way it wasn't his fault. We didn't say a single word. Oddly, I recalled an old book he had passed on to me once. It was about a father who had made a fortune selling Jewish slaves in Europe.

The hillsides were crowned in the white smoke of tear gas. Men and women were running.

I wanted to run with them.

◈◈◈

We spent nearly nine hours before they let us return, but it wasn't until the next day that vehicles were allowed to enter Beitunia. Two young men had died outside the prison that day. They were only teenagers. It was a cold-blooded killing and not the first. And not the last. That day became the first day in a series of events that would change my life in the most unimaginable way.

In the week that followed, Ali left more and more work at The Palace for me to do. I only saw him twice. At the checkpoint he seemed almost invisible to the soldiers. In the attic he was preoccupied, revisiting his already finished efforts. He had told Rafi that he needed to attend to family business but in reality, he wasn't even near his family. When I spoke to Fayez he told me he spent his time with Farrah and her family. Every time I called him, he spoke a lot of how Abdullah's death had affected him and the family of his beloved. His voice had changed. An anger had risen from somewhere deep inside him. Its reasons were easy to guess. We all shared it but kept it subdued. When I think back, I realise how much it drained my soul. To try and suffocate the humiliation. To wrap it in think-blankets and squash it under the bed. To ignore it kicking and screaming at me. The remorseless anxiety of having to find more space for more of it. To box it and put it away. As if it were separate from me.

Come the second week I was getting used to days of solitude. As soon as I ventured into the attic I was in another world, sometimes with the radio for company. Classical *oud*[44] held my hands as I carved

---

44 The Arabic *oud* is a short-neck, pear-shaped type of lute with 11 or 13 strings.

in rhythm with the instrument. Melancholic parts to rapid sequences marked the beginning and end of a love story without a single word sung. With closed doors, the daily commotion of The Palace was but a dull rumble under my feet. I was left to carve my own imaginary tales. There was peace. There was love. There was freedom. I would step back and look at the pillars through the room. The stories wove themselves into the streaming light. I heard them whispered below the rooftops and I watched them streaming upwards to be retold in fine brush strokes on the blue canvas of the sky.

One day Rafi stepped into the attic. Under the blade of my knife, a story of friendship was coming to shape. Two men, who were almost about to kill each other, put down their arms. An angel appeared with two mirrors. The men looked at themselves and then at each other. They realised they had been so blinded by hatred they forgot that they were brothers. I stepped down from the ladder and turned to Rafi. He was gazing intently at the pillar with a carving of two intertwined women soaring towards a man's heart in the sky.

'Do you think Ali will be back?' he asked slowly without looking at me.

'No…' is what I said.

Rafi didn't ask why. He looked around the attic and turned to me with a sigh.

'Beautiful work, Adnan. It's your attic now.' Then he walked calmly away at a steady pace. On his way out through the large wooden door, he stopped and turned with a sunken face. He didn't look at me.

'May Allah be with him…' He closed the heavy door behind him and his footsteps faded away.

I took in the words. The tone of every word went through my soul, paralysing all of my body. The knife slid out of my hand. I heard my tears dropping on the wooden floor, the empty space of the attic amplifying the impact.

14

Café Mount Carmel became my lunchtime paradise. It also became a place in which I understood the choice of freedom. Once you walked through the narrow door you declared that you renounced hatred. I was met with a smile. Being met with a smile in East Jerusalem is not the norm. I didn't go to Mount Carmel for the falafel. I went there because I was able to eat without a heavy chest, without the knot in my guts of anxious thoughts twirling through my mind. Little Mount Carmel had a glass front. And a Palestinian owner. Nobody walked in unless they accepted that those sitting next to them could be either Palestinian or Jewish. But in the east, most guests were Palestinian, as most guests to the west of the walls were Jewish.

It always had me thinking that I was caught in a twisted family feud.

Adam placed the tiny plastic basket with the wrapped falafel in front of me. I didn't look at him as he set it down but he came into view. I was staring out the window, holding the corner of a newspaper between my fingers but without turning the page. My mind wandered in among the people walking outside the window. They were moving fast. I felt almost trampled upon. I shook my head and came back to reality inside the café. I looked down at the paper and my eye caught the falafel. I was about to turn to thank Adam when I saw he hadn't moved. He smiled.

'You're welcome,' he said. 'Where were you?'

'I was…' I stumbled without continuing. 'Thank you…'

Adam left me to eat. I was the only one in the café. I looked out again as I munched the falafel. My taste buds were nudged. The salt and cumin, garlic and chilli as well. The crunchy texture scraped the top of my mouth. I heard the sound as I chewed and felt satisfied as the food eased down to my stomach. I heard the voices of people walking past. Through the glass bits of conversation reached me: '*Who was she?*' '*It was a bad decision my friend.*' '*Damn them all the way.*' '*He's going to get that job…*' I heard the silence as the wave of people thinned out. Tiny birds perched in a tree saw their chance and dived to pick the ground clean. A car horn went off. The birds took flight.

I looked down at the newspaper. An investigation was being launched into the Beitunia killings. Everything had been denied the first week. A frame from a CCTV camera of a nearby Palestinian store showed a young man falling to the ground. He was on his own. Another bullet had taken another young soul. I felt again the warm blood of the young man at the checkpoint. I felt a surge of this sensation through my body. There is no life without freedom.

I took a deep breath and raised my head. I looked out through the window and straight into her green eyes. She must have looked to her side at the exact same time. She was on her own. She stopped and turned towards me. She had a white T-shirt on. Denim jeans. I looked all the way down to a pair of red slip-ons. A shoulder bag swung across her chest. Her black hair was long and straight. The breeze lifted it up as if she was doing it. All the way to the tips to then let the strands drop back down little by little.

She stood there. I sat there. I swallowed. I let go of the falafel with my right hand and placed it in the basket. I could hear Adam stirring behind me. I kept my arm resting and only lifted up my hand. I moved my fingers in a wave. I smiled carefully. Food still in my mouth. She lifted up her hand. Her arm was still down her side. She moved her fingers in a wave. She smiled. Her eyes sparkled.

I smiled. My whole body tingled. I wanted to move. I saw she was shifting her weight. Was she coming in? I didn't know where to take myself. I thought she didn't know either. We kept looking at each other. I didn't feel it necessary to look away. To pretend I wasn't looking. Because I was. And she was. She raised her arm and looked at her watch. I looked at the clock on the wall. It was quarter past two.

Our eyes went back to each other. I smiled. She smiled. Wide smiles. I felt she wanted to say something. She had just begun to walk away when she stopped and smiled again. She lifted up her arm, put a finger on the watch and tilted her head. She was asking me if this was my lunch time. Or so I thought. I nodded. She put her hands down, smiled once more and walked out of the window frame.

My heart raced. My mind even faster. The flood of thoughts with 'why', 'what if' and 'this is crazy', caused a traffic jam. As my mind short-circuited, Adam's face focused my blurred vision.

'She is beautiful,' he spoke quietly.

I was blank. It took a few moments before I could collect myself. I straightened up from the slouched position I'd slipped into.

'She certainly is…' I said. 'Do you know her?'

'No… But I do know she walks past here quite a lot.' He thought for a second, scraped dried dough off his fingers. It crumbled onto the table. He pushed it into a small pile.

'You have to be careful,' he said slowly.

'Why?'

'Do I really have to explain why to you?' Adam raised one of his eyebrows in a frown.

'No…' The word exited my mouth, disappointedly.

He'd told me his story one day. Like this day it was quiet. He had sat down and asked me about my life, my work. And then he opened up to me like Ali used to when we were children. He told me his dreams. What he wanted to be when he was a child. Where he grew up. That he had been ostracised by his family when he fell in love with a Palestinian girl, Gana. He was only nineteen when he became homeless. He had nowhere to go until Gana's uncle offered him work in his café. He wasn't given a wage but a roof over his head. The back of the café had a room with a bed, a TV and a small cupboard. There was a sink where he could wash out of a tub. The café had a toilet for the customers as well. Adam was a bit younger than myself. He had spent five years of his life in the café. To his sorrow, Gana was eventually married to a Palestinian man. Most Israeli women wouldn't go near him because they knew he worked in a Palestinian café. Most Palestinian women wouldn't go near him because he was Jewish. As Jewish as I was Muslim.

'I can help you…' he said looking down at his hand. He thought for a while, then said: 'If she comes back and there are people here, I am sure she will sit at another table. In that case I will flip the sign on the door to closed. That way people can only exit. She will wait until you are on your own.'

'What makes you so sure she will do that?'

'I saw how she looked at you. Do I need to say more?'

'No.'

'Good. If she comes back and there is no one here, she will still sit close to you. I will flip the sign, make the door open from the inside only, take her order, give it to her and then I will disappear to the back. If you need me, just ring the bell. Okay?'

Adam spoke so fast. I became excited, playing out his scenario in my mind.

'Okay.'

Adam got up.

'Wait!' I almost whispered.

'Yes?'

'Why are you helping me?'

Adam's face changed to a lost stare.

'Nobody helped me and then somebody did help me.' His eyes came out of the stare. 'Why not?' He added. He walked back behind the counter and shaved the turning shawarma roll. I got up and went to the door. The long shiny handle was hot. So hot I let go and grabbed it from the bottom part where there was a bit of shade. On reflection, the burning sensation felt like an omen. A reminder of the tingling pain when you don't know how to play with fire.

'See you soon, Adam.'

'See you tomorrow, Nana.'

I smiled and opened the door.

And walked out into the brightness of the sun.

❖❖❖

The next day I walked with giant strides to the café. I had told Rafi I'd extend my lunch break. My hand and fingers were, after all, sore from the hours holding the carving knife. It was Friday so tensions around the old city were high as usual. Most soldiers were stationed around the gates, our faces familiar to each other. None of them motioned me to stop. The *Salāt Al-Jumu'ah*[45] *Adhan*[46] had already been called. Muffled sounds from the thousands of men gathered in straight lines in front of the mosque followed me. They were a jury of conscience but I was the judge. I thought only of my meeting with Linah. What could I expect? Had I read her signs right? I was sure I had. Why did she want to talk to me? Why did I want to talk to her?

Following this train of thoughts, I stopped all of sudden. A man in a suit walked into my back. As I turned around I found his empty eyes, and felt the wind from his discontented puff. I apologised and moved to the side. He continued and looked back, questioningly. What was I doing? Where was I going? There were plenty of other women. Palestinian women with open minds and kind hearts. Intelligent and caring. What was it about this one, I wanted to know? But there was no answer. My self-interrogation and reasoning left me blank. The only thing obvious was the pain in my gut. I don't know why, but right there and then, I took a look around me as I began walking again. Back at the walls of

45 The Friday Prayer.
46 The call for prayer.

the Old City, at people buzzing around me. The light, the smells. My life was connected to that place, a large part of my beating heart as well. But my soul had left, and it told me in a language anyone in the entire universe could understand. The resentment was contradictory. Yet I had seen it, felt it and known it for a long time. The folly of conceits that kept us and still keep us chained in mutual hatred. I knew it because I felt it every day. Like a bad cold that would not go away. The faces that brought it back were ugly. Their voices suffocating me. The reality was a life lived in the past. All I wanted was to be able to breathe freely.

Suddenly I had to stop. There was a pop-up checkpoint straight in front of me. And she was there. Her colleague had his Kippah slightly tilted. He was laughing about something. His face was ugly. His voice distinct. I remembered him from the night the fat man got caught in the door of the bus. I remembered his braying donkey grin. I felt my chest tighten. His curls had grown and his beard was unshaven. He stepped towards me as I approached them. Linah followed him. I could hardly breathe.

I gave him my ID automatically. He took it and went on a full assault show-off.

'What are you doing here?'

'Going for lunch.'

'Where are you going?'

'Café Mount Carmel.'

'Of course. Where do you work?'

'At The Palace in the old city.'

'What do you do there?'

'I work as a carpenter.'

'What is your mother's name?'

'Ghalia.'

'What is your father's name?'

'Khamis.'

'Do you have any children?'

'No.'

'Do you have a girlfriend?'

'No.'

'Do you like fucking men in the arse?'

'No.'

'So, you fuck men in the arse but don't like it.'

I looked at his name tag. It read DICKSTEIN M. I clenched my hands into fists until they hurt.

'If you don't fuck your best friend, you must surely fuck your mother?'

I remained silent and shifted my eyes to his. Inside them I found a scared child.

'Okay. Okay. I get it. You want to play tough.'

'I want to go to lunch.'

'So, answer my questions!'

Linah turned and whispered something to him in Hebrew. I couldn't hear it. His answer was an annoyed 'Sure…' as she turned to face me again.

'So?'

I had been here before. Barraged with the same set of questions. I could have fired a volley of profanities at him and been thrown in the back of the armoured van to spend several days in prison. It would have complicated, if not prevented me from returning to the Old City. The temptation to take the bait and stand up for myself almost defeated me. I wanted so badly to answer it. But I didn't. I was a pawn being played by a pawn. I knew he'd always have the draw to take me out, so I could only look ahead and leave him behind.

I glanced over at Linah. She was looking down, hardly moving. I looked at Dickstein M calmly. He was waiting for my reaction. I resisted. Instead, I let my rage leave through my body as cold sweat.

'I don't fuck men and I don't fuck my mother.'

Dickstein M handed back my ID without a word.

As I walked away I heard Linah's voice but I didn't look back. My tears went backwards, across and into my ears, down my neck. They went down my face and into my mouth.

My tears turned from the salty taste of pain to the drum of bitter fury.

15

The last bit of wood curled under the knife's edge on the second day of June. The last story showed the vengeance of a man for his beloved. Beneath the tip of a mighty sword, a young maiden lay slain. The man's arch enemy, a giant with a large spiky club, depicted a mocking laughter. Following the frames, the man courageously took the monster on. With splinters still showing in the wood, mortal combat took place in the final sequence as both of them perished. Pools of blood flowed in random shapes below their bodies as they both looked up to the sky. There, an angel cried.

My mind wandered. I was missing Ali. Our contact had been only on the telephone. He told me he felt happy. He told me he thought of asking for Farrah's hand. Her family was accepting of them. He told me he'd come back to work during the week once he had finished helping Farrah's father prepare for the olive harvest.

I stepped down from the ladder and took a walk around the room. Dust kicked up under my feet and it didn't take long before the sun created a spectacle of beams. Except for the distant rumble of The Palace, I once again found myself in utter silence. I heard my breathing and my heartbeat, and I heard my stomach tell me it was time for lunch. I took the strides to Mount Carmel once again. Spring had given way to summer and the morning hours foretold how the day would turn out. Sweat streamed down my entire body as the city baked. All around me people's faces glistened in the sun. It was dreadfully hot.

As I pushed the front door to the café open, the airconditioning compressor went on. The hum vibrated through the entire shop front. The place was almost empty. A young woman with black hair tied up sat with her back to me near the wall. A couple on the opposite side. The man was in a shirt and slacks, the woman in a classic skirt. Nearby office workers. I looked up and found Adam smiling at me.

'Badawi seriously needs to change that thing,' I said across the small room as I pointed up to the airconditioning over my head.

Adam didn't reply. Instead his smile receded as he nodded his head towards the young woman on my left. I looked across. I couldn't see her face. Did he mean it was Linah? I took in her hair once more, her figure. She was reading the newspaper, her jaw moving as she chewed. Adam signalled me discretely to stay put. The palm of his hand white from the flour. I pulled a chair out and sat down. Adam quickly made up a falafel sandwich. He came and placed the small basket in front of me. I shrugged my shoulders questioningly. He nodded. It was her.

I ate, watching the couple to my right. The lady suddenly picked up her handbag as the man glanced at his watch and said they were late. They walked past me, opened the door and left in a hurry. The heat from outside swept my back as the door opened. Only the three of us remained. I couldn't wait any longer. I stood up and with the falafel basket in my hand, I walked straight over to Linah's table.

I stood there until she saw me.

'Are you going to sit down?' she asked, as she put her hand up to her mouth, still chewing.

I didn't reply. I gently pulled out a chair facing her and sat down. Having walked over almost unthinkingly, the realisation she was there, right there in front of me, set off a drumming in my heart and my stomach heaved loudly.

Adam walked past us and went to the door. He flipped the sign to closed and set the door lock. As he passed us once more, he glanced and flashed a wide brotherly smile. He went behind the counter and rustled on. The volume of the radio on the kitchen bench rose slightly and then I couldn't hear him anymore.

I didn't leave an inch of her face uncharted as I drew lines across it. I remember it was as if I had the whole day to redraw her in my mind. It was the most beautiful face I'd ever seen. That is how she appeared to me. In her eyes, there was this sparkle of both mischief and kindness, and I was drawn to her like a lion to a lioness. We were studying each other, taking turns to look down at our food.

You can't really eat a falafel sandwich unless you figure out the best or next best position to bite into it. Otherwise, it falls apart—hence the basket.

I watched as she ate the last bit, carefully chewing, meanwhile wiping her hands and patting her lips with a tissue she effortlessly removed from a box on the table. Normally half the content would follow. I noticed the red nail polish was back. She smiled as she chewed, watching me looking at her hands. I still had a few bites to go when she finished.

I remembered watching a television show from London about something they called 'speed dating'. Couples had just a few minutes to question each other and find if their interest and so on matched. They might as well have been visiting a cake shop on a diet. We could have used our time differently but we had already exchanged questions, and I discovered that beyond attraction, our differences were only a matter of acceptance. Right there and then, there were few words spoken but there was an obvious and powerful attraction. The way she stared into my eyes, the way she let me to delve into hers.

'So… Are you going to tell me about the nail polish?' I said, as I put my closed fist in front of my mouth while swallowing the last mouthful. She smiled brightly.

'I honestly thought you knew. We're not allowed to wear red nail polish.'

'I didn't know. What colour are you allowed to wear then?'

'No colour. Transparent or pearl white I've been told more than once, light pink as well. Not sure who wears that though. Or French style it's called—a white strip at the end of the nail, here.' She pointed to the end of her fingernail. She had nice hands. The way she held one in the other made them look strong and soft all at once. Her nails were flat and in proportion with the rest of her hand.

'I thought they only allowed blue,' I said in a teasing tone.

I didn't think about it. I let out my prejudice, albeit a tiny bit. It came without warning. A reaction and not a response. I felt my skin blush. I had a million other questions I could have asked her to connect. Linah's expression changed. I could see she was wondering what to say. She almost spoke, then she stopped and looked at me. She looked at my hands. Then her own. I almost jumped as she removed the tissue from my right hand and took my hands in hers. I felt her pulse through the palm of her hand or perhaps it was mine. I wasn't sure. Her hands were warm and her grip firm. Her fingers were broad and formed a perfect fan with her palms. A small scar ran along the thumb she moved on my skin in small circles. Linah gazed at me questioningly.

'Why are you here?'

It was simple and real and as far as possible from anything I could have imagined her asking me. I felt scared but not like when a gun was pointed at my chest. Scared like when asked to get naked. I stuttered as the words passed my lips.

'I…I am not sure…'

Silence followed for a moment and then our fingers loosened to touch in random patterns.

'Have you thought about me?'

'Yes…'

'When you see me, do you want to know more about me?'

'Yes…'

'Do you find me attractive?'

'I…Yes.'

'Do you think I find you attractive?'

I coughed a short laugh, then I realised Linah wasn't wasting time.

'Yes…' I said, having followed her eyes intently. She smiled.

'Do you want to ask me the same questions I just asked you or do you want me to answer them straight off?'

I squeezed her hands a bit and pulled myself towards her slightly. It wasn't what she had asked me but how she had asked me. The intonation in my voice was forgiving as this time I responded instead of reacting.

'Linah... Are we at a checkpoint here?'

She understood. She realised her own probing manner and put her head down in a fast surrendering move. The large pin which had held her hair up, fell out and the bundle of thick black strands flopped over to cover her face and spread on her arms like sparkling charcoal threads. After a few seconds, she lifted her head, shook her hair backwards and showed me her face again.

'Adnan... I am sorry. I do it all the time. You get so used to talking like this. I even talk to my friends like that sometimes. I...' She stopped. She swivelled her hands, and mine with them, gesturing her innocence.

'It's okay...' I said, 'and you can call me *Nana*.'

She took a deep breath and smiled. 'I like *Nana*.'

I carefully asked Linah her first question.

'Have you thought about me?'

'Yes... a lot... Every single day since that day the young man took his own life. It was crazy... In the midst of all that, every time our eyes met, I felt a rush through my body. Behind my clothes, my rifle, I felt naked.'

I almost choked on my own saliva as I swallowed. I caught my breath and went on.

'When you see me, do you want to know more about me?'

'Yes...'

'Well, you've already answered that...' I said quietly, my heart racing.

'I have...' she replied as she left the words hanging on her lips. Her mouth remained slightly open. I stared at her lips, the curve of them. They were gleaming and wet, the lines moving symmetrically towards her cheeks. She smiled, her pearly white teeth showing. I smiled and felt like a Neanderthal in comparison.

Linah released her hands. She let her fingers run over mine as she slowly let go. The tiny glistening pearls of sweat on my palms felt cool as they evaporated.

'What is it that you do again?'

'I work with wood. Did you already forget?'

'Of course, not. It must be some incredible stories though...' she said as she touched the calloused lumps at the base of my fingers.

I watched her as she took my hands once again. She examined them, lifted them up and turned them around. The front was the same. Scratches, bruises and calloused knuckles. I remained quiet, smiling inside. It felt so good. I felt good. And right there and then, I would have been happy to remain in Mount Carmel for the rest of my life.

'So, when can I read these stories?'

'Any time you want,' I replied without hesitation but with a pounding heart.

Linah took a deep breath, stretched her head and shoulders backwards, lifted her arms high and pulled them backwards with clasped hands. I made out her figure through the white shirt. A white bra pushed her breast upwards embossing them to form a tantalising crevice. I travelled along the contours as a warm elation spread through my body. As she lowered her head, her eyes ran over me. She let out a little laugh as her lips stretched joyfully. She pushed her chair back and stood up.

'I've got to go.'

'Me, too.' I stood up as well.

'I'll see you soon, again.'

'*Insha'Allah*,' I replied, frozen in my place, my eyes tracing further down her body.

She put her hand on the back of the chair and was about to say something. I waited as I saw her look down, apparently with a fleeting idea as she shook her head dismissively.

'*Insha'Allah!*' She said decisively, sending me an unquestioningly beautiful smile.

Then she turned around and walked out of Mount Carmel. In the few steps before she pulled the door open, I watched her long hair waving gently down her back. Her movements spoke through her clothes, demanding my attention to her every shift and stir. The sight of her feet wrapped in soft slip-ons silently gliding across the floor was a novelty to my eyes.

Eyes inured to nothing but the black boots of the enemy.

⟐⟐⟐

After Linah had left, every muscle in my body relaxed and I fell back into the chair. I took deep long breaths as my thoughts battled and my heart pounded. I finally got a hold of myself and walked up to the counter. I yelled out.

'Adam!'

Adam came quickly from out the back of the café.

'So?'

'I didn't pay you,' I said, somewhat distantly.

'I wasn't talking about that! Don't worry about the sandwich. How did it go?'

Adam was curious but I didn't know what to say. For a second, standing there, I realised that I hadn't accepted his friendship yet.

'It went well…'

'*Well*, as in meeting again?'

'I think so… Yes…'

'Well, my friend…' I listened to him intently as he spoke those words. I wasn't used to them.

Not from *an enemy*.

'I hope the best for you. For both of you. She's a beautiful woman. And regardless who she is, she's a woman and you're a man, and that is the way of the universe, no matter how different we believe we are!'

Adam's words were profound. I stood there, silent in awe, the twenty-shekel note in my hand. Adam saw me, put his large hand over mine and pushed it away. I put the note back in my wallet.

'Thank you.'

'You don't have to thank me.'

'I do. Thank you for helping me.'

'Anytime, my friend. Anytime.' Adam gave one of his generous smiles.

I walked out the door and took steady strides. In the distance I could see a small part of The Palace dome. Angels and demons, heaven and hell, the courses of many lives before my own, carved their destinies before my eyes. I felt suddenly scared. I fell into a silent soliloquy, grappling with conflicts between head and heart.

What am I thinking?

What if she is an undercover agent?

But I'm a nobody! That makes no sense. No it's not that…

What was Ali up to? Could she be befriending me to get to him?

This is crazy. Of course, she's not an agent… Or is she?

What am I doing? Even if I wanted to move forward, it would be impossible.

What am I doing?

I don't have her number. She didn't give me hers. Why?

I didn't offer mine. She didn't ask. Perhaps she already knows it?

What am I thinking?

It doesn't matter. I might never see her again. And I don't find her that beautiful.

I do… She is.

She's Jewish.

This can't happen, of course.

But it just did. And it felt wonderful.

I felt no hatred. None.

What am I afraid of? That it turns out to be a lie?

That it turns out to be true?

What AM I afraid of?

That I will have to face myself? And in that self, do I know what is right and what is wrong?

Do any of us know?

Or is the thought of challenging the hatred so fraught we'd rather cling on to it?

Am I really afraid because I know the answer to my own question?
And I wonder, I truly wonder what she is thinking?
Out of everyone else she could have, why me? Why me?
It makes no sense and perhaps that's the most frightening thought of all.
To suddenly have our dreams come true.
And to realise we're making it happen ourselves.
By not clinging on to what we believe. It might not be true.

❖❖❖

I went back to work, unaware that I was walking very fast. Nobody stopped me, not even the soldiers at the entrance to the Old City. I didn't think about it at the time but afterwards I did. I walked with my head high. I felt invincible. Invincible and invisible, as if suddenly, I was not a Palestinian.

My thoughts frightened me. I returned to The Palace, ran up the crooked staircase three steps at a time, opened the attic door and jumped straight to work. The sandpaper was piled in a mess. I knelt and began sorting the different grades. The coarse eighty paper, the finer hundred-and-twenty, all the way up to the finest six-hundred. The higher the number, the smoother the polish.

I'd pushed myself near to the edge, not breathing easily. In time I calmed down. A delicious embrace of kindness folded over me. I allowed it. I let it speak to me. I felt a tear form and saw it drip on my dusty hand, then another one; within seconds it felt as if I had opened the tap to all the pain I had suffered since I came to be Adnan. I was about to stand up, but stayed on my knees as I let go and cried till it hurt, to where I felt the veins in my neck throb as if I were on fire. My vision blurred as tears flooded my eyes before gravity pulled them down like big, warm drops of summer rain.

My voice was quenched. I felt like screaming but I could hardly even breathe. I heaved for air, and finally managed to gasp out a cry. I let go—cry after cry after cry. I felt as if there was a demon leaving my body and I was the exorcist. I stayed on my knees, drooling uncontrollably, gasping for air. Then the physical stress passed and gave way to a divine serenity, such as I had never felt before. I literally lost my senses in that short space of time filled with numerous flashbacks. My mother's face as I woke in the hospital the day Bilal died... Bilal's heroic smile as he passed me the sweets after dinner. The day Ali and I found the giant olive tree and discovered the leaf-spangled hollow at its heart. Ali's ecstatic spirit the day he met Farrah. So many flashbacks.

The lasting one was Linah's sparkling eyes.

I remained on my knees for who knows how long. I wiped my hands and face with my clothes as my breathing settled into a peaceful rhythm. Underneath me the floor was rumbling with the commotion of a throng of departing tourists. Nobody had heard me. Most of the coarse grade sandpaper at my feet was wet. I spread it out across the floor. I took a one-hundred-and-twenty grade in my hand and looked at the carving of the Holy Trinity that Rafi had humbly asked for. I had depicted the Father in the form of a pair of cupped hands pointing downwards and the Son as a thorny wreath while a dove represented the Holy Spirit. Interlocking rings symbolised the unity between them. I took a deep breath and got up, feeling dizzy.

I ran my fingers over the rough texture in preparation but felt myself floating away, light-headed. The sandpaper fell and I rested my head against the pillar. I felt the earth move and the sun pierce the skylight above and swathe my body. My feet let go. I let myself fall backwards, my arms and legs spread as if borne by an angel. It lifted me higher, and light as a feather, I drifted into a sublime repose.

Suspended in a sunbeam.

16

In the days that followed I stayed away from Café Mount Carmel and let myself sink into a peaceful space with time to feel and time to think. I was facing a change. I tried to reach it, to cautiously embrace it. I imagined Linah was doing the same. We knew what had happened. We also knew we were on either side of not just a great concrete barrier but also a psychological trench—elements within ourselves and also in the world around us that sooner or later would unveil us. And without saying a word, we were already hiding.

As if whatever happened and whatever might happen was and would forever, be a crime.

That thought stalled in my mind. However much I reasoned its injustice, I also knew that our lives had permanently changed, no matter what would happen from then on. However, my instinct held that Linah would approach me again, and that was all that mattered. I would welcome it. What could follow would be uncertain and entirely uncharted. I had no plan, no ideas. I wasn't trying to plot out the future. In my peaceful space I was nurturing an emotion that I had thought was almost lost: hope.

The day after our meeting, I spent meticulously sanding edges in the attic of The Palace. When I went back through the checkpoint in the late afternoon, there was still no Linah. The days passed in repetition.

When I went through the checkpoint, my heart thumped. Part of me wished her to be there. To see her and have her see me. To speak to each other without words and be close without touch. To be reassured that what had happened between us was real. And nobody around me would know I had held her hand and touched her finger. The finger that rested on the trigger of the rifle pointing at us. No one would know she had held the hands of a particular young man in the herd. To all but her, I would be just another head. But she wasn't there.

Friday came and things at work were coming together. I had finished sanding half the carvings and I alternated between oiling the wood and more sanding. There was an absolute joy in reading the stories of the times. From the circles of singing and dancing between Jews and Palestinians to messages of faith that were common to every belief.

As I was stepping down the ladder, I heard the squeaking bi-folding doors open. I expected to turn around and find Rafi but instead there was Ali in the doorway. He was smiling and spontaneously, I smiled back. I hadn't realised how much I had missed him. We rushed towards each other, almost running like boys, before meeting in a tight embrace.

'*Habibi* Ali... I've missed you.'

'Nana... You've been with me all along. I've missed you as well, my friend.'

For a second, I almost felt like telling Ali everything. I almost did, but luckily, he let go of me and looked at the large pillar we stood by. He walked around it, reading some of his own carvings, some of mine.

'Nana... It's beautiful...'

'Thank you. May God keep you. I had a good teacher,' I said, pleased.

'But I didn't teach you how to become a master!'

I laughed. Ali's compliments went on and they were genuine. We spent the next couple of hours going through our work. We found details we'd forgotten. We carved shoulder to shoulder, sanded, laughed, ate and caught up with each other's lives. And that's where I made my first decision. To not tell Ali about Linah. I played the hand of injustice. There was no question about it. I could have told him and explained that we'd just met, made excuses for myself. But that in itself was also playing the same hand. I learned something that day and that is, that the changes we wish to make for ourselves in life are only real changes when we find the strength to build them and make them our life. With that courage, we reap our rewards, though I didn't know that at the time.

Ali opened up to me about his feelings towards his mother. He told me about the last incident, with eyes that spoke sadness, contempt and anger. Ali's father had invited Farrah's father over for tea. It was clear where Ali and Farrah's relationship was heading, and it would be the first of many steps to bring their families closer towards a union between the two. Ali's father wasn't traditional but for Ali's sake, he took the formal steps of invitation because Farrah's father was. Ali's mother, on the other hand, did everything Ali asked her not to do. In Ali's words: 'My own mother made a mockery of me.' I once tried to imagine what it would be like, to feel unloved by my own mother. The thought scared me so much, I begged Allah to ward off the devil. I could imagine the pain Ali felt. He also told me about his relationship with Farrah. He said they had *surrendered to each other.* They were in love and when he told me about it, there was no doubt. He straightened himself up and his excitement radiated through his voice, his smile and his large, shiny eyes. Ali had found his soulmate.

Time ran from us, the light signalling the arrival of the late afternoon. I asked my friend to come and eat with me at my parents'. He accepted. We packed our things, left The Palace and walked at a brisk pace to the bus depot to catch the bus to take us back across the Qalandia checkpoint. Even though it was crowded in the afternoon, the same as in the morning, we weren't subjected to the same scrutiny as when entering Israel. However, as we approached the chute to cross back into the West Bank, the queue came to a halt. We looked over at the entering snake queue. At the end of it, an old woman had passed out on a stretcher brought in from the humanitarian lane. She had been brought there by a Palestinian ambulance and was waiting for an Israeli one to take her the last stretch to the hospital. It wouldn't have mattered how critical her condition, countless others have died on stretchers, waiting for the move to take place.

A soldier poked the muzzle of his rifle at the old woman's thigh but to our surprise another soldier suddenly stepped in and fronted him, moving him away from the stretcher. He grinned curiously as he stepped backwards. They were too far away for us to hear what they were saying. The second soldier's figure was that of a woman and she put her hand on his chest, pushing him backwards. She pushed until he was pinned against the wall behind them. Her hair, tucked under the helmet, fell down as the soldier resisted. It was long and black. She pushed her loosened helmet backwards to her neck and poked at his chest repeatedly. The other soldier tried to walk away from the wall but she turned around and grabbed him by his vest.

She was Linah.

An argument broke out. Arms were waved and voices were raised. Soldiers flocked from several directions. I watched as two of them grabbed Linah's arms and dragged her away. She resisted and threw her helmet at the soldier she'd confronted. I smiled when I saw that. He retaliated in the same way. People in the queues began laughing but soon went back to silently watching. The standoff ended quickly and Linah shook off the arms holding her. A superior walked up to her and they stepped into the checkpoint command bunker. The other soldier was kept to the side with a couple of his colleagues keeping him at bay. It looked as if they were buying his side of things, smiling, nodding. He was letting it all out.

What, I couldn't poke a damned old Palestinian hag in the leg?

You didn't need to understand or hear the words to make out what he was saying. A couple of other soldiers came up and ushered us along. ID cards were merely glanced at. The place was cleared, the situation diffused. I looked back at the old woman on the stretcher. She looked straight up, ignorant of what was happening around her. She had tears running down her cheeks. I fell into them, imagining her stream of memories. A childhood, long before checkpoints and men and women with guns. A time of dignity and peace.

Ali was talking about that female soldier. We boarded the bus to continue to Mukhamas. The sound of the diesel engine drummed in tune with his voice. What had just played out was not entirely exceptional. From time to time we'd experience a soldier who was different, who'd talk to us as if we were people and not prisoners. When that happened, I again would feel hope; that there was still a chance of a different life from what I knew. And as long as that light of hope remained, I could keep going. As long as the battle against hatred held on, I could keep moving forward. Never to give up and submit to the occupation. As long as the struggle went on, I could keep my hope of a peaceful existence alive. With that, the jagged separation remained an ordeal of despair.

I watched Ali. He was scraping the dirt from under his fingernails. He smiled to himself. I guessed he was thinking about Farrah.

'What are you thinking about?'

Ali laughed—I hadn't expected that. I didn't know what to make of it. It was both happy and anxious. He kept cleaning his fingernails. He smiled, moved his eyebrows as if reasoning with himself what to do. I remained patient. He turned to me with boyish glee on his face.

'Farrah is pregnant. You can't tell anyone!' he whispered, swivelling his eyeballs left and right as if someone was listening.

I didn't expect him to tell me Farrah was pregnant. I am not sure why I wasn't ecstatic for him, but I wasn't. A part of me looked after Ali like he looked after me. As brothers. Ali and Farrah had only known each other for a *very short time*. I wanted to understand Ali because I found myself full of assumptions. So I put the question to him, but his reply sadly confirmed what I already knew. Ali was filled up with so much pain, he convinced himself that his union with Farrah and her family was the cure. A potion to dissolve the shame inflicted by our daily humiliation under occupation, the cruel barbs his appearance attracted, and the heartbreaking contempt of his own mother. With the sip of a magic tonic, all this was forgotten and gone.

In the dreamy reasoning of romantic love.

17

Monday. I walked through the checkpoint alone with my thoughts and the occasional flash of conversation struck with a familiar face. It was the second week of June and it brought unusually hot nights. Sweating bodies pressed against each other as weary eyes offered unspoken apologies for the degrading reality. It took me five hours to pass. My feet hurt as we were left standing for an hour—as usual, with no explanation.

Rafi caught me at The Palace front door as I entered. He held both of my shoulders and asked me to join him for breakfast. We went into the main dining hall where the food was already waiting for us. I was taken by surprise. For a moment I thought he wanted to let me go, in a kind sort of a way. But Rafi hadn't spared anything. The breakfast was a palette of the best Palestinian dishes. There was warm flatbread, cucumber spears, tomato and sweet onion wedges. Fava beans with olive oil and cumin, crushed salad in tahini, lots of fresh parsley, fried eggs, poached eggs with leek, mushroom and spinach and olives.

I thought it best to wait for him to come out with what he really wanted from me. As I filled myself with great gusto, Rafi allowed a pause in our general conversation and I sensed he studied me for a while, I am not sure why. He spoke his first words quietly.

'I need you for something, Nana.'

I stopped for a second. *Something?* Still chewing, I looked at Rafi and switched to auto-reply.

'*Order me,* Rafi.[47]'

---

47 Arabic way of saying: You are valued. Also can be: I am under your command.

'I'm going away this week. I have some business to attend to in Jordan.'

'Yes?'

'A man will come and ask for a briefcase he forgot here at the hotel. I want you to give it to him.'

'Is that all?' I answered with food in my mouth, somewhat puzzled.

Why was Rafi asking me?

'The briefcase will be in the safe in my office. I will trust you with the code. Here...'

Rafi had already written it down on a small piece of paper. He slid it across the linen next to my left hand and kept his finger on it. I read the code, 0-4-1-4-1-0-0-7, and looked back at him. I didn't have a choice. I finished chewing and swept my teeth with my tongue as I put my finger on the paper. Rafi let go.

'When will this man be here?'

'He will be here on Friday. His name is Mohammed. I am leaving at noon and will be back on Monday, *Insha'Allah*.'

I could have kept asking questions but it was better not to. I realised Rafi was using me because he couldn't ask anyone else at The Palace. I wondered who he was, this man. I wondered why the briefcase was in the safe and why Rafi was keeping the facts from me. But although my head was swarming with questions, I didn't ask.

'*Insha'Allah*.'

Rafi went back to eating. I watched as he stuffed his mouth full of food.

He looked up. His chewing came to a halt.

As did the trust within his distrust.

18

I watched as a black Mercedes picked up my employer and benefactor. It sped off with a muffled drumming on the cobbled road, far beneath The Palace attic. The hotel floors were quiet, guests were either out sightseeing or in the dining hall for lunch. My mind drifted with the pulse of my breathing, louder than the distant sounds from the alleys below. With every breath, disturbing thoughts came and went. After a while the sound of the news from a radio on a balcony alerted me that the clock had struck one. I still had work to do.

The three waiters we meet in life were in front of me. The one we call Love, the other we call Satan and the third we call Death; carved in that order, finally meeting our shared destiny: to order our last meal from the hideous waiter that breathes no life. Until that moment, we are seduced by Satan's eagerness to please, his offering of temptations in real and abstract forms. But we keep returning to Love's childish ways and unceasing torture. Both trying to morph into our souls. The edges around each of them needed sanding. Satan's three-pronged fork that jabs us, firing our earthly desires like the fix of a drug addict. Love's manipulating harp that roils our senses while constantly losing to the fork of Satan which severs its strings; only for them to quickly regrow, leaving us perpetually bewildered.

I balanced on the small step ladder, neatly folded the sandpaper several times before applying it to the wood. I could hear what sounded like a half empty jar of rice being shaken, and intermittently, a tapping noise. I stopped sanding. Nothing. I began again. Another tap. Again. Tap. I gazed around the room. There was nothing different to be seen or heard. I went back to the carving and resumed sanding.

It wasn't until I heard the distinct creaking of the wooden floor that I turned around. Startled, I almost fell off the ladder as I saw her. Standing there was Linah, smiling. I regained my balance and smiled back.

'You didn't tell me you were an artist. It's beautiful…' Linah let her fingers run over a carving of Adam and Eve in the Garden of Eden.

'Thank you… I'm not an artist… I… write stories on wood… Remember?'

'I remember, stories anyone can read, regardless of their own language. Correct?'

'You remember.'

'You're also an artist. Most people can't write like this.'

I stepped down from the ladder and stood at the foot of it. I felt awkward. I was wearing a dusty torn singlet and dirty, once-white working pants I'd used for everything from painting to welding. Dust covered the black hair on my arms. I wanted to at least put a shirt on. There was so much I wanted to do. So much I wanted to say. A moment I knew would arrive, had arrived—as sweetly and surprisingly as I had dreamed.

'I didn't do it on my own. My friend and teacher, Ali, is just as much part of it. But you will see that… You are welcome to look around… It's still rough, though. I still have work to do on it.'

Take a deep breath, Nana! She will think you are weird! Be cool.

'I'd love to, but not now. I'm going to visit a relative, but I was passing by and thought to see if you were truly hiding here.'

'Well you found me.'

'Is that good or bad?' Linah was so direct.

I was encouraged. 'Very good.'

Linah walked around the pillar I was working on. I turned, following her movement. She looked at me and smiled. She had the whitest of teeth. Both of us were smiling. The image of her face, large earrings and black hair flowed like a calm ocean swell.

My eyes fell on her shoulders and ran down her arm to her hand until it disappeared behind the pillar it was touching. As she appeared on the other side her breast lightly stretched her green shirt. It had a big, white peace sign on it. She wore dark blue jeans and the same red slip-ons I'd seen when she was standing outside the window at Café Mount Carmel. I kept going back to the face, her cheeks that widened in smiles that made her eyes narrow.

She was so beautiful.

I kept turning until I could turn no more, and she was in front of me. There was only the small step ladder between us. I could have moved it but didn't. I wanted to move myself but couldn't. I was petrified. Perhaps we both were. Linah pulled her lower lip and bit it gently. My heart raced with déjà vu. We stood there until she swung her cotton shoulder bag in front of her. She opened it and pulled out a large falafel from Mount Carmel. Across the wrapping, the words 'Made in Palestine' were showing. She handed it to me, stretching her arm across the ladder.

'I thought you might be hungry.'

'Thank you.' I raised my arm and held the other end of the wrap. Linah didn't let go of hers straight away. My instincts had been right.

'Didn't you just happen to pass by The Palace?'

'Kind of,' she said.

And did I see a hint of a blush?

A silence fell between us. I felt my body relax, my heartbeat as well. I stepped away from the ladder and so did Linah. Except for the sanding papers on the floor, there was nothing between us. I could smell her. It wasn't a perfume smell but something more subtle, an oil of some sort. And a distinct female scent. Or perhaps I just imagined that. Whatever it was—I liked it.

Linah drew circles in the dust with her left foot. Unconsciously, I flicked it backwards with my right foot like a bull scratching the dirt before the charge. We studied each other. On the surface, we were like two near-identical creatures of opposite sexes. One could have easily replaced the backdrop of the attic with that of an African savannah. We went on, moving our eyes up, down and across each other. Finally, Linah took a step forward. Then another couple of steps and walked past me. We let our hands brush. As she went behind me we meshed them together until we had to let go, right to the very tips of our fingers.

I turned around at the same time as Linah. For a second we consumed each other. She turned around once more and walked at a slow pace all the way to the door. I watched her every step, the graceful flow of her body, the sway of her hips.

When she reached the door, she opened it, turned—and a new aspect of her hit me. Yes, the beautiful creature was blushing.

She shook her head. *This is crazy!* Linah's face widened in a heavenly smile and then she left.

I felt drops of sweat running down my body. My clothes hung suspended from my skin.

I was naked.

19

I read somewhere that time is relative to the distant vantage point from which we are watching. If I could talk to someone far enough away, and see with large enough binoculars, perhaps they would tell me that they could see me as a child or perhaps as a baby. Perhaps they would say they could not see me at all—I was yet to be born. They wouldn't see the walls of separation. They wouldn't see the bodies of women, children and men facing them. None of that would exist for them, not because it doesn't exist but because they're so far away that the reflection of light from that time hasn't reached them yet. They would simply be looking into a past image.

As was I, searching the sky the night after Linah's visit. Tracing through sparkling specks, distant pasts. The light that reached my eyes had travelled so far that to me, that was all it was. Specks of light. And even though I knew I would never reach the places from where that light came, nor know their stories, I was not separate from them. Whatever was happening, wherever it was, I was part of it. We all were.

A profound feeling of empowerment rushed through my being. I realised I was stronger than the pain inside me and I realised my way of dealing with it differed radically from that of those around me. I began admitting thoughts and solutions, for myself, for my people, previously not engaged. The injustices of people towards each other, whoever they are or whatever they are called, concern the whole of humanity; never separated by the colours and flags and borders made by people with agendas and a limited concept of what we, as human beings, are capable of being.

There is no way of knowing the future. If we did, it would make it the past. If all that happened in the world was good, we wouldn't know what bad was. There wouldn't be a need for the word bad. Think of Palestine: if there hadn't been an occupation, I wouldn't have been working at The Palace. If there hadn't been an occupation, Linah and I might never have met.

Linah's visit cast a delicious aura of abstraction over my daily routine. The next day I felt so far away, I didn't register the trauma of having to get out of bed in the middle of the night to start the journey to work. Queueing in the dark turned into fantasy, like a rock star being moshed back above hordes of fans to continue singing on the stage. I met the soldiers with a smile. I could have been taken aside, interrogated, kicked or beaten, thrown into the death room, but it didn't happen. I could see fury boiling inside all of them except for one. One soldier stood out. He was young, part of the border police. He stood on top of one of the high concrete slabs that served as watchtowers. He was resting his chin on his rifle. He had my dark skin colour. Thick eyebrows, long eyelashes, black hair and black eyes. The Star of David was sewn to his shirt and a golden pin decorated the beret on his head. Underneath the symbolism was a living breathing human being with a mind and a heart. Perhaps he knew how to think. Perhaps his struggle was trying to make sense of his place on top of that concrete slab. He lifted his head up, stood up straight and returned my smile.

Right there and then, we shared a tiny ray of hope. It lived within that last inch of integrity. And that last inch, was all we had. All that we have. The only thing that we are left with and the only thing that could set us free.

I never saw that soldier again, but I will always remember him. He was Jewish, of course. Only Jews are allowed to serve. It didn't matter.

To me, he was also Palestinian.

20

I didn't expect Linah to walk in the next day. The doors parted and there she was, her aura so bright it lit up the whole attic. She came every day of that week. Every day, she brought our lunch. She even brought a blanket to spread out so we didn't have to sit on the dusty floor. I couldn't do much about the dust on my clothes but I tidied up so that the attic began to look like the large vintage penthouse it was destined to be.

For a week I felt fully alive. I apologised to nobody. For a week I had flowers and butterflies swirling, as if the cave of the olive tree had come to life inside me. I had never previously felt that way. Besides teenage infatuations and flirtations, hanging out in public places, I had never been so close to a woman. I had never had the chance to have intimate talks in a private setting. And it was private. Rafi was away and besides the expected arrival, at the end of that week—of the mysterious Mohammed who had forgotten his briefcase—no one disturbed us. In many ways, more than ever, the attic at The Palace had become my sanctuary.

Linah was born in Tel Aviv on the 25th of June 1988. This was the same day Hillel Slovak died. He was the guitarist for the famous rock band, Red Hot Chilli Peppers. I was intrigued by the coincidence because I knew the band but didn't know the guitarist. I told Linah about the coincidence of my own birthdate. She had never heard of Naji Al-Ali. Not once. I showed her an image of Handala on my cell phone and she recognised him straight away.

Perhaps it wasn't so strange that we touched on politics first. We wanted to see how strong the bridge was, so to speak. We crossed it several times and were able to reconcile our different perspectives. Neither of us was right or wrong; we simply exchanged facts and views. We once came to a pass in which we had nothing more to say. Our silence turned to smiling and our smiles to laughter. And our laughter turned into an eyeballing, heart-racing, physically charged conviction that whatever we were told we were, we were also fully free to become who we wanted to be.

Inevitably, we recalled our first meeting. That tragic reactionary checkpoint suicide re-emerged as a nagging insult to what we had thought of ourselves. Ultimately, it told us that the only antidote to hatred was what we were creating, right there and then in the attic.

'Why did you look at me? Why didn't you look at Sharon like those around you?' Linah asked me with a quietly fearful voice.

'You helped the pregnant woman…'

'But you were the only one who looked at me.'

'And…?'

'If you hadn't, I wouldn't have seen you. I was checking where Sharon was, and the only eyes looking at me, and not him, were yours.'

'I'd watched you from when the woman collapsed on the ground and you reacted in such a different way from the others. I'd never seen that before.'

'Never?'

'Never,' I said, at the same time questioning whether that was true.

'I've seen kind souls, young soldiers who put their rifle on their shoulder to help an old man through the turnstiles. There was a woman soldier who took the time to get to know the men who went past her daily.'

'So, there are good soldiers?'

'They don't last. The checkpoints aren't there to make things easy or to help us, and any form of kindness is forbidden at the checkpoint. You know this.'

I felt my chest tighten.

'There was kindness that day…' Linah said, almost surrendering in her voice.

'There was. And look at where you are now...'

Linah had been suspended, temporarily, for standing up for the old Palestinian woman the day Ali and I saw her. Her other rebellious move of painting her nails red was retrospectively added to the charge sheet. And most likely, aiding the pregnant woman the night we met, had been noted as well. She expected not to return to the checkpoint but to be posted to field duty at the end of the week. She didn't know where she'd be sent. I didn't know or ask her much about how the military system worked. I listened instead to her telling me about the narrow, poisoned minds of many of her comrades. I recognised the personalities. I felt their hatred. It felt as if Linah had borrowed my eyes for a day. At first, I couldn't see how she could do this.

As the days and hours passed by, I came to realise we can use, not only our minds but also our hearts, to think.

'Do you dream about the man Sharon shot?' Linah's tone was sincere.

I answered gently: 'no'.

'I do. He appears every night. His body flying through the air. His arms spread. His roar... I saw him from the side, but in my sleep he's charging towards me! Nana, it is horrible... It ends in the split second, when either I shoot him or let him fall on me.'

'What do you do?'

'I wake up.'

'But he doesn't want to attack you. He wants to die.'

'I know that.'

'So why do you dream of it?'

'Because I am afraid of it being me pulling the trigger, one day.'

'You won't.'

'What makes you so sure?'

'Because you are not like him. And if you want another reason, your days at a checkpoint are over. They will never let you stand at another checkpoint again. Believe me.'

Linah quietly stared at me, as if wanting to read my mind. Her eyes seemed to circle my face, unfolding every crease, searching the shaded parts.

'I believe you… but…' As Linah was searching for words, I went first.

'I will be honest with you. I wanted Sharon to shoot me that night.'

Linah's reply wasn't immediate.

'Do you still feel like that?'

'No… And, yes… I don't know. I am with you now and isn't this as crazy as the checkpoint?'

Linah nodded, a smile spread across her face.

I went on: 'What happens to us every day could never be called normal. We harden ourselves to keep our hearts alive, but we cannot… I cannot think about it because I'd go crazy if I did.'

'So how do you block it out?'

'I can't. It's like an onion. Another layer is pulled over it. It lives inside me. Sharon and the hatred he spat out that night will not leave me, but I've hidden him underneath layers, both good and bad layers, since then.'

'So, am I just another layer in your onion?' Linah asked after a pause.

I laughed lightly. Linah lit up too.

'This is a new onion to me. I'm still at the heart of it.'

'That was a good answer. A very good answer indeed…' Linah's smile untied the knot in my chest. It loosened her own despair as well.

We were sitting cross-legged opposite each other. So close, strands of her hair kept touching my face. These touches were our embrace, randomly granted. The fire was lit and as it got hotter, we broke out in blushing laughter. Then we went back to silence. I took Linah's hand and we both rose to our feet. I walked her over to one of my carvings. I'm sure we left behind us a trail of smiles with wings on them as we walked.

'Do you read Arabic as well as you speak it?' I asked Linah.

'I was curious about the letters as a child. I had Arabic-speaking friends as a teenager. In short, yes.'

I pointed out a line that went all around a post. Linah kept hold of my left hand as she read it. She only let go when I took her right hand as she came around.

The three things we must never sacrifice in life are our families and our hearts and our dignity.

Above, a man and a woman ran towards each other. Each of them had a man chasing them with a rifle. Between them a big group of children were in an embrace. Two more carvings followed underneath. On one, the children, the man and the woman each reached out to their pursuer with a flower. The rifles were pointing halfway down. On the other and last carving, the men aimed and fired, the flowers were gone but the children, the man and the woman faced the viewer standing straight.

Linah took both my hands again and I gazed into those mesmerising green pools of light. They were shining as tears slowly brimmed. She didn't speak, and for a moment I wasn't sure whether it was right of me to have pointed the tableau out. When we first met, words had left her mouth that she didn't really believe. She was asking me questions in an interrogating way. In this time, as we approached the end of Wednesday, her voice had softened, her shield had lowered. With me, it was just the same. I could feel the hardened steel cap that had been clamped on my heart, opening up. It was happening in the light of day and in my dreams at night. I felt I could almost breathe like a free man. The thrill and wonderment in my soul had me sharing parts of myself that I had kept as the darkest secret before now.

That week became a probe into the scintillating joy and devastating dread sadness of our first meeting. We jokingly pondered how a Palestinian man and an Israeli woman could live out their lives together. We knew we were talking about ourselves. We knew that. What each of us wanted was reassurance. We also knew we needed more time to think out a solution to what seemed like a Gordian knot: the forming of a relationship between two people who are destined to be nothing but enemies.

Linah wrapped her arms around me and placed her head on my chest. My heart pounded as I folded myself around her warm body. My fingers combed through the thick strands of her hair that flowed down her back like a gossamer stream of ebony. I breathed in her scent. She closed her eyes and took a deep breath. Her head in the middle of my chest. I couldn't let go. We remained embracing, for a long time, caressing each other with the whole of our bodies.

Life had kicked me a fate I had never imagined. It hit me, hit us both like a bombshell and blew us so far from its centre, we found ourselves in another world. We rose to our feet and floated carelessly through the Garden of Eden.

Exhausted, we released our embrace and drifted back, our arms and hands touching. So close. Our foreheads nudged each other and our noses touched. We breathed together. Finally, we let our lips come together. Just barely. Waited a bit. Then we kissed.

And in that one long and tender kiss, walls crumbled to the ground.

21

I let go, surrendering myself to oblivion. It was madness. But it was in that madness I discovered what sanity truly is. For the first time I discovered that within me, an entire universe existed. I discovered a world that had been unknown to me. That I didn't even know existed. I was born Palestinian, this is who I am and who I am told I am. But I discovered that behind Adnan, under the shell, lives a human being, a man with a beating heart in his chest. I am no less than anyone else, but *I am also everyone else*. I am who we all are.

The last two days of that week, Linah and I transfused lives. I became Jewish and she Palestinian. We made another world. Everything was possible. I told Linah about the cartoon, Adnan & Lina. It started as a Japanese anime cartoon but it was no coincidence that it flourished in the Arab world. That cartoon is heroically romantic and Arabs are suckers for romance. Adnan is an adventurous eleven-year-old who grew up in a secluded life after an apocalyptic war between two superpowers. He is ridiculously strong and exaggeratedly confident, and knows how to use many weapons to free him from every kind of sticky situation. He is also gentle and kind, the archetypical hero, though a boy and not a man. It's an elaborate plot. A post-ultra-magnetic-weapons war scenario. The continents have been engulfed by the seas and the earth is thrown off its axis. Some people tried to flee in spaceships but crashed back to earth. Only a few survived on a couple of tiny islands that miraculously remained, and on one of those, Adnan was born. After some years he met Lina, one of the few survivors from another island. And so their adventure began. They travel together and it is on this journey that their friendship transforms into a love story which overcomes the conflicts between the people of good and the people of evil.

Linah laughed as I told her the story. She sat on the attic floor with her back to one of the columns and I paced back and forth in front of her, throwing my arms into the air, jumping around and quavering my voice, passionately. But seconds after I finished, Linah suddenly fell distant. She clenched her hands above her knees and stared at the floor. I remained standing in front of her, then squatted until she looked up and our eyes met.

'I'm sorry.'

'For what?'

'For saying my job is to protect my people.'

I remembered when Linah had said that. I flicked through a range of emotions, not finding a means to reply.

'Why are you recalling this now? You were laughing just a second ago…'

Linah didn't look away. The circles in her eyes expanded as she breathed, relaxed and spoke.

'Your cartoon brought back what I already know but try to ignore… That I am not protecting anyone. My people are the evil people. We treat you like animals and we expect you to obey and be quiet. And when you resist, we kill you. I see it every day.'

I didn't know what to say. Linah had plainly laid out the world, the truth. There was no argument. I felt awkward. The amount of good and evil I witnessed daily wasn't segregated into *my people* or *their people*. It was what happened when you showed people two identical circles and told them they were different. My slow reply to Linah came from the heart.

'At the time you said it, I felt anger—but moments later—I had forgiven you. We throw ourselves over the edge, Linah. I do it and you do it. Believe me, I am just as much part of what I'm told I am. But then… I see the stars at night, and I feel the heat of the sun. Its light shows me the colour of my own blood and I see that we are all the same. I know the story I'm told is safer than the story I'm writing myself. The story we're writing here... There's nothing to apologise for, everything to forgive...'

There was a brief silence.

'Thank you. For sharing your heart...' Linah said.

A beautiful smiling flowed between us. I took Linah's hand and helped her get up. I walked her over to one of Ali's carvings. A big, thick wooden ring attached to the ceiling served as a chandelier frame. It hung over a space that would hold a large circular dining arrangement. Ali's idea was that each person sitting underneath could read it. It would bring unity to the table and ward off bad arguments. After all, who would willingly admit to not liking the other? That was his reasoning.

Linah looked up and read the circle out loud as she slowly turned around.

'*An-gels bring-us-our hearts. And- when-a heart-meets-a heart, - the eye-sees no flaw...*'

Linah was silent as she looked at me.

'The first time he carved it was on his sixteenth birthday.'

I waited for her to say something, to perhaps ask a question but she didn't say a word. Instead she slowly walked all the way up to me. Linah was a bit shorter so her head rested perfectly on my chest. She looked up at first, in a flickering observation of my eyes. Then she slid her hands around my body and dropped her head to listen to my heart. Her hands moved up my spine to my shoulder blades, then spread out and drew back to push my chest as she took a deep breath. We kissed, at first gently bringing our lips to touch, then passionately.

The Garden of Eden was on the top floor of The Palace in those last two days of that week. The world outside the folding doors, the world underneath, vanished. We became one, time and time again. We closed the doors, whispered as we smiled and laughed, shared our food, wine and kisses. We made love, and we were neither Muslim nor Jew. We were naked.

I would not understand this till much later but that Thursday evening I walked through the checkpoint as if I was going through an international airport. My ID wasn't a symbol of segregation, it was my passport and the weapons around me were for my protection.

I got back to Mukhamas with less than six hours to sleep before I had to return to the checkpoint. My father and mother were sitting outside the front door. I saw them from a distance. My mother was smiling. My father had just told one of his many jokes. He was bent forward, blowing the surface of the hot tea, laughing with the cough and smoke from the cigarette between his fingers. I stopped and watched them and the world suddenly went silent. Right there and then, in a clutch of apprehension, I thought I'd never be able to sit with Linah like that. The joy in my soul turned to a tightening in my chest. My heart pounded.

Like a tribal drum before the sacrifice.

22

That is what I thought. Perhaps one day. Perhaps not in my own lifetime. However, I would later realise that immediate thoughts, even my own, should not be taken too much to heart.

Friday was no less tense than any other Friday in Jerusalem. The anxiety Linah and I both felt and openly shared, aligned itself with what was happening in the world around us. Mohammed's visit came as an unexpected shift in the tide. I confided in her, suspecting something was going on.

Mohammed had arrived before Linah in the early morning. I had expected an older man. Somehow, with a beard. When I was called to greet a visitor asking for me in the foyer, I met a very young man, possibly in his late teens. He stood straight and had his hands down by his side. Only his head and eyeballs moved around the foyer as I walked towards him. He wore a business-like outfit that was a size too big: a white, short-sleeved shirt and brown slacks, snub-nosed shiny leather shoes. He was handsome and fit.

'Mohammed? I am Adnan.' I extended my right hand. He took it and clenched it. It hurt.

'I am here to collect a briefcase I forgot.'

'Yes, Rafi said. Come with me,' I replied politely.

I walked Mohammed to the office, opened the door and offered him a chair. He declined, walked to the window and looked out over the Old City. He didn't say anything. I noticed he turned his back to me as I opened the safe. Naturally, I was curious. What was it that Rafi was hiding from me? Questions spat out of the fire like red-hot coals.

I placed the brown briefcase on the table. It was heavy for its size, one of those I'd see in office supply stores. My first thought was obviously *money*. But for whom, for what? And who was this Mohammed after all? He turned around, walked briskly to the table and grabbed the handle. He was about to lift it when I spoke.

'Don't you want to make sure everything is fine?'

'I'm sure it is. We trust Rafi.'

Who was we?

'Who is *we*?'

Mohammed did not move. He took a deep breath and faced me.

'I will ask you to tell me what you think is in the briefcase. If you answer correctly, I will not say anything. If you do not know the answer, I will leave you and journey in the name of Allah.'

'Money?'

Mohammed smiled. He took the briefcase and walked to the door, opening it. I stopped him again.

'Are you from Gaza?'

He didn't turn around. There was a brief pause.

'If you find yourself in Gaza, please honour me with your presence.' He turned around and handed me a business card which I took without inspection. He was about to leave but hesitated. He glanced at me from head to toe, then he smiled.

'I'll tell you who *we* are at that time. *Asalaamu aleikum.*'

'*Weh aleikum al salaam*,' I answered in a low voice.

Mohammed turned around and left. Mohammed, the young man from Gaza, left with a briefcase full of money. Mohammed from Gaza was not a young man. He just looked like that.

I became lost in thought until I heard voices in the hallway. I closed the safe and left Rafi's office, shutting the door behind me. With my hand still on the door knob, I read Mohammed's card:

Khaled Abu Mohammed
Import and Export
Gaza, Palestine
+972 55 898 8900

Linah walked through the attic door shortly after. She put her head to my chest and cried. Her tears came out of a nightmare she had had of imprisonment and rape. Not thinking, Linah and I had thrown ourselves off a cliff, not knowing whether we'd hit water that would save us or rocks that would break us. For my part, I had also suffered torments. That morning, I had walked through the checkpoint, feeling like a double agent, fearful that my time was up. That I would be caught out and have my throat slit as a traitor.

It was to be the last time we'd be together at The Palace. Her expectation of being ordered to field service had been right. She would report to duty the following Monday and be taken to a platoon in the Negev desert somewhere. Linah talked about claiming a *profile 21* of mental instability. For a time we fell silent. We had aired the possibility that our days together might run out. It felt all too difficult. It *was* too difficult. We locked the attic doors and made love. It was that simple.

Physically we were perfectly aligned, emotionally we had lost track of our past selves. We were just Adnan and Linah. Two young people in the tingling springtime of love. That wonderful week! That special Friday when age, colour, race, gender, religion, politics, the past, and the future simply did not exist. There was only the magic of physical and emotional fulfilment. Hatred and mistrust were abolished by love. In the only way possible.

We were on the floor. I watched Linah as she ate an olive she picked out of my lunchbox. She licked it so the oil wouldn't drip. She bit off half of it and chewed slowly. I could tell by her smile she liked it. She saw me looking at her, then blushed and grinned.

'What?!'

I waited with my reply. Then I said what I saw.

'You are beautiful...'

'Thank you...'

She intrigued me. There was something about the way she smiled. Something about the way she put the olive onto her lips and didn't eat it straight away. Something about the way she had pulled her hair up around her ear. My mind wandered back. Way back to the day I stood at the bus stop with my father and saw a beautiful girl across the road.

'I want to ask you something… It happened a long time ago… It's crazy and it might not mean anything to you. And that's okay! Or you might have a similar memory but…'

'Just ask me!' Linah stopped me and smiled. I took a deep breath. Butterflies were bouncing off my chest and nosediving into my gut.

'Well, many years ago, when I was a child, I was at a bus stop with my dad. I don't think it's there anymore, but it was on a highway. I remember there was an overpass and shade. I also remember there was a water fountain… Not for us but for… eh… I was thirsty. It was hot. Well, you know what they look like, these stops… Anyway, I saw this school class waiting for their bus. There were a lot of children. They…'

'…were very noisy. And… a Palestinian boy waved at me…'

With Linah's words it felt as if the heavens and the earth had come together. The scene from the past reeled back to me in full focus. Particulars of a long-gone moment in my life became crystal clear. It seemed as if I had found them in a magical book. I flicked through page after page of moving images as I saw again what my eyes had seen that day. I felt again the holding of my father's hand, the pungent smell of the heat, the thirst. And then I saw the little girl again and our eyes met … and she waved back at me.

Linah was shaking slightly, smiling and teary all at once. I moved closer and felt the uncertainty of my own reaction. My limbs twitched and shook. We put our arms around each other. I felt her tears drop down my naked back. I held her tightly, letting my face caress hers, wiping her tears away with my cheeks, tasting them as I kissed her. I moved my hands gently up and down her back, until her skin felt warm. Her breathing slowed down and she stopped shaking. We could not bear to separate. We embraced in silence. All the time, I felt a sublime clarity in my soul. We were reading each other's bodies, our fingertips tracing every contour. We felt the moistness and the warmth, embedded the texture of the other into our hearts.

I have no idea where I found the courage to ask Linah about that day at the bus stop. In a way my heart was telling me it was her, but it was only when I heard her own recollection, that it made sense to me why we have a heart.

We embraced and we kissed for a long time behind that closed attic door. Sounds came in with the draughts, breathing through the cavities of the old building, loaded reassuringly with voices and laughter. We were so close our eyes appeared as large pools of enchantment. A kiss with open eyes, then a kiss of closed eyes. First the vision, then the intensity of contact. We were in the grip of the lover's cry. We wanted to eat each other but the time had come for Linah to leave. She took hold of the door handle. She turned it and was about to pass through when she let go and faced me again.

'*Ata ḳol ḳaḳh yafe.*[48] I've wanted to say this to you for a long time.' Linah's words were followed with a soft peck on my lips.

'*At ḳol ḳaḳh yafa.*[49] I've been wanting to say this *to you* for a long time,' I replied, returning her kiss.

Linah blushed and laughed. Then I laughed and at precisely the same time, we both said:

'Since Mount Carmel!'

Linah gave me a flirtatious glance. Her eyes sparkled. I felt my hair rise in an ecstatic rush that ebbed through the far reaches of my body. We closed our eyes, our lips met and in that moment, we took a giant leap through the darkness of our separated worlds into the open and inextinguishable light of oneness.

It was Friday the 13th of June when Linah and I had our last kiss at The Palace. Then followed a period of agonising uncertainty during which we had only limited contact on the phone. The

---

48 You are so handsome.
49 You are so beautiful.

world around was bleeding. A newspaper in the lobby caught my eye. Three young Israeli teenagers had been abducted. There was a strong presumption of revenge for the Beitunia killings. There was speculation about the teenagers' fate. A convenient braggadocio resounded between the lines. The voice of the Israeli narrator was excited, turned on by his own hatred. There was no doubt. It was time to set the scene. Time for revenge. An eye for an eye would be nowhere near enough.

The sky was clouding over; blood was about to flow.

Palestinian blood.

23

Two weeks passed and the month of July was signalling its arrival. Since the abduction of the three teenagers, there had been a series of revenge attacks. Palestinian children were either kept at home or forced to walk to school with an Israeli army unit watching over them. Fanatical settlers were ambushing them, throwing stones, torching their homes and shooting at them. There was no doubt: the purpose was to kill. The settlers were even attacking the children's Israeli army escorts; but no action was taken against them. It was an ominous exhibition of the overall strategy. To divide and conquer, to get rid of all Palestinians. The settlers, in their own rabid and unsubtle way, serve this vision with steadfast barbarity.

Linah went away and I went back to my own solitary company at The Palace. I was alone to finish the work Ali and I had begun months earlier. I thought of Ali a lot. I missed his company, missed having a brother-and-soul friend in my life. I was happy for him, though. He had called me on the last day of June and announced he and Farrah were formally to consummate their marriage at a wedding set for the 11th July. I laughed and told him to slow down, but I also knew they were in a hurry. Farrah's belly would begin to show. Traditionally, the couple are expected to consummate their marriage on the wedding night. However, for most couples, being cheered out the door in the midst of the celebration to go off and have sex, is the most unromantic tradition of all.

Ali and Farrah had already taken their vows at the mosque in Budrus; only Ali's father and Farrah's family had been present. I felt the pain in Ali's voice when he spoke to me about it but I also heard the joy. He was letting go. His voice conveyed the serenity of a man who was overcoming the sense of shame inflicted upon him by his own mother. And to a degree, by his brother as well. Fayez remained the pillar in Ali's life. He called me several times to make sure I would attend the wedding. He had a suit sent to our home in Mukhamas and invited my parents as well. We would rejoice with family and friends from the villages of our childhood.

In the two weeks after Linah left, the drums of war went into a roll. She sent me text messages when she could, telling me they were being prepared for a military operation. I pieced it together as most people did. The news chanted the call for a war against Hamas; chanted the euphoria of hatred and revenge. I'd find myself catching the tightening knot in my chest, feeling my heartbeat rise as it shrank. The vicious punishment of an entire people did not fit this three-victim crime.

On the first day of July, Ali and Farrah walked hand in hand the distance from the village of Aboud to our olive tree. They made love, cocooned in The Palace of Angels as wind swirled around them. It cooled their sweating bodies as they drifted off to sleep, entwined like twins in a womb. When they opened their eyes, they shared their dreams, their imagined future together. They kissed in the privacy of the bower before they climbed down and began walking home. At the dirt track near the village they parted in a proper way. Ali went south and returned to his father, awaiting him on a chair outside his childhood home. Fayez embraced Ali with a smile and observed that Farrah must have been wearing a beautiful scent. To marry his son and provide a place for the newlyweds to spend their honeymoon, the landlord had left them the house for the entire month.

Farrah walked to the north. Her parents were waiting for her to return from her walk, but she didn't arrive. An hour later she was found halfway down the track from where she and Ali had parted. Farrah had been savagely raped. Her face was blue from the blows she had received. Her head rested like an angel's—in a deep halo of blood. A shot had gone through her skull and left her staring at the stars in the darkening hue of the sky.

And the angels fared along with the sunset as they turned black in sorrow.

⧼⧼⧼

We buried Farrah late the following day. Her body had been quickly removed and we made sure the Israelis would be told simply that she'd died. If we reported a killing, there was no telling when the body would be returned. She had been raped and brutally murdered and no Israeli authority was going to help find the perpetrators.

Although the wedding hadn't been officially consummated, neither family objected to Ali's demand to be part of the washing and shrouding of her. But at the rite, he did it all himself and wouldn't let anyone else touch her. Fayez was told he'd been washing her as if he was caressing her. He talked to her, asked questions about what she'd like to do on their honeymoon. Farrah's family prayed to Allah, asking Him to protect Ali's soul. They prayed as they watched and cried.

He didn't hear them. As he closed Farrah's eyes and wrapped the shroud around her, he left himself with her. His fists clenched tight as a demon entered the void inside him. I tried arousing him, but he was forever gone. I had never seen anyone stare at a shrouded corpse as much as Ali did when Farrah was laid to rest on her side. After the prayers were read, he wouldn't let anyone throw soil on her. We kept pleading with him to give her peace, but he stood fast at the windblown graveside, gripping the shovel as if it were a weapon. Finally, without a word, he scooped a mounded load, lifted it up and held it. Tears in every colour of the rainbow flowed down his face to form rivulets along the bulging veins of his arms. They finally blotted the tension of the dirt and soaked the earth around Farrah. He shed the load and with each spadeful that followed, tears left Ali until there were no more. His eyes turned matte and it was the last I would ever see of my old friend, Ali.

Fayez approached me shortly after.

'May God provide her with a place in heaven…'

'If Allah wills it…' I replied and watched Fayez light a cigarette. I sensed he wanted to speak.

'What would you like to say to me, Fayez?'

'Am I that obvious?' He laughed with tears in his eyes. Then he quickly calmed.

'Are you able to keep an eye on Ali for me?' His tone was almost pleading. I took a deep breath.

'I'm not sure I'm able to…'

'Why?'

Why was a good question although the answer was riddled with pitfalls. I had a love within myself that I kept a secret. A love for one of the enemy; and in the eyes of hatred, the enemy has no face. There are no individuals. Everyone becomes prey as poison fills the mind and heart of the hater. This is true, even for people not directly fighting each other. Religions, races, cultures and even ideologies stand equally condemned when they are seen as deficient. I couldn't answer Fayez's question with honesty; I didn't know when I could or if I ever could. I looked over his shoulder and saw Ali standing in the centre of the thinning crowd of people. The cries of revenge had subsided, and Ali hadn't moved. His fists were still clenched, his jaw clearly grinding as he stared at the mound of dirt at his feet. I looked back at Fayez. And within me I mustered words that served no more than comfort and hope. Which was all I had left in me.

'I don't know where Ali is right now, Fayez. I have to allow him the time to grieve…'

'I'm not asking you to stay with him. Just let me know that he is safe.'

'I will honour your wish, Fayez.'

Fayez bit his fingernails and smoked his cigarette in sequential puffs. He hadn't finished. He looked at me once more, then found the words he stood by, speaking them in the most heartrending tone.

'Two men I call my children, Nana, but he's my *only son*…' He put his right hand before his eyes and wept.

Tears ran between his fingers as the smoke from the cigarette floated over his bald head.

Ali overheard him and turned to us. His eyes bore a hole through my chest.

There, pounding, my fear was exposed.

24

The first week of July felt like a wound-up spring; everyone knew that its release was imminent. The hatred intensified, refuelled and primed for explosion. A lust for retaliation and vengeance was mounting. We would have a full-blown display of what one human being can do to another when he believes he is God's only chosen, and he only can be right. Because God didn't create us equal.

Ali disappeared after Farrah's funeral. I called him from work. At first the phone kept ringing, then I couldn't get through at all. I kept my phone on me all the time. I checked the signal, the answering machine, but there were no words from him. I went to visit Fayez later in the evening, but he just cried and pleaded with me to keep searching.

'Let me know he's well, Nana... Please...'

Ali was nowhere to be found. Nobody knew where he was. My father and I put out the word that we were looking for him. Most of that day, my phone was quiet. When it sounded, it was an odd call from a distant friend who wanted to connect. My mother also called and asked me to bring her some groceries on my way home. I waited and worked hard. My mind worked hardest as I smoothed the last edges of drawings and words. I was finished at The Palace.

One of many revenge killings made it to the news channels. A sixteen-year-old Palestinian boy had been murdered by Israeli settlers the same day we buried Farrah. The Prime Minister, Benjamin Netanyahu, used the killing to further mock the Palestinians by denouncing their violence. His way of putting an end to it would take on an entirely new meaning as a fresh wave of retaliation attacks was launched from Gaza. Both sides called them rockets but the silently whispered nickname for these weapons was *stormwater pipes*. Both sides needed each other.

It was the first Friday of the month. I wanted to leave The Palace. As much as I loved their beauty, a feeling of isolation crept up as the engraved stories around me became my only company. Rafi knocked and opened the attic door as I was cleaning up. I'd sent him a text telling him the work was complete. I sneezed from the dust as I turned around.

'*Sa*-ah-ah-*laam*, Rafi. I'm sorry about the dust.' I suppressed another sneeze and rushed to open a window. Dust played in the sunlight before escaping out the window in a wraith-like motion.

Rafi walked around with a bright face as he examined the carvings. There was no single narrative but stories that nudged one's perceptions and toyed with ideas about the eternal questions of life. No matter where you'd turn, there would be a story, carved as letters in numerous shapes and as indented drawings in the timber. Rafi stopped and read one of Ali's earliest pieces.

'*Bury me so I can be free or silence me to save myself.*'

A woman handed a man a spade. He dug a hole and lay in it. On his back he smiled as an angel flew off with an oversized tongue of his. The woman kissed the man and in the end they lay side by side in the grave, staring at two angels crying above.

Rafi eyed my dust covered body from head to toe. He held an envelope in one hand. I glanced at it. He noticed, raised his hand and looked at it himself. Then he turned to me.

'Adnan... First of all, thank you. The work is incredible ... I love it. I just love it.'

'You're very kind, Rafi. I'm so glad you feel like that.'

Rafi handed me the envelope.

'This is for you. I've given the same to Ali, not because he's worked as hard as you but because I knew he needed the money for his wedding.'

I gasped. When had he spoken to Ali? Why hadn't Ali told me? He had already given it to Ali? When? A storm of thoughts went through my mind. I opened the envelope and there were two and a half thousand Shekels in new notes.

'Thank you, Rafi. You didn't have to...' My heart was racing as I kept my calm.

'You deserve it.' Rafi cleared his throat and continued.

'I don't have much work here at the moment... As things look, it might all blow up soon and... Then it will be very difficult for you to come here every day... More difficult than what it already is... I have to let you go, Nana... But you already know this...'

Yes, I knew it. Rafi wasn't saying anything I hadn't expected. On the contrary. That he had let us work for so long and spent so much money on the work in the attic, was in itself prodigious. He wasn't apologising but he wasn't glad to let me go, either. For a man who befriended many and trusted few, his decision was straightforward. My response was equally sincere, though driven by curiosity. Much as I appreciated support and kindness, I couldn't stop thinking about Ali. I hadn't told Rafi about Ali's disappearance.

'I understand... Rafi...'

'Yes?' Rafi's voice sounded helpful.

'When did you give Ali his bonus?'

'At the end of last month. In fact, I left it for him at the reception. They told me he'd picked it up the same day Mohammed came to pick up his briefcase. Didn't you know?' Rafi looked surprised.

I felt my stomach turn. It felt as if a cauldron of agony had been emptied over my head. The impact on my emotions was overwhelming. Ali had been here but hadn't come to see me? Why? Then, what if he had? Or had he? My thoughts turned inwards. Could he have opened the door and found Linah and me naked? Perhaps he had seen the thrill in my eyes as I wrapped my tongue around my Jewish darling's erect nipples, or as I drank from her flowing nectar? Perhaps he had stood there watching, hearing her sweet moans as she took me inside her. Watching our bodies entwined in pleasurable rhythm, hearing our heavy breathing? Out of this swirl of thought, I gave Rafi an answer.

'No, I didn't know... Ali hasn't said anything...' My voice trembled as a chill went through my body.

Rafi freed two plastic chairs from a stack, set them before us and gestured towards them. We sat down.

'Nana. Where's Ali?' His voice was concerned.

'I don't know.'

'That's strange. Why? Ali is like your brother.'

'I'm not sure, Rafi... We are all very worried about him. After the death of Farrah's brother, I fear he began walking down a very dark road.'

'I sensed that... But what about Farrah? He is in heaven with this young woman. What's she like? I can't wait to meet her.'

In heaven? He didn't know Farrah had been murdered.

'Rafi... The rest to your life. Farrah is dead. She was killed outside Aboud. Settlers, without a doubt...'

'Allah have mercy upon her soul!'

'We buried her Wednesday. Then Ali disappeared...'

'Disappeared? First you tell me Farrah is dead, then you tell me you can't find Ali. Jesus, Nana! Is there anything else you haven't told me?'

The world was crumbling around me and in front of me sat Rafi. I knew he was shifting between the dark and the light. Who else to unknot this ganglion of conflict with? I decided to pull the rope and hoped I held the right end.

'I'm in love with a Jewish woman. She's a soldier. And she's probably getting ready for war, as we speak.'

Rafi looked as if he was stuck in a time warp. As if someone had presented him with Netanyahu's head on a platter and told him he could split it with an axe. He was literally speechless. We sat there tracing the lines along the wooden floor. We followed them until we reached each other's feet, looked up and were finally staring into each other's eyes.

Of all the people I had imagined talking to about Linah, Rafi was the last. I hadn't even thought of him. Now I had told him and with that, I had surrendered all of my secrets. I had wanted desperately to breathe again, and in an instant all my fears were gone. He leaned back in his chair, ran both his hands through his silver-grey hair and thought for a long time. All the while, he didn't say a word. He looked back over his shoulders towards the door and back again. His spine arched as he put his hands on his knees and tightened like a bow as he sat up straight. He voiced his response in a determined, slow and unexpected way.

'Life… It never fails to surprise me…'

I imagined his mind was sorting through a barrage of questions, as was mine. It was my turn to ask questions. I opened up calmly.

'Rafi, who is Mohammed? The young man who came to pick up the money from you? Who is he?'

Rafi dropped his jaw. The knot was definitely being untied.

'So Ali *did* tell you about him.'

'Ali?' I was confused. What was Rafi saying to me?

'Yes, Ali… He met Mohammed the day he came to get his money. The same day Mohammed came to pick up the briefcase.'

'The briefcase full of money?' I struck with my sword. I hadn't thought.

Rafi hesitated momentarily. He pierced me with questioning eyes.

'Yes… Why are you asking me about Mohammed, then? You already know…'

'No, I don't. I guessed it when Mohammed came to pick up the briefcase. He gave me a card that had the name of someone named Khaled. Then he left. I had no idea he had met with Ali that day…'

'Mohammed told me that Ali had made the arrangements with him, so… I thought you knew…'

'Which arrangements? With Khaled? Or with Mohammed?' I was bewildered. The confusion and sensation of having a knife pushed through my back was gut-wrenching.

'Khaled is Mohammed's father. Mohammed works for him…'

'Which arrangements, Rafi? What is Ali up to?' My voice trembled.

'He's going to Gaza. Khaled will get him in. Mohammed is his voice here, in the Sinai, in Gaza…'

'And the briefcase?'

'*Fighting*, Nana… Death is the cheap part of it…'

'Why is Ali going?'

'Why do we kill, Nana? Because otherwise we ourselves will be killed.'

Then I spoke before I thought.

'Did you kill your father?' My fear flared up like a lighthouse on a dark stormy sea.

'Would you like the key to the basement?' Rafi was surprisingly calm.

'I'm sorry, Rafi.'

'Don't be. You are scared. Your best friend, your brother, has gone behind your back.'

'Maybe he's trying to protect me.'

'Let's say he was. Why?'

'Because I'd follow him!'

'Nothing is stopping you.'

'Where is Ali, now?'

'Mohammed will know…'

'Where is *he*?' I became irritable.

'Calm down. I'll give you his phone number. He'll be either here or in Ramallah.'

Rafi took out his cell phone from his trousers and scrutinised it, cursing at the many Mohammeds in his contacts, finally, finding the right number. He dictated it and I pressed the digits on my phone. A piece of the puzzle was in my hand; I felt nauseated.

'Rafi?'

'*Yes?*'

'Why did you put Ali in touch with Mohammed?'

Rafi was about to reply but stopped. He took a deep breath, sighed. Another stop. Then he dropped his elbows to his thighs and stared at the wooden floor. He repeated the sequence. Finally, he sat straight and said the words. There was no wavering in his voice.

'Ali came to me, Nana. I promised him I wouldn't tell you. He said he wanted to honour the death of Farrah's brother Abdullah with revenge. But he was lying; there was something else in his eyes. The same thing as when he approached me before that time, and I sent him walking. So, he began staying away. His reasons were the same, though. He wanted blood…'

'Why?'

'Do you want me to reply to that?'

'No…'

Rafi excused himself to me. He got up and walked towards the door. Before he opened it, he turned to me.

'Love is a beautiful thing, the only antidote to hatred. But… Don't be afraid to ask me if you need… eh… *Help*… And don't wait too long… You never know what might happen… *Tomorrow*.'

The way he said it would not leave my mind. Rafi, I was coming to realise, was a fixer. A man who worked both sides. A man whose social skills were his means of survival. He was well-connected and he had a lot of friends. And likely a lot of enemies as his friends.

I couldn't tell whether I was sitting or standing, sleeping or awake. I was in a vacuum without direction. The knot had been untied and the rope was around my neck. A fuse had been lit inside my head and a bomb was set to go off. I wanted to blow myself into two pieces. One for each of the loved ones of my life.

I imprisoned the child who let the frog go.

25

Tomorrow came and the bombs were already falling. The distant sound of fighter planes blended with the breakfast TV news. Seven men had been killed and bombs had been dropped on Gaza overnight. The one-and-a-half-second clip of a man running with a blood-soaked child slumped in his arms, flashed across the screen. The flatbread between my fingers disintegrated as my fists closed in anger. My parents watched in silence, not saying a word. My mother prayed in whispers and my dad kept anxiously rubbing his forehead. The warlords dived into their stockpiles of hatred but it was no real fight. It was an onslaught. How could they possibly call it a war? No matter how much faith the resistance held, the almighty juggernaut of the Israelis was becoming nothing but a wild, merciless killing spree. The underdog standing up to the über-bully could only result in one-sided devastation. As the news flicked back to camera flashes and politicians, the text at the bottom of the screen changed.

Netanyahu says it's time to 'take off the gloves' against Hamas.

I went up to my room and sat on the bed. I found Mohammed's number. I had saved it as *Mohammed Ibn*[50] *Khaled*. But as I was about to call, my mind wandered off. My elbow rested on my thigh and I stared at the cellphone display. I moved my thumb and located Linah's number. My heart thumped in my chest as I pressed the call button. I put the phone to my ear and waited. It took a little longer than usual and suddenly Linah's voice sang into my ear. It was the answering machine. I hadn't heard it before. It was the first time I'd tried to call her. I didn't pay attention to what she was saying,

---

50 Son of.

just fell into the musical stream of her voice and floated along. The *beep* at the end of her message pulled me back to earth and I almost dropped the phone as I hit the red button and hung up. A couple of seconds must have been recorded. I pushed the call button once more. And, again, fell into the flowing embrace of her voice. She was right next to me, talking into my ear, kissing it gently. The end was expected this time. I waited a second before I exhaled and spoke.

'*Shalom*... It's me, Nana... If there are a few missed calls from me it's because I love the sound of your voice...'

For a moment, I hoped for a reply. I wanted to say more and then I didn't. I hung up and kept looking at the phone. I wished she would ring. I wished for so many things to be different while I was sitting there. But as I scrolled downwards again to Mohammed's number I knew things were about to change—though to what, I did not know. I pressed the call button. It took even longer than when I tried Linah's number. He answered.

'*El Salaamu Aleikum*.'

'*El Salaamu Aleikum*... I am Adnan. We met at—'

Mohammed cut me off.

'I was told you'd call me. We can't talk on the phone. Wait outside *Osama's Pizza* on Rukab street in Ramallah. Pretend you're looking at the menu in the window. Do you know this place?'

'Eh... No... But I'm sure I will find it.'

'Good. Go there as soon as you can and wait. Someone will come to meet you. They are listening to this call, I'm sure you know that. Leave your phone at home so they don't know when you are leaving.'

'I understand.'

'*Salaam*.' Mohammed hung up before I could reply.

Salaam... I said to myself as my mind wandered off. I would probably not have been able to call him if Rafi hadn't told him. The way we would meet was the usual. He knew the Israelis were listening, so he made it so they couldn't be everywhere all at once. Waiting on the street, having a stranger meet me, most likely going through a number of people before actually meeting him. Just in case we were important to them, which would only rest on the absurdity of their imagination.

Muhkamas, the Qalandia checkpoint and the Ofer prison are very close to each other and within a ten-kilometre radius of Ramallah. The city is home to the Palestinian seat of government and one of the hardest to access. A network of roads, none of them in Israel, link the city's roads with those of Jerusalem and those built for the Israeli settlers in the West Bank. The roads also connect the settler *islands* to Israel through *hassle-free* settler checkpoints which aren't usable by Palestinians. It's a confusing display of how separation works, practically. Or doesn't.

I caught a *servees*[51] that took me through the Jaba junction then north into Ramallah. Tyres burnt at the Hizme checkpoint. Boys were shooting pebbles with slingshots at soldiers. Tear gas went the other way. The young men ran. Traffic moved slowly as Israeli tanks formed a bottleneck on the road. Clearly, the soldiers were under orders to avoid a major confrontation as they hardly reacted while stones were pelted at them from all around. Fighter jets were in the sky and people turned their heads as they approached or roared overhead. The bombs they carried under their wings would be released over Gaza. As we snaked our way through the tanks and armoured vehicles, a shower of stones was launched by a group of young men hiding between burnt-out cars and large blocks of concrete. The driver read them the way a fisherman reads waves on the sea. Not one stone hit our yellow minibus.

The *servees* made its way through the hustle and bustle of Ramallah, the driver stopping at random as passengers asked to be set off or others hailed him to get on. I decided to get off near the city centre, like most of the others. Numerous buses converged in a yellow swarm with hordes of people filling the spaces in between cars, shopping bags and kids dragged along in a stratum that adults

51 A minibus, typically a converted van.

could only see if crawling on their knees. A large group of people were gathered, as a demonstration was about to start. At their forefront was a bearded man surrounded by even more bearded men in suits. He yelled passionately into the microphone, sounding the cry of resistance, pleading for the world to stand up for the Palestinian people. As I walked behind him, he chanted words the crowd repeated so loudly my body throbbed.

'FALASTINE HU'RA!' FREE PALESTINE!

As the chant receded, other chants rose in the distance from smaller groups in the crowd.

'Khaybar, Khaybar ya Yahud, jaysh Mohammed sawfa ya'ud!' Khaybar, Khaybar you, Jews, the army of Mohammed will return.

The slogan evoked the story of the battle between the prophet Mohammed and the Jews of the town of Khaybar in ancient times, a battle the Jews lost. My steps hastened while at the same time my mind questioned the need to resurrect the past.

Isn't subjugation for peace really what is asked of us now. Isn't that always the oppressor's preference?

I found Osama's Pizza. It was a small place, typical, with the usual steel shutters that were rolled up to just above the door height. To its left was a clothes shop, to its right a staircase. There were no people inside and it looked as if the place was only just opening up. Perhaps someone was in the back. I spotted the tiny menu in the window: an A4 sheet with the different types of pizzas served in small, medium and large. Another, much larger menu hung inside with a selection of snacks and salads.

Life goes on during conflict. People still eat and drink, talk and laugh. I remembered Bilal and the day he put his hand down his pocket and pulled up small rocks instead of coins. I remembered his laughter, then my own laughter and I remembered Omar, the owner, laughing until tears came out of his eyes. I remember the Israelis watching us, undecided what to do. We were three *men*, though I was a child, laughing our hearts out while looking at rocks on the counter. We had seen the soldiers before. They knew who we were but even with rocks in front of us, we somehow managed to disarm them with our laughter. I remember they turned around and walked away. I stood outside Osama's grinning as I remembered this moment from the past, in another place. My grin froze as I imagined that the soldiers had kept walking and had never returned. I cursed my imagination, the gullible child inside me. We were still fighting. Bilal's dreams hadn't come true. Someone else had taken them. Omar's laughter had been silenced. His son, Ahmed, threw a lump of dough at the back of a soldier who hadn't paid for his shawarma. The soldier swung around and fired a single bullet right through his heart. Ahmed died on the spot; the soldier was never charged. Instead, the army sued Omar. It was at the beginning of a preposterous zero-tolerance policy. They claimed the food had been unclean and the soldier had to be relieved of duty for several days, costing the Israeli taxpayer as much as what Omar's life depended on, his small shop.

'What were you grinning at?'

A door opened to the right of Osama's Pizza and a boy poked out his head.

'Nothing... What's your name, my son?' I said in a fatherly voice.

'Adnan. Just like you. Come with me.'

The boy spoke like a little soldier. He was short, just about a metre in height. I hesitated, then moved towards him. He exited the door and walked up the road. I followed him as he took small hasty steps, almost jogging.

'How old are you?' I asked him as we walked.

'I'm nine. Almost ten.'

He stopped all of sudden, and with his index finger moving quickly, he directed me closer to him.

'See that green Mercedes over there?'

'Yes.'

'Go and sit in it. If no one has shot you after five minutes, someone will come to you.'

'Just like that?'

'Yes. Go in peace.'

Nine-year-old Adnan moved in hasty steps back down Rukab street and disappeared through the door he had come out of. I turned around and looked at the old green Mercedes. My thoughts couldn't collect. Either I would walk forward or just walk away.

But I couldn't walk away. In large strides I went up to the car. I closed my eyes before I opened the passenger door. Perhaps the whole thing would blow up and that would be it. But it didn't. I remained for a moment with the door open, looking at the light brown seat. I got in, closed my eyes as I sat down and shut the door. It was quiet. I listened to my breathing.

The chanting from the demonstration was all I could hear from the outside. It came in waves. The gaps between the crests and the troughs were short. The speaker's voice rose passionately until the crowd erupted in a roar, then followed a short inaudible murmur, again followed by an amplified chant. The energy soared, driven by a blast that would suddenly surge like wind in the sail to push the rage to greater heights.

Allahu Akbar! Allah is great!

The streets outside were on fire. Lives were bursting with rage. I felt my own bitterness mixed with the feelings of having been deceived. And the self-reproach of having deceived the world around me. The fighting was bringing out the worst character in ourselves. The diabolical, boorish and vengeful. The scavenger beast that feeds on the soul-shredding affair between *Us* and *Them*.

I saw myself in the side view mirror.

And there was that creature.

26

Morning clouds still hadn't lifted, and the air was hot and muggy. Sweat was running down my back. I rolled down the window and took a deep breath, stared out and traced the cars parked along the sidewalk. At the far end, a man was approaching. He moved in a slow and painful walk. I studied him from top to bottom. Nothing appeared to be missing. It was only his walk that was awkward. Every time he took a step, he'd shift his weight onto his walking stick and throw his right foot forward. The limp was hard, almost a snap in his spine. He was fit, though, muscles contoured through his T-shirt and across his chest Arabic letters read:

WE DON'T WANT TO FIGHT,
BUT BLACK IS THE SEA,
UNTIL WE ARE FREE!

His beard was neatly shaved around his almost square face. Black hair on fairly fair skin with a set of emerald blue eyes that found my own and dilated.

As he came near, he went through the narrow space between the bonnet of the car I was sitting in and the rear of the car in front. He pulled himself across and slithered around, holding onto the side of the car until he reached the side mirror. Supporting himself against the car, he put one hand around the mirror and the other to me, palm facing up.

'May Allah give you wealth, may he provide you a life in safety and happiness. May Allah have given you a kind heart… May Allah—'

'May Allah keep you and keep you safe!' I interrupted, not moving my eyes away.

He stopped his iteration. Then he began again.

'May Allah…'

I interrupted once again, my voice sincere.

'*Insha'Allah*, Allah will provide you with happiness, good health and fortune. But, good man… Surely you have something to offer me. I see Allah has given you two hands. Surely Allah has also given you a fine physique and, no doubt, a fine mind—or am I wrong?'

He put his hands down and stared at me. I thought the time wasn't right for a discussion, that I should perhaps give him something and send him on his way. Then I noticed the healed shrapnel scars on the hand he lowered. Scars covered his whole hand, and as I made out, part of his face that hadn't been shielded by it when he was injured.

I felt like an idiot sitting in the car asking a beggar to make his own way. I was about to ask him how much he needed, when he walked away. I watched him in the side mirror. Snap, step, snap, step, snap, step. Eventually he was just a tiny man in the window and it almost looked as if he walked straight. I leaned forward to take a better look in the mirror but was startled by the driver's door suddenly being pulled open. A woman sat down in the seat. She slammed the door shut, put keys in the ignition and turned to me.

'*A'Salaamu Aleikum,* ya Adnan.' She extended her hand and I shook it briefly. It was warm. My eyes went from hers, sparkling brown, and flashed down to her legs. I noticed my own action with a twinge of embarrassment. Since I had met Linah, my mind had opened up to a different level of fantasy. I had lost my innocence. The woman turned the key and the engine started reluctantly. She pumped the gas a few times with a satisfied smile and glanced down at the gear stick, shifting it to D for drive. The car jolted a bit. She smiled again, this time to me as well and turned the wheel.

'Who are you and where are we going?' I asked her.

'I'm Lina. And you're Adnan!' Then she grinned. 'We're going on an adventure.'

I felt a sudden flush. Had Rafi told them about Linah? Where was I going?

'Is your name really Lina? And how do you know I'm Adnan? We've never met before.'

She laughed and her profile grew with it. Her cheeks lifted and her lips stretched, showing pearly white teeth. I could smell her perfume. It was subtle to the senses, but there I was, feeling a burning attraction rushing through my veins. This awareness came with a touch of guilt.

'Is Lina not good enough for you? And do you think I just get into any parked car and drive away with a guy I don't know? Come on, Adnan… Come on…'

'I didn't say your name is not good enough. On the contrary, I like it a lot. I just thought…'

'What? That we knew the name of some girlfriend of yours? Adnan… Come on…'

I wanted the seat to swallow me. I remained silent and looked at her while she was driving, swearing at the traffic, honking, telling an older lady to watch out when she crossed the road. I looked away when she saw I was looking at her. She had the widest smile looking at me. I couldn't help but think I knew nothing about women in the cities.

'You are a very handsome man. And fit too!'

She took one hand off the wheel and squeezed my left biceps hard. I jolted and pushed myself up and back in the chair. She didn't care. Her hand moved across my chest and over my abdomen, all the way down to my belt and up again. Her hand moved in circles, the fingers occasionally pressing in. I pushed back with my legs and sat up straight, tensing every muscle.

'What? Have you got a girlfriend or something? In any case, very nice…'

'What are you doing?'

'By Allah, are you really asking me?'

She spoke while navigating her way through the crowds. We had gone around the demonstration and were slowly headed north, as far as I could make out. I answered, although I was confused.

'What if *I* touched you like that, now?'

'Tell me, are you man or a boy? Hold on! Let me have a look.'

She turned to me for a short moment and blinked an eye. Was she flirting with me or just *pulling my leg*? Her hair was as black as coal, long and wavy. It contrasted with her light-hued eyes.

'Okay, you *are* a handsome man... What else could it be...?' She thought for a while. 'Ah, got it. Where are you from, Adnan?'

'I was born in Budrus but moved around the villages as well...' I suspected she was talking about my apparent innocence. I caught her as she was about to laugh.

'Lina, just because I'm from the country doesn't mean I don't know anything!'

'Oh... So, you do?'

'Yes... But what is it to you, anyway? And how do you know I'm Adnan?'

Lina smiled. Looked at me briefly again. I so liked her eyes. They were courageous, independent. She was right, she was very different from the girls in the villages. And I was very different from the men in the cities. Ali was, too, as were all the men I'd grown up with. Our fingers worked terribly on smart phones. I was reminded of that every time I shook hands with someone from the city.

We approached a barrier, one of simple construction. A gate followed by a couple of steel shelters for shade. Concrete barriers were placed to form two lanes, and at the far end were used to block the exit. A couple of soldiers stood guard in a small cubicle and another three soldiers stood further on.

'This is Beit El checkpoint. It's only open to those authorised. We're not allowed to exit here but we're still going to go through it, so don't speak and pretend you're *my customer*.'

'Your customer?'

'Didn't you say you knew it all?' Lina pursed her lips as if kissing me and smiled.

'*Yalla*, be serious about it. They're bombing Gaza today, so they'll be on alert. Mind you it looks very quiet here, right now.' She took her foot off the gas and the car slowed down.

I leaned over and put my hands on Lina's shoulders. I turned to her ear… Big shiny rings hanging from them. With the movement of the car, my nose touched. That wasn't deliberate but it was deliberate when I moved my head down to her neck, touching. Her skin was smooth, her body scent underneath the perfume tantalising. I kissed her softly on her neck.

'I said customer, not boyfriend!'

'Sorry.'

'It's okay… It was nice.'

How does a customer kiss? I didn't know, after all…

We pulled up next to two soldiers. I remained leaning on to Lina, took her straight black hair between my fingers and played with it. One of them smiled widely and walked forward to meet the car at the tilting gate. He glanced at me but eyed off Lina in an amorous manner. Lina cut the engine.

'David! David!'

'Shalom, Lina… What are you doing here, Hot Stuff?'

'David… You're going to make me blush!'

Had my world suddenly been turned upside down? Was this really happening? Lina was speaking fluent Hebrew. And their laughter…

Lina leaned out of the window and David crouched down with the butt of his rifle resting on the ground between his legs. She whispered to him.

'David… I need to take this guy back to Shiloh, but I can't exit south. Not today… Can you help me out again?'

'Lina… Out of all days, today?'

'I'll make it up to you… Aren't you the man in charge?'

David's face lit up in excitement. Lina quickly ran her index finger from his nose to his chin, firmly pushing his lower lip down until it let go with a light pop.

'Let me see what I can do…'

David walked over to the other soldier. Spoke to him for a minute, then he waved his arm in the air like a helicopter to the men further down the checkpoint. I watched through the window as one of them got on to a forklift and moved the concrete slab to the side. He banged the trunk of the car. Lina pulled the lever below and it opened with a hollow bang. The other soldier stood right in front of us. Lina popped the bonnet.

Without turning her head Lina whispered to me.

'Don't say a word!'

I wasn't going to. Why had she mentioned Shiloh? That place was a settlement. Another soulless dot on the map, strategically positioned with strategically laid streets, and strategically occupied by settlers as a statement of Zionist supremacy. I glanced up in the mirror and thought it couldn't be my looks because I looked Palestinian. Or did I? I felt a shiver throughout my body. Could it be that I resembled the Israelis so much that it had kept me out of the death room? Could I pass for a Jew? I glanced at the rear-view mirror once again and in it, I saw my profile. My nose which I had compared to Ali's protruding one, was after all large. It was as rugged as our faces. My beard was about a week old. My skin fair from working indoors.

David came back up to Lina and put one arm on the roof of the car. His right arm held his rifle with a finger still on the trigger. He leaned forward and eyed me out before turning to Lina.

'I'll call you next week…'

'Make it before noon.'

David banged the roof of the car and Lina turned the key as the tilt gate was lifted. Rifles pointed to the ground as we drove through the checkpoint. Eyes peered at us. Lina's turned to me.

We exchanged the stare of betrayal.

27

The only official crossing between Israel and neighbouring Jordan is the King Hussein Bridge. It's also named the Allenby Bridge, a reminder of British imperialism and the governor, Edmund Allenby. From Ramallah we headed north and then east. I didn't have a Palestinian passport nor papers to exit the crossing that serves as the only exit-entry point for West Bank Palestinians. I'd have to get to Jordan by crossing the Jordan River and then head south to cross the Aqaba to Sinai in Egypt to then head north to Gaza through the tunnels. I wondered why Rafi hadn't extended my work permit—he knew I was going after Ali. Perhaps he knew it would be too difficult for me making it through the border tunnels into Gaza without being caught. A lot of questions were going through my mind.

We headed to Al-Auja. There, Lina told me, someone would accompany me across the Jordan River. I wasn't asked whether I wanted to or not. Lina told me, and that was all I knew at the time. I knew nothing of where Al-Auja was, except it was very close to the Jordan River, a large village that has lived on farming for centuries. The area is arid; the only reason there are people and villages there, is because it has natural springs and deposits of ground water.

We drove through the village and headed north along the main road. After a short way, Lina pulled up at a restaurant, Abu Hussein's. I was hungry. The stop came at just the right time. Lina picked a table in a far corner and a young waiter brought us a couple of menus. Lina did all the talking. He took her order as he looked at both of us, glancing conspicuously every time he looked up from the small notepad in his hand.

'Why?' I asked.

My tone was calm. During the hour or so it took us from the checkpoint, I'd hardly spoken a word; Lina had done most of it. The only outer reminder of what we were doing or where we were heading was the frequent roar of fighter jets. My thoughts were tumbling over, and out of the blue, I expressed them.

'Why? Why do we choose to do what we choose to do? Why, is always a good question…'

Lina understood. She replied for herself, without any hesitation, in a remarkable monologue.

'Because I see the emotions I stir in them; and I'm not afraid of *them*, either. I see the enmity and the jealousy and all the responses that are involved. Of course, I'd die for another line of work, but I can't think too much about it. It's too unnerving. I keep going, even if it breaks my heart. Besides, some of the men who have had me, the men in power, would never allow me to do anything else.'

I didn't speak for a while. I watched her staring preoccupied into nowhere, not knowing whether to speak at all. In the end, I replied.

'We all have a broken heart but there is no need to step on it…'

Lina didn't hear me. She was still replying to my aired thoughts.

'It is habit… Everything we do is habit, even fighting each other. And even that becomes routine. We are caught in our habits of routine because we function in habit. Our habits of ideas, concepts, the habit of being a Palestinian. Or a Jew…'

'That's dangerous…' I said, quietly. Lina went on.

'Yes, we are afraid of danger, aren't we? And to be aware of habit has its own danger.'

What an unusual woman, philosophising while on an undisclosed journey.

And she kept talking.

'We are afraid of not knowing, aren't we? Of not being certain… But… There is great beauty, a great vitality, in not being certain. Security and fear is insanity. None of us want that, still what we do is, we break one habit and create a more pleasant habit…'

'So, why don't you do that…?'

'Because it would break my heart.'

And with that Lina threw a piercing stare straight into my eyes. She had heard me after all.

I was a carver of wood. Lina carved into men's hearts. And the uncertainty of not knowing the meaning of that, I found insanely attractive. The allure of it lay in my sudden fantasy of her carving my heart as it beat. It didn't mean treachery, rather, fearfully resisting the hooks of desire.

And I harboured this fear in rapt fascination.

28

A man, tall and wide, climbed out of a grey car. The car left straight after. The man took firm strides towards the entrance of the restaurant. A group of boys were playing soccer, raising swirling dust clouds on the parking lot. The leather ball, worn to a flannel look, rolled to the man's feet. He flicked it up in the air, let it drop between his shoulder blades, down his back and kicked it back to the boys with his heel. This was a man to watch. He wore a plain white V-neck T-shirt and black cargo pants. His head was almost box-shaped with a well-groomed beard. It wasn't until he opened the entrance door and saw us that I recognised his piercing emerald-blue eyes. He walked towards us as Lina rose to meet him. I stood up as well.

He whispered something to Lina before turning to me. She remained standing with a disappointed expression before walking to the back of the restaurant towards the toilets. The man turned to me.

'*Asalaamu aleikum*. I am Salama,' he thundered, extending his hand. When I took it, his firm grip hurt.

'*We'aleikum a'salaam*. I am Adnan. I see your leg is better...'

'Hahaha!' he laughed. 'We had to make sure. We're still here. True or not?'

He was right. If either of us had been watched back in Ramallah, we'd both be dead. Period. Salama sat down and poured himself a glass of water. He flipped the mineral bottle and showed me the brand. It said *Mekorot*. The Israeli water corporation which steals the water below the West Bank. Palestinians are forbidden to access the aquifer. Springs that once sustained villages like Auja have dried out or been systematically destroyed. The Israeli settlements drain the underground to fill up their swimming pools, irrigate their farms and water their livestock. The Palestinians are left out to dry.

'We must pay for the water of our own land.' Salama drank the water and set the glass down.

'Have you finished eating?'

'*Alhamduallah.*'[52]

'*Yalla*, let's go for a drive.'

'What about Lina?'

There was a moment before Salama replied.

'Don't worry about her, Adnan. Lina doesn't belong to anyone…'

'What makes you so sure?' I felt an anxious anger in my chest.

Salama leaned over and composed an almost Godfatherly voice.

'Adnan… Lina is a beautiful woman but she has been opened by the enemy. He didn't love her of course… And when he abandoned her—she came to me. She wanted to join the fight. We asked her to use herself as her beauty is her best weapon, and she agreed. She will sacrifice her soul until it one day will be drained. Until then, she lets the enemy empty himself inside her as he tells her their secrets. But one day they will find her out and kill her. That is God's punishment. The same punishment that commands us not to touch her. Do you understand?'

The heartless cruelty of Salama's reasoning. The stupendous unchallenged tribal minds of the world I grew up in but hadn't chosen. I felt like screaming out my feelings for Linah, my yearning for her and watch Salama's face turn as my words spilled treason. But I didn't. We were enemies to each other. Enemies to ourselves. All of us. I swallowed and gave what I knew was the right answer.

'I understand.'

Salama grabbed the car keys on the table and I left enough money under a plate to tip the waiter effectively. We walked outside and got into the Mercedes. Salama drove fast. We went further east, away from the main road. A dirt track took us away from the scorched

---

52 *Al-ḥamdu li-llāh* or *alhamdulillah*, also known as Tahmid, is an Arabic phrase meaning: Praise be to the Lord, sometimes translated as: Thank Lord!

hills and past flat, wasted farmland. Through the afternoon haze we looked across a parched brown valley. In the distance, green-grey vegetation marked the course of the Jordan River. For a moment, it seemed within easy reach. Salama stopped and left the engine idling.

'There's an electric fence, a minefield, and of course the Israeli army,' he said smiling. 'When night falls, you will cross safely. *Insha'Allah*...'

'You're not coming?'

'No, Atef will meet you.'

'Who is he?'

'One of my men.'

I thought of Lina for a second and I'm not sure why, but I trusted Lina. A part of me wanted to help her escape. From both her enemies.

'Can you let Lina go as well, at least to Aqaba? A couple travels easier, I'm sure you agree...'

Salama turned his head swiftly. He had clearly become annoyed with me. I stared into his eyes. In there, I saw doubt. The doubt behind the words we choose to believe but fear to question.

'It appears you do *not* understand, Adnan, but so be it...'

I didn't reply. Salama didn't say another word. He started the engine and we went back to Abu Hussein's. He asked me to stay in the car. He went inside and walked up to Lina. He didn't sit down, just dropped the keys on the table in front of her, said something briefly and went up to the counter where he paid to use their phone. Shortly after, the same grey Peugeot that had dropped him off, came and picked him up. He walked past me, turning his head towards me as if I was prey to the hunter. He got in the car and it took off, covering the entire parking lot in a fog of dust.

I looked through the windows. Lina hadn't moved her eyes from me. They smiled. My heart raced in excitement between Lina and Linah.

Both, just like myself, enemies to their own.

⬥⬥⬥

'May Allah be with you.'

The young waiter removed the plates and cups that had piled up on the table. He didn't look at me. He just said the words, took the dishes and walked away. Lina had stepped outside, her cell phone to her ear. She was laughing, smiling, throwing her head back as she ran her fingers through her hair. She had a friend on the phone. I could hear her voice through the glass, in between the cars whooshing by in the background. The restaurant was about to close for the day. Lina had told me Salama would tell Atef to arrive *some time* after it closed.

As the sun sank behind the horizon, the sky turned to a blaze of fire slowly extinguished by the encroaching darkness. Yellow light covered the parking lot as we waited in the car, watching the staff leave one by one. A couple of older men sat with cups of tea outside, waving them off one by one. Eventually, they expressed their parting and left as well. In the distance, the sound of jets kept breaking the silence. The occasional car passed behind us. Lina and I hadn't exchanged a word for a long time. I was so tired that I reclined the seat and closed my eyes.

Her lips touched mine. Just barely. They were soft. I didn't want them to let go, I wanted them closer. I wanted to kiss them deeper. But they withdrew. I found myself literally swimming in the green of Linah's eyes. I reached the magic ring around the iris and held on to it. Behind my back, the freckle in the middle of the yellow line was beating like a heart. I let go and swam towards it. As I got close, I felt it draw my own heart towards it.

It seemed as if Linah was talking to me. I must have said it out loud.

'Linah... Where are you?'

And then I felt a pair of lips touch mine. I opened my eyes and looked straight into Lina's eyes. I gasped a quick and deep breath. Then she kissed me again. I didn't kiss her back but I didn't resist either. I let her lips touch mine, not letting go straight away. Lina's eyes went inquisitively back and forth between mine. She was going to kiss me once again but pulled herself back to the driver's seat.

'Who's Lina? Or is it, Lina-h?'

Lina gave me an unevadable look. Her question took me by surprise. She didn't know, but she had just found out. It was a sharp question I wasn't ready for and my silence spoke for itself. My mind raced to conjure an answer but as I turned my head, seeing her with her back against the door staring at me, a car pulled up behind us. The headlights blinded me and I put my hand up to my eyes. I heard a door open, Lina turned and put her hand up as well. We couldn't see anything but a trained high beam and the diesel smoke in its outline. The door slammed and the lights turned away to disappear with red tail lights trailing south.

A man opened the rear door and got in.

'Good evening, Atef…' Lina said, without looking at him.

'Good evening,' he replied and looked at me. 'Adnan?'

'Yes.' I extended my hand and he shook it.

'Adnan and Lina. *Yalla beena*,' he said, laughing.

I could hardly see Atef. In the dim light he had a gentle appearance, most likely in his forties. He had a moustache and a deep voice and seemed to smile most of the time. A fatherly smile. He kept praying muffled prayers to himself as Lina pulled out of the car park and drove down the same way Salama had taken me earlier. She drove slowly with the lights off. Halfway from where Salama and I had stopped, there was a deserted Bedouin tent at the foot of the hill. I'd seen it earlier. It barely rested itself on two pairs of pillars. We parked under it and got out. Atef crouched down and began drawing on the sand.

'This is where we are now.' He drew a cross and a snaking line further away that indicated the river.

'We will walk away from the road along the foot of the hill. If you hear a buzzing sound, stop and crouch down. Do not lie flat. Make yourself into a ball.'

Histrionically, Atef's body language followed his words. He had a lot to tell, everything in one go; we would not be able to speak when we got nearer the border.

'There are a few short tunnels under the electric fence. The army finds them as they patrol and blow them up. So, we dig new ones when we can. Tonight people will be digging to the north, so we have to try our luck south. Once we find a tunnel, I'll bid you farewell and ask for Allah's protection for your journey. I will see you appear on the other side. Here you must not stand up. There is a path the military uses for patrol. There are mines on both sides. Crawl on all fours, following the sticks. The chopsticks! You must not deviate from the chopsticks! There could be a mine just to the left or just to the right. Keep the stick between your knees and keep moving! If one is missing, look further for the next one or slightly to the sides. But always move in a straight line between the sticks and be careful when you cross the dirt path! Do not move too fast or they will see you. Do not stop! They will see you. There are cameras and sensors but they will not be triggered if you do as I tell you. Just keep moving until eventually, the rocks and sand underneath you will turn into mud. This is the marshland. Keep crawling. Keep following the sticks! They will take you through the bushes. It's dark and it's scary and your arms may sink deep. Don't panic. Once you reach the river, lie flat in the water. There are snakes, but splash lightly and they'll go away. Avoid swallowing the dirty water. Once you reach the other side, look out for the Jordanian army there. Once you've crossed their path, you'll find yourself in between farms. There are no mines there. Keep heading east until you see an old water well. Bilal will be waiting for you there with phones and food. Any questions?'

Bilal...

Besides the childhood memories that momentarily flooded me, I had a feeling that I hadn't thought about what I was doing at all. I hadn't questioned where I was going. I hadn't told my parents that I had left. I imagined my mother worrying herself sick. A war had begun. Bombs were being thrown over Gaza and I was about to cross a minefield. I didn't even have a backpack or a phone. All I carried was my wallet. I watched Lina leave her bag and phone in the car for Atef to hold. She wore jeans and sneakers; she, too, didn't ask a single question.

We walked behind Atef. He walked in a steady, calm pace. Lina faced the ground. She was preoccupied, in another world from mine. I was heading towards a river. Heading towards Ali. I wasn't even sure whether I was trying to find him or trying to find answers for myself.

I looked up at the stars. The universe is there, but because we sleep at night, we rarely realise we're part of it and not so very far from it. It just looks far away when we see it and during the day it remains hidden from us. But it's still there, just like our emotions attached to it, attached to us.

Our emotions that we can't always trust.

◈◈◈

It was the deepest breath in my life when I floated out into that smelly water. It was cold and I strained every muscle in my body to avoid hyperventilating. I turned onto my back and glanced at Lina as she watched me being carried out by the stream. She followed suit, and in the short time it took to cross the slow-moving trickle of a once mighty river, there was peace. Sweat poured from the front of my body while ice-cold water cooled my back. The easy roll of moving through the water brought the stars closer, so my breathing relaxed. With small movements I propelled myself across. In my peripheral vision I saw the umbrella of vegetation behind my head encroach upon me like tall, leafy stick figures. I was frightened and turned around, swallowing a bit of the river before settling on my knees. I stared into the stalky shore bushes as I spat the foul water out. Turning around I found Lina floating towards me. I put my arms out in the water and let her drift on to them. She looked back and nodded as I lifted her to a sitting position. We crawled through the stalks, the water receding until my hands abruptly felt the softness of the riverbank. Feeling relief, I stood up and saw dim village lights in the distance. Then I felt my legs give in and I sagged to the ground. Lina was still on her side in the mud, staring at me with open eyes. We were exhausted.

'I am cold … And thirsty…' she said, slowly. Then I could hardly believe it when she started giggling. Then I started chuckling along with her. Finally, we both turned on our backs and simply laughed. Then we faced each other again, glowing with the warmth of our blood rushing, the cold streaks of water on our faces blending with the steaming lines of sweat. Our eyes fixed on each other as my pulse rose and my blood surged, setting every cell in my body on fire. I didn't have to wait for her move. It came instantly. Her lips touched mine in one impetuous move as her eyes held me transfixed. I responded. I kissed her back. At first gently, then passionately. For a moment, between here and there, our attraction found its only way to discharge.

We separated slowly. Our bodies rolled apart, resting on our backs once again. Our eyes were the last to let go before we turned to the sky of the night. We lay there without a word, with thumping hearts and racing minds. When I spoke, my breath had finally retreated to a peaceful draw.

'Come on… Let's find Bilal before he leaves again.'

We got up and supported each other on shaky legs. My knees hurt and I could feel warm blood running down my right shin. At the same time, Lina whispered, 'I'm bleeding, I can feel it…' The stalks on the edge had turned into razors as they broke under our weight. We hurriedly crossed the dirt road without seeing any patrols. Against the backdrop of a small lightbulb, there was an old classic stone-lined well. It was probably serving more as a village hangout than a functioning water source. An old Toyota Sedan was parked next to it with a man in the driver's seat, smoking a cigarette. It had to be him.

The man had already seen us. He must have, because he got out and walked towards us. We stopped because we weren't entirely sure. He was taking fast steps. I could only see his outline, but he was round and short. He reached us, panting, and stopped, almost startled.

'*Ya Allah*, I have to stop eating so much!' He bent and grabbed his knees to catch his breath before standing straight again. He looked at me and then, curiously, at Lina. He had a large moustache that in contrast to the dim reflections in his eyes, looked uninviting.

'They didn't tell me there'd be two of you … And by the grace of Allah, look at your state … *Yalla*! We have to get moving before anyone sees us. I have clean clothes in the car … But not for you.' He looked at Lina. He raised his index finger gesturing an idea, 'Ah, I know! But *yalla*!'

I opened the car door and noticed the tarpaulin across the velvet back seats—he knew what to expect. I helped Lina get in first. Bilal turned to us as he started the car.

'I'm Bilal. And you must be Adnan.' He looked at me.

'*Marhaba*[53]… And this is Lina…'

'*Ahlan wa sahlan*,[54] Lina. You have lit up Jordan! What a fortuitous occasion. Tomorrow I have a guest from the Emirates visiting in Amman. A business man… He will value your company deearrly…'

Lina glared at him through the mirror and remained silent. Even to the uninitiated, the words left his mouth with a smudge of dirt behind them.

'We will go to my sister in Amman and tomorrow I will take you to Aqaba.' Bilal was talking to me.

'*Insha'Allah*,' I replied. I was exhausted.

'Lina, you will stay with her until I return.'

Lina's eyes turned matte, similar to Ali's after Farrah's death. When I saw that, I felt a merciless stake drive through my body. The

53 A way of saying, welcome, also used as a general greeting.
54 Yet another way of saying, hello/welcome.

eyes of vengeance are a window to the rage within. A sharp weapon pointed at both ends to maim or kill. Each end pronouncing the judgement of the avenger's wrath.

I slowly pulled the stake out of my body. My heart pounded and my head spun.

Lina's silent anger crackled like fire through the grinding of her teeth. Bilal took his eyes off the mirror, stepped on the gas and drove us eastwards through the darkened village. I saw the devils outside the car, swirling like ghosts, chasing the angels that were rushing to hide in my heart.

Avoiding their searing forks.

29

Lina had left during the night. She'd placed a small note inside one of my shoes. I saw it when Bilal came to pick me up.

I would never have made it out without you. Thank you. You tore down the shield around my heart. Believe me, Adnan… It turned into an adventure after all…

Lina

PS. I hope she deserves those kisses of yours…

She had kissed the paper, leaving me with a lipstick stamp that I ran past my nose. It smelt like berries of some sort. After the three dots, two dots and a half circle formed a smiley. I smiled back, folded the paper and put it in my wallet.

Bilal wasn't happy that Lina had gone and kept asking where to, saying the police would arrest her and so on. His bet on her had fallen through. Amal, his sister, had taken a liking to Lina, letting her sleep in her own bed and finding her clothes from her younger years to wear. I had suspected Lina was planning her exit. I had closed my eyes and fallen asleep, hearing their voices going through Amal's wardrobe.

Bilal didn't say much as we drove south. He kept lifting his hands off the steering wheel, talking to himself, rehearsing what he would say to his customer, I suppose. Bilal's legs appeared shorter than they should have been. He'd pushed the seat forward to the steering wheel, almost touching his belly. His ears were large and blubbery, his chin double, at least. Amal had given him two bags with food and drinks for us. Earlier she had also prepared for me a delicious breakfast that sufficed for a long time. Bilal kept eating, at the same time smoking a stack of cigarettes. In the four to five hours it took us to reach Aqaba, he almost went through a packet.

When we reached the town, we got out and walked up a narrow staircase in a dun-coloured apartment block. The sea could be seen and smelt through rectangular cut-outs in the wall, sparkling a deep blue in contrast to the scorched brown mountains of the Sinai, in the background. I stopped, put my head out and took a few deep breaths as we walked up. I was in my first foreign country. It was the first time I'd seen the sea and was struck with a wave of fear, sheer exhilaration as well as utter freedom in not knowing where the wind might take me. I was looking for Ali, but suddenly, there and then, I found myself looking for myself. And I was there, somewhere out there. I didn't yet realise the pull of the sea, its ability to awaken a sense of adventure. For the very first time, I could have stepped outside the prison of my own life. But I didn't. I was being led and I let myself be led. I wasn't ready to escape.

I looked up at Bilal, panting, in front of me. We were heading to the seventh floor and every last step was an ordeal for him. In the car he'd briefly mentioned I would need papers to get into Egypt, but I didn't expect to be taken into a passport workshop. First, they took my picture, then I waited. The room was empty with no windows and chalked white walls. I didn't like it. I knew everyone was making money, but I also knew that Rafi must have paid—or perhaps someone else who had a debt with him. Whoever saw a chance for profit got involved. Even when it was two legs and two arms that could hold a gun and wanted to fight. Nobody cared what the reason.

I picked up my passport and looked at it curiously. It said I was a Jordanian. I had few references to passports, but it looked very well made. When Bilal told me it was a real stolen passport, I became more than curious, I was anxious. I wasn't just being made into some fictitious character other than who I was—that would have been bad enough. I was, all of a sudden, supposed to assume the identity of another real person.

Bilal took me then to a hotel where a small bus was waiting. The driver opened the door as I shook Bilal's hand and bid him a safe journey home. He handed me fifty American dollars for the visa and food and told me *a man named Mohammed* would wait for me at the port in Nuweiba. Neither of us mentioned Lina. Then he turned around and left.

The bus had the airconditioning running cold as I entered and about three dozen happy faces stared at me. They were red from too much time in the sun; men and women of all ages, nationalities and colours. I was planted in the middle of some foreigners heading to the Sinai on holiday. Greeting them, I found an empty seat as the driver took off on the short ride to the port. I had barely a smattering of English but caught the words *Gaza* and *war* spoken by some people as they looked worriedly towards the horizon. I had never been on a holiday but I was used to tourists. I knew they didn't know any better. Most of them arrived with a bag full of TV-fear, often annoyed when events scrambled their plans. I wondered if any one of those around me cared for what was happening in Gaza? I wondered if I myself cared. Gazans, I'd been told, were different from *us*. I thought of going with the tourists. I could spend a week on the beach and then disappear and make a life for myself. I'd heard Egyptians were like Palestinians, but I'd also heard Gazans were like Egyptians. It occurred to me that I was just like everyone around me. I had wondered the same in Jerusalem. Perhaps I was indifferent to the young men throwing stones? I wasn't doing it myself. Most people seemed indifferent to *them*—the stone throwers. The tourists didn't think to photograph them either, and as soon as the last stone was thrown, the cameras were back in action. The shopkeepers, often the stone throwers' relatives, smiled as trading resumed and money changed hands.

Before boarding, my passport was checked with no questions asked. The officer didn't even look at me. We left the port. The ferry was large and sleek. There was a lounge with mounted screens. Many eyes were already glued to the American soap that was playing. The only outside area was the rear deck. I walked out and watched the blue turn into white as the propellers churned the water to push us forward. The shaded side was crowded. I remained in the sun and watched Jordan retreat into the far background but grabbed the railing as the ferry began chopping through the waves. The steel bars were burning hot, but I kept holding on. Soon water was splashing over them, cooling them, cooling my hands. I closed my eyes. Droplets sprayed my face with salty water. I licked it and tasted the sea, dreamt my way into the blue and imagined the silent blue world underneath the keel where escaping your enemy depends on the strength of your heart.

The sun turned the sea crimson red as the ferry docked in Nuweiba. I disembarked onto the concrete jetty and followed the long line of westerners. There were a few Arabs scattered, most of them Egyptians, with their distinctive accent. They separated into another line. Both went through the passport control, a square structure with two officers next to each other on either side. The officer at the passport control glanced at me, flicked through the pages of the passport as if shuffling a deck of cards. He was tall, very dark skinned with almost black eyes, all in contrast to his incredibly white uniform. He asked me rudely where my visa was and without waiting for my reply, he slid the passport through a fist-sized arch in the tinted glass separator to the next counter. He waived me along to it, dismissively, without a word, without a glance. I took the few steps and faced the plain-clothed man sitting below counter-height. He licked a couple of government stamps and stuck them onto a page in the passport in almost mechanical speed and rehearsed motion. In exchange for twenty-five American dollars, I was allowed entry. The stamp hit the paper hard as the wonky table underneath emphasised the sorry residual aftermath of colonialism. The man handed me back my passport, between two of his fingers. I took it and walked away, glancing back at the scene, the familiarity.

Mohammed waited for me outside the restricted area of the port. It was young Mohammed who had collected the case at The

Palace. He was leaning against the bonnet of an old Fiat, texting on his cell phone. I saw the Egyptian plates partly covered by his legs and noticed the car was empty. I remained standing and as the crowd quickly dispersed and the area emptied. Then he saw me and signalled as he walked towards me.

'Gratefulness to Allah for your safe arrival. We meet again.' Mohammed shook my hand firmly.

'May Allah keep you. Thank you. And I had a feeling we'd meet again.'

'*Yalla*, we are in a rush. Let's continue talking in the car.'

The engine of the old Fiat squeaked direly as Mohammed drove off. The road towards Taba was turning dark. The mountains created a mud-coloured wall behind his silhouette, reflecting the red of the ocean to the south. Before long, we were engulfed in darkness, only to have light from the flickered high beam of cars travelling the other way.

We didn't speak for quite a while. I was waiting for Mohammed to say something as he sped through the night. His phone kept beeping and he replied as he drove. The noise of the wind through the open windows played a harsh monologue. It was only when we turned north from Taba to head to Rafah, that he spoke.

'Forgive me. I had to reply before we head north. There is no reception for Egyptian phones until we reach Rafah. We don't use Israeli numbers here. In Gaza, yes.' Mohammed concentrated for a few seconds as a couple of army trucks drove past.

'Are you hungry? Thirsty?'

'Yes, to both.'

Mohammed reached behind him and passed me a plastic bag. I fished out two large pieces of tinfoil. One had wrapped sandwiches in it; when I opened it, the smell of Egyptian *ful* filled the car. From the other, I stuffed myself with delicious *Taemeia*[55] and pickled capsicums. There was coffee in the thermos and full bottles of

---

55 Egyptian falafels made with crushed ful beans instead of chickpeas.

mineral water littered the back seat. The car was obviously used for transports.

'When we get to Rafah, we'll leave the car with Salah. He will drop us off at one of the tunnels. I don't know which one as the Egyptians are blowing up every tunnel they can find. *From you to Allah Sisi. From you to Allah...*'[56]

'They are talking about clearing people away from the border now. Levelling hundreds of houses so no one can build tunnels under it,' Mohammed paused and added: 'And we call ourselves brothers and sisters...'

It was a voice of disappointment and anger. In the hours we spent driving north, he told me about his family. About his father Khaled, one of the most influential men in Gaza. That he lived in Egypt with his wife and two children but that the rest of his family were on the other side of the fence. He surprised me about the tunnels. I had only thought there were a couple but Mohammed told me there were thousands. Most houses had an opening to one under them. Before the siege people built them to get to their relatives, then as times changed they became a necessity for survival. When they were bombed, the Israelis didn't just disarm the fighters. They also cut supplies for everything imaginable needed to keep a society running. Even cars were smuggled through the tunnels—dismantled in Egypt and reassembled in Gaza. Tunnel transport had become an imperative.

As we approached Rafah, the army presence increased. The sounds of fighter jets in the distance were frequent. Strips of light from homemade rockets went up in the air, some short-lived, others reaching further. In seconds they were answered by jets roaring in the opposite direction. Ominous blasts could be heard. I was scared when we were stopped, my heart was racing. Armoured cars, a couple of tanks and lots of soldiers were gathered around the road into Rafah. Mohammed glanced at me and told me to be calm.

---

56 A phrase asking Allah to judge someone; implied is the forgiving of that person.

'I'm Egyptian,' he said and smiled. 'And you're my friend from Jordan, visiting.'

The soldier gazed at Mohammed's ID. He took my passport and handed it to a superior who flashed a torch on it. I heard a barrage of questions. He was rude and fat and seemed annoyed.

'The general wants to know why your friend has come today?'

'Haha! Tell him because the water is warm in El-Arish this time of the year.'

'You know what he means…' The soldier was young, polite and spoke gently to Mohammed.

'*Habibi*, just tell him the truth. How would we know the Jews would begin to bomb?'

'They began yesterday. Were you not here? Does your friend not hear the news?'

'*Habibi*, are they bombing us?'

'No.'

'Okay, am I allowed to take my friend to my home where my wife awaits him with supper or are you going to keep us here?'

The soldier went back to his superior who waddled over to Mohammed.

'Show me your wife is waiting for you!' He gloated all over, proud of his obvious intelligence.

'Here!' Mohammed flicked through his phone and turned it to him. A text message from his wife asked where we were and said supper was getting cold.

The general's face was disappointed. He told the soldiers to check the car and walked away.

'We're okay. They have to flex their muscles, but they're *thick*.'

The soldiers opened the boot, ran mirrors under the car and eventually waved us through.

The yellow lights of Rafah reminded me of the checkpoint I had dragged myself through so many times. In the distance, behind the dusty trees, there were watchtowers, dunes, tanks, fences, barbed wire and behind it all, everything appeared to repeat itself.

I doubted that we could cross. I was silent as I looked at Mohammed, who was smiling. He was almost home.

'Once the children are asleep, you will cross to Gaza. *Insha'Allah!*'

I wasn't confident about the *Insha'Allah* part but I said it to myself, as well.

Insha'Allah.

The street was dusty and full of children playing football. Occasionally, they stopped and turned to the sky as a rocket took off. They yelled to each other as if it were part of the game.

'Wait, wait! There's another one. Look!'

The rockets were unguided. Several had fallen across the border into Egypt to cause little or no damage. Mohammed pulled up in front of his home. It was a two-storey house adjacent to a row of similar court-enclosed homes. A young man sat at the front door next to two children who jumped up and ran towards us screaming.

'Baba! Baba!'

Mohammed jumped out of the car and knelt on one knee. He embraced the children with closed eyes. Amal, his wife, came out the front door. The young man also rose and walked towards me.

'*Ahlan wa sahlan*. I am Salah.'

I got out of the car. His face had numerous scratches and his hands felt like leather. He was young and fit like Mohammed, the muscles on his shoulders flexing visibly in the yellow street light. As we were shaking hands, the sky above our heads lit up. Salah didn't turn his head but watched me as I briefly looked towards the light in the sky.

With his children, Faisal and Thaera, around him, Mohammed went up to Amal and gently pushed her back through the front door where they flirted openly before he kissed her, out of sight, as is prescribed. Seeing Amal smile at Mohammed, Linah's smiling face flew into my mind's eye. My heart sang a sad tune of longing as she appeared and faded together with the flashing of the battle lights above. I caught my breath, stopping the well of emotions from rising.

I knew I could have turned around in Ramallah the previous day. And I could have turned back before I went into Jordan with Lina. Or I could have taken a different path when I woke up there—and found she had left. Or we might have even gone somewhere together. Away from Bilal. We couldn't and we could… There were so many escape routes, so many options. I could have disappeared amongst the numerous Palestinian camps in Amman and tried to find one of my uncles there. I could have taken a different turn several times, but I took none. The reason I didn't, comprised a stew of emotions. It simmered away, and I was hoping that it was only a matter of time before I'd find the remaining ingredients to turn off the heat and let it settle.

Or perhaps it would erupt, cascading torrents of convulsions.

30

Some of the tunnels dug from Egypt into Gaza were monsters. A concrete-encased hole would serve as the drop-in point. Whoever needed passage would pay the fee and use a hoist, manual or electric, to lower the human or other cargo down to horizontal level. Here, workers—or soldiers, if there were weapons—pushed it across. Some tunnels were narrow and dark. Others were large, with concrete walls, which you could walk through. Some even went into Israel and were feats of engineering, kilometres long, well-lit and ventilated. Some provided phone reception. Weapons, groceries, livestock, vehicles, fuel, building materials were all desperately needed in this open-air prison. People relied on these lifelines under the desert floor. And as always, when there was a need, there'd be people benefiting from that need. Mohammed and his father, Khaled, were some of those people and, I suspected, Rafi and his connections.

I remembered Mohammed's large eyeballs the first time I saw him at The Palace. I had watched how they moved, almost independently of his face. Now, with the three of us gathered on the living room floor setting after supper, I watched how his dark honey-coloured irises with random flecks carefully studied me as I dozed off. They were almost hypnotising. He kept turning them onto me as he discussed with Salah which tunnel we would use.

I closed my eyes and saw myself falling into a large hole. The wind howled in my ears as I stared into a pitch-black abyss. My breathing was rapid, anxious, and my heart pounded. I wanted to stop falling. Suddenly there was a white dot. I tried to make it out but before I knew it, everything went white. With force, I was dragged out of my sleep as I struggled uncontrollably for a moment, before calming down.

The lightbulb in the ceiling hung from a single wire. It was dazzling bright. I turned my head away, closing my eyes again. All of a sudden, the redness in my shut eyelids disappeared. I opened them and found Mohammed standing over me.

'Good that you got some sleep. It's time to wake up. Here, get dressed and meet me outside. *Yalla*.'

He threw a pile of clothes onto my guts. I gasped as the air came out, and rolled onto my side. I looked and saw him walk away, already wearing black boots and black pants. His walk was the same. Hands down his sides, determined. I felt the exact opposite: on the floor, bewildered. There was a world in what was happening around me that I didn't know much about. That I wasn't sure I wanted to know about. I sat up and stared at the clothes. Then I glanced at myself, at what I was wearing. The plain jeans and shirt that Bilal had given me.

At a too-rapid pace, I was moving onto another stage. One upon which I didn't know how to play the part. And the obvious question was *why* I was going. I didn't have an answer…

I had to keep on moving.

I tightened the belt around my waist and turned around to the window in the living room. Against the dark of the night, my distorted reflection looked like a stranger. My head spun with pressing questions I knew I couldn't answer. I might never have them answered. In a short time I'd be across the border. My intention was to bring Ali back home but I wasn't sure if he'd even talk to me. Would he want to kill me or expose my affair with the enemy? Would he stand with his comrades while forcing me to face the foe like a target at a country fair? It would be sweet revenge for my treason—to watch me die at the hands of the enemy I had gone to bed with. Now the 'war' had begun and people were already dying, I'd just be another head, another count. Without identity, without importance. Just another dead Palestinian with his face in the dirt. Perhaps my mother would see me in amongst the morgue mugshots. My mother! A lump moved up through my guts. It was something I absolutely had to do. I had to contact my mother. My father.

The engine was already running with Salah behind the wheel. Mohammed was outside the front door, texting, with a serious face. As soon as I stepped out, he turned to me.

'*Yalla*! The crossing is ready. We have to hurry.' Mohammed walked towards the car.

'Mohammed, wait!' He turned around and came back.

'What?'

'I want to speak to my mother.'

Mohammed looked me in the eyes. He saw the fear, the questions and the doubt. He looked at his watch, checked with his phone and handed it to me.

'Be quick.' He left me and went to sit next to Salah, who leaned his head forward to see what I was doing.

I dialled the number but it came back faulty. Then I realised I'd forgotten the country code. We were on an Egyptian network. I dialled once again. While it rang, I sat down on the front steps of Mohammed's home, waiting. It cut out after a while. My hands began to sweat as I tried again.

'Allo? Allo?' My mother's voice sounded worried.

'Mama. It's me. Nana.'

The screaming and calling my name lasted for what seemed an eternity. She called my dad and they asked me questions without listening for an answer. Every time they asked if I was fine, I said I was. I wanted to hear their voice, to connect and tell them I loved them, but I couldn't get past their frantic worry. Finally, I cut through.

'Mama! Baba!' I yelled and they stopped talking. Mohammed and Salah turned their heads and stared. I didn't care. Sweat ran down my body. I shook from my head to my toes.

'I just called to tell you I am fine and that I love you. I am going into Gaza and I hope to find Ali, well and sound, and bring him back… That's all.'

My mother cried and called to Allah repeatedly for my safe return. She walked away in the end, then my father cleared his throat and spoke with a choked voice.

'Please let us know you are safe as soon as you can. I will pray for you. May Allah be with you. I love you, my son.'

He hung up before I could reply. I collected myself on the steps before I got up. As I did, I felt dizzy. I wanted to run back into the house, find a dark room and throw myself to the ground and cry.

Ali had chosen his life; I had chosen mine. But in friendship and love, there is a bond that transcends reason. That was what was driving me, but I didn't know it that night. And although I didn't entirely believe my own thoughts, they were so full of guilt and fear I couldn't think straight.

Where I was and was heading, became increasingly blurred. I felt the tears in my eyes as I walked to the idling car, opened the door and got into the back seat. I handed Mohammed back his phone and Salah glanced at me in the mirror with warm eyes. He asked Mohammed, in a whisper:

'*Tawakalna ala Allah*?'[57]

'In the name of Allah, the one who is the most gracious, most compassionate.'

We drove for a few minutes, through alleyways and dusty streets, heading north between farms and buildings. Except for a few people around some small corner shops, Rafah was quiet. Salah pulled up next to a shop that had its shutters down. He doused the lights of the car and we waited in silence. I looked out as the night followed suit. There were no planes or rockets, only stars.

Over Gaza the sky was dark and so was the earth.

◈◈◈

The roller shutters of the shop opened slowly and stopped halfway. Two men appeared. Both of them put their heads out and waved us in. They looked worn and dirty. Salah started the car and Mohammed turned his head to me. I nodded, and we got out. Salah drove off back into the night while we walked into the building as

---

57 Posed here as a question: Are we trusting in Allah? Or, In Allah we trust?

the shutters closed behind us. I stood in the dark until a flashlight came on.

The shop had been cleared, except for a thick rope dangling from a windlass in the middle that two men operated, and labelled crates of food and medicine, as well as clothes and other items to go through the tunnel. As soon as the empty hoist would come up, we'd climb onto the board one by one and be lowered down. From there we'd crawl or walk with bent backs for about half a kilometre. Mohammed had outlined the crossing procedure during supper. There was no talking in the garage. Only the sound of the winch squeaking and the panting of the men could be heard.

The empty board appeared and Mohammed jumped onto it. The two men applied their bare feet to a footbrake as he went down swiftly. As soon as he tugged the rope, they quickly wheeled the board back up. When it appeared, I jumped on and held the guy ropes above my head. Like that of a child on a roller coaster, as I was dropped down the tube, my heart pounded and my stomach lurched. The scent of the hot hemp rope mixed with the smell of the damp earth. With each breath, as I descended, the air became even more pungent and heavy.

Mohammed's torch lit up from underneath. I looked down past the board and saw the ground approaching. As I touched down, I got off and tugged the rope. Mohammed signalled for me to follow him as he began to walk ahead. I understood why he was so fit. He walked fast, his back all the way forward with bent knees. I was in pain after a few moments but kept following him. Light came from ahead so he switched off his torch. Small light bulbs were strung along the wall that lit up the underground. Sweat poured down my back and I felt as if I was suffocating. There was very little oxygen in the tunnel and the temperature was like an oven. From where we had entered, we descended slightly before we began climbing once more. Past Mohammed I could hear voices in the far distance. The ground directly under the exit appeared as a white-lit platform. It looked like a helicopter landing pad. Mohammed paced resolutely ahead. There was only a single thick rope at this end of the tunnel. He put the rope between his legs, tugged it and went upwards into the strong light.

When I stood in the centre and looked up, the light was so fierce, I could hardly see anything. I covered my eyes with my arm and squinted to see if the rope was reappearing. There was the distinct hum of a generator and voices at the top, but I couldn't make out what they were saying. The sounds all blurred into an indistinguishable hum.

Then the voices stopped, and I could only hear the whir of the generator. The rope dropped again. I took hold of it, put it between my legs like Mohammed, and tugged it. I was lifted off the ground, but my ascent was much slower. There was a light squeak from the winch as I stared into the wall of the vertical tunnel. An intricate pattern to reinforce it had been made with concrete; almost like tiny squares that interlocked, mesh-like.

I didn't expect to, but my body shivered as I passed an elaborate carving in the concrete—a man was pulling up what seemed to be the devil from a well. Another carving saw him signing a pact with this devil, laughing. And in the final carving, he met his Maker and was depicted as a man praying for forgiveness. I wanted to yell to whoever was pulling to stop, but it was too late. I had reached the surface. My eyes were level with the rim of the hole. A hand was extended and looking closer, I felt a tremor of recognition. I tried looking up, but the man's face had the bright light behind his head. There was only a silhouette.

As my hand took a hold, I knew who it was. I trembled with fear and almost fell off the rope. He extended both his hands and pulled me up with great strength. As my eyes adjusted to the light, he appeared to me in a halo, like an angel from our imagined heaven.

There was no one else in the room; I allowed the surge of tears. Ali put his hands on my shoulders and I took hold of his arms. Tight in our grip we pressed into each other, as if in a wrestle but it didn't take long before tears dropped from Ali's eyes, too. He let go. We both put down our arms and looked at each other.

We didn't say a word. It was Ali who first moved in for an embrace. I didn't hesitate.

'I'm sorry, my brother. I'm sorry, Ali.'

It was the first thing I said even though I still believed I hadn't done wrong. It was an apology of confusion and guilt for a crime I hadn't committed. My fear spoke.

And Ali didn't reply.

◈◈◈

I saw that Ali's eyes were still dull, that the blue that used to shine on the black had vanished. There were dark rings underneath that fell to sunken cheeks. The short time he'd been away was already taking its toll. His clothes looked as if they were tailored to suit him. They showed his strong figure from his torso through to his boots. He had begun to grow a beard before Farrah's death; now it had grown to be dense and well-trimmed. In pure black, it followed the sharp lines of his cheekbones and widened his already wide jaw. He was dressed in black, his beard was black and his hair was black. Even his boots were black. He was still in mourning, and not just Farrah's death but also the reality of his own life. And beyond that, the reality of Palestinians in Gaza being killed like sitting ducks, unable to flee the iron ribbon of land they were caged in.

I thought we'd get a chance to talk but there was no time. Ali had been told of my arrival and had asked to receive me when I came up from the tunnel. In a flash of prescience, he had asked for the room to be cleared. He had told his comrades that I would either stay or that he would personally lower me back into the hole.

He got straight to the point:

'Why are you here?' But I felt he already knew the answer.

'I came for you, Ali.'

'Why?'

'Because you are my only brother.' I held myself together, but I could tell right away that whatever I said, it didn't matter.

'I will always be your brother. We are connected in our souls, until eternity.' Ali took a deep breath. 'They said you were looking for me. Mohammed told us yesterday.'

'Hmm... Mohammed. Why didn't you tell me about him? Even before Farrah died...'

Ali's eyes narrowed as his mind viewed its secrets. They bore into mine to give the answer I already knew.

'Let's not talk about this now. There's no time. We are heading northeast tonight. We can talk on the way.'

'Ali... I don't want to fight. I came for you—'

'I'm not coming, Nana. *There* is the exit if you wish to return. It will be up to you to make your way back down the tunnel or try your luck to the east, into Israel. There are still a few tunnels left there.'

It had been such a short time, but my friend, brother and soulmate was irrevocably committed. He had come to fight. His eyes were flint-hard, lustreless.

Ali was not there with me; he was somewhere else. I could not reach his soul. I had thought I could, but I couldn't. I had believed I could make him see the madness of war, heed the calling of his own beliefs. All his stories were of love, not of hatred and death. I was watching Ali betraying himself. And at the same time, it struck me that *that* is what we all do. It's part of how we are trapped in the reality we create for ourselves.

My time at the tunnel entrance was running out. Obviously, I had to make a decision before the others came back. More bombs would be falling. We could hear them in the distance. Deep, like a dull thunder without the rumble.

We were arguing without words. Ali's eyes had changed, and I drew a line around every contour of them. They were windows to another world. I saw the reflection of the room with all its tools of war. I also saw in them the way to turn back, to escape, the rope dangling above the tunnel entry.

I could go into combat with Ali, I thought. Alongside him, to protect him. That way, he'd have no doubt of my allegiance. Fight and share the weight of the brutal anvil of war. Fight with him knowing he'd eventually want out from the valley of death. My mind was in turmoil. My mother's call *to keep my soul healthy* found its way through. A caution not to throw myself in with Ali's surrender to hatred. I knew it was dark. I knew it was sinister. It was a pact with the devil and the devil knows nothing of forgiveness. But against a terrible wrong, there is no greater instinct than to fight.

I pushed my mother's words aside. The gate was open for me to break out from the boiling frustration of living as a prisoner in a society of prisoners to which the world has deliberately turned a blind eye. I reasoned why I had come so far. Why I had fled and escaped and why I had returned. Why I had smuggled my way back into this trap of bitter resentment. The answer had come and my heart gave a thump of resignation. My focus had narrowed but my vision remained wide.

The wall of separation crumbled and Linah appeared. She waved at me but with her arm fully extended. I waved back and watched our smiles meet. We walked towards each other through a mass of people. There were no watchtowers, guns, waiting areas or turnstiles to pass. Our lips met without fear in an embrace of love. Our fingers entwined and her red nail polish shone in the sun. Children were flying kites in the four parts of the Palestinian flag, red, black, white and green. Illuminated by the sun, they surged like vivid scarfs towards a dazzling white dove, outlined in the dark sky-blue of the Israeli flag.

I wanted the walls to come down. I wanted to reach into Ali's soul and show him what it could look like. I wanted to believe I could make it happen. I wanted everything to be right without knowing how to do it right. I had nothing more than the hope, which at that time only existed for me.

I decided to stay. And yes … I decided to fight.

31

More than a week had passed since I had entered Gaza. I had joined Ali in the small group he'd been assigned to with two other men and brothers, Ghassan and Ghanim. They were young—in their twenties and experts on rockets and rifles. Together we went from stockpile to stockpile, fixing rockets that wouldn't fly and rifles that jammed. The two brothers taught me everything or so it seemed. Every time I learnt something knew they stressed its importance and had me doing what they showed me. The result was simple, crude and effective.

Within a week, I was a nervous wreck. Several times the brothers didn't know what was wrong with the rocket and it blew up as they launched it. Then we had to run. Next, we'd have the Israeli drones swarming in the skies above. As soon as a rocket was launched, they'd lock in on the launch site as their target and, if they weren't able to take it out, a fighter jet would follow within minutes. The surrounding buildings, the launch site, anyone alive—all of it would go up in a pulverising blast. I felt I did nothing but run. Everybody was running—we weren't the only ones. Once I was running next to Ali. I can't remember where we were exactly. I looked behind and I saw this man. He would have been in his thirties. He was thin. He was carrying his son on his shoulders. His wife had hold of their daughter by the hand and they were running in front of him to get away from the imminent shelling. The brothers ran into an open garage door ahead and I turned to the family and pointed them to it. They ran towards it. At the same time a drone flew over and whoever was flying it miles away, saw me. Hadn't he seen the family? It banked sharply and returned. Ali, Ghassan and Ghanim came outside. We fired at the drone and scored a hit. Pieces came off but it still flew away.

Then another drone turned towards us in the distance. As we ran, I yelled back to the father to take his family and run away from us. He trembled with fear and his wife looked terrified. The children were crying, almost screaming. I'll never forget that moment. None of us were given time. The drone operator launched a missile that hit a building right between us and the family. The blast was deafening. The shockwave blew out car windows and pressed me to the ground. Flying debris lacerated me in several places as I closed my eyes. Through the smoke and dust, through the pounding of my own heart, I heard the screams of the father. He was still screaming when I was able to squint through the haze. The man was kneeling in front of his lifeless wife and daughter. His son stared blankly at him and at the torn corpses of his mother and sister; his legs shook uncontrollably but there were no tears, no crying or screaming.

Ali helped me off the ground. He glanced back at the stricken family and didn't react; kept supporting me as we walked away. As we walked away from four victims, alive ones and dead. With his profile close, as I stared at Ali a voice spoke up inside me. This was not my Ali. Not the kind, principled, natural leader I had known since we were children. He had become a different man. Hope had been crushed out and what was left was the hard shell of Farrah's never-wed widower. Ali had turned. What had been, was no longer.

Our lives were no longer inextricably linked. The angels Ali had carved in our Palace of Angels had sprung from a loving heart that now had stopped beating. Hatred had turned Ali into an agent of the devil with an all-consuming inferno in his chest.

His angels had had their wings cut off and had fallen from the sky.

◈◈◈

When the shelling was near it was impossible to sleep, but when it was far away, I let go and drifted off. I wasn't sound asleep, but

I wasn't awake either. I was somewhere where dreams didn't exist. Somewhere, walking on the edge of a sea of nightmares. The drones and fighter jets were paradoxically my saviours. With their own ordnance, they pressed me to seek the answers to a torrent of questions: asking why we kill each other and why we can't ever see that it doesn't work—never has, never will.

We were in the hinterland of Abasan Al-Saghira, a village on the eastern outskirts of Khan Younis. The Qassam Brigades had a structured network of safe houses throughout Gaza and we were in one of them. It had a small stockpile of Qassam 1 rockets. They were the smallest rockets, yet big enough to make it to the settlements across the border line to Israel. There were also bullets, both for American M16 rifles and for Russian Kalashnikovs. In the daytime, this was a clothes factory.

Ali had no trouble sleeping. I found him up against a wall with a smile on his face. He had a muffled snore and his head appeared perfectly poised without flopping around or falling to either side. I couldn't decide whether to close my eyes again or keep watching. There was something familiar about Ali there, sleeping. I felt I could approach him, just like when we were children. Ghassan and Ghanim were sleeping as well, so keeping my sitting position, I quietly shuffled close to Ali, using my hands to push off the ground.

His cheeks, beard and dangerous-looking face were defined in the moonlight. I noticed then that his breathing had changed, but he still startled me when he whispered without opening his eyes. It also scared me.

'What do you want, Nana?'

I held my breath for a few seconds before letting go. My mind cried out to make the most of my chance.

'I want to talk to you.'

'About what?'

'About what we haven't talked about. About this. About us. About Linah...'

Ali held his breath for a few moments. Drops of sweat ran down the valley under his prominent Adam's apple. Then his eyes opened halfway and the blackness in them shone as he faced me.

'Why? What is there to talk about? She is a beautiful woman—'

'So, you did see us?'

'Yes.'

'Is that why you didn't tell me about Mohammed?'

'No.'

Ali was calm with his answers. He was whispering every word which came to me clearly. His appearance was frightening but a still greater impact was made by his voice. The voice I had so admired. After a moment, he went on:

'If I'd told you anything, you would have followed me...'

'We're brothers, Ali.'

'No, Nana, we're not. I love you, as such, but we're not brothers. Brothers don't keep secrets from each other.'

'I've already apologised, Ali.'

'I haven't.'

'What do you mean?'

'I mean, I *am sorry* that I didn't tell you about Mohammed. About coming here.'

'Well I found out.'

'I had a suspicion you would...' Ali smiled as he said it. He opened his mouth and was about to say something. He stopped for a second, then asked in a forgiving voice.

'What about Linah? It looked... Very serious to me...'

Ali surprised me. His tone was not judgemental, not what I had expected. I had expected to hear about judgement, obstacles, challenges, laws, many things. A multitude of reasons why I should never have gone near Linah.

My time had come to say my piece and I said it truthfully.

'She's a beautiful woman, Ali... I love her smile. The very fact of her being makes me *feel alive*. She's got a good generous heart and she makes my heart laugh. She doesn't say a bad word about anyone and... is a bit of a rebel!' I smiled when I said that last bit.

Ali looked straight into my eyes. He smiled back.

'You're in love with her, Nana… When will you see her again?'

The question surprised me.

'I don't know. I mean I'm here now. Come with me, Ali… Let's go home—'

'What home? *This* is my life now. This is where I'll stay until I die. I'd rather die standing than surrender to anyone. Even to my despicable mother.'

This hatred. I had taken myself to it, although I wanted to be as far from it as I could. I felt Ali's pain and his loss, but this wasn't my life. None of this hatred was my life anymore.

Ali went back to asking about Linah.

'Why didn't you tell me about Linah?'

'Because I was afraid, Ali. Afraid because she is the enemy—'

'Not to you… So, she's not the enemy.'

Here was Ali being forgiving yet full of hatred at the same time. In the darkness, I felt a sudden peace. Ali surprisingly didn't have his emotions and thoughts mixed up; my own fears, my own thoughts, were put to shame.

I had lost my old reflection in the mirror of my conscience. In the mirror of all the conflicting emotions of my life. Constantly having to choose between who is a friend and who is a foe. I wanted to see a new reflection. One of *who I am.*

Ali's words said it clearly. He wasn't denying another person the freedom to choose. Every man and every woman embodies a potential bond. But in a war, it's an easy choice because there is none—it's all laid down—either you, or the enemy.

Both the enemy that lives within ourselves, the enemy that fights within ourselves, and the enemy that we want to kill.

For its resemblance to ourselves.

◈◈◈

Ali closed his eyes and went back to sleep. I sat looking at him for a long time until fatigue got the better of me and I lay down. The floor was barren concrete, a pillow of torn cardboard for my head.

I closed my eyes.

Tacitly, Ali had told me to leave. To go and find Linah and get myself a life. His words had come from exhaustion. He was almost delirious, yet they made sense: '*The God is One and the life is One. Either it comes or it goes.*'

Tears trailed down my cheeks as Ali's response untied the knot in my soul. I was standing at the edge of the cliff. I could stay there and hold on to what fears I had or I could jump and trust the parachute would float me to a soft landing. My faceless conscience was right, I would see my real self in the mirror when I was ready. I didn't want to see the old reflection again because it had never been mine anyway. All of a sudden it made sense.

I drifted off to a café that was bathed in sunlight. Not Mount Carmel but with a similar setting. Linah was waiting for me. She faced the windows and smiled as I opened the door. I walked up to her and she stood up. We hugged and our lips met in a soft kiss.

There were people around but they didn't look familiar, nor did the man behind the counter. A young woman who was waiting on the tables politely stood by for me to sit down. She asked me what I felt like ordering. I had an iced coffee and a slice of chocolate cake. Linah already had an order. She opened her handbag and showed me a picture of a turquoise beach. Behind the beach, there was a simple hut, backed by a tropical forest. She suggested, by expression, that we go there and make love.

It was a world of my dreaming. It didn't exist. It was a snapshot from Linah's words, from her world. The world that I can't tell you about for I know nothing of it.

In the darker parts, angry men featured, reminding me I was in a war. The voice of Ali repeating he wasn't coming, telling me to head back home. To find an exit under the Israeli border and return to Mukhamas. There was also a humming of drones that maybe came from inside my head or possibly from the ravaged heavens above. In the end it didn't matter.

Either it came or it went. Either I'd wake up or I'd not. I let go and jumped and as I fell, I realised I wasn't falling at all. I had found steady ground.

The path I wished to walk.

◊◊◊

The blast rocked the walls so that bits of the concrete roof fell down. We had no warning, just the incoming screech of the shell. A tank across the border only a kilometre away had fired. I scrambled off the floor, dizzy and disoriented, and heard Ghassan yelling that Ghanim was injured. A knifelike piece of concrete had cut through his pants and torn into his right thigh. I pulled a length of cotton from a pile of discards, wound it around his thigh, and tightened it until the bleeding stopped. Ali was right alongside me. We lifted up our wounded comrade and all four of us ran outside. The building had taken a direct hit and so did the building ahead of us. Children ran in their pyjamas down the street, their parents carrying the smaller ones or dragging them by their arms. A man in his underwear ran towards us, calling for his mother and father. Terror was etched on his face.

We kept running. Fighter jets flew over the rooftops towards the west. They banked and circled sharply, launching their missiles. Blinding white lights cut through the deep blue of the morning sky and turned into balls of fire on impact. We kept running. Left, an explosion—right, two more. We ran back again, like rats being chased through a maze. The bombing was indiscriminate. Lives were obliterated in front of my eyes and I didn't know if I'd make it for another step. The images of the dead mother and daughter clung to me, chasing me. The horror and devastation in the eyes of the father. I could not cope any longer. I had reached the point of emotional collapse. I cannot explain my emotions as I passed three children who were staring at the sky in broad daylight. What I witnessed in that passing second, I can. They were all facing the same way. Perhaps they were holding hands the moment they were killed. Their clothes were on fire and tongues of flames were licking their way up to their heads, the wind whipping them furiously and bearing the unmistakable smell of burning flesh.

Panting, I stopped and stood next to Ali. He seemed unaffected—or perhaps he hadn't even registered the sight of the children. We looked out over the border. Tanks were advancing with lines of soldiers alongside them. Aerial bombardment was not enough—the Israelis were massing on the ground. They travelled fast. Ghanim and Ghassan hid behind a building and signalled across the road to Ali. They were motioning the shape of a rocket in the air and pointing to one of our stockpiles. One they could use to retaliate. We had rockets hidden all over the place to save the fighters from having to carry them around and lose mobility. The launchers were simple steel structures, like curved steps from a children's slide. The rockets lived on solid fuel made from sugar and fertiliser. The explosive was also made from fertiliser and the detonator was a spring-mounted nail.

The Israelis, of course, knew about the stockpiles, so they bombed away at every house, hospital, playground, outhouse and henhouse that might hold one. No matter what else was inside. Women, men, children. They were Palestinians.

Ghanim supported his limping brother and took the direction he had signalled. Ali and I headed northwest. Inland and then north, towards Gaza City. We were on foot and light. The only weapons we carried were an automatic rifle and half a dozen clips. The Israelis moved in platoons, with a short enough space between them to be able to support each other on the flanks. Ali told me that once we came between two platoons, we would have our chance to retaliate.

It's hard to be philosophical when someone's trying to kill you, but I *did* have a rifle in my hands. I reasoned that if I didn't make it out of Gaza, I'd end up using it, perhaps to defend myself, at worst in my life's final moments, in a blood-lusting rage. I was running and my mind was racing in conflict with itself. I had to choose between myself and my brother and friend. Then running, it all became clear: I had already chosen life, already chosen love, already chosen not to be the enemy, already chosen not to be the victim. This was my strongest intention, my resolve. But whether I could bring it off, was another matter. I hadn't decided when to leave Ali.

And Ali was a dangerous man to be with.

◈◈◈

Ali was aching to kill people. This was his chance. He was driven by hatred and I knew that once hatred takes hold of a man, he is lost. His eyes were on fire, feverish, as if unwrapping a long-wanted gift. Before us, we had an army advancing, full of contempt, with sophisticated weapons and equally eager to kill. They were not offering peace, and unlike us, they were not defending themselves. Neither were we. We did not have the weapons to defend ourselves.

Any real damage our rockets caused was random and minimal. The rifles in our hands were all we had. Surely, we could take a life or two. But inevitably, we'd die. *It would be suicide, perhaps reactionary but suicide, nevertheless.* But where would we go when there was no escape? Gaza is a big prison, with the Egyptian army on one side and Israeli forces on every other side, even out at sea. The only way to enter or exit is under the ground or to apply for permission to enter or transit Israel, which would almost certainly be denied with no reason given.

After moving north for an hour, Ali and I reached a small empty square at the eastern end of Qarara. Ali unfolded a hand-drawn sketch of the place. The houses around it were marked with family names, in red for those who did not co-operate. He turned the paper to match the buildings in front of us. As I looked up, I saw the centre of the square with its small enclosed garden patch, full of rubbish.

The grass was reduced to a few grey patches and in the centre, a small water fountain lay in pieces. A tap had been attached to the end of the pipe that had run through it. I tapped Ali on his arm and pointed to a concrete angel that had broken off the basin. It was beautifully crafted. Two angels had held up a heart, but the concrete had broken right through their arms so that only their hands were attached.

'Look… The angels—'

I didn't get to finish my sentence. Ali either didn't see the beauty in it or he rejected the part of him that did. The time, the place, the predicament was wrong—or perhaps it was paradoxically right. Right for him, not me. Finding moments of sanity, moving beyond the insanity of war, was what kept me alive. Ali's eyes flicked on the angels and quickly reacted, flashing dismissal of a withered part of his soul. He turned his attention back down to the paper.

'You're living in a dream… If you want to give them an angel, *there* is the border.' He nudged his head in the direction. 'I suggest you go *underneath* them and find someone who might… eh… Listen…'

Ali had put the pieces together. He knew what was on my mind. He pointed to a square on the drawing. It said, 'entry'.

'I believe this tunnel is still working. It will take you to a field south of Kisufim. If you make it, you have to wait until nightfall before exiting and even then, it's doubtful you'll make it back home.'

'Allah will open the way.' I said it without thinking. Ali glanced at me, puzzled. For the first time in my life the words felt real. The only place where our Gods could possibly roam, must be where our souls aren't surrendering to the poison of impiety. Whether in their name or not.

The time to leave Ali came in a way I could never have foreseen. He moved ahead of me, darting from building to building towards a house across the square where rockets would be stockpiled. I wasn't far behind when the missile hit. It came from a helicopter suspended above the border fence. There were many helicopters and we couldn't have known one had its eye on us. I heard the sound of a speeding object and before I could react, it hit the building in front of Ali.

The blast was furnace-red, a fireball that scorched everything around it. Ali, in that instant, was torn open across the waist and hurled backwards. The shock wave struck me with colossal force. I felt needle-like fragments ripping through my skin as I flew backwards through the air and hit the ground. I could hardly breathe. I couldn't hear anything except for the loud pumping of my heart, the sirens in my ears. I was staring at the blue of the sky, dropping in and out of sight through the passing smoke. It seemed to last for many minutes before my senses came back. The world slowly became audible again and a feeling of being paralysed went away. My breathing grew deeper and my consciousness returned from the unnerving sensation of being unconsciously awake.

I looked to the left and right. On one side, there was the centre square with houses around it. On the other side, I saw smoke and fire. I pushed myself off the ground and sat up. Pain shot through my thigh, right next to where, decades earlier, one of the bullets that killed my cousin Bilal, had gone on through me. I felt something sticking out the back of my thigh and pushing against the ground. It was a small piece of steel, part of a concrete reinforcement bar. It had to come out. The visible bit was half as big as the palm of my hand. I grabbed it, closed my eyes and pulled. It came out easily and I exhaled in relief, no barb, no gushing blood.

Alhamdulillah…

Then I saw Ali. He was just metres away; what met my eyes was a horror scene of summary mutilation. My breathing choked, my senses were stifled. Was I alive, was I dead? Ali's face was clean gone, lipless, glaring white teeth. His skin was peeled back, right over his blackened skull. His eyeballs stuck out and one drooped to the side. His legs were gone, and his entrails hung out, dirty, below his waist. His skin had burnt through his clothes or the other way around. It looked as if the black fabric had been pressed into his body, crusted in patches of blood. I vomited, painfully on an empty stomach, and the tension in my body released itself as belching tears. Impulsively, I moved towards him, putting my hands in front of me to crawl. But for every inch I gained, I stopped. Tears were blurring my vision and mucus was dripping from my nose. I wanted to get closer, but my body wouldn't go. I had to look away. Every time I tried to move, I felt a terrible weight, as if standing on a cliff's edge and held back by fear. Terrified, I almost screamed when his detached body convulsively shook and settled at last, deathly still. At peace.

Ali was no longer. His life, so close to mine, as a friend and brother, had ended before my eyes. He died full of hatred, losing everything from nothing. He didn't deserve such an ending. I had found the germ of tenderness, still there, deep in his heart. But it didn't stand a chance under the dense, miasmic burden of vengeful hatred and distrust that sits on this world of ours. The world that gave birth to us. The love with Farrah, the bond they had shared, was no different from that desired by every one of his enemies, by every living breathing human being. Ali had once taught me how to patiently depict the joys, sorrows, wonders and mysteries of life. He had expressed his dreams and hopes, sharing his thoughts with those who listened. He came so close to what we all strive for. Happiness. But he never made it. I saw Ali and I saw Bilal, my cousin. I saw them as I was, on my knees in sorrow, and that is how I said my last farewell to both of them.

My love for them will never die. But I knew, almost as if called from the blue sky above, that neither of them went to heaven. Neither of them was a martyr in my eyes because their desire for justice had been usurped by a malignant lust for revenge. And in that, they resembled their enemies rather than the noble men they had been—two men I held to my heart. I let go of my admiration for Bilal and I let Ali's soul return to the ether, return to Allah. Perhaps *His* benevolence would give Ali the forgiveness I could no longer give. I stood and picked up my rifle with feelings of disgust and defeat. I turned my face away from Ali as I walked past him.

The hand-drawn map had been lost, but even with it, I would need luck and time to make it to the tunnel entrance. The tanks could be heard coming close from behind. Ahead of me there was yelling. Challenges to fight. I felt the sting in my thigh as I limped desperately to get away from the imminent battle. The square with its small houses was encircled by higher apartment blocks. The sun glinted against moving weapons in distant balconies, high up.

The one thing on my mind was to get to that entrance. I saw an opportunity to hide between the tall buildings. If I made it, if the tunnel was still there, if it hadn't been blown up, I, at least, had a chance.

To get out of the hell I'd put myself in.

32

That was it. Men and women were rushing towards each other to kill one another. I don't know who got in position first, but the Israelis had the tanks, the helicopters and the laser-guided missiles. The tanks fired their shells straight into the sides of the apartment buildings. They blasted holes the size of trucks in them and debris flew everywhere. Every explosion left a scene of devastation. Then there were the helicopters, hovering birds of prey, with night vision, heat-seeking hi-tech predatory powers. They plotted paths for the missile-firing drones which could get at targets that were out of the helicopters' reach.

As I was running, I felt like a chased goose. I had to make the tunnel entrance before the next bomb. It was my only hope even though I wasn't sure I could find it. I was in double jeopardy, fleeing both sides. I didn't want to be seen by either the al-Quds Brigades or the al-Aqsa Martyrs' Brigades or any other brigades—but, of course, I was. Several times voices yelled at me as I dashed from wall to wall, pretending not to hear. My ears hurt from clamping my hands over them and from the explosions. As the bombing stopped, the soldiers moved in.

A bullet hit the wall in front of my face. I turned instinctively. Behind a broken-down wall, two Israeli soldiers were taking cover. I raised my rifle and fired a shot. The recoil punched the butt into my shoulder. More pain. I ran. More shots were fired. I stopped under a window and ducked as a rifle poked out and fired several rounds across to the position of the soldiers. My eardrums almost burst. I hadn't seen the marksman. His eyes looked angrily down at me as he motioned with his hand for me to move out of the line of fire.

This made sense and would bring me closer to the tunnel. He wore a balaclava. His eyes were like Bilal's. On fire.

I took off with my back to the invading troops and got to a wide street where I pressed myself against a wall. I only had to run across this street, past one tall building and there would be the house, hopefully, with the entrance. I could see it from where I was standing. The absurdity of scurrying to a hidden hole in the ground, to escape from a living hell, to escape back into a prison.

Another bullet cut my shoulder as it whisked past to hit the wall. I jolted back and put my hand to the wound, the blood warming my skin. I was in an alley between two townhouses, pinned in my position, needing to get away from it fast. If they couldn't kill me with a bullet, they'd eventually get me with something bigger. I edged towards the street and peeped around the corner of the house. Straightaway, I saw soldiers—and the moment I did, they fired at me. I pulled back, held my rifle around the corner without looking and fired several shots. Then I took a chance and spurted across the street and kept running into another alley, gunshots following. There was a door to my right. I opened it and entered a garage underneath a house. I ran across, opened the door on the other side. Another alley. I didn't stop; I ran back out towards the street. In the last few steps, I moved slowly, with bullets coming from the side. The two Israeli soldiers were also pinned, exchanging fire with the fighters higher up.

Panting, I glanced at my rifle. I was scared knowing I was close to death. Any bad or unlucky move could finish me off. I checked the clip in the rifle, counted my bullets. I had roughly a couple of hundred left, spread over six clips, taped together in doubles. I was determined to survive, but whatever that meant, whatever was happening around me, I learned something about myself that day. Much as I had lived a cramped life under occupation, I did not hate these people. I felt sorry for the occupiers. They were right there upon us—but unable to defeat us. The power of the small against the mighty gave me hope. I knew the occupation would never defeat me. I would never succumb to hatred. The devil might offer me the suckering pleasure of power, but I would never take it. Angels filled my heart and, though in tears, they were realistic angels and let me fight for my life. I picked up my rifle.

I marked the position of both sides and in my head, I drew the way to the tunnel. I had to run to the car parked on the street, hide behind it, then dart across to the next adjacent alleyway. If I could make it around them, I could reach the house with the tunnel. I waited for a break in the shooting, then ran. The Israelis fired and were shot at themselves by the men above and behind me. I was waiting for the next burst of fire when the Israelis suddenly turned and ran back to where they had come from. I was kneeling on one knee, about to stand up, when a bullet tore through the trunk of the car. I threw myself to the ground. Ali had taught me that on my first day in Gaza. I held the rifle in front of me. Two soldiers came running from the side of the house where the men had covered me. One in front of the other. He was about to take aim when I fired first. It all happened in a flash. A spat of bullets on fire left the muzzle of my gun. I flexed my arms against the recoil and momentarily closed my eyes. When I opened them again, the soldier was on the ground. The other one had disappeared. I looked up and the men in the building pointed to the alley. The soldier had dodged around the building and would try to engage me from behind. I got up and went back to where I had just come from. There was no cover, I was in the narrow alleyway between parallel streets. I hid in the doorway of the garage halfway down and waited. Within a short time, I heard footsteps approaching and my heart raced in big heavy thumps. Adrenalin coursed around my body like a drug and I felt a high as the first soldier went down. I'd never before had that. The thought of another kill, another win, and another escape made me feel as if I was about to be freed from the pain and torments of my life.

I heard the boots. There was uncertainty in the way they moved, quickly coming close. Running, stopping, running again. I could hear the breathing, a scared panting. It got louder. I heard the clearing of a throat. A small sound, almost like a tiny squeal from the heaving of air. It sounded familiar somehow. It didn't matter. My sweating left hand held the hot steel, my right shaking, as I put my finger on the trigger.

I lifted the rifle to my chest, aimed straight ahead and jumped out.

33

It wasn't me. It was my trembling hand that pulled the trigger. My heart stopped as the bullet left the muzzle of the rifle and went straight through the soldier's collarbone. The soldier was a woman. And in the oneness of Allah, it was Linah! I hadn't had time to think. I hadn't had time to stop myself. My hand had shaken so violently. I had pulled the trigger before I even felt the pressure on my finger. We both froze as the crack of the bullet deafened the moment. She dropped her rifle and slumped to the ground. I had never expected that I would be looking into Linah's eyes. Eyes that stayed on me as the bullet went through her.

There was a slow-motion aftermath, which became all too real in a flash. As Linah fell, she twisted around with her hand against the wound.

'Nana! Nana! Nana!' she cried.

She was twisting her head back. Our eyes kept meeting, kept confirming what had happened in this bizarre snap of time. I gasped, shocked, as I looked down at her and at the rifle in my hands. I looked behind me, in front of me—there was no one else.

The shock of finding Linah tumbled in my mind, with the horror of knowing I had shot her. My thinking then became clear. The world coalesced into a single, pulsating, homogenous entity—*Linah and me*. I threw myself to my knees.

'Linah! I'm sorry! I'm sorry! I'm sorry!'

I was oblivious to our surrounding dangers. I was frantic. I had wildly jumped on the express elevator, straight to hell. Linah looked at me, her eyes angry, as if she wanted to kill me. Then they changed and spoke the unwritten language of despair. The failure of a fate that had brought us back together in the most tragic of ways. Then another change. Her eyes turned to joy and flooded with tears. Tears that trickled down her cheeks in rapid drops, like the waving movement of a waterfall.

Her eyes smiled through her anger and pain.

'Take off my helmet, you stupid man!'

I quickly released the clip under her chin. The helmet dropped backwards. Her hair fell out like the mouth of a river, spreading its lustrous arms into the sea.

'Sorry, Linah. I am sorry. Sorry—'

'Stop. Shut up!' Linah was in agony.

'Help me. Hide me.'

She was telling me to hide her so she could call for help. I looked behind and ahead once more, couldn't see anyone. I got behind her and put my arms under her shoulders.

'Be careful. It hurts!'

I lifted her, dragged her back through the doorway and rested her on the concrete floor behind the door. I knelt next to her. She turned her head to me, and I fell into her universe once again.

'I've missed you…' Linah whispered.

Then even in this dire strait, she could surprise me.

'And all I want to do now is hit you!'

I couldn't speak a word. Tears fell from my eyes while my heart yelled out an agony I'd never felt before. I didn't ask nor did she. Instead, I bent over and our lips met as if destiny had set them up for that very moment. We remained in unison for longer than was prudent. We were alone with our heartbeats until our lips parted in the softest way. Perhaps there is healing in a kiss. Perhaps kisses could embrace and compose the world.

Linah had a micro-chip implanted in her shoulder. She told me to get out fast, told me that as soon as she didn't move and didn't report back, they'd send soldiers looking for her. They'd already be coming for Yona, the fallen man I had shot.

I had no choice but to leave Linah. It was her only chance of surviving. We couldn't know how badly hurt she was. She was losing blood.

'Go!' Linah's tears were rippling down her cheeks. She turned her eyes to the ceiling high overhead.

I took her hand, kissed it, pressed it gently and let it down next to her. I had a last glance before I pushed myself off the ground and walked out the door. I didn't look back. I picked up my rifle, still on the ground outside, and ran away from the shooting.

I felt invisible, as if being alive was a figment of my imagination. The only thing that seemed real to me was Linah. The life I was stuck in was madness and my only sanity in this madness was an unconditional emotion that transcended all others. The emotion that is indisputably the only antidote to hatred.

The only cure for our common insanity.

34

I made it to the entrance. Nobody was there and I went in, down a long rope ladder. I felt my way through the tunnel, walking cautiously with my head bent, one arm on the wall, one in front, the darkness so dense I might as well have been blind. It was a weary trek in the turbulent company of my frantic mind. When the ground shook from an explosion, my eyes opened wide, in a turmoil of fear and hope. Fear of the tunnel collapsing and entombing me. Hope that the ceiling would break open and let in some light. There was neither. After walking over one and a half kilometres under the ground, I finally made out a distant speck. Then a promising thin strip of light that proved to mark the exit. It had a steel door with steps welded on which were filled with dirt to blend in with the surroundings. Nobody was around. I peeped out and saw in the distance that there were the fields and greenhouses, just like Ali had said.

I stayed there in the dark until the strip of light faded with the sun, then I pushed the door open and crept out.

From back over Gaza came the roar of explosions. Plumes of fire lunged into the heavens. Fighter jets churned the sky with thunder and the air straight above me sounded like the cracking of whips. I started crying. Sobbing without restraint, picturing the devastation, the screaming, the flesh-tearing earthly trauma. A legacy of death, sorrow, pain and anger. The dread might of Israel crashing down on Gaza, the underscoring of its violent oppression. Palestine's own holocaust.

I was crying because I had left behind the two people I loved most. Sitting there in the dark, my back against an olive tree and with implacable stars looking down, I felt my soul disintegrating.

I had brought myself to hell on earth, failed in my mission and had come out none the better—without Ali, and maybe like a mindless myrmidon, I had maimed the woman I love without fulfilling my dream of redemption and peace. Ali had carried his prison on his shoulders. He wouldn't let it go and when he died, he took it with him, his guts hanging out. The devil hadn't told him of that when they sealed their pact in blood. The devil handed Ali the knife of hatred and set him the impossible task of using it to carve out his future.

I left Gaza without Linah. Before that, we had known we had to be separated for a time. I had felt it wouldn't be long before I heard from her. But shooting her and leaving her wounded, I could never have imagined; though no less imaginable as falling in love with her in the first place. And then, I had no way of knowing whether she would live or die. I would have to summon the courage and be a warrior of patience to see myself through my inner turmoil.

I stayed under the olive tree until the first break of light. I had tried to rest, but it was impossible. Beside the deafening din of the bombing, pains tore increasingly through my body. I crawled to a nearby orchard. There, I gorged on avocados lying on the ground. The privilege of the starving. There was *fresh water* in the taps so I quenched my thirst. I was crawling—kept crawling, right until I lay in the ditch of the highway leading to the old Kissufim crossing. There were heavy troop movements but also a lot of taxis dropping and picking up personnel. I waited for ages, covered in dirt. Nobody expected anyone to be there, no one looked. It took an unnerving length of time before I summoned the courage to signal a driver whom I thought might help. I raised my head, and slowly put up my hand.

He must have been a hundred feet away. Talking on his cell phone, the driver saw me, looked in his mirrors and motioned for me to wait. I ducked out of sight. As soon as the coast was clear he drove forward and opened the passenger door. I crawled in and curled up on the floor. He obviously knew I was a fugitive. With barely a word, he covered me with clothes, newspaper and boxes of avocados from the backseat. I was lucky. I will never forget the hands of this man, Halabi, the Palestinian-Israeli taxi driver who delivered me from the danger I was in. He gave me clothes, he knew where the checkpoints were, and he knew how to avoid them. Halabi drove me back to Qalandia where I put myself in the hands of the border police at the checkpoint. I told them I'd lost my work permit and had been beaten by settlers. They cuffed me and laughed, told me to shut up or they'd take me back there. I took a chance on Rafi and told them to call The Palace to verify my identity. One of the officers called. When he asked whether a man by my name worked there, Rafi didn't reply straight away. The officer thought the line had gone dead. In the end Rafi's voice came over and said yes, I did. I was let through the checkpoint. My bloody thigh was eyed suspiciously but nobody cared. I was Palestinian.

I was in the throes of segregation, back at the checkpoint. It felt like coming out of a time capsule. The metallic clang of the turnstiles, the steel bars, the barren faces of people whose caged minds had lost even a sense of freedom. The images returned as if they'd never left me. I felt the sadness and the humiliation build up, and then the anger. I walked, tilting forward in the customary posture, my head facing the ground, only looking up when asked to.

As to our street in Mukhamas, I found my parents sitting outside with a group of neighbours, watching the news from Gaza on TV. My father was the first to see me. He stood up. His lips moved. '*Ya Elahi…*'[58] his voice trailed off. My mother saw him looking, she followed his eyes and when she saw me, she burst into screaming, scaring everyone around her. She jumped up, pushed her chair and some people aside, and ran towards me. Before she'd even reached me, her tears were streaming. She grabbed me by my arms and hugged me, pulling me tightly against her body. She kissed my cheeks, kissed my forehead, the circles in her eyes expanding into

58 Similar to 'Oh, my God'.

a supernova of love. She must have thanked God a dozen times before the kissing stopped. When she had calmed down, I stepped in with a big hug of my own. Throughout my life, throughout the torments of body and mind, through all our travails, the closeness of my mother was a portal to heaven, sweet with comfort and peace.

My father stood by with dignity, awaiting his turn. He could not hold back his tears and when my mother stepped back, he opened his arms and gave me a father's embrace. He kissed me on my cheeks four times, as men do when they greet in sincerity. And I, in all this emotion, I was oblivious to the people around me. All three of us were. Embracing my father, I felt like a boy, an innocent child whose parents' love is the light of his life. Then I opened my eyes and saw our neighbour Al-Fattah, the local shopkeeper Abd Al-Raheem and his wife Hoda, standing behind us. They, too, were crying. All of us were crying, and like most Palestinians, at the heart of our life, the communion of people amidst hardship is our greatest strength. It's our lifeblood and the very essence of what makes us Palestinian.

The day I returned, I decided to become the warrior I wanted to be and not a classical weapon-wielding combatant. Weapon-bearers exchange pain and injury, and the only party sure to benefit is the arms manufacturer. I had never previously carried a gun, and the day I did, I put a bullet through the woman I loved. That day I returned, I was all at once a child in the arms of my parents and an adult, knowing who I wanted to be. That day, I understood what it meant to me to be Palestinian.

What it meant to call my home, Palestine.

35

I tried calling Linah a couple of weeks after I returned. I had no other way to get in touch with her. But the answering machine kept coming on. Then at the beginning of September, the line stopped working. The same day it happened, I called Rafi. He hadn't contacted me although he knew I was alive. He was reticent when I asked him about contacting Mohammed.

'Why do you want to speak to Mohammed?'

'I wanted to know if he has any information on wounded or killed female soldiers?'

'Are you worried about your Linah?'

'Yes...'

'Mohammed is dead, Nana. He was killed the same day as Ali...'

The hopeful faces of Mohammed's children flashed in front of my eyes. I felt dizzy and dropped my head between my thighs. Mohammed, the not-so-young young man, was gone. I asked Allah to have mercy upon his soul. My conversation with Rafi ended in silence.

The next day he called me. I answered, wondering what else he would have to say to me. He cleared his throat several times and then he asked if I would return to The Palace. That was unexpected. He wanted to convert the basement into a banquet hall. I accepted, suspecting I would be covering more than empty ground with the Turkish marble slabs he envisaged as a floor. I wasn't sure what I'd carve at the base of the giant pillars that reared up through the building. And I wasn't sure whether I wanted to be near Rafi again. I wasn't sure, but I accepted. I accepted, because all I could think about, was Linah.

And whether I had killed her.

36

I didn't want to be anywhere else at that time. I had found myself back in the checkpoint queues, but they had become objects of pity rather than contempt. The humiliation, once torment, I now shrugged off as routine. The prison guards had also become the prisoners, for me, and I walked with my head high, my back straight. I put all my faith in seeing Linah again and dismissed the possibility that I had taken her life. My gut instinct told me I had not, but I didn't really know. I wanted her alive and in my arms. But if I had killed her, I needed to know. Inside, I was in turmoil.

Rafi handed me the keys. I thought this was perhaps to help him fully conceal his secret. At least that's what his eyes said. I opened the doors to the basement with Yaser. He was the only man prepared to work below the ground level of The Palace. The others uncomfortably declined. The rumour about Rafi and what he had hidden under The Palace had travelled far. Yaser was a gentle giant. He was two metres tall and almost twice my own width. He smiled all the time, even in the middle of the night, going through the checkpoint. The Israeli soldiers didn't say a word to him. He smiled when we opened the doors and he smiled when we turned on the floodlights and found the obvious marks of a grave.

Café Mount Carmel was open, and I walked in. Everything looked the same. I looked towards the table where I had sat with Linah. A young couple were there. They appeared to have ordered the same food. A falafel sandwich. They were Jewish and were speaking Hebrew. The young man stopped as he saw me step in. He smiled, I smiled back. He went back to talking to his girlfriend. I looked up towards the counter. The radio played the tunes of the *oud* that had kept me company at The Palace. Behind it, I found Adam, shaving what was left of the shawarma roll, preoccupied.

'Business must be good…'

'Yes. It's been busy today. Hold on and I'll be right with you. What would you like?'

Adam turned around and grabbed a pen and the floury notepad on the counter before looking at me. I smiled. His face went from stunned to smiling, and on to laughing.

'Nana! My friend! I'm so happy to see you!'

Adam came around the counter, opened his arms and embraced me. I returned the embrace, somewhat startled. I hadn't expected it.

'I'm happy to see you too, Adam. You look well.'

'Thank you. Where is…?'

'Do you mean the young woman? What was her name…? Eh… Eh… Linah?'

'Yes, her…' Adam looked surprised, he looked suspicious. He knew I was being deceptive.

'I don't know. Haven't seen her since I finished the work at The Palace. Have *you* seen her?'

'No…' he said, in a disappointed tone.

Taking my order, he served me my sandwich at the table then went back to his work behind the counter. I saw his reflection in the window, looking at me. I had hurt him.

I went back to Mount Carmel every day and every day Adam would take my order as he did from every other customer. With a courteous smile, professional. We only exchanged superficial small talk. I'd sit at the centre table and read the newspapers while I had my lunch. Every time the door opened I'd look up hastily, then quickly look down again. I'd see Adam watching me in the reflection; he knew that I knew he was watching me.

I went back, day after day, waiting for Linah to walk in through the door. But she didn't. The only thing that arrived was autumn outside the window. It was succeeded by winter. The checkpoint queues in the night turned colder and colder. Every day was a déjà vu. Every day became a fight with myself; a fight I was determined to win.

It was a couple of days before the end of the year when I decided to stay at the café after it closed. Adam asked me to leave but I asked him to sit down. He closed the door first. Then he sat down and silently waited for me to speak. It took a while. I stammered to begin with, wasn't sure which words to choose but then I let go. I told him *everything*. After I had finished, Adam pushed his chair back and stood up.

'Thank you for sharing.'

'Thank you for listening.'

Adam's eyes glistened as I said those words. They were more sincere than any apology I could have given him. We had accepted each other's friendship and it became the day I turned the tide. I stepped onto the path of the reality I wanted to create for myself.

I stepped into my new future.

37

I'll never forget that day. It was raining. The water was sheering sideways as the wind gusted through the city. I had finished my lunch and fell slumped in my chair, preoccupied with the passing umbrellas outside the café. Women clung to them as they fought to keep dry. There were also young men who walked against the onslaught of water. They closed their eyes and leaned into the wind, their soaked jackets drawn all the way to their chins. Children struggled to walk behind the legs they were following. The birds had gone and the trees were now shaking skeletons against the wretched grey sky.

It was in the middle of January. My work in the basement at The Palace with Yaser was coming towards its end. In a matter of weeks, I'd be out of work. My patience had come a long way. For over four months I had attended Mount Carmel with hope in my heart. Slowly, however, hope was fading, despite my determination to keep it alive. Every day I'd bid Adam a brief goodbye and leave with a slumped head. I'd look down the street in either direction, thinking Linah could be arriving at the exact same time. Every day I looked at Adam, initially I asked, then after some weeks it was just a glance and an answering shake of the head. One day he sat down with me and asked me for how long I was going to wait. All I could say was, as long as I could.

I stopped thinking about all the possible reasons why Linah hadn't called me, and I continued to deny that she could be dead. I maintained this stance until doubt eventually began wearing my allegiance to patience and time—a place in which I became who I wanted to be. One night, I told my parents about Linah. To my absolute surprise, their sorrow for my torment was spontaneous and could not have been more real. My parents asked me why I had hidden my love for this woman. Moments later they gave the obvious answer to their own question, and my mother said she'd pray that I'd find Linah soon. It took me a long time to see why I had expected a different reaction. Eventually, I concluded that growing up, I simply hadn't been listening to them. I hadn't taken in fully, who they were and what they wished for me in my life.

Back to that rainy day. Drooped in my chair, I lost my focus on the slashing rain outside. The drops on the glass windows trailing, the figures of people walking, the cars passing—all were a blur. The grey backdrop was dotted with wet and faded clothes. Among the procession, a figure or two would stop. A woman and her child, through the blur, a girl with ponytails and a red jacket. They took my mind back to the day of the crazed soldier at the checkpoint. Mother and child quickly left and were replaced by two skinny men. Their forms were vague as they moved towards the door which opened. The wind barged in with them as well as the smell of cold rain. They ate quickly, spoke loudly and left. Then another figure appeared. Arms down the side, hands sticking out of a full body poncho. It was blue with big red dots and moved closer to the window. I didn't move, but the figure did. Towards the door. And the door opened. The wind came back as well as the smells. Including the unmistakable scent of a woman.

My field of view only stretched to the door. As soon as she entered, she was out of my sight. I heard her raincoat move about before it stopped and came towards me. I was still in my daze when only the coat came into my vision. She walked in the aisle between the row of tables and chairs adjacent to the window, and when she came in front of me, she turned to face me.

All I saw were the red dots on the blue vinyl straight in front of my eyes. I was staring into a full-frame canvas. The synthetic fabric moved in waves. My vision was still blurry. Right until I saw her hands poke out of the poncho.

And when I saw the red nail polish, my heart drummed, and I almost fell off the chair. I heaved my breath as if I was falling off a cliff. I pulled myself up, kicking off with my legs, flashes of the faceless woman in my dream flicking by as the chair scraped backwards against the floor. Adam's reflection in the window caught my eyes. He stood with an open mouth, his hands down his sides, staring. I followed his line of sight and saw who he was looking at, who I had been waiting for all this time.

It was Linah.

I stood up. We might have embraced, but instead we fell into the depth of each other's eyes. Her tears overflowed and dropped on the raincoat with a hollow tap. My short breaths calmed down. I countered them with a few long ones as I composed myself. We were silent, studying each other. Linah hadn't changed. She looked exactly the same. She didn't smile, not at first anyway, but then she suddenly stretched her lips. And when she did, her eyes drowned in her tears. I smiled back, all choked up, about to burst out crying. Linah took quick steps around the table and opened her arms. I kicked the chair further away and took her in my arms. Her head fell onto my chest as she closed her eyes. We embraced tightly. Both of us crying. I put my head to hers and breathed in her scent. She let go, looked up and we put our lips together.

Adam paced towards the door and closed the latch. He turned off half the lights in the shop and cleared his throat to get our attention. I looked at him. His eyes were wet.

'Let me know if I can get you anything before I leave you.'

'Thank you… Can you make me something warm?' Linah asked, wet and sniffing.

'Thank you, Adam.' I said.

'I'll make you a hot chocolate. And stop thanking me. Both of you.'

Linah took off her poncho. She was wearing her dark jeans into red rainboots. We both giggled when I looked at them. An earth-coloured woollen jumper covered her lovely body. We stood there for a while, our hands touching. I moved my hand up her arm, around her shoulder, along her neck. She closed her eyes and tilted her head sideways. I ran my fingers into her wet hair, down again. She shivered as the cold water ran down her back. She put her hand to my face, traced my chin with her fingers, then my lips, nose, around my eyes. She let her hand fall down and across my chest before returning it to mine. We lost any doubts we might have had in those first few moments, loving each other in silence, holding hands. Still standing.

As I sat down, Linah pulled the chair around the side of the table and kept hold of my hand. It was only when Adam brought her the hot chocolate that she sat down. She put her chin on her hand, set her elbow to rest on the table and gazed at me, smiling.

'You almost killed me!' She snapped the words, but playfully.

'It wasn't me!' I pleaded, cringing.

We both chuckled. Then I turned serious as my mind impulsively formed a question.

'Why didn't you call me?'

Linah's tears flowed once again. She thought about her reply carefully.

'I wanted to, but I couldn't. I spent two weeks in a hospital before they let me go. I don't know why. The bullet, *luckily…*' She smiled as she said it. '…didn't do much damage. The blood was from it cutting a vein. I was fine. Really.'

Linah looked at me. Perhaps my guilt shone through my eyes. It came out as tears and I felt warm and sweaty. My body shook. Linah leaned forward, kissed me softly, reassuringly, leaned back and continued.

'I was taken to a military prison after that. They wanted to investigate how Yona had been shot.'

'Did they suspect you? Surely not?'

'Well, as it happened, yes. They said that I ran away. Yona testified against me.'

'I spent almost six weeks in that prison. The verdict was, I hadn't done my duty. I should have covered him to begin with, then stayed with him, helped him, us. It's a long list… So in order to get out of it quickly, my lawyer recommended I pleaded mental instability. They sent me to a military hospital where I stayed until Christmas. Then I was discharged back to my parents in Tel Aviv. Discharged from the hospital, discharged from the army. At last!'

We both laughed. I had so many questions for Linah, but I didn't know where to start. I told her my story. What I had seen. What I had done. I told her about Lina.

Lina, what could have happened to her? Whenever I thought about Lina, I was always more than a little sad.

I told her about why I went to Gaza and how I was swept along by the madness before I could even think about it. How everything had its reasons and how I had come to the café every day, determined in my heart, that she was still alive.

'When I came here today, I felt quite sure I'd find you here.'

'It's been every day since I went back to work at The Palace.'

'In the attic again?' Still in tears, Linah threw a cheeky smile. Possibilities.

'No, in the basement. With Yaser, who is twice my size. At least! That's a story for another day.'

One question was paramount in my mind. It was clanging away like a rod inside a big brass church bell. I knew it was shared and part of it had already been answered. We wanted to stay together. Linah was the woman I wanted to share my life with. But the *reality* of my life wasn't what I wanted. It was not what I wanted to offer Linah. Not with checkpoints, walls of segregation and being seen as a threat to the people around us.

'What now?' I asked. Linah had an answer ready. More answers, in fact. She didn't hesitate.

'I've already told my parents.'

'Told them what?'

Linah had everything thought out.

'That I've met you and that I might leave the country.'

'Is that the only thing we can do?'

'It's our only solution, *right now*. One day it will, hopefully, be different. Have you got a better idea?'

Linah knew the answer to her own question. No, there wasn't a better idea.

'Where would we go to?' I answered.

'Anywhere, as long as it's peaceful! Anywhere, where we don't have to hide!' We both laughed.

The hours passed by, one after the other. We hadn't moved, hadn't eaten. We reconnected, joined our souls and bonded them with the strength of our mutual spirit. We had cleared our biggest hurdle. I felt as free as the wind, free of anxiety, free of doubt. I'd come to this café for months, waiting for her. If I had to leave her again, it would be when I closed my eyes to hers for the last time. I took her hand from the table and kissed it, looked up to her eyes and spoke.

'Will you marry me?'

'Are you sure?' I couldn't have expected any other reply. Then she jumped up. I hadn't expected that. She flung her arms around me and gazed earnestly into me, as if searching for the truth on the bottom of a deep well. Her answer came decisively.

'Yes.'

It was that simple. A yes.

38

Our war-torn separation resumed with the confirmation of our beautiful union. Our brief episode of love—a blessed meeting of opposites could have faded into a wistful memory. Perhaps never knowing if death had intervened or why the other had not made contact. But barriers were cleared and doors were thrown open to a world of possibilities. My parents stood by us at every step and my fear of not being able to rejoice with Linah in their presence was dispelled. Alas, Linah's parents' response was more complicated. Paradoxically, they were from a family of post-Holocaust liberals, believing in human rights and equality. Except, we would learn, for marital unions. They were utterly distraught, as upset and anxious as much of the society they lived in. They rejected her as their daughter. One day with me, Linah re-enacted her mother's fury.

'You just can't marry a man who is not Jewish. And Arab, on top of that. She clenched her fists and shook them, her face flushed and tightened into a mask of exasperation. *And even if he converts, which he won't because he's a Muslim, he'll never be a real Jew!'*

The prospect of our sharing our beliefs was so alien to them, they concluded that anyone so minded just could not be their daughter. I could not understand it and I could never empathise with this view; how people could cling to a love-blocking attitude that is so traumatic to themselves.

Linah and I embraced our paramount realm of unity. We accepted it in the simplest terms possible and held on to its strength and its life-giving uncertainty. We broke the habit of being ourselves. Each in our own way, we became stronger than the world around us. We had found our sanity in its madness. We had courageously challenged who we were, and in our distance apart, we opened up and surrendered to the only force that sustains life.

The power of love.

❁❁❁

An olive tree may live for hundreds of years. Even a thousand. It's a palace of green, spreading branches that symbolise peace. It feeds us and makes us healthy. As every child that enters the world brings hope, an olive tree brings unity. Harvesting it requires many hands, many hearts and many smiles. Many seeds fall to the ground but only a few sprout. Out of those, one will grow old and carry strong branches. Beneath them, a man will question his place in the universe. In life. A woman will appear who will offer him a mirror in which to reflect himself. But he will not want it.

'Why don't you want it?' Linah asks me.

'Because I don't need one. We are it, you and me.'

'How?'

'*We are it*. Leave the world to reflect itself in us.'

We stand under the giant olive tree. As I kiss Linah, the wind picks up. It rustles the leaves above and we hear the creaking of branches. The lavender moves around us like purple waves. The olive limbs droop down to our feet. They form a staircase that goes up to a set of entwined twig doors. I, Adnan, take Linah's hand and we climb up those steps. There she kisses me and the doors open to us.

To *The Palace of Angels*.

AFTERWORD

The end of my story feels like the right place to start. It was a beginning more than an end. We went to Amman after I got my Palestinian passport and a week later, we held our breaths when we opened my fake Israeli passport. We didn't speak a single word and didn't make a single sound as we boarded the plane to Vienna.

On board, I was so tense my legs went numb. I thought of the wait with my parents in the van outside the Ofer prison. So I got up because I could. I curiously wandered to the lavatory in the front of the cabin and opened the narrow door. There, I stood looking dumbly at the seat until another passenger asked if I was going to use it. I stepped aside and the man walked past me. He looked like the braying soldier at the checkpoint but was dressed like a rabbi—long curls, thick glasses and everything. He stared at me suspiciously as he closed the door and pulled the latch shut. I watched as the small sign slid across to a red and backlit 'OCCUPIED'. I found myself staring at a word. A word that triggered an avalanche of emotions. I dismissed a feeling of suffocation that was mounting and walked back to my seat, and Linah.

Her eyes glowed and she was as beautiful as she still is, as she was the first day I saw her. But there were no bars between us anymore and neither of us were prisoners. Before we left, my mother gave me a set of keys to never forget to fight for my right to return home—a sacred human right Israel denies us. I keep the keys around my neck all the time.

Naji al-Ali was killed the day I was born. His work lives on. It depicts the harsh reality of the occupation, the atrocities of the occupation and the duplicity of the foreign powers that permitted that theft. His most famous character, Handala, is the cartooned refugee child who remains true to himself—the symbol of my people's struggle for justice and self-determination. He has bare feet like the Palestinian children who were in the refugee camps after the Nakhba. Naji al-Ali was forced to leave Palestine and grew up as a refugee in the 'Ain al-Hilweh' camp in Sidon in Lebanon. He created Handala in 1969, in his own reflection, often shown with a key symbolising the hope of returning home, always with his hands clasped behind his back, signifying the rejection of the unjust 'solutions' posed to the Palestinian people.

The place of my birth marked the triumph of the small against the mighty, years later. In 2003, the people of Budrus rose up against Israel's erection of a concrete barrier which would cut through their lives. At that time, the wall would have divided my people, cut through our cemetery and forced the children to pass it on the way to school. It would have destroyed the farmland they had lived off for centuries. They resisted peacefully, unarmed villagers swarming in endless demonstrations like mosquitoes. Only the IOF[59] resorted to violence. Violence that demonstrated that even when Palestinians were peaceful, time and time again, the IOF were not— they, in fact, carried out the orders of a brutal and oppressive regime.

Some Israelis recognised the courage of the demonstrators and stood side-by-side with Palestinians. Palestinians protected Israeli activists from Israeli soldiers and the Israeli activists voiced the cry of my Palestinian people. It was a union of supposed opposites—evidence of human oneness. Activists from far corners of the world joined the small population of demonstrators, with Palestinian women at the front. Palestinians across all factions united and, after almost a year of non-violent resistance, the mighty elephant, Israel, backed off. The wall was still built but the line was re-drawn, away from the village of Budrus. The leader of the resistance, Ayed Morrar, had made it right. With a kind heart and a courageous mind.

---

59 Israeli Occupation Forces.

If you want to see the power of the small against the mighty, put an elephant in a room with a mosquito.

This wall was not simply meant to stop violent incursions into Israel, but was covertly designed to impose a state of paralysis. The wall came up and was still the prison wall the Israelis intended it to be. But more than that, it stands as a symbol of Apartheid and tyrannical oppression—oppression of people robbed of their land, their homes, their culture and even their lives. A forced separation designed to strangle any dreams and hopes of peace and co-existence, feeding a poisoned atmosphere where bigoted leaders on both sides depend on each other to keep the separation alive. But one day they will fall.

One day we will see the checkpoints disappear. They are as degrading and as dehumanising as the surrounding regime of guards, patrols, regulations, queues, curfews—and guns. Palestinians live in a prison state—with drones continually looking down—and are controlled by the Israeli ID card system which is the administrative core of the Zionist policy. The laws surrounding them are virtually the same as the *pass laws* that South Africa had during its Apartheid era, but uglier still.

Palestinians are divided from each other. There are East Jerusalem Palestinians, West Bank Palestinians and Gazans. East Jerusalem Palestinians have access to Israel but can have their ID cards revoked without warning if they live or are considered living outside East Jerusalem. Often, families are purposely torn apart when one member's ID is revoked and changed to a West Bank ID, forcing the family to move to the West Bank. East Jerusalem, the heart of Palestinian life, was annexed by Israel in 1967. The wall that began being built in 2001 through it, around and between the homes of my people in the West Bank, is the embodiment of Israel's denial of our right to live together.

I had a West Bank ID which meant I could only live in areas that made up less than half of the occupied West Bank. I was barred from living anywhere else in Israel and I could not vote. To go anywhere outside the West Bank, I had to pass through the eight-metre high reinforced concrete separation barrier at a checkpoint. My work was in East Jerusalem, roughly ten kilometres away so I had to pass the Qalandia checkpoint daily, with thousands of others. The regime at the checkpoint itself is arbitrary and random. The rules are unstated and constantly changing. I needed a permit to pass but only my employer could apply for it. I had to then apply for another permit to pass the checkpoint to pick up my working permit which came in endless forms, usually only lasting a few days, subjugating me and every other Palestinian to the humiliation of a torturous obstacle course. If I didn't manage to return at the end of the day, I'd be given a curfew and required to repeat the ordeal. Sometimes I'd get there and find a soldier yelling through a megaphone, telling us the checkpoint was closed. Sometimes the checkpoint was simply not staffed so we'd have to wait for hours. Sometimes I was just not allowed to pass. No reason given. My nerves were often frayed, and my heart was pounding every time I approached the checkpoint. Things could change from day to day, even from hour to hour. The uncertainty and total control was, and still is, the torture.

The separation barrier, the West Bank barrier, the security fence, the Apartheid wall—is over seven hundred kilometres long. Its name in Arabic is literally *the wall of race separation*. It is condemned by the UN and the International Court of Justice found it to be a violation of international law. Somehow, though, that escapes redress.

The countries that founded those institutions fail to enforce their own policies. There are no economic sanctions or military or other interventions. Instead, these nations trade openly with Israel, buy their drones and turn a blind eye, except for strenuous gymnastic exercises at the UN and public comments of concern, to the continuing annexation of Palestinian land and the advancement of the Zionist agenda of creating a purely Jewish state.

Almost at the bottom of the ladder are the Gazans. Their ID card means they cannot live anywhere outside Gaza and entering Israel is only by special permission—in effect, rarely. Even medical cases are, with few exceptions, denied entry for treatment in Israel. A Palestinian living in Gaza is being treated like a prisoner and the tiny strip of land is under siege. Israel controls who and what goes in or out—it occupies Gaza.

Outside this system, are every Palestinian man, woman and child who have fled the ethnic cleansing and brutal occupation. They are barred from returning to their own home—because they are not Jewish.

The state of Israel was set up at the cost of the Palestinians. The first Zionist Prime Minister, David Ben-Gurion, declared it a Jewish state and the constitution reads that it is for Jews only. That same year, the Universal Declaration of Human Rights was drafted. It came in the fallout of the Second World War, the Holocaust horrors and with the millions of refugees displaced worldwide. On December 10, 1948 the General Assembly of the United Nations adopted and proclaimed *the Universal Declaration of Human Rights.* Article 13 of this declaration says:

Everyone has the right to freedom of movement and residence within the borders of each state.

Everyone has the right to leave any country, including his own, and to return to his country.

The world lets Israel—with almost total impunity—break its most important declaration, what has been proclaimed as the highest aspiration of the common people. Israel flourishes its weary cry for redemption and the world, in paralysed apathy, colludes with its brutality and oppression.

There was nothing that could have ever prepared me for what I witnessed in Gaza. People called it a war. But how could they? It was a massacre and a demolition. For seven long weeks the world watched and did nothing as the Israeli army killed more than one and a half thousand civilians. Men, women and children were killed in their beds, cut to pieces by bombs and missiles. More than five hundred and fifty of those were children. They had names and hopes and dreams; they were told fairy tales before bedtime.

For seven weeks drones and fighter jets made their nights a nightmare, and every day, the Palestinians opened their eyes to a world of death.

Perhaps they would have survived, perhaps the leaders of the world would've been outraged, had they been five hundred and fifty dogs.

We all, disregarding the name of our God, deserve to know there is a better way. We deserve a new reality where we all live together in peace. I'm part of my country and it is Palestine to me. To Linah, it is Israel. Do not ask us where we are from. Ask us where we wish to go, who we wish to become. We are part of this planet, part of the universe. Part of me, however small that part is, is a part we all share. It lives within us all—holds our integrity as human beings.

That part of us that will free us from ourselves.

For Linah and me, for us to share a life together, we had to leave. We went to northern Sweden where the only prison is the darkness of winter. Compared to the turnstiles and yellow of the checkpoint nights, compared to the horror of children, men and women being slaughtered before my eyes, compared to the daily humiliation and punishment for no reason, it's as bright as the sun on the clearest summer's day.